MIDNIGHT SEDUCTION

Walker's eyes dropped to Skye's hands when she touched the first button. The material parted and he had a glimpse of the hollow of her throat. A second button was undone and more of her skin came into view. She undid another. Then another.

"Skye." His voice had a deep, raspy quality to it. It also held a warning.

"Mmmm?" She sounded innocent even as she played the temptress.

"What do you think you're doing?"

"Flirting?" she asked hopefully.

Walker pushed away from the window. His palms grazed her arms, her shoulders. Skye leaned into him and raised her face. Her lips parted as she stood on tiptoe and reached for him. Her fingers threaded at the back of his neck and she pulled gently, bringing him closer. Her mouth closed over his, hungry and searching.

She was lifted, carried. She felt the edge of the bed at the back of her knees. He pushed the gown over her hips. It spread like a dark green pool at her feet. When she was tumbled backward on the bed, she pulled him with her. She kissed his jaw, his cheek. She pressed tiny, tasting kisses along the length of his neck.

Skye kissed him again. Softly. Slowly. "One of us has too many clothes on," she said.

It was gratifying, Walker reflected, that they thought so much alike.

Books by Jo Goodman

Published by Zebra Books

JO GOODMAN

ALWAYS IN MY DREAMS

ZEBRA BOOKS
Kensington Publishing Corp.
http://www.kensingtonbooks.com

> *For Walter . . . for helping me think about family.*

One

"You want me to *spy* for you?" Mary Schyler Dennehy was incredulous. Her wide eyes and raised brows complemented her tone. Even her jaw remained a trifle slack as she stared in wonderment at her father.

"Don't be so melodramatic," Jay Mac said dismissively. "Spying is not a word I would use."

Skye cut a sideways glance at her mother. Moira offered drily, "It's certainly the word *I* would use." A sweet Irish brogue took the sting from her sarcasm. "I don't think I like the sound of this, Jay Mac. It's dangerous."

Skye's mobile and expressive mouth closed and flattened. She snorted a bit indelicately. "I don't care *this* for danger," she announced, snapping her fingers to emphasize her point. "It's just that I can't believe Jay Mac is asking me to be a spy."

On anyone's list of the rich and powerful, whether in New York or in the country, John MacKenzie Worth's name was always placed prominently. He was the founder of Northeast Rail, a transportation system that had long outgrown its name and expanded west beyond the Mississippi to California, Nevada, and Colorado, following the trail of gold and silver discoveries. He owned prime real estate around Central Park, an investment that was returning itself a hundredfold as those who could afford it bought land and built their brown and gray stone mansions uptown. He sat on some of the most influential boards in the city, counted among his friends six senators, five congressmen, and a president, got away with his very public feud with the mayor, and was often consulted by other men of industry. Even more frequently Jay Mac was sought as a financial backer by those with interests in science, art, and politics. He gave generously to worthy causes, which generally left out all things political.

With rare exception John MacKenzie Worth, known simply as "Jay Mac" to most of the country, was regarded with respect and something akin to reverence.

The rare exception took place in the stone palace he had built on the corner of 50th Street and Broadway. Behind the spiked iron gate and manicured rose bushes, he was also known as Jay Mac. But here, surrounded at various times by his five daughters and their mother, the nickname decidedly elicited more affection and amusement than awe.

Jay Mac's attention darted between his wife and his youngest daughter. Moira was quite serious in her objections, but Jay Mac was just arrogant enough to think he could handle her. Skye, on the other hand, for all that she looked appalled by his suggestion, was clearly intrigued. He knew how to interpret the glint in her bright green eyes and the hint of a dimple on either side of her wide mouth.

"This is *not* dangerous," he said to both of them.

Moira remained uncertain, but wanting to be convinced. Mary Schyler was trying to hide her disappointment. Jay Mac believed his confidence was well founded. He had them both. The trick was to allay the fears of one while making it an adventure for the other.

He rose from the dining table and went to the side-

board. While he was pouring himself a tumbler of Scotch
Mrs. Cavanaugh entered the room to judge the success of
the meal. He heard his wife commend the cook for her
special attention to the fish. Skye commented on the pine-
apple sorbet and asked politely if they could never have
it again. Moira admonished her daughter's distressing
lack of tact while Mrs. Cavanaugh merely chuckled. There
was something comfortable about the scene that had just
been played out behind his back, something reassuring
in his daughter's cheerful directness, his wife's gentle
scolding, the cook's laughter, and his own enjoyment. For
an instant he felt a pang of alarm at the thought of sending Skye off. She was the last of his daughters, the only
one of his five darling Marys still at home. What would
it be like without her?

He quelled the momentary rush of fear by asking if
anyone wanted a drink. Moira and Skye refused, taking
tea instead.

"What do you call it if it's not spying?" Skye asked,
when her father had returned to the table. She absently
tucked a wisp of flame-red hair behind her ear. It
slipped out again almost immediately.

"Investigating?"

Moira looked at her husband sternly over the rim of
her teacup. "Are you telling or asking? I'm not certain
I know by your tone."

"Investigating," he said more firmly. He took off his
spectacles and rubbed the bridge of his nose between
his thumb and forefinger, a gesture that was meant to
convey that he was slightly annoyed at Moira's inability
to grasp the difference. "Skye would be investigating
the whereabouts of the invention. I thought I had already explained myself in that regard."

"I'm certain you thought you did," Moira said, with
a touch of asperity. "But you can see that Skye thinks
it's spying, and I don't disagree with her."

Before Jay Mac could counter, Skye broke in. "Please, Mama, I want to hear Jay Mac out." For a moment it looked as if Moira would object, and although her eyes remained worried, she gave in with a brief nod. Skye thanked her with a wide, dimpled smile, then turned to her father. "Tell me about the invention."

"It's an engine, or more precisely, a particular part of an engine."

Skye asked innocently, "What part? The wheel, the cowcatcher, the smokestack?"

Jay Mac returned his spectacles to his face and gave his daughter a hard look, wondering if she was pulling his leg. "I mean the motor," he said. "The engine of the engine."

"Oh," she said, her voice small. "Sorry."

Behind her cup, Moira permitted herself a smile. For a moment it looked as if Jay Mac regretted broaching the subject at all. "What's so special about this engine?"

"The fuel it uses. The inventor swears it won't be powered by steam. It's going to use a petroleum byproduct. Something similar to kerosene. It will be incredibly powerful, lighter and faster than anything in use today. It could change the way we all think of transportation. You can't imagine the application possibilities." Jay Mac's voice rose slightly as his excitement grew. "This is something scientists are working on around the world, not just in this country. There's a push to develop some kind of steam turbine engine, not the lumbering impractical ones that exist today, but something streamlined and efficient. The impact of that invention would be enormous and yet I can honestly say that it pales in comparison to what would be possible with the engine this inventor has proposed."

Jay Mac paused to let his words sink in. Skye was impressed. Moira looked interested in spite of herself. When he spoke again his tone was quiet and grave and hinted at things he would not share with just anyone. "Rockefeller's interested. You can imagine the implications for a company like Standard Oil. John D.'s already made one fortune on kerosene. Think of his profit if he's able to use products that he's now virtually throwing away."

"Westinghouse?" asked Skye. She saw her father was surprised that she knew the name. It was hard to know whether to be insulted or pleased. She had generally worked hard at giving the impression that she was mostly frivolous. She conceded now that perhaps she had worked *too* hard. "Air brakes," she added, to make sure Jay Mac knew it was no fluke. "I may not know what Rennie knows about them, but I would have had to have been deaf not to know it was an exciting time for Northeast Rail."

At the mention of Rennie's name, both Jay Mac and Moira smiled. Mary Renee must have been about seventeen, they recollected, when George Westinghouse had patented his air brakes. For Skye's sister, who had wanted to be part of Jay Mac's empire from the inside and had realized that dream, the invention of the automatic railroad air brake was a milestone.

"Rennie did go on about it," Moira said wistfully. She turned her thoughtful gaze to her husband. "I imagine you've shared this latest news with Rennie and Jarret."

Jay Mac shook his head. "Very little, actually. They've been in Colorado and Nevada since this came about and it isn't something I've wanted to trust to the telegraphers. In fact, I haven't wanted to put much about it in writing. There's a lot at stake, too much, perhaps, to include even the most trusted men in my employ."

Moira frowned. She smoothed back the temples of her dark-red hair, not because there was a strand out of place, but because she needed to do something with her hands. She remembered very well what had happened only a few years earlier: Jay Mac had been the target of a murder plot that would have wrested control of Northeast Rail from the family's hands. How could he say this wasn't a dangerous business? Her sigh, as well as the militant look in her eyes, expressed the words she would not utter aloud.

Once again Skye managed to head her mother off. She was leaning forward in her chair, the perfect oval of her face animated with excitement. "Do you want me to steal this invention for you?" she asked, with more eagerness than was either ladylike or strictly moral. Out of the corner of her eye she saw that her mother was appalled. Skye made a half-hearted attempt to appear abashed. It didn't fool anyone. In front of her eyes Jay Mac's hair seemed to take on a more grayish cast.

"I don't want you to *steal* anything," he said, just managing to swallow his drink without choking. "I want you to bring it back to me."

Confused, Skye merely stared at her father. Moira's comment underlined her own confusion. "You'll have to pardon me if I fail to distinguish the difference."

Jay Mac set his tumbler on the table. A damp ring of water beaded on the polished surface. "You can't steal something that already belongs to you," he explained patiently.

"You *own* this engine?" asked Skye.

He nodded slowly. "Bought and paid for every part of its development."

"Then why don't you have it?"

"I fully expected to get reports from the inventor on his progress. This is by no means a finished product. It has never tested reliably, but my early information has always led me to believe he was on the right track and getting closer. I've asked for the current status, but I get little in return that's straightforward." Jay Mac shifted in his chair. "I'm concerned that he's backing out of the project, or worse, that he may even have thoughts of selling the idea elsewhere. That's forbidden in my contract with him. I want you to find out if my fears are founded. And if you can get the plans, or the engine, all the better."

Moira simply sank back into her chair and crossed herself. "Dear God," she said quietly. "I can't have heard any of this correctly. This is something you should be sending one of your men on, Jay Mac, not your youngest daughter."

Skye bristled. "Mama, how could you?" she asked, wounded. Her mother has always been supportive of her daughters in whatever they wanted to do. Traditionally, it had been Jay Mac who was the fly in the ointment.

He had been fiercely protective of all his children, planning, prodding, pushing, usually in directions they didn't want to go. He had opposed his oldest daughter's decision to enter a convent, but Mary Francis had held her ground and did as she wanted. He had tried to guide Mary Michael's career as a newspaperwoman when he'd realized she would be a reporter with or without his support. When he'd attempted to buy her a job on the *Herald,* she had promptly accepted a position with the New York *Chronicle.* Mary Renee had had to prove herself twice over to gain a position as an engineer with Northeast Rail, and Mary Margaret was going to medical school because of her husband's support, not her father's.

He had been just as iron handed in his machinations to see them married and settled. Mary Francis had slipped away from him, but Michael, Rennie, and Maggie had given him some frustrating moments as they'd tried to avoid his openly manipulative touch.

Skye's ambition was vastly different from that of her sisters. Thus far it had kept her out of her father's sight. She had no desire to serve God, inform the public, build bridges, or care for the sick. Skye wanted to be an adventuress.

Though it was not precisely a lofty goal, it was nonetheless one for which she felt eminently suited. Indeed, in her own manner Skye was just as singleminded in her approach to realizing her dreams as any of the Marys before her. She had decided long ago what skills were most needed for adventuring and had set about mastering them. Skye Dennehy was an excellent horsewoman and a crack whip. She rode sidesaddle in public and astride in private. In her phaeton she was completely at ease leading a high-spirited team on a rollicking ride over farmland just north of the city, or keeping them tightly in check on a crowded city street. People remarked that she had a passion for it. To Skye it was merely one means to an end.

Skye studied art and antiques and architecture. She devoured books on the history and geography of the places she wanted to go. Like riding astride, she did it outside the public eye. Even her family did not suspect the extent of her learning. Maggie had been the scholar. Skye was the scamp.

She was confident they would have encouraged her endeavors but found some way to discourage her plans to apply them. It was easy to be secretive about her accomplishments. She wasn't doing at all well in her final year at school. In fact, she was failing most of her university classes and had no intention of returning in the spring.

It wasn't that she couldn't do the coursework. Quite the opposite. With rare exception she found her private plan of learning had advanced her far beyond what was expected by her professors. With little to challenge her, Skye avoided most of her classes and arranged tutoring in activities that interested her.

That was how she'd become proficient in the use of weapons. Skye was not only accurate with a bow, she could fence and was comfortable using a variety of guns. The advent of winter had curtailed her sailing lessons on the Hudson, but she had recently found someone to teach her all about photography.

"Tell me about this inventor," Skye asked her father. "What sort of person is he?"

Jay Mac leaned back in his chair and picked up his drink. He rolled the tumbler casually between his palms, choosing his words carefully. "Serious," he said. "Yes, that rather describes him. It's difficult to know what the man is thinking. The plans he outlined to me were brilliant, though. Brilliant."

Boring: that was the word that came to Skye's mind. The man was boringly steady and dull, and probably too smart for his own good. She'd met a few men like that at social gatherings. Invariably they couldn't talk about the weather without describing what they intended to do about it. She practically yawned.

Moira said, "Now, why in the world would a man like that want our Skye around?"

One corner of Skye's mouth kicked up. Her mother's question wasn't terribly complimentary, but it was something Skye had been wanting to know.

Jay Mac sighed. "He doesn't want Skye around. He doesn't know her or anything about her. His social circles, such as they are, are vastly different than Mary Schyler's. What he needs is a housekeeper. Skye would be perfect."

Skye raised one brow. "As a housekeeper? I don't think so, Jay Mac." She stood, gracing both her parents with another innocently dimpled smile. "But I'd make a wonderful spy." Skirting the table, Skye dropped a light kiss on her father's cheek. "Let me think about it. Right now I have to be going. The ball's up in the park, the skating's wonderful, and I'm meeting Daniel in— " she glanced at the clock on the sideboard, "— oh my, I'm already late." She quickly came around the table and gave her mother a kiss. "I should be home before ten, but don't give it a thought if I'm a little later." Skye didn't give anyone a chance to respond. She hurried out of the dining room, crisp petticoats rustling beneath her brushed wool skating skirt.

Jay Mac looked at his wife. "Your daughter's a flibbertigibbet, ma'am, I'll never get used to it."

"*Our* daughter," Moira said, "is a breath of fresh air. You can't harness her."

"I'd be satisfied if she'd sit for ten minutes."

Moira ignored his attempt to sidetrack her. "I think you'd better tell me what's really going on. I won't have Skye exposed to any danger, and I can't believe that you would, either. There's something not quite right, and I don't think it has anything to do with that inventor. You're hatching a scheme . . . I just know it."

"Scheme?" he asked, with an exaggerated show of innocence. Chuckling, he took Moira's hand and bade her rise. He came to his own feet and casually rested his hands on either side of his wife's waist. He liked the way she automatically laid her palms on his arms and raised her face to him. After thirty years together, she only seemed more beautiful to him. "Let's go into the parlor."

Moira stood on tiptoe, kissed her husband on the mouth, and let herself be led out of the dining room. Under her breath she added, "Said the spider to the fly."

"What was that, darling?"

"Nothing, Jay Mac. Lead on."

"He wants you to be a *spy*?"

Skye continued to lace her skates, not bothering to spare a glance at her companion. "Don't be so melodramatic," she said, echoing her father's words. "This is Jay Mac we're talking about. My father, remember?"

Daniel Pendergrass shook his head. "I'm not likely to forget." He brushed a bit of crusted snow from the tip of one skate. "He hates me," he said forlornly.

"Now you're being ridiculous. He doesn't hate you.

When you think about it, he hardly knows you." Skye looked up from her lacing and grinned at her friend. "He hates the *idea* of you." Daniel's forlorn look became morose. Skye laughed. "We wouldn't suit, Daniel. We both know that. We've known it since our very first kiss."

Daniel's pale cheeks flushed with color. "Do you have to bring that up? I didn't know what I was doing. I'm sure I'd do it better now."

Skye finished with her skates and thrust her hands into her ermine muff. "That's because you've been practicing with Evelyn Hardy," she said, without a trace of jealously. She stood up. The park bench wasn't comfortable enough to allow them to linger in conversation. A cold wind was blowing across the pond. The skating party they'd been invited to join was circling on the far side of the ice. Skye could hear their laughter. "Come on, Daniel. Your friends are waiting."

Daniel watched Skye Dennehy step gingerly onto the ice. By the time he came to his feet she was already moving away, her sweep across the ice both confident and graceful. He adjusted his hat over his fair hair and tightened the scarf around his neck. Tall and lanky at 22, it seemed that he hadn't yet grown into his skin. His course across the ice was much less graceful than Skye's and infinitely less confident. But he was a good sport, amiable, and humorously disparaging of his own shortcomings. Skye assured him, in spite of the fact that she wasn't interested, that he was also quite handsome. He grinned. Evelyn Hardy thought so, too.

When Daniel reached his group of friends, Skye was skating by herself, intent upon cutting a perfect circle in the ice. Daniel's easy grin faded. It was no accident that she was alone. Skye's presence was merely suffered by most of his friends, permitted because he invariably insisted upon it. She had chosen her words deliberately earlier. The group of skaters they were about to join were *his* friends, not hers. Skye was skating at the pond at his invitation, not theirs. It seemed incredible to him that anyone still cared she was a bastard.

Skye looked up as Daniel approached and promptly lost the line she had been tracing. "See what you made me do?" she said. "You took your time getting here." If she was hurt by her exclusion from the others, she didn't show it. Her features were made lovelier by her animated smile, the brightness in her green eyes, and the color in her cheeks. Her hat was set forward at a jaunty angle and a fringe of white fur touched her forehead. Not far away, a bonfire on the bank cast all the skaters within its circle of light in a gold and orange glow. Where Skye's hair peeped out beneath her hat and scarf it was like a flame.

He held out his elbow and waited for her to slip her arm in his. He thought tonight she seemed to grasp him more tightly, as if he had extended a lifeline. Daniel studied her face again. No, there wasn't a hint that anything was wrong. Skye would never let anyone see what she was feeling; she rarely let anyone know what she was thinking.

"What happened?" he asked, as they skated toward his friends. Someone called out his name and he raised a hand in recognition.

"Nothing happened."

"Skye."

"Nothing happened," she repeated. "Exactly that. They cut me dead."

Daniel shook his head, hardly able to take it in. His friends were not often so deliberately cold to Skye. He looked around as they joined the pairs of skaters crossing the ice in a large circle. A band played on the bank, loudly enough for them to match their movements to music, but not so loudly that it interfered with conversation. "Hi, Charlie. Alice." He cast a quick smile over his shoulder so as not to misstep. "You remember Skye Dennehy, don't you?"

Charlie looked distinctly uncomfortable. His adam's apple bobbed as he swallowed hard. Alice offered a wan smile. "Skye. It's a pleasure." They offered their greeting in unison, and as if shocked by the volume of it, they bent their heads and concentrated on their footwork.

Skye's laughter was bright and unfettered, but she leaned closer to Daniel. "I've known Alice Hobbs since we were 6," she whispered. "And just last week Charlie confided in me that he intended to ask for her hand." Behind them, Charlie and Alice had left the circle and were waiting to join it in another place. "What's wrong with everyone?" she asked. She had been snubbed before; in fact, she took something of a perverse pleasure in forcing people by the very act of ignoring her to acknowledge her existence. This was different. There was something almost vicious in the way she'd been cut out tonight.

Daniel shrugged. "I'll be damned if I know," he said. The band on the shore struck up another tune. The introduction of a banjo increased the tempo and the skaters picked up their pace. There were bright flashes of gold and crimson as the women whirled, their skirts lifting to reveal white petticoats and flannel leggings. Now it was Daniel who leaned into Skye for support. She held him securely and made certain their feet didn't cross paths. "I'll never understand it. The circumstances of your birth are hardly your fault."

Skye knew that Daniel meant well. In truth, it made no difference to him. She had sensed that from the very beginning, which was why he probably knew her better than anyone outside her own family. But he was naive about it. She could have pointed out that his parents had never invited her into his home, although they would have been pleased to have made Jay Mac's acquaintance.

The circumstances of her birth, as Daniel referred to them, had taken on a new twist in recent years when John MacKenzie Worth had actually married his mis-

tress. It had made some difference to New York's social
elite that he had seen fit to make a match after the
death of his wife, although behind closed doors they
had blamed him for her suicide. Prior to Nina's death,
Jay Mac had openly kept Moira Dennehy as his mistress
and had raised five bastard daughters with her.

Skye was no more accepted in the social circle of her
peers than her mother or sisters had been; she merely
worked harder at it. There was an awkward transition
when Jay Mac married Moira, but by then people were
so used to cutting out the Dennehy women no one knew
quite how to stop. Then there was the fact that Skye had
not been moved to take "Worth" as her own surname.
She had grown up as a Dennehy. She was not enamored
of the idea of replacing it with something else.

That last thought brought Skye back to her earlier
conversation with her father. "He's got some sort of
plan up his sleeve, you know."

Daniel's light brows came together as he frowned.
"Who? Charlie?"

"No, not Charlie. I don't care about Charlie or Alice
or any of the others." Which was more or less the truth.
"I'm talking about Jay Mac. This inventor business is
just a bit suspicious. It's not like my— " Without warning, Daniel's left foot slipped to the side and caught the
blade on Skye's right skate. They wobbled, clutching
one another, scrambling to hold their balance. Somewhat to Skye's amazement it was Daniel who managed
to compensate, his lanky figure folding and unfolding
like the pleats of an accordion. Skye went down with
an unladylike *oooff* and sprawled across the ice on her
stomach. Her face was protected by the ermine muff
she had managed to raise at the last possible second. It
cradled her head on the ice while she caught her breath.

She was vaguely aware that she and Daniel had become the center of some confusion and attention. A

few couples had managed to avoid bumping into them
as they had teetered on the ice, but two others not paying attention had gone down hard. Skye heard her
name used like a curse. She smiled, closing her eyes as
she took a quick inventory of body parts. She sensed,
rather than saw, Daniel hunkering down beside her and
the beginnings of a crowd gathering around them both.

"Skye? Are you all right?" he asked, touching her
temple. "Where do you hurt?"

She opened one eye and said drily, "All over."

"Is anything broken?"

Skye was still taking inventory. She stretched her legs
and rotated her ankles. "Nothing's broken."

"Do you think she'll lose the baby?" someone in the
crowd whispered, loudly enough to be heard.

"She shouldn't have been skating," said another.
"She probably wanted to be rid of it."

"I think she fainted," said a third.

The conversation around her was so absurd, so patently ridiculous, that at first Skye had no idea she was
the subject of the scandalous speculation. It was the
stricken look on Daniel's face that made her take notice
of the talk and eventually apply it to herself.

"It's happened before in her family," a voice whispered knowingly. The confidential tone was carried on
the back of the wind to all parts of the gathering circle.
"Her sisters, you know."

"Not all of them, surely. Isn't one a nun?"

"Why do you think she went into the convent?" came
a reply. It was said with the authority of gospel.

"My mother says this is the final straw," said a young
woman. "I'm not allowed to accept any more invitations
if *she'll* be there. It doesn't matter who her father is.
My mother says it's what happens when a Protestant
like Jay Mac takes up with a Catholic." There was a
small pause, as if the speaker was shuddering. "If she

knew about tonight . . ." She let her voice drift away, allowing her friends to imagine the consequences she might suffer if her mother heard about this incident.

Skye was too angry to be mortified. Did they think she was deaf? She held out her hand to Daniel. "Will you help me up?"

He took her hand and her elbow and assisted her into a sitting position. "You're certain you're all right?"

"I will be, as soon as you get me out of here." She hardly recognized her own voice. The words had been said through clenched teeth.

The crowd began to disperse as Daniel helped Skye to her feet. His own balance wasn't steady but no one offered to lend a hand. Looping his arm under Skye's, he supported her as they skated away from the party to the edge of the pond and the bench located on the perimeter. After she sat down he knelt in front of her and began loosening the laces on her skates.

"You shouldn't pay them any attention, Skye," he told her. "They were speaking without thinking."

Skye's low chuckle was humorless. "They were speaking *exactly* what they were thinking."

"They were showing their ignorance."

Skye had nothing to say to that. "How do these rumors start?"

He shrugged. "It seems as though there has to be someone to scapegoat."

"But this time it's me."

Daniel pulled off her skates and found Skye's shoes under the bench. "Put these on. I'll take you home." He sat down beside her and wrestled with his own laces.

"Remember the masquerade at the Bilroths' last month?" Skye asked.

"Of course I remember." He had had his share of attention as a buccaneer. Skye had had hers because she was one of two women to faint in the hot and crowded ballroom. The other was Mrs. Spencer, a matron in her sixties who was said to suffer a heart condition. Daniel supposed that that was the origin of the rumors.

Skye saw by his changing expression that he understood. "I suppose it's easy for people to think the worst of me." She sighed. "Though, truth be known, there are a lot worse things than being pregnant."

Daniel blushed at her plain speaking. "Watch your voice," he cautioned her. "People will hear."

"What if they do?" she said recklessly. She raised her voice purposefully and repeated, "There are a lot worse things than being pregnant."

Daniel wanted to slink off the bench and into a nearby snowdrift. Skye's timing had been perfect. A lull in the music permitted her voice to carry across the pond unfettered. He saw several people in the skating party glance in their direction. "You've convinced them now."

"They were already convinced. They probably think— " she raised her voice again, "— you're the father."

Daniel turned on her, yanking his scarf away from his face. "Skye! That's not amusing!"

She couldn't find it in herself to be contrite. "Would you be ashamed to be the father of my child?"

"Don't be ridiculous," he said, dismissing her.

Skye had expected a fervent denial from him, not some comment on the absurdity of her statement. "Daniel?" She turned toward him, studying his profile. "*Would* you be ashamed?" she asked softly. She watched the play of emotion on his face and heard in his hesitation an answer for which she wasn't prepared. "Oh, Daniel," she said sadly. "You, too."

He sat up a little straighter, defending himself. "You haven't let me answer."

"Yes, I have." She finished slipping on her shoes and picked up her muff. "It's all right. Don't give it another thought. I know I won't. It's not as if I wanted to have a child by you so I don't know why I'm disappointed. Perhaps it's just because I thought you were my friend."

"I *am* your friend."

"You wouldn't be ashamed." She stood, turned her back on Daniel, and began walking away. He called to her, but he was tangled in his skate laces. Skye didn't look back. When she heard him call again, she increased her pace. It was important to get away from Daniel right now. What his friends thought only touched her a little; Daniel's silent admission seemed more like a complete betrayal.

Skye found one of the paths in the park and kept to it. Where the snow hadn't been cleared it was crusted, and her leather boots made a crunching sound as she hurried along. She concentrated on the sound, trying to block out more intrusive thoughts, but she was only marginally successful. In the silent spaces she heard the condemning voices. She not only heard what they had said; she imagined she heard the reproachful things they'd all been thinking.

In her mind she heard them call her mother an Irish Catholic whore. The way they said it it was difficult to know which word carried the most disapproval. Skye heard old, familiar phrases like "The apple doesn't fall far from the tree," and "Like mother, like daughter." It didn't matter that Moira Dennehy and Jay Mac Worth had been together for more than a quarter of a century, that her mother had loved no other man. She was a whore, her five daughters bastards; and while Jay Mac's wealth and considerable influence sometimes altered the way the Dennehys were treated, it did little to change what anyone thought of them.

The family had weathered scandals more damaging than this little rumor, Skye thought, but it was the first one that had touched her so personally. She wondered if her father had heard the rumor. Was that why he was offering her the opportunity to get away?

It was something worth considering, and Skye promised herself she'd confront her father directly on the matter. He'd scowl at her straight talking, probably waggle his finger at her for being impudent, but she'd be able to see through his bluster to his heart. She'd know if he was lying.

A sound behind her caught Skye's attention, stopped her musing, and halted her in her tracks. She felt the hair rise at the back of her neck as the crunching sound came again, this time closer. She had wanted to believe it had been her own feet making the noise, that the sound had been an echo of her own steps. She had to stop pretending that now.

Skye stepped off the path and moved into the shadowed area of some pines. The evergreen canopy sheltered her. She hugged the rough bark of one tree, making herself nearly invisible. She couldn't even say why she was suddenly wary, why she suspected it was someone other than Daniel sharing the path with her. Her breathing became light and shallow. She waited and watched.

The man who came along the path had established a pace that was both hurried and somehow restrained, as if he wanted to run but was holding himself back. Skye saw him pause not far from her grove of trees. He never once looked in her direction but cast a backward glance over his shoulder. It was then she realized she had never had anything to fear from him, that he wasn't following her, but that someone was following *him*.

His breath seemed to hang in the air a moment as he considered his options. He blew on his ungloved hands to warm them while his eyes darted around, looking for protection in the bushes and trees. Skye could hear another set of footsteps approaching, then realized it was at least two men, perhaps more. She almost called to the man on the path, beckoning him to join her, when she saw he had made his decision not to hide or run. He was turning in the direction of his pursuers, his fists clenching and unclenching lightly at his sides.

His body crouched slightly, his lean frame coiled in a way that made him seem powerfully wound. His feet weren't planted, his shoulders weren't braced, he held himself lightly and loosely, giving the impression of lithe tensile strength. He wore neither a hat nor a scarf. In the moonlight his hair only appeared dark and overlong at the nape where it brushed the collar of his coat. His profile was clean shaven and stark, the lines of his face hard. He was so still that he might have been a statue.

They came upon him suddenly. There were two of them, Skye saw, relieved that there weren't more, though why she should be favoring the lone stranger she couldn't say. They were both burly, hard muscular men with shoulder spans that seemed as wide as they were tall. They both wore wool caps that covered their hair and ears. One cap appeared black, the other a lighter color, probably yellow in daylight. Their faces were broad and their cheeks were hidden by large side whiskers. Their chins were bare.

"There he is!" Black Cap yelled. They charged forward as if expecting their quarry to turn tail and run. When he didn't, they didn't stop to think what it might mean.

Yellow Cap leaped first, throwing himself at his prey to drag him to the ground. Skye pressed her knuckles against her mouth to keep from shouting a warning. As she watched, the man simply and gracefully pivoted to one side and Yellow Cap pitched forward, flailing at the air until he landed belly down on the path. He grunted hard, the warm air spilling from his body and misting in the moonlight.

Seeing what happened to his companion brought Black Cap skidding to a halt. "You all right?" he called.

There was a muffled groan. Black Cap accepted it as a signal that no real harm had been done. He gave his full attention to his quarry, circling slowly, elbows bent and gloved fists raised in a fighting posture.

Black Cap closed the circle, jabbing and thrusting with his right. The other man feinted, easily dodging and ducking the intended blows. A left hook sailed above his head. A right jab missed his ribs by inches. Skye saw Black Cap become frustrated and make his punches wilder and harder. Yellow Cap was on his knees, pushing himself upright. He staggered for a step or two, found his land legs, and threw himself into the fight.

With Black Cap and Yellow Cap both punching and jabbing, their victim had to watch his front and his back. He was able to avoid their throws, bobbing and weaving, until both his assailants were fairly growling with anger. Without a word passing between the two of them, they closed in again. Then Black Cap managed a swing that connected. The stranger's head snapped back and he lost his footing for a moment, pushed backward by the force of the blow. Black Cap came at him again, this time aiming for his ribs, but his victim was already recovering.

From Skye's vantage point she thought the lone man's movements were so precise they almost seemed choreographed. He twisted and feinted with the powerful grace of a dancer, his hands and arms part of the same motion as his legs. He struck like a snake, coiled in one moment, then unleashing a terrible fury in the next.

The stranger used his right hand like a cleaver, chopping Black Cap hard on the curve of his neck and shoulder. Black Cap's heavy coat wasn't enough padding to absorb the power behind that blow and his knees buckled under him. He groaned, as much in surprise by the attack as in pain.

Yellow Cap stepped back, confused by his victim's tactics. The distance he put between himself and his quarry prevented the stranger from using his arms. Yellow Cap couldn't have anticipated that the stranger might use his legs.

Skye's eyes widened as she saw the stranger leap feet first. His right foot connected with Yellow Cap's midriff. Before Yellow Cap could take stock of what had happened, the stranger's left foot followed through, shoving Yellow Cap backward with enough force to push the breath from his lungs. Gasping for air, Yellow Cap dropped to his knees again, this time clutching his middle. When his head dropped forward, exposing the vulnerable back side of his neck, the stranger struck again, this time with the same cleaver-like chop he had used on Black Cap. Yellow Cap toppled sideways and lay groaning for a moment before his body jerked once, then was completely still.

Skye's gaze lifted from Yellow Cap's motionless body to his partner's. Black Cap charged the stranger from behind. She opened her mouth to yell a warning and in the next second realized it wasn't necessary. The stranger seemed to have an awareness beyond what his eyes could see. He pivoted and stepped out of the path of Black Cap's charge. At the same time he reached out to grab Black Cap by the scruff of the neck and the small of the back and pushed, using Black Cap's own considerable weight and speed to force him even further away.

Black Cap stumbled and fell forward, collapsing on all fours just a few feet from where Skye stood. She remained perfectly still in her hiding place, afraid to even draw a breath. Black Cap shook himself off, much like a shaggy, sopping wet dog after a bath, then he scrambled to his feet, turned, and charged again.

It seemed to Skye that the stranger waited until the last possible second to step out of the way. Black Cap was once again helped along in the direction he was already going. This time he skidded on the ground on his stomach and face, his broad chin pushing clumps of snow out of the way like a plow. For a moment he remained still and Skye thought he just might have the good sense not to get up. It wasn't to be. She winced as Black Cap pushed himself into a kneeling position, swiped at his icy chin with the back of his hand, and looked over his shoulder at the prey who had become the predator.

"You're a nasty bit of business, ain't you?" Black Cap muttered. "You afraid to face me with your fists?"

The stranger stood his ground, saying nothing.

"That's what I thought." He reached into the pocket of his coat and pulled out a derringer, a deadly weapon in the right hands and at close range. "Then go up against this, you bastard."

The stranger didn't wait until Black Cap finished his sentence before he attacked. His lithe body was a blur of motion, spinning, flying, leaping. A single kick dislodged the gun from Black Cap's hand. His wrist, devoid of all feeling now, was trapped beneath the stranger's foot. A second solid kick to Black Cap's gut drove the breath from his lungs. Black Cap collapsed and never saw the blow that centered between his shoulder blades. His body shuddered once, then was as still as his partner's.

The stranger stepped back and paused, looking at his felled attackers. Skye thought he might be using the time to catch his breath, but he wasn't winded in the least. He simply seemed to be indulging in a moment of detached curiosity.

Skye watched him take his fill. He shook his head back and forth slowly, as if he could not quite believe what had taken place, or at least couldn't comprehend the stupidity of his assailants. Although his back was to Skye, she imagined that she could see his mouth curved in an ironic sort of half smile.

"You were never in any danger, ma'am."

Skye started, blinking widely. She looked around, her

eyes darting to shadows on the other side of the path. It didn't seem possible that he intended his comment for her.

"Or is it 'miss'?" he asked.

Mary Schyler inched away from the pine tree but not out from under its protective canopy. "Sure and I'm thinkin' it's none of your concern," she said cheekily, affecting her mother's lilting Irish brogue.

He turned toward her and the moon shining on his face gave Skye slender evidence of a smile that was a bit menacing in its coolness. "You're right," he said. "You'd better be on your way."

Skye didn't want to leave the safety of the sheltering pines. She was merely a shadow to him and she wanted to remain that way. "You first." He ducked his head and she thought the action hid a more fulsome smile. She wished she could see him better, yet to do so would have compromised her own anonymity.

"I need to look after these men, don't you think?" he asked her.

Since both Black Cap and Yellow Cap seemed to be perfectly unconscious, Skye could only imagine what his "looking after" might entail. "You're going to kill them?" she asked. "Right here in the park?" She thought she heard him chuckle. The low, husky, back-of-the-throat sound sent a shiver up her spine, yet she recognized it wasn't fear that she felt, but something just as elemental and infinitely more intimate.

"I'm going to tie them up."

Remembering what Black Cap had pulled out of his pocket after reaching inside, Skye held her breath as the stranger's hand slipped into his own overcoat. A normal rhythm resumed when he held out a length of rope and dangled it in front of her. "You were prepared," she said.

"I've learned to be."

She wondered what sort of man he was that he had

anticipated a walk in the park to be so fraught with danger. It occurred to Skye that she didn't even know which side of the law he was on. "Why were they after you?" she asked.

"Sure, and I'm thinkin' it's none of your concern," he said, echoing her earlier words as well as her accent.

This time she heard the smile in his voice even if she couldn't see it. He was amused by her and that didn't set well with Skye. "I could scream," she told him, "and bring down the beat cops on your head."

"You could," he said. He knelt beside Black Cap, drew out a knife, and cut off a length of rope. In short order he had the man securely trussed, his hands behind his back and one of his own gloves stuffed in his mouth.

Skye couldn't say why she was still standing around, except perhaps because it was the most exciting thing that had ever happened to her. It was practice of sorts, she supposed, for being an adventuress.

Out of the corner of her eye she saw that Yellow Cap was stirring. She started to call out a warning, then saw it was unnecessary. Once again the stranger seemed to have anticipated trouble. He turned on his haunches, saw Yellow Cap's struggle, and neatly clipped him on the chin with his fist. Yellow Cap's jaw cracked and his head struck the frozen ground with a thud. Skye winced.

"So you *can* fight with your fists," she said when she'd recovered her voice. "Just like a Dublin street brawler."

The stranger merely shrugged and began tying up Yellow Cap. When he was done, he dragged the unconscious man toward Skye's hiding place.

She retreated quickly. "What are you doing?" she demanded. She wished her voice could have shown more anger and less fear.

"I'm moving him off the path," he said calmly. Even the exertion of dragging Yellow Cap's considerable bulk to the hiding place hadn't winded him. He came within a few feet of Skye but he didn't once turn in her direction. After leaning Yellow Cap against the rough trunk of an evergreen, he shifted his attention to Black Cap and repeated the procedure. He completed his activity by kicking up snow where it had been pressed flat from dragging the bodies. In less than a minute he had obscured the trail to the bodies.

When he was standing on the path again, he glanced once in Skye's direction. "You'd better go before they come around and you're discovered with them."

Skye hesitated, waiting for the stranger to move on.

"I assure you they won't be half so gallant as I am about a lady's welfare."

She blushed and her husky brogue deepened. "You do me credit, sir, callin' me a lady, but I'm not so fine as all that."

The stranger was quiet a moment, considering. "Then perhaps you'd agree to go somewhere with me. There'd be money in it for you."

"You mistook my meanin', sir; I said I wasn't so fine as a lady, but that doesn't mean I'm a whore."

The stranger was stunned into silence, then he chuckled lowly. "And *you* mistook *my* meaning. You could help me if— " He stopped. There was a shout of rowdy laughter somewhere along the path behind him. More than one person was part of the vocal fray. Someone called a name. A woman giggled in response. A joke was finished and there was more laughter.

"Go on," Skye urged him when the stranger hesitated, looking in her direction. "Get out of here." She would have repeated herself, but he needed no second urging. He vanished almost in front of her eyes.

Skye came out of her hiding place just as Daniel and his friends came upon the grove of pines.

"Skye!" Daniel said, halting in his tracks. "I thought you'd gone home."

"And I see you lost no time in chasing after me," she said sarcastically. She glared at his friends. They didn't have the same grace as Daniel to look sheepish. Her eyes touched everyone in the crowd. Louisa Edison and Alice Hobbs were gaping at her. Thomas Newman's laughter had been trapped at the back of his throat. Charlie was staring at the ground. Richard Mill and Amy Scott seemed to wish themselves elsewhere.

Skye was suddenly fiercely angry. Angry at Louisa and Alice for staring at her as if she'd grown another head. Angry at Thomas for not sharing his laughter. Angry at Charlie and Richard and Amy for being embarrassed. But most of all, Skye was angry with Daniel for not supporting her. She was a lady and she had never given them any reason to think otherwise.

The words simply came tumbling out. "What if it had been the baby, Daniel?" she asked. "What if something had happened to the baby?"

There was a collective gasp from Amy, Alice, and Louisa. The men were staring at Daniel, their looks registering something between horror and admiration.

Skye turned her back on them all and marched away.

Two

"Skye! Wait for me!" Daniel looked at his speechless friends and made a quick apology. "She's making it up," he said. "Just to give you what you want to hear. I swear it!" He took off running. "Skye!"

She didn't turn her head, but she didn't increase her speed to avoid him, either. "Did you make excuses for me?" she asked, when he came abreast. "Perhaps you told them I'm a little out of sorts because of the baby."

Daniel grabbed her elbow but she shook him off. "You're being unreasonable. Why you purposely want to feed their silly speculations, I don't know. You're determined to make yourself an outcast."

Skye's hands clenched inside the ermine muff. She bent her head against the wind as they left the park. "I've always been an outcast, Daniel. Tonight's merely the first time it's been so openly discussed." She spoke so softly that Daniel had to bend forward to hear her. "There's nothing for me in the city; there never has been. I don't know how I always knew that, but I did. I've never wanted anything so much as to get away from here."

Daniel stepped to the edge of the sidewalk and waved down a hansom cab. He gave the driver Skye's address. "What about school?" he asked, as they climbed aboard.

She shrugged. "I don't want to go back for the spring term."

"But—"

Skye turned to Daniel and gave him a frank stare. "Don't you think Jay Mac already suspects that's the case?"

"It hadn't occurred to me."

She gave a short, humorless laugh. "That's because you don't know him as I do. He's not only realized I intend to fight him about returning to school, he thinks he's a step ahead of me. That's what his amazing offer was about this evening."

"You mean he dangled this in front of you in the hopes you'll choose going back to school over being a housekeeper?"

Skye snorted indelicately. "You really don't understand how he thinks, do you?"

"I suppose I don't."

Removing one of her hands from her muff, Skye patted Daniel's arm. "It's all right. He's my father, after all, and I've had years of opportunity watching him work on my older sisters. He has the best of intentions, you understand. He wants to be certain we're always well cared for."

Daniel sighed. He raised one leg and rested it casually on the seat opposite him while he slouched restfully beside his friend. "Do you know what, Skye? I think I'm glad I bungled that first kiss with you. I'm not sure I'd want John MacKenzie Worth for my father-in-law."

Skye leaned into Daniel, laying her head against his shoulder. "You wouldn't, Daniel," she said feelingly. "You really wouldn't."

He laughed at her heartfelt comment. "You don't think you'd be worth it?"

"Oh, God. I *know* I'm not." She glanced up at him. "You saw what happened this evening. I can't leave well enough alone. If people give me an opening to make a public fool of myself I not only take the opportunity, I *thank* them for it."

Jo Goodman

Daniel grinned. "You're worth it," he said. "I'm the one not up to snuff." Before she could contradict what he knew to be the truth, he said, "I still don't understand your father's plan."

"The story about the engine and the inventor . . . that's just smoke and mirrors."

"Smoke and mirrors . . ."

"Sleight of hand," she explained. "A magician's trick to hide what's really going on."

"And what's really going on is . . ."

"Is Jay Mac wants me to experience complete boredom. He supposes that after a few weeks or months as a housekeeper for some fusty old man, I'll be begging him to allow me to finish school."

"So the adventure he's offering you is all a lie."

Skye nodded. "Precisely. Jay Mac's lies don't get much bigger."

Daniel noticed that Skye was smiling. "You don't seem angry about it. I wouldn't have thought you'd like being manipulated like this."

"I don't. But if I look on the bright side, I can be glad Jay Mac tried to bribe me with something I find appealing. It means in his own way he understands what I want. He wasn't nearly so accommodating with my sisters."

The swaying motion of the hansom quieted as the cab slowed in front of the Worth mansion. Daniel helped Skye out of the cab and escorted her through the iron gate to the front door. "Will you take your father's offer, then?" he asked.

"Probably. I wasn't certain I would when he brought it up, but after this evening . . . well, it's better that I go off somewhere to have the baby."

"Skye!"

She graced him with her mischievous, dimpled smile. "I can't behave myself," she said. "It's not in my nature." Standing on tiptoe, she rested her hands on

Daniel's shoulders and kissed him on the cheek. "Go pursue Evelyn Hardy," she told him. "She'll make you happier than I ever could."

A moment later Daniel was alone on the stone steps of the mansion, bathed in the yellow light coming from the towering arched windows. What Skye had said about Evelyn wasn't true, he thought. If it were, he wouldn't feel so ineffably sad.

Hunching his shoulders against the wind, Daniel ducked his head. The hansom cab was waiting to take him home.

Moira looked up from her needlepoint as Skye passed the parlor entrance. "You're home early," she said.

Skye backed up a few steps and remained framed by the dark wood of the doorway. "It was uncomfortably cold for skating," she lied, removing her hat and muff. She tucked both of them under her arm. "Where's Jay Mac?"

"In his study. Where's Daniel?"

"I sent him home."

"He's a nice young man."

Not wanting to give her mother any reason to hope, Skye nodded absently. "Has Jay Mac talked any more about his idea?" she asked.

"Almost nonstop since you left," Moira said. Her smile was indulgent. "I banished him to the study."

"What do you think?"

Moira didn't hesitate. The lines at the corners of her eyes and mouth deepened as she said sternly, "I think it's as foolish an idea as Jay Mac ever gets in his head."

Skye laughed. "We agree, then. What do you think I should do?"

"Whatever will make you happy."

Moira's answer gave Skye pause. She leaned against the door frame and tucked a tendril of bright-red hair

behind her ear. Her green eyes darkened with speculation. "You don't think I'm happy?" she asked.

The lines of Moira's face smoothed as she stopped
working on her embroidery. "I think you're making
yourself miserable working at being so happy. Sure, and
it shouldn't be so hard."

Skye's mouth sagged a little as her mother neatly
summed up what she had been feeling for months, perhaps years. "Then you wouldn't mind if I didn't return
to college?"

"You've got to want it for yourself, Skye. Just because
your sisters went doesn't mean you have to follow in
their wake."

"Perhaps if it weren't so confining," she said almost
apologetically.

"It's not the classroom. You're confined if you're not
moving." Sensing her daughter was about to interrupt,
Moira held up one hand to cut her off. "It's no good
telling me you think otherwise. Mary Francis, Michael,
Rennie, and Maggie all had direction. They were going
somewhere specific. Whereas you . . ." Moira's gentle
smile touched her eyes. "Whereas you, Mary Schyler,
want to go everywhere."

"I do, Mama, I really do." Her voice had the sound
of youth, earnest and eager.

"Then you have your father to deal with, not me."
Moira bent her head and examined her needlework.
"Look at this. I've used the wrong thread on this rose."
Moira didn't expect a response. She knew she was alone
and that Skye had gone in search of Jay Mac.

Skye pushed open the door of the study, not bothering
to knock. Jay Mac was at his desk. Behind him flames
were crackling in the fireplace. A number of books were
stacked haphazardly on one corner of the desk and the
rest of the surface was covered by ledgers and papers.

Jay Mac pushed his spectacles up the bridge of his

nose and looked up as Skye closed the door. "Too cold for skating, I imagine," he said, leaning back in his large leather chair. The soft burgundy padding cushioned him as he situated himself comfortably.

"Something like that," Skye admitted.

"That Pendergrass boy isn't still skulking around, is he?"

Skye gave her father a small smile. "No, Papa, he's gone home. I think he's a little afraid of you."

"What?"

"Don't pretend you're surprised. You like it that way." Skye didn't give him an opportunity to deny it. She dropped her hat and muff on a chair and followed it with her coat, draping it over the back. She walked over to the fireplace and held out her hands. "Did you know that Daniel's friends think I'm carrying a child?" she asked bluntly.

Jay Mac's broad face took on a ruddy cast. He clutched the pen in his hand so tightly his knuckles went white. "No, I didn't know," he said carefully.

Skye recognized when her father's temper was strained to the limit. "It's not true, Jay Mac. I just wondered if you'd heard the rumor. I thought perhaps it was one of the reasons you suggested that I go live with this inventor for a while."

"Well, it wasn't. I never heard that nonsense. Who's repeating it?"

She shrugged. "I imagine most everyone. Daniel's friends let it slip this evening. It was the first I'd heard. I fainted at the Bilroths' masquerade. Remember? I told you and Mama about it."

"I remember. Daniel brought you home. You both said it was stifling hot in their ballroom."

"It was. But I suppose other people put a different construction on events."

Jay Mac turned in his chair and faced the fire. Skye

was a slender silhouette against the flames. "Perhaps this isn't the best time for you to leave the city."

She turned, surprised. A wisp of hair fell across her brow and she pushed it back. "What do you mean? I thought you wanted me to go."

"I did . . . I *do*. But I wonder if it's a good thing for you. It will support the rumors. Everyone will think you've gone away to have your child."

Skye knew he was thinking of Maggie. It was what her sister had done when she had had to face the real dilemma. "If I stay, people will assume I had an abortion."

Jay Mac's lips flattened. "I can't say that I like your plain-speaking."

"People will believe what they want to," she said. "That's all I was trying to say."

"I didn't say I didn't understand it," he pointed out. "Just that I didn't like it." Jay Mac took off his spectacles and cleaned the lenses with a handkerchief from his breast pocket. The action was more indicative of the fact he was thinking than of his spectacles being smudged. "You and your sisters have had to deal with a lot of sly rumors over the years," he said quietly, almost sadly. "If I could have known . . ."

Skye perched herself on the arm of her father's chair and rested one hand on his shoulder. "What would you have done differently?" she asked. "Not loved Mother? Not had children with her?"

He shook his head. Life without Moira was unimaginable. Life without his five daughters would not have been nearly so joyful. "There's nothing I could have done," he admitted.

"I'm glad to hear it." She meant it. Regret was wasteful. "Now, if we agree there's nothing to be changed in your life, perhaps we can agree that it's time to change something in mine. I've decided I'd like nothing better than to spy for you."

"Mary Schyler," he said sternly. "If you think—"

She patted his shoulder. "I know. I know. You don't want me to spy. You want me to steal." Skye felt her father's shoulders rise and fall as he sighed. "All right. What you really want me to do is become a housekeeper for—" She paused, waiting for Jay Mac to fill in a name.

"Jonathan Parnell."

"Jonathan Parnell," she repeated thoughtfully. "I think I could be a housekeeper for Mr. Parnell. How would I acquire the position?"

"There's no trick to it, Skye. You'd have to apply."

"Do you mean he's advertised?"

"In this morning's *Chronicle*. It's what gave me the idea."

That gave Skye pause. She would have thought her father had been working on this plan for weeks, if not months. It was not like him to leave things to chance. Skye had supposed he would have already thought of a way to make certain the position was hers. She wondered if she could believe him. "Do you have the paper?"

Jay Mac pointed to the newspaper neatly folded on one corner of his desk. Skye left her perch on his chair and picked it up. It took her a few minutes to find it. When she did, she looked up, surprised. "This address is in the Hudson Valley."

"Where did you think I was sending you?"

"I don't know." But she had hoped it would be somewhere more distant than upstate New York. Her brows came together and her mouth flattened as she read the ad again. "Why, this house can't be far from our summer home."

He heard her disappointment. "It's not."

She glanced up, thoughtful now. "It seems I remember someone buying the Granville place. It wasn't so many years ago. You don't mean . . ."

Jay Mac was nodding. "Parnell's the owner."

Skye's eyes widened. "But that house is haunted!" As soon as the words were out, Skye was flushing with embarrassment. It was an old tale, something she had heard rumored for as long as Jay Mac had made the valley their summer home. That had been every bit of fifteen years. "Rennie said so," she finished lamely.

Her father laughed. "So you *do* remember those stories. I wondered."

Skye leaned against the desk, her arms crossed casually in front of her. "How could I forget? It was a source of speculation every summer." She smiled now, remembering. "Would the Granville ghost leave his house and come for us? Rennie assigned us all watch duty. I took first watch because I was the youngest."

Jay Mac's laughter deepened. "Do you really think any of your sisters kept vigil after you?" His eyes crinkled at the corners as he took stock of Skye's expression. "You never suspected, did you?"

"Those *brats!* I can't believe they . . . yes, I can . . . it's just like them. Especially Rennie. Wait until I see her! I used to sit at the windowseat in the attic for two horrifying hours looking out for that ghost! I thought I was protecting them and all the while they were having a laugh at my expense!"

Jay Mac thought he couldn't laugh any harder, but Skye's outrage was very real. One would think her sisters' prank had happened yesterday, not a dozen or more years ago. He was forced to pull out a handkerchief and dab at his damp eyes. "Forgive me," he finally managed to say. "It's just that . . ."

"I was such a *fool*. Yes," she said tartly, a little hurt by her father's amusement, "it was a good joke on me."

"Mary Francis put a stop to it."

That didn't appease Skye. "I think I was ten when Rennie told me I could stop keeping watch. By then I was actually volunteering for it. Everyone let it go on for years."

"You can take that up with your sisters," he said. "Your mother and I didn't know a thing until it was stopped. Then Mary Francis made everyone confess."

"Thank God she had a conscience," Skye said feelingly.

Jay Mac cleared his throat and looked a little uncomfortable. "I believe Mary Francis was tired of carrying you down from the attic after you fell asleep during your watch." He shrugged apologetically. "At least, that's the story I remember."

Skye snorted indelicately. "It will be a pleasure plotting my revenge," she said. "And after all this time, surely surprise is on my side."

Jay Mac could almost feel sorry for his other daughters because he was confident that Skye would think of something. His eyes fell to the newspaper again. "You intend to respond to Mr. Parnell?" he asked.

It took Skye a moment to understand her father's question. Her thoughts had gone spinning in another direction entirely. She picked up the paper, rolled it, and tapped it lightly, thoughtfully, against the edge of the desk. "I'll compose a letter this evening. I suppose I shall need references."

Jay Mac had already considered that. "I've talked to Dr. Turner and Logan Marshall. They would both be willing to write letters of recommendation."

"And all of it done today. Imagine that. You were very certain of me."

He shook his head. "I was hopeful."

"This means I'll be missing the spring term at school."

"Is that a sacrifice?" he asked. "I didn't think you were enjoying yourself."

Skye couldn't remember that her father had ever thought she should attend college to enjoy herself. His lecture had invariably included the fact that she should study harder. "It's not a sacrifice. I wasn't doing very well."

"That's not because you're not smart enough," he said.

Suspecting that he was warming up to a speech, Skye leaned forward, dropped a kiss on her father's cheek, and bade him goodnight. In the hallway she called the same to her mother before tripping lightly up the stairs.

Skye's bedroom was in a separate wing from that of her parents. At one time she had her sisters on every side of her. Now she was alone. Some nights she missed the sharing and confiding, the laughter and tears, but this evening she didn't mind them being gone. One of them might have tried to talk her out of going to the valley. Someone, probably Rennie, would have brought up the Granville ghost and tried to frighten her out of her plan.

Skye caught her reflection in the mirror above her vanity. Her mouth was lifted at one corner in a half smile. She shook her head, laughing at herself. That ghost. From the moment she realized her destination was the Granville house she'd felt a thrill of fear that made her instantly feel all of five again. And not only fear. There was curiosity that was almost like a hunger. Excitement squeezed her stomach and heart. It was the kind of anxiety that skirted the edge of panic and gave her restless energy instead.

She'd felt that same way in the park tonight, not when she was surrounded by Daniel and his friends, but when she was hiding in the pines, watching the stranger face his enemies.

Skye sat at her vanity, dropped the newspaper among her perfumes and creams and rouge, and took the pins from her hair. As she threaded it with her fingers, her hair was like fiery silk against her skin. She massaged her temples, easing the tension that had begun to form there.

The stranger. She had managed to put the incident

behind her, but not the feelings. She wanted her life to be that exciting. It hadn't seemed earlier that being a housekeeper for Jonathan Parnell quite fit the bill. Now, thinking of confronting that childhood ghost, for all that it was only a story meant to scare her, it seemed that a door had been opened to her. There was no sense in not stepping through it.

Skye unbuttoned the throat of her velvet bodice. Flipping open the paper again, she reread Parnell's ad.

Housekeeper desired for year-round employment. Small staff. Must be able to do both heavy and light work. Room and board. $50 per month. Please reply to 224 Brooke Place, Baileyboro, New York.

Heavy work . . . she wondered if he expected his housekeeper to move the furniture as well as dust it. The wages were less than her father gave her for an allowance, but she would survive quite nicely in Baileyboro. There was no place in the hamlet to spend her money. Small staff. She remembered the Granville home as being every bit as big as anything ever built on Fifth Avenue. It was curious that he didn't require a full staff.

Skye got up from the vanity and turned down her bed. She lighted a lamp on her small writing desk, then went to the armoire and withdrew a nightgown and robe. The nightdress had a border of eyelet lace on the neck, sleeves, and hem, and pearl buttons on the bodice. The material was so voluminous that Skye always felt she was being wrapped in a cloud. The very feminine cut of the nightgown disappeared as Skye slipped into her comfortable old robe. The plain cotton wrapper, shiny at the elbows, worn at the hem, and frayed along the sash, had certainly seen better days, but Skye couldn't part with it.

After belting the sash, Skye sat down to compose her response to the ad. It took her several attempts to find the right words. She didn't want to sound too young or inexperienced, afraid that if Mr. Parnell suspected she was young, she might not even be granted an interview. The references from Dr. Turner and Logan Marshall would help, but she had to pass muster first.

Unaware of passing time, Skye looked over her last draft and decided it was worth recopying in her best handwriting. She stretched, arms flung wide, back arched, before hunching over the desk again like an accounting clerk. She had just set pen to paper when she heard a thud belowstairs.

Skye paused, cocked her head to one side, and listened. Out of the corner of her eye she could see the clock on the mantel. It was after one, too late for either her father or her mother still to be up. Mrs. Cavanaugh and her husband had long since retired to their apartment above the carriage house. There were no other servants living on the property.

But there was the unmistakable sound of footsteps.

Rising gingerly from her chair, careful to be quiet, Skye padded barefoot to the door. She fingered the worn threads of her sash as she moved along the hallway to the backstairs. Below her there was silence again. She waited, barely breathing. Just at the point she began to believe she had imagined it, she heard movement again.

It was not possible to know the precise location of the noise. As Skye stealthily made her way down the stairs, she kept hoping she'd find her father in the kitchen with a glass of warm milk, or Mrs. Cavanaugh returned from the carriage house because she'd had a sudden urge to bake bread. Neither explanation seemed particularly likely, and when she reached the bottom of the steps she learned that neither was true. The kitchen was dark and empty and the sounds were coming from somewhere down the hall behind her.

Skye had not considered a weapon until now. She picked up a butcher knife from the wooden cutting block and went into the hallway. There was silence again and Skye learned firsthand how it was possible for silence to be deafening. Blood rushed in her ears, her heart slammed in her chest, and her imagination was marching ahead double time. Having no clear idea what she would do if confronted by an intruder, she went on, opening one door after another, peeking in each room, then stepping back when she found no one.

Outside her father's study she paused again, this time pressing her ear to the door. She crouched and looked through the keyhole. There was a vague light in the room and it startled her until she remembered there had been a fire in the grate. It was only the dying embers, she realized, and turned the handle.

It took a single step into the room to know she was not alone. She felt the presence of another person, the warmth of a body nearby, the tension of fear, the barely audible hum of controlled breathing.

Skye's knuckles whitened on the door handle. She tried to slam the door with herself safely in the hallway, but a foot wedged itself between the door and frame. She opened her mouth to scream and almost immediately something capped the sound. It took her a moment to identify the thing over her mouth as a hand and the texture and smell against her skin and nose as leather. As she fought for breath, another hand captured her wrist and squeezed. In the same motion she was dragged back into the room, her weapon useless now in nerveless fingers. She dropped it as the door was pushed closed behind her. The knife made no sound when it fell on the oriental carpet.

The realization that no one could hear her, or had heard her, made Skye redouble her efforts. She kicked backward, connecting twice in her struggle, but the hold on her never relented. She tried to bite and actually managed to get the leather glove between her teeth once before she sensed a creeping blackness on the edge of her vision. The pressure in her chest became enormous and she clawed at the hand over her mouth. The last thing she remembered was a voice near her ear, the breath hot and damp, telling her to hush.

She didn't imagine she was unconscious long. When she woke she couldn't move or see and she could breathe only through her nose. It was odd, she thought, that she could recognize the cloth that bound and gagged her as scraps from the robe she'd been wearing. She tested the binding at her wrist and ankles. It wasn't tight enough to eliminate circulation, but it was more than sufficient to keep her from getting free.

"You're awake."

The voice came to her from across the room. It was only a husky whisper, but she had no problem making out the words. Skye's response was to become still again.

"I'm not going to hurt you."

Except for a nearly imperceptible lessening of tension, Skye didn't move.

"Just so you know."

She wished he wouldn't talk to her. She couldn't respond, and nothing about the low, sibilant voice was particularly comforting. Turning her head toward him, Skye strained to see through the scrap of thin cotton that covered her eyes. The residual firelight wasn't enough for her to make out more than shadows. The intruder appeared to be in the area of her father's desk. Skye could hear him shuffling papers and opening and closing Jay Mac's drawers.

What was he looking for? She started to ask and her tongue pressed against the ball of cloth that filled her mouth. Her nose wrinkled as she tried to push it out.

"There's nothing you can do."

He was not apologetic. In fact, he sounded smug, as if her helplessness satisfied him. Skye heard nothing from him for several minutes and supposed he was reading. Behind her back she twisted with the binding on her wrists.

"Is there a safe?"

Skye heard papers being shuffled again and a drawer was closed. There was a finality about the sound that made her think he was done rifling Jay Mac's desk.

"A safe?" he repeated.

This time he was closer and there was agitation and some impatience in his voice. She hadn't heard a chair move or his steps across the carpet. He was so quiet that she wondered what he'd done to draw attention to himself in the first place.

"You can't see, can't move, can't talk, but I know you can hear."

He was hunkered down beside the sofa where she was lying. His face was close to hers. Skye instinctively tried to move away, pushing back against the cushions.

"The safe?"

This time the whisper was menacing. Skye shook her head. There was no safe in the house. Her father kept his important papers at the offices of Northeast Rail.

"There's no safe in the house?"

Skye nodded. She expected him to move away, but he stayed where he was. A hand touched the crown of her hair. Skye flinched. The hand was moved slowly, slipping over her temple and cheek. The leather was cool, and she turned her face to avoid it. "Mr. Worth keeps documents at his office?" she was asked.

It seemed to Skye that it would have been more natural for him to call Jay Mac by name or refer to him as her father. That he didn't suggested to Skye that he didn't know there was a relationship. Why would he? she wondered. He had no reason to think she was anyone but a servant.

His hand moved from her face to her shoulder and rested there. She could feel the soft leather of his glove through the eyelet lace. Would he be touching her so freely if he knew she was Jay Mac's daughter? Skye squirmed. The hand was moved to the curve of her breast and now Skye's entire body stiffened. She held her breath, more afraid in this moment than in any time since entering the room.

"The Worth Building?" he asked deeply, angrily. His thumb flicked the tip of her breast.

Skye shook her head violently. If he had assumed she was a servant, he couldn't really expect her to know more than the fact there was no safe in the house. She sensed his silence, his thinking.

"All right," he said finally. He was slow to remove his hand from her breast, letting it glide under the curve, then along the plane of her belly. "But give this message to Jay Mac." He waited until Skye slowly nodded. "He doesn't own me."

Above the cloth that bound Skye's eyes, her brows rose a fraction.

"He doesn't own me."

There was icy anger in the message. Skye flinched again, this time from the tone. She indicated her understanding with a curt nod, her chin jutting forward aggressively. His low chuckle took her by surprise as did the touch of his hands, now resting over hers. His gloved fingers tugged at the binding. She felt the cloth being unknotted and loosened. When she was free, her wrists were taken and massaged lightly, then the intruder helped her sit up.

He might have expected her to rip at the cloth covering her eyes or mouth, but Skye touched neither with her newfound freedom. Blindly she swung out with her hand and unerringly found the intruder's face. The force of her blow knocked him back. He stumbled before regaining his balance, but managed to come to his feet before

Skye yanked at the cloth on her face. By the time she could see again, she could only see him leaving the room.

Gagging, Skye spat the wad of cloth out of her mouth. She caught her breath, held onto her stomach, and came to her feet. She started to give chase only to be reminded painfully that her ankles were still bound. Her fall was caught by the edge of the sofa and her flailing arms protected her face. She cried out, hoping her mother or father would hear her. The sound that came back to her was the front door opening, then being slammed shut.

Her fingers fumbled with the knots at her ankles. She loosened them enough to push the bindings off her feet and raced for the front door. At the top of the wide staircase behind her she heard Jay Mac call her name. Ignoring him, Skye threw open the door and charged out onto the icy sidewalk. The front gate was swinging shut. She flung it out and went to the curb, looking up and down Broadway. A carriage was turning the corner onto 49th Street. Two pedestrians paused to let it pass. A milk wagon was heading north, the steel cans rattling on the wagon bed as it passed.

Skye saw nothing suspicious. No one was running. No one was alone. She forgot the unseemliness of her attire until the milkman turned his head to stare at her and kept on staring. She looked down at her bare feet. In the light from the gas lamp her nightgown had taken on a yellow cast. Wind buffeted her, making the gown swirl about her legs. Her flame-red hair whipped across her face. Brazening it out, Skye made an exaggerated curtsy to the driver of the milk wagon before stepping back inside her yard. She danced on the icy pavement as she shut the gate, suddenly aware of the bitter cold.

Turning around, Skye started back to the house. Her father was waiting in the open doorway. Behind him she could see her mother perched on one of the lower steps of the staircase. Both her parents looked anxious.

"Skye? What's going on? What are you doing out here dressed like that?"

Sighing, Skye stepped onto the stoop. She looked at the way Jay Mac was braced in the doorway, one arm blocking her entrance. "I think I'd rather come inside to discuss it." She ducked under his arm. "Mama, we should go in the parlor."

"Let me get your robe, Skye," her mother said. "And your slippers." She started back up the stairs.

"Just slippers," Skye called after her. "My robe . . . never mind . . . the slippers will be enough."

Jay Mac closed the front door and stamped his feet to warm them as if he had been outside himself. He hustled Skye into the parlor and started a fire. Moira returned with her slippers and a woolen throw blanket for Skye to put over her lap.

"There was an intruder," Skye said when her parents sat down.

Moira could not sit back on the sofa. She was on the edge, her hands clasped tightly together. "Your father thought he heard something. I told him he was imagining it."

Jay Mac touched his wife's hand. "It's all right, Moira. There's been no injury." His eyes narrowed on Skye. "Has there?"

She shook her head slowly, wondering what she was being asked, then realizing the intent of her father's question, Skye shook her head more vigorously. "No, Papa, no injury. I surprised him while he was searching your desk. He tied me. That's all." Almost all, she thought. She couldn't bring herself to say more. She could still feel the gloved hand resting lightly on her breast. The sensation was so vivid that she wanted to look down at herself.

Moira's voice rose shakily. Her brogue was thicker. "Tied you!"

"Mama, I'm fine. It was something of Jay Mac's that he wanted."

"There was only one man?" asked her father.

"Yes. Only one. He never found what he came for." She hesitated, wondering what she could or should say in front of her mother. Her father seemed to understand and with the merest glance communicated for her to hold her thought.

"Moira," he said. "A cup of tea would be nice. Skye looks as if she could use one."

Moira Dennehy Worth looked from father to daughter. "I'm no one's fool, Jay Mac, and I won't be treated like one now. Sure, and I want to hear what she has to say, same as you." Her tone brooked no argument.

"There was a message," Skye said. "For Jay Mac." Her father remained perfectly still, waiting. " 'He doesn't own me.' That's what the man said."

Moira frowned, turning to see her husband. "What does it mean?"

Jay Mac's pale brows were pulled together. He scratched his temple, thinking. "I have no idea." He met Moira's eyes, then his daughter's. "I honestly have no idea."

"I want you to send for the police," Moira said, looking at the clock. "Liam O'Shea will be another forty minutes making his rounds. I don't want to wait that long for help. Someone should search the grounds now."

"I'll dress and go out, Mama, if it will make you feel better, but I think the intruder's long gone." Skye spoke to her father then. "It's still a good idea to get the police. Your offices at Northeast may be in danger of being ransacked. He wanted to know where you had a safe."

"You told him?"

She shook her head. "I couldn't talk. He gagged me." She saw her mother's horrified look and went on quickly.

"He didn't really expect me to know. He thought I was a servant."

Jay Mac patted Moira's hand. "I'll send Mr. Cavanaugh to find O'Shea. Skye, you're not to go outside again, dressed or not." He stood. "Do you have a description of the man?"

"No. I was blindfolded." She heard the catch of her mother's breath and rushed to reassure her. "I'm *fine*. Really, I'm fine."

Moira remained skeptical, studying Skye carefully. She pointed to Skye's wrist. "Sure, and I don't remember seeing that bruise before."

Skye followed her mother's eyes to her wrist. There was indeed a bruise forming. "I had a knife. He forced me to drop it."

Now Moira sat back on the sofa. She crossed herself and whispered, "Mother of God."

"I'm getting Mr. Cavanaugh," said Jay Mac. "Skye, don't say another word to your mother. Better yet, make *her* some tea." He hurried out of the room.

Skye sat forward. "Mama? Would you like some tea?"

"A little whiskey wouldn't be amiss."

She smiled. "All right. I think I could use the same. I believe I'm actually trembling." She held out her hand and watched it quaver. "What a night this has been." Skye got up and went to the dining room. She returned with two tumblers splashed with whiskey and handed one to her mother. "Did Jay Mac tell you what happened at the skating pond tonight? About me being pregnant?"

"I thought your father told you not to say another word," Moira said drily. "I'm sure I don't want to hear any more."

Skye smiled. Obviously her mother knew the story. "Well, then, I finished my letter of introduction to Mr. Parnell." Moira's look was blank. "The inventor."

Moira nodded. "I see. You're going to go through with it. I wasn't certain if you would."

"It will be fun," she said. "If only to foil Jay Mac's plan."

"You know he has a plan?"

"He always does. I can't imagine this would be different." Skye curled her legs under her and pulled the blanket around her shoulders. She sipped her drink. "Is it the inventor? Does Jay Mac think he would make a good husband?"

Moira found a reason to smile. "That would be like him, wouldn't it?"

"He hasn't told you?"

"He never confides those kinds of plans. I didn't know about Rennie and Jarret or about that awful mess with Maggie and Connor until it was much too late. He knows I don't approve of that sort of interference."

Jay Mac returned. He was holding the butcher knife in one hand. "Mr. Cavanaugh's gone for the police. I've looked in the study. It appears nothing was taken." He held up the knife. "Oh, and I found this on the floor. What were you thinking, Skye?"

"I suppose I wasn't," she admitted. "At least, not clearly."

Jay Mac could only shake his head. "I need a drink." He disappeared into the hallway, taking the knife with him.

The beat cop arrived ten minutes later. He was followed in short order by two more policemen from the station. Mr. Cavanaugh waited on the outskirts of the gathering until Jay Mac assured him he wouldn't be needed again.

Skye made her statement still wrapped in the throw blanket, then Moira hustled her off to bed. Jay Mac went with one of the policemen to the Worth Building, while another stayed on the premises to guard against the intruder's return. Liam O'Shea went back to his beat, alert now to danger in the neighborhood.

Skye rubbed her feet against the cool sheets as her mother tucked her in. She didn't protest Moira's fussing. The act was reassuring for both mother and daughter.

Moira sat on the edge of the bed and touched Skye's forehead with the back of her hand. "You're still chilled," she said, her brow furrowing. "I hope you're not coming down with the ague. Sure, and you were outside in your bare feet without much more than a stitch of clothing on."

Taking her mother's hand, Skye held it firmly between both of hers. "I'll be fine, Mama. It's been an adventurous night, is all."

Moira's reply was a noncommittal grunt at the back of her throat.

Skye smiled. "Good night."

For a moment Moira didn't move. She studied her daughter's flushed face, the cheeks that looked as if excitement had burned color into them, the contented shape of her full mouth, the brightness of eyes that were so brilliantly green they'd shame a shamrock. Moira didn't think she was being prejudiced by blood ties when she thought her daughter, in the space of a few hours, had transcended mere prettiness, even beauty, and become simply radiant.

Moira felt the ache of tears pressing at the backs of her eyes. She blinked to hold them back. "Oh, child," she said softly, leaning forward to kiss Skye's cheek. "You're a piece of work."

Skye started to ask her mother what she meant, but Moira was already removing herself from the bed and turning back the lamps. Rolling on her side, Skye stared at the crack of light beneath the closed door until it, too, was extinguished. She heard her mother's light footsteps recede in the hallway.

Skye was almost asleep when she realized she hadn't told anyone about the encounter in the park, yet in retrospect, she knew the oversight had somehow been intentional.

It was the secret knowledge of this stranger, a man whose face she had not seen, whose voice she had barely heard, that she hugged to herself as she drifted slowly to sleep. It was the stranger who became the unifying thread in the fabric of all her dreams.

Jonathan Parnell was an attractive man. His appeal for some rested partially on his very aloof, almost forbidding posture. While not precisely cold, he was nevertheless only marginally interested in what others were doing or saying. Not only could he be alone in a crowd, he cultivated a serious, reserved air that shielded him from incidental or frivolous conversation.

His hair was a pale yellow color that camouflaged premature threads of platinum and gray. In the sunshine it could still have the brilliance of youth. His blue eyes had dark indigo centers that lent his expression a certain opaque flatness that could be remote or merely mysterious. His features were sharply chiseled, with fine aristocratic lines defining his jaw and chin.

Parnell's mouth bore a distinctive stamp of disapproval as he entered his suite at the St. Mark Hotel. Walker Caine was sitting on a wide overstuffed armchair facing the door. The perfect stillness of his face, the hard look of slightly narrowed eyes, was the only indication of anger that Parnell could observe. In their brief association he had learned Walker's fury was more like lightning than thunder.

Walker Caine didn't move. He watched Parnell remove his hat and coat and hang them on the rack just inside the room. "A woman?" he asked.

Two fingers were raised. "Plural."

The shape of Walker's solemnly set mouth didn't change. He said evenly, "This isn't going to work, Mr. Parnell. I can't protect you if you won't follow my instructions." He stood, coming to his feet in a single easy movement. Reaching in his pocket, he withdrew a roll of bills. "This month's wage. I haven't earned it." He held out his hand.

Parnell didn't make any attempt to take the offering. He studied Walker Caine with dispassionate interest. "You can't quit," he said finally. "There is the matter of my life."

Walker shrugged. Jonathan Parnell was his senior by fifteen years but tonight he had acted with the sense of a fifteen-year-old. "This trip to the city was made against my advice, but you did agree to certain rules."

"This trip was a necessity," Parnell said. "I needed supplies for my work . . . things I couldn't have ordered." He made a brusque, impatient gesture with his hand and brushed past Walker in order to get to the sideboard. "I've already explained that. I hate to repeat myself."

Walker remained unmoved by his employer's irritation. He thrust the roll of money back in his pocket and turned to watch Parnell pour himself a drink. Walker shook his head when he was offered the same. "Where did you go?" he asked.

"The Seven Sisters. It's a— "

"Brothel."

One pale golden brow was raised and Parnell studied Walker again, this time assimilating different information. "I see," he said slowly. "You're familiar with it." He wondered how Walker satisfied his own needs. He couldn't recall seeing Walker demonstrate any interest in the female staff, but he was aware there was interest in the other direction. He supposed that some women found Walker's slightly crooked nose an intriguing flaw.

His stare became vague again, introspective. He would never understand women.

"Not intimately."

"Hmm?" he asked. "What was that?"

Walker repeated himself calmly, giving no outward sign that he was annoyed by his employer's inattention. "I'm not personally familiar with the brothel."

"Oh." He wondered if Walker Caine ever paid for his pleasure.

Walker wondered why Parnell paid for his. Yesterday's simple walk through the lobby of the St. Mark should have been enough to show Parnell that he was interesting to the opposite sex. Or had he really not noticed? "You should have remained here while I was out. I wasn't gone long."

"Did you get the things I asked for?"

"Some of them. A few shops were closed. Someone else wanted exact specifications that I couldn't give."

Parnell sighed. "I told you."

"I know. I'll escort you around tomorrow."

Parnell knocked back half his drink. "Tomorrow, eh?" he asked, one corner of his mouth lifting in a sardonic smile. "I suppose that means you're not quitting."

"I suppose it does," he said without inflection.

Nodding, Jonathan Parnell rolled the tumbler between his hands. "You'll be as happy to return to the valley as I."

"You're safer there. We both know that."

"I was thinking of my work. I'm anxious to get back to it."

Walker was silent, waiting. Parnell rarely talked about his project and his work area was off limits to Walker. Details about the project were rare. After a few moments Walker realized Parnell wasn't going to say anything about it now. "I want to get the rest of your supplies in the morning and get out of the city by noon. It's better if we travel during the day."

Parnell nodded. "That's fine. I'm not anxious to tempt fate again."

Walker was alert to the phrasing. He hadn't missed the reddened mark on Parnell's cheek, either. It made him want to touch the side of his own face. "Again? Was there an incident this evening?"

Finishing his drink, Parnell cleared his throat before he answered. "No. Tonight was . . . uneventful. I was referring to previous threats on my life."

"Then you were lucky. The people who want your invention wouldn't hesitate to put a whore in the Seven Sisters if they thought you might go there again."

Parnell considered that. "Intriguing thought. You think I was followed?"

"I know I was." He watched his employer's eyes cloud over, then become distant. "Don't worry. I lost them. No one saw me purchase any of the things on your list."

There was a hint of relief. "Secrecy is everything."

"So you've said."

Putting down his drink, Parnell raked his hair with his fingers. "I know. That's why you're going to be surprised at something I've done."

Walker doubted anything Parnell did could really take him off guard. He had planned too carefully for that. He hadn't yet reached his thirtieth year, but he wasn't inexperienced at his work. "What's that?" he asked politely.

"Before we left the valley I placed an ad with the *Chronicle* for a housekeeper. It was in this morning's paper."

Walker realized he'd been wrong. He *was* surprised. One of his tawny brows rose and his head cocked to the side as he simply stared at his employer. "Jesus," was all he said.

Three

Walker Caine poked his head into the hallway from the parlor. There were three women sitting on padded benches in the foyer. Only two of them looked up. The third, the one whose bonnet could not quite hide a beacon of startling red hair, kept her eyes on her lap. Was she daydreaming? he wondered, or merely shy? Uninterested, or deaf? Perhaps she had given up hope. The women who were staring at him had anxious eyes, fidgeting hands, and uncertain yet eager-to-please smiles.

It was the same posture, the same nervousness, the same hint of desperation that he had witnessed all morning. Until now, the parade of women seeking a position with Jonathan Parnell had seemed endless. Walker couldn't recall specific faces or fashions. Neither did he remember particular women for their age or experience or marital status. What he could not forget was their common need for work. Thus far, none had left the old mansion with any promise of it.

Ducking his head back into the parlor, he turned on Parnell. "You've three left to choose from. You do plan on hiring someone today, don't you?"

"I thought I would," he replied. He fanned the résumés and letters of reference in his right hand like playing cards and studied them. "None of the applicants seems quite as right in person as she does on paper. I'm not so hopeful as I was this morning."

"Perhaps if you told me what it is you're looking for," Walker said. He tried not to sound impatient. He'd asked the question earlier and received no concrete answer. He didn't really expect one now. "There hasn't been one woman interviewed who wasn't qualified for the position."

Parnell nodded. "That's true. But no one's really stood out, has she? Each one's like the next. And we have to think of Mrs. Reading. The housekeeper has to be able to work with her."

Corina Reading was Parnell's cook. She didn't come with the house, but one could be forgiven for thinking so, such was her proprietary nature. "If you didn't want to disappoint Mrs. Reading, you should have let her conduct the interviews."

"But then she might have disappointed me," Parnell said gravely. "It's very much a two-way street, don't you see?"

Walker didn't see much of anything. He held his thoughts in check. There was nothing to be gained by taking his employer on. It was, after all, a concession on Parnell's part that Walker was permitted to sit in on the interviews. It took only a brief reminder of the threats on Parnell's life to make Walker's argument a convincing one.

A lock of tawny brown hair fell across Walker's forehead. He raked it back and waited for Parnell's directions.

"Bring in Miss Staplehurst first," Parnell said, making a sudden decision. "Let's see what she's about."

Skye Dennehy knew she didn't want the position any longer. She'd known it almost the minute she'd taken her seat with the other hopefuls in the foyer. A single glance at her rivals for the job told all she needed to know about who really needed work and who didn't.

She considered getting up and leaving right then, but several of the women began talking among themselves and Skye could not think how to excuse herself gracefully. So she stayed and listened . . . and learned from the snippets they shared that it would have been criminal to vie for the position they were seeking. Jay Mac had obviously not given much consideration to that aspect when he'd suggested Skye apply. She couldn't believe her father would condone taking work from someone who needed it just to teach her a lesson— and Skye was thoroughly convinced that a lesson was what Jay Mac had in mind when he put her on the train to Baileyboro. She tried to get him to say as much at the station but he was being particularly inscrutable and she did not press hard for an answer.

Skye leaned back against the wall just as Annie Staplehurst was taken in for her interview. She felt the back of her bonnet being crushed, but she didn't lift a hand to correct it. Even knowing the entire thing was resting askew on her head didn't prompt her to remove or right it. She yawned widely and shut her eyes. It was only after the pocket doors were closed and Annie was safely inside the parlor that she permitted herself a small smile. She was perfectly aware she was under some scrutiny from the man who'd come to fetch all the applicants. Skye wasn't certain she knew how to get the job at the Granville mansion, but she was fairly certain she knew how *not* to get it. If the man was Jonathan Parnell himself, so much the better. He'd looked at her for a moment as if she had three heads.

* * *

"I thought she was fine," Walker said, speaking of the last woman. "And the one before her . . . Miss Staplehurst . . . she was also quite good. Mrs. Reading wouldn't find her too pushy."

"I'm uncertain," Parnell said. "She may not be able to manage the others. It's hard to know what to do. I actually considered offering her the position, but I thought it would be better to meet everyone. Didn't you tell me before you brought her in that there were three left? That means there's one more— unless she's bolted."

"She's still there. Sleeping, I think."

"Sleeping?" Parnell asked. He gave a short laugh. "That doesn't do her much credit, does it?"

Walker stretched as he rose to his feet. He wasn't used to so much inactivity. A day spent sitting, even in the comfortable confines of an overstuffed armchair, had cramped his muscles more than a day of riding ever had. "I'll send her on her way."

Parnell shook his head. He leaned toward the marble-topped table at his end of the sofa and quickly sifted through the résumés. "No," he said. "This is someone I want to meet. She once worked for Logan Marshall."

"The publisher of the New York *Chronicle*?"

"Apparently so. That's impressive, don't you think?"

Impressive, Walker thought, and from what he'd seen, unlikely as well. He wondered if she had lied on her résumé, as he suspected several others had. "It makes you wonder why she'd seek a position here," he said.

Parnell had dropped the résumé back in the pile and was lighting the tableside lamp. He paused just as the wick caught. Flickering light licked at the shadows on the wall behind him and cast an orange glow on the platinum threads running through his hair.

"No," he said deliberately, "it makes *you* wonder why she'd seek a position here. You're suspicious of everyone. But then, that's why I hired you, and that's why you're sitting here now." He seemed to remember what he was doing suddenly and blew out the matchstick in his hand before it burned him. He replaced the glass globe on the lamp. The indigo centers of his eyes darkened and widened. His assessment of the man he employed to guard his back was frank. "You've suspected every woman I've interviewed today of doing me in with a feather duster. I think you've earned your wage." Parnell's slight smile was condescending. "Now relax a bit and bring this last one in."

Walker Caine nodded once. "Her name?"

"Miss Mary Schyler Dennehy." He chuckled lowly. "It's quite a mouthful, isn't it?"

Walker repeated only the surname, then went to the door and called Skye in. She wasn't sleeping, as he'd suspected she might be. That would have been an improvement on what he witnessed. Instead, she was lying over the padded bench, her bustle tilted toward the ceiling as she fished for something under the seat. If she sensed him behind her, she gave no indication of it. She wasn't modest as she twisted this way and that, trying to retrieve whatever it was that had been lost.

Walker cleared his throat. His palm itched to lay a well-placed thump on the bustle and the behind it decorated. "Lose something?" he asked.

Skye twisted around and bolted upright. Her right hand was a closed fist around the object of her search. "Hatpin," she said triumphantly.

"Yes," he said drily. "I see that."

Since she'd opted to play the fool, Skye could hardly take exception to being laughed at, even when the tone was delicately edged with sarcasm. Still, she had an urge to stick the hatpin into the pompous ass and deflate him on the spot. She quelled the impulse with some difficulty. Adjusting her bonnet, she secured it with the pin and stood. "My turn, I see."

"Very good."

It wasn't what he said, but the way he said it. Skye's green eyes narrowed briefly as she studied his still, calm features. She had always imagined her own father played his cards very close to the vest. This man wasn't even showing the deck. Suddenly Skye felt very young, very gauche. There was something here she didn't understand and wasn't certain she wanted to.

Walker knew the moment she had been put firmly in her place. A hint of rose stained her cheeks and her eyes slipped away from his. He almost regretted it because he'd found something both amusing and admirable about her. "This way, Miss Dennehy." He gestured with his hand for her to precede him into the parlor.

Jonathan Parnell stood as Skye entered the room. "Please," he said, and introduced himself. "Won't you have a seat? And some tea, perhaps?" He glanced past Skye's right shoulder to Walker. "You'll bring Miss Dennehy some tea, won't you, Walker? Enough for all of us, I think."

This was different, Walker realized. Parnell hadn't offered amenities to any of the other women. He hadn't even stood before or offered his name. Walker assumed he just didn't think it was necessary. For some reason Parnell thought it was important now. The change in Parnell bothered him. He wanted to protest about getting the tea, then thought better of it. Hoping he could make it quick, Walker stepped back into the hallway and slid the doors closed behind him.

Skye didn't particularly want tea but it seemed that since entering the room her mouth had gone dry and her tongue clove to the roof of it. She must have made some sort of murmur which had been taken for an assent. She was peripherally aware of the doors shutting behind her and of being left alone with Jonathan Parnell.

He was not the fusty old inventor she had imagined.

During the past three weeks, while waiting to hear for some reply to her letter of inquiry, she'd given some thought to the man her father had described as intense and brilliant. Nothing she'd imagined had come close to the reality of the man before her. Certainly his blue eyes, with their deeper indigo centers, were intense. And the way his pale yellow hair caught the lamplight and highlighted strands of platinum could be called brilliant. She just didn't think her father could have meant *those* words in *that* context.

She realized she was staring and remembered herself. It was rather startling to discover that in spite of the difference in their ages, she felt nowhere near so young or awkward with this man as she had with the one who'd hovered by the door. Parnell was formal but gracious. Skye found herself sitting at Parnell's second suggestion that she do so. The chair was warm. Belatedly she was aware she'd taken the seat that recently had been occupied by the other man.

"No, stay where you are," Parnell said. "On his return Mr. Caine will be comfortable over there." He pointed to a narrow wing chair a few feet from where she sat.

The chair looked stiff and unyielding, a place where one could perch but never relax. She imagined that Mr. Caine had not been asked to give up his chair to anyone who had come before her. Skye wondered anew if her father had made some arrangement with Mr. Parnell.

She made a point of looking around the parlor. It was difficult not to be aware of the clutter that fairly seeped from all corners. Every surface was covered with fringed shawls and clusters of ornate figurines. Chubby porcelain cherubs crowded brass candlesticks for space on the mantel. The burgundy brocade drapes were heavy enough to ensure that no amount of sunlight faded any of the fabrics on the chairs or sofa. They were even closed against what little sunlight remained in the late winter afternoon. Oil portraits and landscapes of the Hudson covered the walls on either side of the piano. Sheet music lay haphazardly on the upright's top and bench. The metronome had been turned on its side.

A tower of papers littered the table on Parnell's left and other documents were precariously stacked near his feet. A tray of partially eaten biscuits had been slid under the sofa. Coffee stains marred the antimacassar on one arm of her chair and both of his. The apron of the fireplace was covered with a fine dusting of ashes and the delft tiles were streaked with soot. None of the fireplace tools were in their rack; they were all leaning against the hearth, waiting to be used or toppled.

In spite of the rush of heat from the fireplace, there was still the cloying odor of dampness in the room, a mustiness that a brigade of maids might find too challenging.

"Shall we begin?" Parnell asked.

Skye noticed that he seemed oblivious to his surroundings. Perhaps this room was a test of sorts, she thought. The applicant who didn't blanch at the work confronting her got the job. Skye felt very certain she was blanching.

Watching Schyler carefully, Parnell sat back in his chair and crossed his legs casually. From the table beside him he picked up Skye's letters of introduction and reference. "You're younger than I would have imagined from your experience."

It was a comment for which she was prepared. "I was fourteen when I began working for the Turners," she said. "I was employed first as a companion for their young daughter. Dr. Turner was away a good deal at the hospital and his wife had many responsibilities with the auxiliary. I lived in for several years and by the time Amy was too old to need someone to stay with her, I was indispensable."

"Yet you left . . ." he prompted.

"Yes, when Amy was sent to finishing school. The Turners would have kept me on, but I was ready for a change. I was very well recommended to the Marshalls." Some small part of Skye's conscience was truly appalled at how smoothly the lies came. Three weeks of practice had given the words just the right pitch and cadence. She could almost believe she'd done the things she said she had.

"The *Chronicle* Marshalls?"

"That's correct. Do you know them?" It was not the sort of thing one asked of a prospective employer. Skye knew it. She hoped her bald question would make her seem too aggressive and too pointedly interested in the affairs of others to be suited for the position.

"I know of them, of course. There has been some interest in doing a piece on my work. Marshall's wife was an actress, I believe."

Skye nodded. The arrival of the tea prevented her from inappropriately adding a bit of salacious gossip.

Halfway across the room Walker paused, noting with a small scowl that his chair was occupied. He elbowed aside some papers and photographs to make room for the tray, then turned to look at Skye, his eyebrows raised.

"I'd be happy to pour," she said. Half expecting him to take her chair when she came to her feet, Skye supposed she should be grateful that he merely hovered over her while she completed the task. She exhibited none of the usual grace she could muster for the serving and managed to splash both of them with hot tea. "Here," she said, handing him a cup and saucer. "Take that." And when his hooded gaze narrowed slightly she knew he had caught the insolent nuance in her voice. She turned quickly and passed another cup to Jonathan Parnell. "Cream, sir? Or sugar?"

"Neither," he said. The smile that edged the corner of his lips upward opened fully as he glanced at Walker.

"But I believe Mr. Caine is a little put out that you didn't ask him."

Skye pretended she hadn't meant the oversight. "Forgive me, Mr. Caine," she said apologetically. "Cream or sugar for you?"

"Neither," he said tersely. "But thank you for asking."

She couldn't miss that his voice was too cold to be in any way sincere. Ignoring him, Skye returned to her chair and let Walker Caine fend for himself. She wondered at his purpose in the interview, why he was permitted to stay at all. He hadn't the deference of a good butler but seemed less a friend to Parnell than an employee.

Walker sat not in the wing chair, but on the arm of it. Out of the corner of her eye Skye noticed that his long legs were stretched out in front of him, crossed at the ankles. The delicate proportions of the china cup and saucer did not seem at all incongruous in his large hands. The lean fingers were turned lightly, almost gracefully, around the fluted edges of the saucer. He was studying her closely and making no effort to pretend he was doing anything else. "Insolent" was one word that came to Skye's mind. "Insufferable" was another.

Parnell watched Skye's attention drift away, then come back to him. When he had it fully, he spoke to Walker. "Miss Dennehy was telling me that the Marshalls she worked for are indeed associated with the *Chronicle*. You know Logan Marshall, don't you?"

In three weeks of preparation Skye hadn't once considered the possibility of being caught in her lies so quickly.

"I worked for him on one occasion," he said.

"You're a reporter?" Skye asked. She sipped her tea to cover her hard swallow. Her sister Michael had worked for Logan Marshall at the *Chronicle*. Had they known each other?

"No," he said. "Not as a reporter. I did . . ." He

paused, searching for the right phrase, "investigating for Mr. Marshall."

Skye managed to replace her cup in the saucer without telltale clatter. "I see." She turned to Parnell. "I supervised a staff of ten with the Marshalls. My initial position with the family was very much like the one I had with the Turners, then their housekeeper took ill and I took over."

Parnell glanced at Skye's letter and noted the dates she had supplied. "You didn't stay with them long."

"No. She recovered nicely and there really wasn't a good place for me there once she had. I enjoyed the children, of course, but I was prepared for more responsibility."

"There aren't any children here at all," Walker pointed out.

"I suspected as much, Mr. Caine, when I entered the house. Children lend something special to a home. This house hasn't had it for many years."

"I wouldn't know about that," Parnell answered. "I've only lived here a little over two years myself. The townspeople still refer to it as the Granville Mansion, although I renamed it Brooke Place almost immediately."

"It seems as though it may be a house with a past," she said, glancing around the room, this time seeing more than the obvious clutter. The furnishings were old but solidly made, with the ball-and-claw feet of another era. The floors were dark oak, the grain running seamlessly from wall to wall. Where the end tables were exposed, she saw the rich green-veined markings of quality Vermont marble and the cut and polish of a skilled craftsman. She wondered which among the dozen portraits might have come with the house and which one might be the Granville ghost who had kept her up on humid summer nights.

"Yes, I think this house does have a past," Parnell said. His eyes became opaque as his thoughts seemed to draw him inward and he looked off past Skye's shoul-

der. She was fascinated by his withdrawal and wondered
where his thoughts had taken him. He collected himself
suddenly and offered a small smile in apology. "You're
not afraid of ghosts?" he asked.

"I've never met one," she said uneasily. She wondered
if she could force her voice to crack or stutter to emphasize
her unsuitability. It was nothing new for Skye to embarrass herself in the pursuit of something she wanted— or,
as in this case, something she didn't want. She'd once sat
through an entire meal with spinach wedged firmly between her front teeth to discourage a suitor. Her eyes
widened and she let a shiver rattle the teacup and saucer.
She pitched her voice higher. "This house is haunted?"

"So they say," Walker told her, watching her carefully.

"Mr. Caine is exaggerating," Parnell said dismissively.
"We've heard the story from one or two of the townspeople. The help here pays it no mind."

She made a gesture which encompassed the room.
"Your *help* here pays little mind to anything, Mr.
Parnell," she said. "So I don't know that I'd use them
to support my case." There was a choked sound from
Walker Caine, but she couldn't tell if he was swallowing
laughter or outrage. Perhaps he was one of the help
after all. "There are some forces I'd rather not tempt.
I can manage the squalor . . ." She paused and looked
significantly at Walker. "I can even manage the help,
but I won't attempt to manage what's not of this world."

There was a moment of silence while she let it sink
in. She wasn't surprised when Walker was the one who
broke it.

"That's that," he said.

She could almost hear him rubbing his palms together, washing his hands of her. She waited to hear
what Jonathan Parnell had to say.

"You're rather forthright, aren't you, Miss Dennehy?"
he said. The back of his knuckles brushed his chin as he

considered her. "No one else has commented on the state of the house, though I think squalor is overstating it a bit."

Skye gave the parlor another swift glance. "Not to my way of thinking," she said bluntly.

Parnell leaned forward and dropped his forearms on his knees. When he spoke, it was the voice of a man who'd made a decision. "You're exactly the breath of fresh air this stuffy mausoleum requires."

"Mausoleum?" she asked hollowly.

That raised his slight smile. "A poor choice of words. Tell me, Miss Dennehy, what would you need to convince you to take this position?"

Skye wasn't certain she was hearing correctly. "You're offering it to me?" she asked.

"If you want it."

"But the ghost," she said.

He waved a hand in the air dismissively. "Walker will get rid of it. You do that sort of thing, don't you, Walker?"

"It will cost you," he said, without inflection.

"That's all right, then, I can afford it." He looked back at Skye. "Consider the ghost exorcised, Miss Dennehy. Now will you take the position?"

She hesitated, thinking furiously. Jay Mac's hand surely was in this. There wasn't a good reason for Parnell to hire her except that Jay Mac had arranged for him to do so. She certainly hadn't distinguished herself in the interview. Her father apparently was determined to see that she sit only one term out of school. He probably was even responsible for the state of the parlor. There was something deliberate about the grand mess. The clutter, the soot, the marred floors, the dusty drapes— it had probably taken days just to get the right effect. She could almost hear her father telling Parnell, "Don't make it easy on her. Give her lots to do, the more menial the better. She'll be grateful to go back to school."

Skye considered all the women who had come before her, who didn't know that their fate was set because of her father's manipulation. It wasn't fair they'd been given false hope just to teach her a life lesson.

But then, Mary Schyler Dennehy was not her father's daughter for nothing.

Walker Caine sensed trouble the moment he saw her back stiffen. In profile she looked almost regal with her small chin raised and the shape of her jaw defined by a smooth, angular line. A tiny muscle worked in her cheek, hinting at her resolve. Her hands were folded neatly in her lap, but there was tension in the bloodless knuckles. The braced set of her shoulders thrust her breasts forward and showed the curved smallness of her back. He remembered her in the hallway bent over the bench, all bustle and backside.

She really should go home, he thought, and somehow knew it wasn't going to happen. Once he'd suspected she was indifferent to gaining employment; he was certain now she had changed her mind.

"How many people were you intending to hire?" he heard her ask Parnell.

"Why, only one. I have other help."

"You may understand that I beg to differ," Skye said, motioning to the room again. "How many do you employ?"

"Five. Six, if you include Mr. Caine."

Walker shook his head as Skye's attention swiveled to him. "Don't include me," he said. "I wasn't hired to polish the silver."

"As long as you're housebroken," she said sweetly, "you can stay." Not giving Walker a chance to respond to her outrageous remark, she turned back to Parnell. "I will take everyone else in hand, and those who can't be trained are out on their ear. I'll brook no interference from you."

"Mrs. Reading stays," Parnell said. "She's the cook and she's been with me for years."

Skye reinforced her condition by remaining silent and continuing to stare at Parnell. "I'll want to hire one woman immediately. It's imperative that I have the respect and loyalty of at least one person."

"Afraid you can't earn it on your own?" Walker asked.

Parnell shot him a sour look, but Skye ignored him. "The wage mentioned in your ad isn't sufficient for me, but it will do nicely for Miss Staplehurst. I'm certain the house is big enough for lodging her and her small son. You knew she had a child, didn't you?"

Walker Caine sighed. "We do now." He wondered how he'd lost control of everything. He knew Parnell was going to meet her demands, although he didn't understand why. "Can't they stay in Baileyboro, like most everyone else?"

"She really can't leave her boy alone, and it would be a hardship to hire someone to stay with him. He won't get underfoot and we'll find small jobs for him. Remember, I've experience with children." My God, she thought, I *do* believe my own lies.

"I don't like it," Walker said, shaking his head. "Mr. Parnell, I think we should talk."

That suited Skye. She needed time to think calmly and rationally. When she saw Parnell was preparing to object to Walker's advice, she interjected, "I'll just take this tea back to the kitchen while you discuss whatever it is you have to. Don't give it a thought. I can find my own way." Like a bird swooping down on its prey, Skye scooped the tea tray and fled the room.

Watching her go, Walker shook his head again— not so much in negation this time as in simple disbelief. He pushed away from where he had been lounging against the wing chair and held up his teacup. "She forgot this."

Parnell smiled and indicated his own. "Mine, too."

Each man conspicuously set his cup and saucer where the tray had been. "How serious are you about hiring her?" Walker asked, even though he thought he knew the answer.

"The position's hers, if she wants it."

"Demands and all?"

"Demands and all," said Parnell. The strong, handsome features had become still, the eyes watchful as Walker Caine considered his position. "What are your objections?"

Walker didn't answer immediately. He went to the fireplace, picked up the poker, and idly jabbed at the hot and glowing underside of one of the logs. Flames leaped from the spot and spread along the length of the wood. Walker slipped the poker into its rightful place on the brass and iron rack and turned to his employer. "If you've been listening to me at all since returning from the city, you're already aware of some of my objections." He raised one hand, cutting Parnell off. "But I'm going to enumerate them again." He ticked his points off with his fingers. "You're taking unnecessary risks by inviting strangers to live in this house with you. When you realized Mrs. Reading wasn't up to the task of taking care of the house and directing the staff, you should have told me what you had in mind before placing that ad. You don't know anything about the women who traipsed in and out of here today and it's no good pointing to their references. I'm not much of a gambler, Mr. Parnell, but even I'd wager that the content of most of that paper is lies and only fit for burning."

"Including Miss Dennehy?" Parnell asked.

"*Especially* Miss Dennehy. Did you observe her hands? They're soft and smooth, and the nails are manicured."

"Perhaps she wears gloves when she works. Or maybe she delegates."

"Or maybe she's never lifted a finger to do more than pour tea."

"That's an absurd idea," Parnell said dismissively. "Why would she apply?"

"My point exactly."

Parnell considered that. "You think she's a killer?"

"You still think this is amusing," Walker said. His dark-brown lashes shadowed his eyes as he stared at Parnell. He thrust his hands into his pockets and leaned back against the mantel. Though the posture was casual, there was nothing but tension in the line of his shoulders. He was successful in shrugging most of it out. "The point is, I don't know what she is, and neither do you."

"That's where you're wrong." He shared none of Walker's concerns and none of the tension. "I know everything I need to know about her."

Walker Caine raised one dark brow coolly. "Based on . . ." he prompted.

"Things I don't have to tell you," he said. "You're just going to have to trust me. She's the one I want. She's not going to hurt me."

"Then why go through the charade of having interviews? You had her letters. You asked Mrs. Reading to respond to all the inquiries when you could have hand-picked her."

Parnell stood. "I had to see her." He shrugged and raised a faint smile. His voice was calm and quite thoughtful now. "She's worth seeing, don't you think?"

That gave Walker pause. "You're hiring her because she's a pleasure to look at?"

Jon Parnell rubbed his chin with the back of his hand. "I didn't exactly say that, did I?" His eyes narrowed and he managed to convey in a single glance all the impatience he felt. "Miss Dennehy's the one I want. You don't need to know more than that. I'm convinced she'll do a good job for me, and my instincts haven't let me down yet. I hired you, didn't I?"

Walker refrained from commenting that Parnell didn't

know him half so well as he knew Miss Dennehy. There was no sense in casting suspicion on himself. "All right," he said finally. "I can see your mind's made up."

Parnell nodded. "I'll leave the details regarding her employment to you, but give her what she wants."

"The salary?"

"Yes."

"Hiring Miss Staplehurst?"

"That, too. She can run the roost, for all I care. I need to get back to my projects."

Walker knew Parnell meant he had to get back to his projects *right now*. He'd once witnessed Parnell leaving the dinner table in mid-bite when an idea had struck him. On that occasion he'd stayed in his workroom for almost twenty-four hours before stumbling, exhausted, to his bed. Walker's hooded eyes followed Parnell's progress across the room and stayed on the door after Parnell had left, waiting for Skye Dennehy's return.

She appeared in the doorway a few minutes later carrying her bonnet. Walker was aware that as far as a weapon was concerned, he didn't have to look any farther than her hat pin.

"Come in," he said, when she hovered at the entrance.

Skye stepped forward, reaching behind her back to close the doors. "Has Mr. Parnell changed his mind?" she asked, fingering the brim of her bonnet. She wondered if she'd be relieved or disappointed if he had. It was hard to know what to sensibly do when she was so caught up in getting back at her father. Getting away from Jonathan Parnell and Walker Caine hadn't made her decision measurably easier.

"No," Walker said, studying Skye again. "Have you changed yours?"

Her chin lifted slightly, giving her answer the edge of a challenge. "No."

Walker nodded once. "I see," he said softly. His gaze

didn't stray from her. She was more nervous than she would have liked to project, he was certain of that. The fullness of her lower lip was marred by the way she worried it between her teeth. It wasn't until she felt his eyes on the betraying gesture that she consciously abandoned it. His attention wandered over the hint of color in her small oval face. She wore small jet drop earrings that brushed her neck as she turned aside to avoid his scrutiny. Her brows and lashes were several shades darker than her flame-red hair. They were drawn together now over a pair of eyes that were deepening to a cool emerald hue as the silence between him and her was drawn out.

She turned on him suddenly. "Are you purposely trying to make me uncomfortable?" she demanded.

"Yes," he said. One corner of his mouth lifted and a single dimple took the sting out of the arrogant smile. "Am I succeeding?"

Skye tore her attention from the cocky set of his mouth and stared at his nose instead. It was slightly crooked from a previous break. She hoped that getting like that had hurt like hell.

Walker pointed to the hand that was clenched at Skye's side, then to his nose. "If you're having thoughts about resetting it, you'll have to get in line."

At being caught out, Skye's fist opened spasmodically. However, she made no apology for what she'd been thinking. "I imagine it's a long line," she said.

His smile deepened. "You'd be right." Walker motioned to her to have a seat. "Mr. Parnell's gone to his workroom and left me to finish this hiring."

Skye sat in the armchair she'd occupied earlier and immediately felt the disadvantage of Walker still standing. "Why?" she asked. "It's clear you don't want me here."

Walker didn't attempt to deny it. "That's true."

Skye watched him push away from the wall and come toward her. He had a rolling, graceful walk and his approach, even on the old hardwood floors, was nearly silent. He stopped a few feet in front of her and Skye had no polite alternative save to raise her face to meet his eyes rather than his groin.

"I don't want you here," he said. "And it's just as well you realize it, because I'm not going out of my way to make things easy for you. You should also realize that I work for Mr. Parnell, the same as you, and when he says *he* wants you here, then— " he shrugged, "— I ignore my better judgment and do what he says."

"I'll remember that," she said after a moment. "It must be difficult to have a position where you have to yield to someone else's judgment."

The gold flecks in Walker's eyes seemed to splinter. "Meaning you'd quit before you'd do that."

"Meaning exactly that."

He was silent a moment. He sat down, taking Parnell's chair, and chose his words carefully. "Then you must have many more prospects than the score of women who preceded you here today."

"Perhaps I do," she said, her tone neutral.

Walker picked up her letter of introduction from the table beside him and glanced over it. "Your experience isn't so different from that of the others. In some cases, you've a lot less."

"I'm sure that's true."

"So why do you think Mr. Parnell's hired you?"

"Because I'm a breath of fresh air?" she asked, forcing a dimpled smile. It faded as abruptly as it appeared. "Is it important? He wants me."

"My thought exactly." He paused a beat. "And you? Do you want him?"

Schyler blinked. Her mouth opened, then shut.

Her surprise amused Walker but he was suspicious. "I wonder if you're as young as you look," he said. "Or a very good actress."

He didn't mean young, she thought. He meant inexperienced.

"I see you understand," he said.

She did. Perfectly. Skye wasn't going to give sanction to the conversation by making a comment. It was only left for her to change the subject. "Has there been a decision on hiring Annie Staplehurst?" she asked.

"Mr. Parnell is willing."

"But you have objections."

"To everything."

"She needs to live here," Skye said.

"I understand that." He paused, thoughtful. "Did you know Miss Staplehurst before today?"

"No. I met her while waiting to be interviewed." Skye's nose wrinkled slightly. "Actually, I didn't introduce myself at all. I just listened to her talk to some of the other women." She needed the work. It was why Skye made Annie a condition of her own employment.

Walker leaned back in his chair and stretched his legs. The tip of his shoe nudged one of the paper towers aside. An avalanche of documents slid across the floor. He made no move to gather them and crossed his arms in front of him instead. "You're a curiosity, Miss Dennehy."

"Am I? That's interesting. I was having similar thoughts about you."

"Really?"

Skye noticed he didn't offer to answer any of her questions. She went back to the matter at hand. "Is Mr. Parnell willing to give me the authority I'll need to maintain his household?"

"I believe his exact words were, 'She can rule the roost.' "

"And the salary?"

"You could have asked for more."

Skye wished she had—not for herself, but for Annie. "Mr. Parnell must be quite wealthy."

One corner of Walker's mouth lifted, but this time the arrogant smile held no charm. "You're in danger of disappointing me, Miss Dennehy. I was certain you knew that already. From what I can tell, you've worked only for wealthy people."

"The Marshalls certainly had money, not that it had any bearing on my working there. I was employed by the Turners first, and they were hardly rich."

"Most people would consider a doctor of Turner's status quite well-to-do. After all, he runs Jennings Memorial. It's interesting that you don't."

Skye realized too late that she had been incautious in choosing her words. Then she wondered if it mattered. If Jonathan Parnell really was in league with Jay Mac, it wouldn't be long before he brought in Walker Caine as well. "Do you really care what I think, Mr. Caine?"

He smiled fully. "No," he said. "I suppose I don't."

"Very well, then. Will you drive me into the village? I left my bags at the station. I'd like to get them and also see if I can catch Annie before she leaves."

"Hank will take you in. He looks after the horses and the carriage."

"That's fine."

"I'll have rooms prepared for you and Miss Staplehurst."

Skye stood and looked pointedly around the parlor. "Please, don't trouble anyone. If this serves as an example of the quality of the work here, Annie and I will be better left to our own devices."

Walker followed her glance. "You know," he said, more to himself than to her, "it's only gotten this bad in the past few days."

Skye heard him and remembered her earlier thought that the cluttered effect had been contrived for her benefit. "That, Mr. Caine, is something that doesn't surprise me in the least."

Watching her precede him out of the parlor, Walker wondered what she meant by that.

Annie Staplehurst was so effusive in her thanks that Schyler was embarrassed. Half a dozen times during the ride back to the Granville mansion, tears welled in Annie's eyes as she spoke of her good fortune.

"You may have a change of heart," Skye told her finally. "I had an opportunity to see some of the other rooms, and the downstairs parlor is one of the *cleaner* areas."

Taking a handkerchief from under the cuff of her sleeve, Annie dabbed at her eyes and nose. Both were more than a little swollen and red, evidence that Annie's weeping had been going on before she'd had good news to cry about.

Skye estimated that Annie Staplehurst was a few years older than she. It was difficult to know with any certainty because lines of worry and fatigue had set permanent creases at the corners of her gray eyes and her mouth had a perpetual downward bend. Her hair was light brown, without any highlights to give it shine or luster. She was large boned and would have been solid looking if it weren't for the fact that her skin was stretched tautly across broad cheekbones and wrists. The effect was one of fragility rather than strength.

If, even in her happiness, Annie's expression was on the dour side, the same could not be said of that of her son, Matthew. He was a lively handful, scooting back and forth along the leather carriage bench so as not to miss anything on either side. He was a few months shy of his fourth birthday, but as far as Skye could tell, it was the only way in which he was shy. He had no hesitation at all about crawling onto her lap and carried on a relatively one-sided conversation with no encouragement from his mother.

When his name was mentioned, he had a habit of lowering his head slightly and looking out as if he were peering over invisible spectacles. Sometimes he'd cock his head and give Skye a mischievous sideways glance that thoroughly entranced her.

"He's got a bit of the devil in him," Annie said apologetically, when she saw the look. "Not that he's a bad boy. He doesn't really give me any trouble, but you can see that he thinks about it."

"He's a lovely little boy. You're very fortunate to have him."

Annie's face softened. "I am, aren't I?" She hesitated. "Do you have any children?"

Skye shook her head. "I'm not married." Immediately she cursed her incautious tongue. "I'm sorry. I didn't mean . . . I don't . . ."

Annie patted the back of Skye's hand and nodded knowingly. "I understand, Miss Dennehy. Don't give it another thought. You're too kind to have meant it cruelly."

"Still, it was thoughtless," she said. "And stupid. I'm a bastard myself. I should know people don't have to be married to have children." She saw she had shocked Annie into speechlessness. "I don't usually announce it so openly, but it's nothing I'm ashamed of either. My parents loved each other. They still do."

"That's the thing," Annie said wisely, nodding. "I surely did love Matt's father." She sighed. "It just wasn't meant to be."

Skye didn't ask for details. She wanted it to be on Annie's terms if more was confided. A rough patch in the road jolted the carriage. Skye neatly caught Matthew as he tumbled off the bench. He grinned cheekily. "You liked that, didn't you?" she said.

He nodded and wriggled out of her grasp, scrambling back onto the bench in the hopes that it would happen again.

"We'll have quite a bit of work to do tonight to get

settled," Skye told Annie. The sun had already set and the wind was rising across the ridge where they were traveling. Skeletal limbs of the naked trees were thinly frosted with ice. A crusty layer of snow gilded the ground when moonlight broke free of the thick cloud cover.

"As far as I can tell, there are only a few of us living at the mansion. Mr. Parnell is there, of course, then there's a Mrs. Reading— the cook, whom I haven't met yet. Mr. Parnell seems eager to keep her, so I hope she's everything I expect a cook to be. Our driver is Hank Ryder, and he has a place for himself in the carriage house. There must be at least three other people who comprise the help, but none of them showed a face while I was touring. I suspect they've gone home for the evening. You may as well know that no one was particularly pleased about the idea of you and your son living at the house. Mr. Parnell accepted it, but Mr. Caine tried to change his mind."

Annie nodded. "I understand. We won't be any trouble or call undue attention to ourselves."

"I'm certain you won't."

"What exactly is it that the other man does?"

"Mr. Caine, you mean?"

"That's the one."

"I'm not certain. He's rather odd. Enigmatic, actually."

Annie covered her mouth as she giggled.

"Why are you laughing?"

Her pale complexion suffused with color. "I really shouldn't say, but since you asked, I thought he was a handsome one."

"You're right," Skye said evenly. "I don't think we should discuss it."

Annie straightened. "I'm sorry." Her gray eyes clouded as she looked warily at Skye.

It was the fear tingeing Annie's expression that made Skye realize the power she wielded. They hadn't reached the mansion yet and Annie was already thinking she might be dismissed. "Please, Annie, don't give it another thought. I'm the one who said he was odd. I shouldn't have said it." Skye thought Annie seemed at least a trifle relieved.

"What about Mr. Parnell?" Annie asked. "Do you know anything about him?"

"Not a thing. It wasn't discussed in my interview. What about yours?"

She shook her head. "I heard in the village that he's some sort of inventor. Do you suppose that's true?"

"It may be. He retired to his workroom while I was there."

"I never worked for an inventor before."

"Neither have I," Skye said. "If you think about it, he's just a tinkerer who's been luckier than most." That description probably gave Jonathan Parnell's talents short shrift, but Skye was not certain she wanted to think kindly of him— not without knowing what his role was in Jay Mac's plans. Walker Caine seemed to think he knew the reason Parnell had hired her and it wasn't a reason Skye would have considered on her own. If it were true, perhaps it absolved Jay Mac. In some ways it was a little flattering.

Skye shook her head, wondering where the truth lay. It would have been just like Jay Mac to suppose that Jonathan Parnell might make a suitable son-in-law. He was steady and serious, qualities her father would have liked to see settled on her. The score of years difference in their ages might have given Jay Mac some concern, but he would put it aside if he thought Parnell could rein in his daughter's impulsive nature.

Skye sighed. Jonathan Parnell was interesting, even attractive to her, but they would never suit. She wondered if she could possibly sit through another dinner with spinach between her teeth.

Four

By the time Skye's head touched a pillow, she was exhausted. Not so surprisingly, she found sleep elusive. She turned on her back, stared at the ceiling, and began counting the day's successes instead of sheep.

She did not number acquiring a job as one of her accomplishments. She did, however, believe that getting work for Annie as well as a place for her and her son to stay was one of the best things she'd ever done. She had also managed to scrub down the small suite she was shown for her own use, put clean linens on the bed, and set a good fire in the fireplace. As she burrowed into the thick feather mattress, these things seemed like remarkable achievements.

She had met Mrs. Reading and established her position in the house by insisting the cook prepare a special meal for Annie and her son since it was late when they returned to the house. The grumbling in Skye's stomach reminded her that she'd satisfied her own hunger with only a cup of warm milk and some bread. The sprinkling of cinnamon and sugar had added flavor, but not much substance. Graveyard stew, her mother had called it, and she had served it when one of the Marys was feeling out of sorts.

Skye's mind wandered quite easily from graveyard to ghost. She smiled weakly, remembering her attempt to show fear during the interview when the Granville ghost was mentioned. She could have made a more effective show of it now, she realized, watching angular fire shadows flicker on the ceiling. She turned her head quickly as the french doors shuddered against the rising wind and something scratched a pane of glass.

She laughed at herself, albeit a little uneasily. It must have been a tree limb she heard at the window, she told herself, or a stray cat looking for an entrance.

Skye rolled onto her side so she could face the fireplace. There was comfort in the snapping flames and glowing embers. The walnut wainscoting held a dull reflection of the fire, and Skye's thoughts strayed to how vibrant that reflection would be once the wood was polished. Amused by the notion, Skye smiled sleepily as she snuggled into her pillow and comforter.

Somewhere between rehearsing her speech to the staff and plotting revenge on her father, Mary Schyler Dennehy fell asleep.

"I'm Miss Dennehy," she said to the staff gathered in the kitchen. "As you know, Mr. Parnell hired me yesterday. You may not be aware that he has given me complete authority. I intend to use it to see that this home is restored."

Skye paused to purposely examine each face turned in her direction. Her eyes slipped over Annie quickly because she knew she had an ally there. Hank Ryder was sitting beside her. He was nodding slowly, his narrow face somber. He'd been helpful yesterday, Skye remembered, in getting their valises and packing the carriage. He required some direction and she suspected he was a little dull, but his movements were quick and efficient. Hank had a thin, wiry body that had already proved its strength by hauling Skye's baggage to her room as if it were so much fluff. He was also a willing worker. She didn't expect to have difficulty with him.

The twins were another matter. Daisy and Rose Farrow were robust young women with apple cheeks and cherub smiles. The expression in their eyes, though, was watchful and sly, and Skye reasoned they were reserving judgment until she proved herself. They might be willing to work hard for her if she took them in hand; if she faltered, they would be slackers. She suspected it was all they had been thus far.

Jenny Adams was in her fifties, older than anyone else in the room. She had a selection of mending in her lap and a thimble on one of her fingers. Her hands worked absently but competently as she returned Skye's stare. She was thin lipped and her eyes were narrowly spaced. The look she gave Skye was frankly skeptical.

When Skye's focus turned to Mrs. Reading, she felt the entire attention of the room shift with her.

Corina Reading was a petite, small-boned woman in her early thirties. Her features, from her bow mouth to her wide-lidded sloe eyes, were very nearly perfect. The slightness of her build, the sheer delicacy of her frame, gave the appearance of fragile femininity. Her thick ebony hair was pulled back off her face and captured in an attractive black netting. She wore a serviceable black gown that was tightly fit to her narrow shoulders and tiny waist.

Before meeting Mrs. Reading, Skye had never considered that a cook might look any different than Mrs. Cavanaugh, the woman of ample proportions who had been working for Moira and Jay Mac for better than twenty-five years. Corina Reading's hourglass figure made Skye wonder if the woman sampled anything she prepared or if what she prepared was any good at all. Acknowledging to herself that this was a narrow view, Skye still opted to withhold final judgment until she had sampled breakfast herself. The cup of warm milk and bread last evening was no test of Mrs. Reading's skills in the kitchen.

Corina Reading stood and offered a small smile in greeting. Her dark eyes fastened on Skye and didn't waver. "I think I can speak for everyone here when I say we're pleased you've taken the position. Your predecessor was . . . well, there's nothing to be gained by speaking ill of her." Her bow mouth relaxed, removing the imprinted smile from her face. "My duties are exclusively those having to do with this kitchen. I don't believe you'll find me lacking in that regard."

Skye was very aware that Mrs. Reading was defining her territory and her responsibilities. In her place she'd have done the same and could even admire the woman for asserting herself. But Skye also sensed a challenge and knew she could not let it pass. "That's very good, Mrs. Reading," she said coolly. "Of course I'll respect you by telling you directly if I'm displeased with your work." She saw the cook's eyes narrow fractionally. "Now," Skye went on, "has the staff had their breakfast already? I know I haven't had mine."

Rose Farrow spoke up. "Daisy and me—"

"Daisy and *I*," Skye interjected. "You must learn to be particular about your speech, Rose."

"*We* have breakfast before we come out to the house," she finished.

Skye asked Jenny, "Do you do the same?" The older woman nodded. "And Hank, what about you? You live here."

"Miz Reading . . . excuse me, ma'am . . . *Missus* Reading lets me get somethin' for myself in her kitchen."

Smiling, Skye turned to Corina. "How very kind of you, Mrs. Reading. However, I think we'll try something different from now on. Breakfast for staff will be served at six-thirty. Everyone will eat here. I think it will prompt a better start for the day and we have a great deal of work ahead of us. Annie will help you with the preparations, since she's also living here." Before there could be any protest, she asked, "What time do you serve breakfast for Mr. Parnell?"

Corina Reading's complexion did not flush when she was annoyed. It went pale as salt. Her speech had a tendency to take on a staccato sharpness which she narrowly managed to hold in check. "Mr. Parnell takes his breakfast when he sees fit."

"Then you're very flexible. How admirable." Skye's smile didn't waver. "And Mr. Caine? I don't see him here this morning. Does that mean he's considered apart from the rest of us?"

Jenny Adams looked up from her mending. "Mr. Caine will be in directly. He's an early riser."

Skye checked the timepiece in her shirtwaist pocket. "It's gone eight already," she said. "That hardly qualifies as early rising."

Annie Staplehurst made a face, scrinching her nose and pursing her lips together. Her head shook in a quick, reflexive negation. Rose Farrow poked her sister in the ribs and Daisy's hand came to her mouth to hide her silent laughter. Hank revealed a gap-toothed smile. Jenny softly clucked her tongue. Corina Reading's face was as satisfied as the cat who'd got the cream.

Skye didn't have to turn around to know who was standing in the doorway behind her. "Won't you come in, Mr. Caine?" she asked, unruffled. "I was just learning something about your morning routine."

"So I heard," he said drily. Walker pushed away from the door jamb and entered the kitchen. He was wearing black trousers and a crisp white shirt. His vest was black with gray pinstripes, and when he pulled a chair out and straddled it the vest rose slightly, revealing red suspenders. Walker rested his forearms on the top rail of the chair and made a show of looking around the kitchen. "I came for breakfast. Mrs. Reading usually has it prepared by now."

"Don't I just," Corina said sweetly.

"In the future, Mr. Caine," Skye said, "breakfast will be served for the staff at six-thirty. We hope you'll join us."

"Miss Dennehy," he said patiently, "at the risk of having you think better of me, I have to tell you that at six-thirty this morning I was already riding into Baileyboro on some business for Mr. Parnell."

Skye dealt Daisy a stern sideways look when the young girl giggled again. "Then you probably would have appreciated something to eat before you left," she said.

Walker's eyes darted between the cook and the new housekeeper. He held up his hands palms outward and indicated he wasn't going to step into the middle of their dispute.

"Mrs. Reading will see to it," she said briskly. "Rose and Daisy, I want you to work with Jenny this morning in the downstairs parlor. We may as well start there. Hank, you'll help them as called upon to move furniture." Skye wore a plain white apron to cover the front of her dove-gray skirt. She reached into the large center pocket and withdrew a piece of paper folded into quarters. She handed it to Rose. "You read, don't you, Rose?" When the girl nodded, she went on. "Good. I've made a list of things to be done in that room. I'll check on you from time to time."

Walker decided it must be true that some people were born to lead. He managed not to show his amusement as Skye turned out the troops. He noticed that even the twins were looking lively under Miss Dennehy's command. They fairly marched out of the room with Hank nipping at their heels. Jenny gathered her mending and followed at a slower but still purposeful pace.

"Annie, you can bring Matthew here to the kitchen and we'll find something to keep him busy. He can't like being confined to his room." As Annie left the kitchen, Skye turned to Mrs. Reading. "Do you have a menu prepared for the remainder of the week?"

"Yes."

"Well, I'd like to see it later. Perhaps you can give me information regarding your budget this afternoon. I'll want to see the condition of your larder then. I noticed yesterday that the road from town is in rather a poor state. I can imagine there are times when it's impassable. I want to be certain we've planned for that possibility." Skye looked down at Walker, effectively dismissing Mrs. Reading. "I need to tour the house, conduct an inventory, and familiarize myself with the keys and closets. I realize that accompanying me is not part of your regular duties, but I wonder— "

Walker was already coming to his feet, his body unfolding with little effort and much grace. "Of course I'll show you around." He glanced at Mrs. Reading. The cook's jaw was rigid. "Will thirty minutes give you enough time, Corina?"

"That will be sufficient," she said tersely. She turned, her small back as stiff as an iron rod, and went to the sink to prime the pump.

Walker ushered Skye out of the kitchen. "We'll do what we can in thirty minutes, then finish after breakfast."

"That's fine with me," she said. "I'm hungry as well, and Annie's little boy hasn't had anything since last night."

Leading Skye down the hall, Walker's first stop was the dining room. He tugged on the pocket doors, which required some strength to open. At the first creak Skye began scribbling in the small leatherbound pad she car-

ried. Walker stood in the doorway while Skye moved
about the room, eyeing the condition of the room's contents as well as the room's structure and arrangement.

"I was impressed back there," he said, crossing his arms
casually in front of him while he leaned against the door.

"Oh?" she asked, continuing to inspect the darkly
stained oak sideboard. It was cracked in places where the
wood had been allowed to dry. She remembered Mrs.
Cavanaugh instructing the servants to fairly bathe the furniture in lemon oil. The sideboard was in need of the
same attention. "I certainly didn't set out to do that."

He grinned. "I have no doubt. Still, you gave a good
account of yourself. You're in a difficult position."

Skye shrugged to mask her surprise. She didn't expect
Mr. Caine to be sensitive to anything about her predicament with the staff.

"You seem to have an idea of what you want to accomplish here," he noted.

"This home must have been lovely once, Mr. Caine. I
think I have an appreciation for what it might be again."
She closed her pad and looked up. "I'll come back to this
room later. Will you show me something else now?"

"Of course."

The site of the Granville mansion dated back to pre-
revolutionary times. Then, the house had been two
rooms with a detached kitchen. Just prior to the war
the structure had burned, and it had been rebuilt in
the grand colonial style. By Fifth Avenue standards the
original house had still been quite small, but subse-
quent owners, all descendants of the Granvilles until
just recently, had made additions to accommodate their
expanding families or their individual tastes. Skye
thought the dining room, library, and parlor were all
part of the oldest structure. The length of the hall joining the kitchen to the rest of the house made Skye
suspect it had probably been a separate building until

relatively recently. There was also no easy way to pass food from the kitchen to the dining area, a feature that surely would have existed had the rooms been joined at the outset.

Other recent additions were the breakfast room and the second parlor. The breakfast room had bay windows which faced east and brought in the morning sun. The second parlor was a vast room that seemed to have been used for entertaining large gatherings, perhaps a reunion of Granvilles or the village itself during the Christmas season. The condition of the room, the drafts that seeped in under poorly insulated and warped window frames, the water-marked ceiling, were evidence that it hadn't been a site for entertainment in many years.

Looking around the room, imagining what it might have been like with gaily dressed women circling the floor and hothouse flowers decorating its borders, Skye was moved to sigh a trifle wistfully.

"It must have been something," Walker said, following her gaze.

Skye had forgotten she wasn't alone. "Is it ever used?" she asked.

"Not since I've been here. But I don't think Parnell used it before that."

"Then you didn't arrive with him."

"No, I was hired only a few months ago. He'd lived here some time before that."

Skye wished he'd come right out and say what he did for Mr. Parnell. His exact position seemed to be cloaked in secrecy. "Mrs. Reading was with him then?"

"That's right. The twins came after I did, but Hank and Jenny were hired not long before." He checked his pocketwatch. "And," he drawled, snapping the watch shut and replacing it, "speaking of Mrs. Reading . . ."

"It's time to go back," Skye finished for him. "I could use your help after breakfast, Mr. Caine. If you would—"

"It's no problem. Parnell's still in his workroom. I checked on him before I came to the kitchen." He paused as she brushed past him to get to the corridor. "I'd be happier about the prospect if you'd call me Walker."

She hesitated. "I don't know if that's—"

"And I'll call you Mary."

Skye shook her head. "You'd better not, not if you expect me to answer. No one calls me Mary. I've always been Skye. Mary Schyler, if I'm in trouble."

"All right . . . Skye."

Throughout breakfast Skye tried to understand how she'd been maneuvered so simply. It didn't go down nearly as well as the warm biscuits and soft-boiled eggs.

"You make the best biscuits, Corina," Walker said, splitting his second one in half. "And brew the second-best coffee." He leaned toward where young Matt was sitting and made a show of sharing a secret. "*I* brew the *best* coffee," he whispered loudly enough for everyone at the table to hear. "Black as oil and thick as Mississippi mud."

Matthew giggled, slapping his hands on the table in approval. He cast one of his adorable sideways glances at his mother. Annie cautioned him to be quiet with a finger to her lips.

"He's fine," Walker said. "Don't reprove him on my account."

"We all know you have few manners, Walker," Mrs. Reading said without humor. "But the boy's mother may want better for her son."

"Now, Corina," he said, attempting to engage her with a devilish grin. "You're being too harsh on me, and *I've* just complimented your biscuits."

In spite of that grin, Skye noticed that butter didn't melt in Corina's mouth. She was angry with Walker Caine for some reason that Skye couldn't fathom. Skye also noticed that Walker simply shrugged off her annoyance. It made her wonder what sort of relationship might exist between the two of them.

Skye made a point of complimenting Mrs. Reading on the meal. It didn't mollify the cook in the least.

"I'll be right back," Walker told Skye as he pushed out his chair. It scraped harshly against the floor and caused most everyone to wince. "Sorry. I need to check on Mr. Parnell again."

Skye wondered why that was necessary and why it fell on Walker Caine to do it.

"Don't bother," Mrs. Reading said. "I'm taking breakfast to him. He's probably asleep at his work table."

"Thank you," he said. He looked at Skye. "Do you have to address the troops again, commander, or can they go about their work based on this morning's instructions?"

Skye flushed, but she didn't comment. "I'm ready to see the rest of the house." She was quiet until she and Walker were mounting the main staircase to the second floor. "That was uncalled for," she said.

"What?"

"You know very well what. I won't have you undermining me in front of the others. I don't care if you don't make it easy for me here, but I'm damned if I'll let you get in my way."

Walker's tawny brows kicked up. He stopped on the step below her as she continued. When she turned around she was at eye level, facing his brown and gold-flecked eyes with brilliant fire in her green ones. Walker tapped her on the tip of her nose. "You, Mary Schyler, are a regular harridan." His hand dropped away and he tripped up the steps lightly, not stopping until he reached the top. "Are you coming?" he asked.

Skye's full mouth flattened momentarily. "I *knew* he was being too nice this morning," she muttered.

"What was that?"

She simply shook her head, not deigning to repeat

herself. Besides, she had a pretty good idea that he had heard her the first time.

The tour of the mansion's upper two floors was accomplished relatively quickly. Skye refrained from asking many questions and settled for a cursory inspection of each of the bedchamber suites, the linen cupboards, the upstairs sitting room, and the servants' quarters on the third floor where Annie and her son had been given space.

There were two staircases giving access to the upper stories. The grand stairs at the front of the house narrowed considerably when they curved to reach the third floor. The enclosed steps at the back were narrow to begin with, as they'd been constructed primarily for servant traffic. There were things she learned about the house on her tour that she didn't share with Walker Caine; things she thought she might investigate when she had the luxury of being alone.

Mrs. Reading had a suite of rooms in the northern wing of the house. Walker Caine occupied a single bedchamber in the same hall. Skye had not realized it last night but she had been given rooms which adjoined her employer's. The rooms which weren't in use had been allowed to grow dusty, and in some cases mildew had rotted the rugs and draperies. The muslin sheets shrouding the furniture were of marginal value, as they had been disturbed over time and now only partially covered the dressers and wardrobes.

The occupied rooms had fared better. Mrs. Reading's suite was well appointed and clean. Walker's was furnished spartanly by comparison, but it was neat. Walking into Jonathan Parnell's room meant stepping over discarded clothes, leftover trays of food, a puddle of water from the washbasin, and a small mound of quilts that had been kicked off the bed. Skye merely shook her head and beat a hasty retreat.

Annie Staplehurst had made a good beginning of righting the servants' quarters. Skye was satisfied that in the end Annie and her son would be more comfortable on the third floor than on the second.

They were passing her room on their way back downstairs when Walker said, "You know he blew his brains out in there, don't you?"

The image was enough to make Skye's stomach roll over. Learning that it had happened in her room kept it spinning. "What are you talking about?" she asked weakly, though of course she knew—probably better than he did.

"Hamilton Granville, the mansion's ghost. Mr. Parnell gave you his rooms."

Skye could only stare at Walker.

He used his forefinger to close her mouth for her. "That's better. Gaping is not particularly attractive—even for you."

She was still too stunned to notice there was a backhanded compliment in his words. "He gave me that room intentionally?" she demanded.

"He told me to put you nearby. I gave you that one." He jerked his thumb to the doors on the other side of the corridor. "I suppose I could have given you one of those." There was no apology offered.

Skye managed to school her features and asked flatly, "Have I done something to give you a dislike of me, Mr. Caine?"

He pretended to consider the question seriously, then shook his head. "Nothing comes to mind, Skye." The genial smile he had offered faded as he studied her upturned face. A stillness settled over his features. "In fact, it's quite the contrary. I have very selfish reasons for wanting you to go," he said. "This is no place for you." He held her wide eyes for a long time. His head lowered fractionally, nearing her upturned face.

Abruptly he pulled himself back and started to go.

It took Skye a moment to regain her voice. "Wait a minute," she called after him. Her voice sounded strained to her own ears and she was aware of her racing heart. "Where can I get keys to the closets that were locked?" she asked.

He wasn't surprised she was ignoring his warning. "I suppose you'll have to see Mr. Parnell about the closets. I've never known anyone to go in them."

A lock of red hair had fallen over Skye's forehead. Exasperated, she blew upward to get it out of the way. "But where can I find Mr. Parnell? You haven't shown me his workroom."

"It's in the cellar," he said. "But you can't go in there."

"Into the workroom or into the cellar?"

"Either. That part of the house is off limits to everyone but Mr. Parnell, Mrs. Reading, and me. The quickest way for you to be out of here on your ear is to venture down there."

"I'm surprised you told me, then."

"So am I," he said softly. "So am I."

Skye didn't see Jonathan Parnell until dinner, when he invited her to share his table. She considered objecting, knowing it wasn't her place as his housekeeper to join him, but it seemed the Granville house operated best with a certain lack of convention.

That afternoon Skye moved from one task to another with a sense of purpose. She was honest enough to admit to herself that her motivation had less to do with the work ahead of her than avoidance of what lay behind her. With her chore list in hand she was able to sidestep discreetly any contact with Walker Caine.

From time to time she lent a hand in the parlor,

where the work was proceeding at a slower pace than she would have liked. She did observe that no corner was left unattended. Jenny Adams and the twins were thorough, even if they weren't quick.

After luncheon, Skye sat with Mrs. Reading and reviewed the menus. It was obvious to Skye that the cook put thought and effort into planning Mr. Parnell's dinner. The courses were varied in taste and texture and temperature. They were diverse in color and presentation. Skye found it interesting that Mrs. Reading attempted a formal dinner. Mr. Parnell's erratic schedule made it almost impossible for anyone to know if he would be available for the meal. It made Skye wonder for whom the dinner was really being prepared. Walker Caine did not appear to share his employer's intensity when it came to work.

Although Skye complimented the cook's work, she saw that Mrs. Reading didn't care a whit if she approved or not— she intended to go on as she had. While Skye made several suggestions regarding the purchasing of supplies to better stock the pantry, she had no wish to argue over the execution of them. In dealing with the cook, Skye realized, she would have to choose her battles carefully. She felt certain she had given a good account of herself as someone to be reckoned with.

After her meeting with Mrs. Reading, Skye took time to prioritize the general house tasks. She followed this by completing her inventory of the dining room and beginning another of the library.

She was sitting at the inventor's massive mahogany desk when Jonathan Parnell himself came in to escort her to dinner. He didn't announce himself but entered the room silently, so that when Skye looked up from her work she had to wonder how long he might have been watching her. It was a little unsettling. Although he smiled in greeting, she had the oddest sensation that something had disturbed him. She had no way of knowing if she'd been the source of his agitation or what she might have done to cause it, but she had no doubt she'd glimpsed it in the dark centers of his eyes.

The shutter came down quickly on his expression as Skye rose from her chair and made her way around the desk. "It can't really be time for dinner, can it?" she said. She was aware that her hair had loosened from its pins and that strands of it curled unflatteringly around her temples and ears. She pushed back at it impatiently, tucking what she could under the hair that was still secured. "I haven't had a moment to change. I'm not— "

He interrupted her apology by indicating his own attire. He was wearing a pair of loose-fitting black trousers and a white shirt creased in all the wrong places. The sleeves were rolled up to his elbows, and a streak of grease peeked out from under the folds. His collar was open and he wore neither a vest nor a jacket. "If you change, then I shall feel compelled to do the same . . ." His smile held the same hint of roguish charm Skye had witnessed the previous day. "And I'd rather not."

Watching that smile, Skye was uneasy. "By all means," she said smoothly, covering the vague sense of disquiet. "You should be comfortable in your own home."

"I'm glad you feel that way."

Skye steeled herself against his ability to make her feel as if she were the one making the gracious concession. If she weren't careful she'd be thinking of herself as a guest and not as an employee. Perhaps it was all part of her father's grand design, but it was not any part of what Skye wanted for herself. When Parnell held out his elbow, Skye shook her head quickly and refrained from taking it. "You're very kind, Mr. Parnell, but I've had my doubts about joining you at all. I hardly think accompanying you to the dining room on your arm is necessary."

"I see," he said softly, studying the resolve in her

features. Both his brows raised slightly. "Very well. But one does crave conversation around here. I hope you'll grant me that. Walker is typically so taciturn at dinner."

Skye was aware she stiffened at the mention of Walker's name. She tried to cover her reaction by pretending to have difficulties with her apron strings. Unfortunately, her diversion meant that her employer was moved to assist her.

"Problems?"

Skye's head jerked up. The drily amused voice didn't belong to Jonathan Parnell but rather to Walker Caine. He was standing in the hallway on his way to the dining room. His faint smile bore witness to his thoughts concerning the tableau in front of him.

"She seems to have her strings tied in a knot," Parnell said amiably. "Deuced if I can get them undone."

Walker watched Skye's discomfort rise at the very thought that he might offer to help. "It seems I was right," he said consideringly. "It *is* possible for your face to rival the color of your hair." If anything, the color of Skye's complexion grew brighter.

Parnell's fingers stopped mangling the apron strings while he got a better look at Skye's flushed profile. His deep chuckle joined Walker's. "He's right, you know. Rose red."

"How very kind you both are to point it out," she said. Stepping away from Parnell, Skye twisted her apron around and made short work of the tangled strings.

In the dining room she was seated to Parnell's right while Walker took his usual place on the left. The courses were served by Rose and Daisy, who, perhaps because of Skye's presence, were apt to be a little clumsy.

Dinner started with a cold clear soup and was followed by creamed soup with artichokes. Fish continued the meal, then thin slices of rare beef roasted in a red wine. The potato croquettes were served with wedges of baked tomatoes and garnished with a sprinkling of cheese. Cold asparagus and stuffed crepes came next. Throughout the meal a variety of wines were served to stimulate or cleanse the palate. Sorbet, salad, and an assortment of cheeses completed the meal.

Skye was aware of the expense of putting this particular dinner on the table. She hadn't questioned Mrs. Reading about the budget, deciding that Mr. Parnell was one she needed to see. From her own experience of spending childhood summers near Baileyboro, Skye knew that a menu as diverse as the ones she'd been shown required importing a great deal of food from the city. Her own family, though Jay Mac could well afford it, chose to live much more simply when summering in the Hudson Valley.

Jonathan Parnell, it seemed, chose to have certain amenities of the city wherever he lived. Skye began to understand why he was particular about keeping Mrs. Reading in his employ.

"I should very much like to see your wine cellars," Skye said, sipping her Madeira. Throughout dinner the conversation had been primarily shared between Skye and Parnell. Walker had not been purposefully excluded, but he had made no effort to add anything to the discussion. His interruption now was unexpected.

"I've already told her the cellar is off limits," he told Parnell. Though he spoke to his employer, his cold warning stare was meant for Skye.

"Have you?" Parnell asked idly. "You do look out for me, don't you?" He rolled the stem of his wineglass between his fingers and leaned back in his chair. "Mr. Caine's quite right, Miss Dennehy. I generally don't like anyone in the cellar."

Skye's lightly feathered brows came together. "I'm not certain I understand. I thought an inventory of your wines would be a reasonable request. Mrs. Reading doesn't have a list of your stock."

Parnell tapped his temple with a forefinger. "Mrs. Reading has it up here." He laid his hand on the table. His fingers were long and lean, the nails clipped short and nicely shaped. "However, I've seen that you appreciate fine wines, and for that reason alone I may be willing to make an exception."

It took Skye a moment to understand the import of his words. She had been staring at Parnell's hand though she couldn't say what about it she found intriguing. "You'd make an exception?" she asked.

"No." It was Walker who answered, not Parnell. It was clear from his tone he did not expect to be countermanded.

Skye ignored him and looked expectantly at Jonathan Parnell, clearly indicating she thought it should be his decision.

Parnell sighed. "Mr. Caine's right," he said. He offered the observation with a certain heaviness in his tone, as if he were reluctant to offer it at all. "It's not a good idea. The fewer people with access to the cellar, the better."

Out of the corner of her eye Skye saw Walker relax his grip on the arm of his chair. Loose now, he drummed his fingers lightly against the scrollwork. "Of course," she said. "It shall be as you wish."

Parnell particularly liked that phrasing. His eyes lightened appreciatively. "Tell me, Miss Dennehy, have you worked for anyone besides the Turners or the Marshalls?" he asked.

The question came out of nowhere and Skye was caught off guard. All day long she had been wrestling with the problem of Parnell's collusion with her father. One moment she was certain it was a fact, in the next she had grave doubts. Did this man know who she really was, or didn't he?

Polite prevarication seemed in order. "Why do you ask?"

Walker spoke up. "Mrs. Givens didn't know *Moët et Chandon* from *Montrachet,*" he said.

"Mrs. Givens?" she asked, stalling to formulate her answer.

"The last housekeeper."

"Oh, I don't think I heard her name before." Her eyes drifted back to Parnell, who had originally posed the question, subtly putting Walker Caine in his place again. "I'm not surprised about Mrs. Givens, though. She doesn't appear to have known much about managing a household. My impression yesterday was that your staff was lacking in discipline, perhaps even skill, but I've discovered today that responsibility for the condition of this house can't be laid at their feet."

"I'm learning that myself," Parnell said. "She would have had me believe quite differently— " He paused to offer a slight, self-effacing grin. "That is, when I paused to notice anything was out of order at all."

Skye used the opportunity to skillfully redirect the conversation away from her own experience. "What is that you do exactly?" she asked. "One hears rumors, but I don't know what to believe."

"I tinker a bit," he said, shrugging.

Mr. Parnell's being modest," Walker said. "He holds twenty-seven patents and has four pending."

"Five," Parnell corrected. "It was the paperwork on the fifth that you delivered to the post this morning."

"Then you *are* an inventor!"

Parnell gave a start at the strength of her surprise. "Well, yes," he said, a trifle bewildered. "Someone has to do it, I suppose."

Skye's dimpled smile was apologetic. "I'm sorry. I imagine my astonishment didn't seem very flattering. It's just that one never knows what to make of rumors, and since it was never mentioned during the interview . . ." Her voice trailed off as she raised the wineglass to her lips. "I can understand why you don't want just anyone in the cellar. Do you have a work in progress?"

Walker's eyes narrowed and his considering look also held another warning. "You're full of questions, Miss Dennehy."

She flushed and began to stammer an apology to her employer.

"It's quite all right," Parnell said. "I don't mind in the least."

"Mr. Parnell," Walker said warningly. "I don't think—"

Parnell's head swiveled in Walker's direction and his blue eyes were as severe and frosty as his tone. "I was *going* to say that as much as I enjoy discussing my work, in this case— at this stage of the invention's development— it simply wouldn't be wise." He looked back at Skye. "This is not meant to reflect badly on you," he told her. "It's simply a rule I have regarding my work."

"Perfectly understandable," Skye said. "I've heard that obtaining a patent is quite a competitive endeavor."

Parnell nodded. "There were 13,000 patents a *year* issued during the seventies. I've heard the number has climbed to 21,000."

"Goodness," Skye said. " 'Competitive' hardly describes it."

"Exactly so."

Skye resolved then and there that she was going to see what Parnell was working on. If it looked in any way like an engine, then it supported her father's story and his reasons for sending her to Baileyboro. If it didn't exist, then she was right to think Jay Mac was up to his old tricks.

Getting to see the inside of Parnell's workroom wouldn't be nearly so difficult if it weren't for Walker

Caine. She had begun to see that he functioned as some sort of protector for Parnell. She would have to get past him to view the workroom. Skye was philosophical about it. She supposed every junkyard had its guard dog.

"You might let us in on the joke," Walker said.

Belatedly, Skye realized she was smiling at the image of a snarling, mangy stray answering to the name of Walker Caine. Skye put down her glass quickly and blotted her smile with her napkin. "I assure you," she said, "it was not worth sharing." She saw that Parnell accepted her words at face value. Walker, on the other hand, remained unconvinced. Glancing at the clock on the mantel, she added, "I have to excuse myself, Mr. Parnell. Thank you for the lovely invitation to dine."

He was on his feet immediately, helping Skye with her chair. "Of course you'll join us again."

"Oh, no. I couldn't. Really. It's very kind of you, but it's not my place at all. I'm sure you can see that." Her eyes pleaded with him not to make the invitation a second time.

"Very well, Miss Dennehy. You must do as you see fit." His hand brushed her shoulder lightly as she rose from her chair.

His touch startled Skye and set a small shiver through her. She quickly ducked from under his hand and avoided his inquiring gaze. "Thank you again," she said softly. It was a strain not to flee the room.

Parnell watched her go. When the door was closed behind her he said, "She's very curious." It was a statement about her personality, not about the fact that she asked too many questions.

Walker knew Parnell was thinking out loud, that he didn't expect a comment. It didn't stop him from responding anyway. "I don't trust her," he said tersely.

Parnell sighed. "So you've said. You can't fault her

work, though. Mrs. Reading reports she has everyone jumping."

As it came from Corina, Walker suspected it was more of a complaint than a compliment. "All the same, I'm going to keep an eye on her."

Parnell's brows rose slightly and his voice was somber. "See that it's all you do."

Skye was preparing for bed when there was a knock at her door. It was already quite late, a few minutes after midnight, but she had stayed up to prepare a list of things she wanted to do the following day. Compiling the tasks took longer than she had expected. As was often the case with Skye, her mundane thoughts were interrupted by her imagination— the bane of her existence, her father would have said.

Parnell's workroom continued to intrigue her. She wondered what a tinkerer's sanctuary might look like. Her own vision of it included a table cluttered with thingamajiggs and whatchamacallits. A scrap heap of tin whirlykabobs were piled in a corner. Dusty reference books on the physical laws of nature were stacked near the door. The walls were gray and the small casement window had had its panes painted a sickly pea-green shade so no one could see in. There would be hammers and nails and levers and awls. There would be magnets and iron filings, copper and lead pipes, jars of acids and salts.

Parnell himself would sit on a stool in the middle of the chaos, his distinguished, handsome features remote as he considered the weighty problem of harnessing the elements. He'd probably lightly stroke the bottom of his chin and his blue eyes would gaze at nothing in particular on the opposite wall. He'd be seeing something else entirely, something in his mind's eye that no one entering the room could possibly fathom. His brows might draw together and the indigo centers of his eyes would darken with his deep thoughts.

Suddenly he would jerk upright, his wide shoulders braced as though he'd felt a blow. A hand would come up and he'd be moved to speak aloud: *"Eureka!"*

Skye wondered if people really said that when they made a discovery. She certainly never had. Then again, she reminded herself, she had never really made a discovery.

The knock at the door came again, this time with enough force to rouse Skye from her musings. She put down her pen and slipped into her robe. "Who is it?" she asked, coming to stand near the door.

"Walker," came the low, laconic reply.

Skye was frankly shocked. Did he really believe she was going to give him entrance? She'd been privy to the scandals involving her sisters, and if she'd learned nothing else, she'd learned that trouble usually started when one let a man into a bedroom. "I'm not opening my door to you," she said. Her eyes fell to the door handle as Walker twisted it. "Go away!" she told him. Frantically she tried to remember if she'd locked the door or if the key rattling in the keyhole had never been turned. Bracing one shoulder against the door, she threw her weight into it just in case.

The handle fell back to its original position. "I need to talk to you," Walker whispered.

Skye didn't respond immediately. His hushed voice unnerved her for a moment. She felt an odd rise of panic and couldn't precisely name its source. He wasn't going to hurt her, was he? He hadn't made any threat, yet she felt threatened. "Go away," she repeated. "I'll scream— I swear I will!"

On the other side of the door, Walker paused in reaching for the key to her room. Her reaction was all out of proportion to his request. She no longer sounded

as if she was concerned for her modesty or her repu-
tation. One would think she was concerned for her life.
"For God's sake," he muttered, "I believe you. Go to
bed. We'll talk in the morning."

Skye didn't relax until she heard his footsteps recede
down the hallway. She fell back against the door, her
heart slamming in her chest. Looking down at herself,
she could have sworn she saw the front of her nightgown flutter with each wild beat.

Skye caught her breath and returned to the small
writing desk by the fireplace. She had no more work
to do, but the thought of climbing into bed now was
unappealing. She didn't think she could sleep.

Her fingers idly traced the crisp edge of the writing
paper she had been using. It was a tempting notion to
write to her father and tell him that whatever scheme
he had up his sleeve, he hadn't counted on the likes of
Walker Caine. Skye found a measure of satisfaction in
knowing her father hadn't thought of everything.

She abandoned the idea of writing at all. A letter to
her mother, even if she used her mother's maiden
name, wasn't safe from Walker. Skye wouldn't put it
past him to read anything she wrote before posting her
letters. Correspondence would have to wait until she
could send mail herself.

Skye's gaze drifted toward the door again. She wondered why he had come. "No doubt he thought he'd
steal that kiss he wanted earlier." She placed two fingers
against her mouth as she realized she'd spoken aloud.
The fingers were pressed to her lips for a moment, long
enough for her to consider what his mouth might have
felt like against hers.

Outside, the deep of night had made the french
doors a mirror of black glass. Skye caught the movement
of her hand in the window. She turned and stared at
her reflection. She could almost feel the heat rising in

her face. Walker Caine wouldn't have had to steal the kiss. She would have given it to him.

"I'm mad," she said softly, turning away from the windows. "Absolutely mad." Shaking her head, finding humor now in her reaction to Walker's knock at the door, Skye promised herself she'd apologize in the morning. She would have to do it carefully, without allowing him to glimpse how perfectly confused he made her. She'd never been so uncertain of herself as she was around Walker Caine.

Skye could scarcely believe it when there was another knock on her door. "I told you to go away," she called, raising her voice. There was a long silence, then a hesitant knock this time, more like a scratching than knuckles rapping against the wood. That certainly didn't sound like Walker. He was not so tentative.

"Who is it?" Skye asked cautiously, approaching the door.

"Annie. I've brought you— " She gave a little start as the door was flung open and Skye practically pulled her inside. The tray in her hand bobbled and she had to juggle it to keep the contents from overturning.

"Goodness," Skye said. "What do you have here?" She shut the door behind them and took the tray from Annie's hands. "Did you really bring this for me?"

Annie nodded. "I mentioned to Mrs. Reading that I saw a light under your door earlier. We thought you might like something. I was already on my way to the kitchen to get some milk for Matt. He's restless this evening."

"Aren't we all," Skye whispered drily.

"What?" Annie tilted her head.

"Oh, nothing. It wasn't important." She elbowed aside the papers on her desk and set the tray down. "I'm surprised you saw my lamplight. I'd have thought you'd use the back stairs. Certainly they're a more convenient route to the kitchen from your rooms."

Annie blushed and dropped her eyes. "You won't say anything, will you?" she asked quickly, giving Skye a furtive glance. "I don't like using the back stairs. *He* used to use them, you know."

"*He?*"

"You know," she insisted. "The ghost."

"*Oh,*" Skye said, drawing out the word. "You mean Hamilton Granville."

"Yes. That's the one."

Skye explained patiently, "Annie, Mr. Granville was the master of this house. I doubt he used the servants' stairs much. He probably considered it demeaning."

"That's what *I* said when Rose told me. But *she* says Mr. Granville had a particular reason for using the stairs." She didn't elaborate but waited for Skye to guess her meaning through a show of brow wiggling and suggestive glances.

"I see," Skye said slowly. "You mean he was intimate with one of the servants."

"Exactly so!" Annie said triumphantly.

Skye found it difficult not to laugh. "So his ghost haunts the staircase, is that it? He's looking for his lost love?"

Annie nodded hard. Her gray eyes were wide and quite solemn.

"Well, that's a relief," Skye said, tapping her heart with her palm. "I was worried he'd be in here." Annie's brows went up in question. "Didn't Rose tell you?" Skye asked. "This is where he blew his brains out."

Five

After Annie left, Skye moved the tray to her bedside and climbed in under the comforter. She regretted teasing Annie, but the opportunity was too delicious to pass up. The poor woman couldn't leave the room quickly enough. Skye thought it was especially thoughtless of her since Annie had been so nice to bring the tray of warm milk and buttered bread. Annie had even remembered cinnamon and sugar. Mentally adding Annie Staplehurst's name to the list of apologies she was making in the morning, Skye settled back against the headboard, surrounding herself with a pillow throne.

She broke the warm bread heel into small chunks and dropped it in the milk. As she added cinnamon and a pinch of sugar, her eyes strayed toward the door. The chair she had propped against the handle appeared to be quite secure. Skye laughed a little uneasily, feeling something of a hypocrite for teasing Annie, then barring her own door.

It's not ghosts I've a mind to keep out, though, she thought. In her mind she could hear her mother's comforting accents. "Sure, but he's a flesh-and-blood man." Wrapping her hands around the mug, Skye raised it to her lips and pressed its warmth against her smile.

* * *

She was cold. A small shiver went through her, prickling the surface of her skin. Her fingers clutched spasmodically but grasped only the sheet beneath her. Where were the quilts? The comforter? She tried to extend her search but couldn't seem to raise her hands. When she shivered again, it was as much from rising panic as from the cold.

Something touched her face. Instinctively she jerked her head away. The touch came again, light against her skin, brushing her from one corner of her eye to the tip of her chin. It wasn't human flesh that made the trail, but something silky, something as insubstantial as gossamer.

The whisper of it across her skin made her want to cry out. She willed herself to open her mouth and force the sound. The thing grazed her lips, stilling her voice.

She moved her head again, another sideways jerk to avoid the brush of it. Her throat was exposed. She felt the naked arch of it as the touch of butterfly wings beat softly against its length. Something drifted across her bare shoulders. It lay still against her skin for only a heartbeat, then it moved like a fog across her flesh, touching her breasts, her ribs, then lower, so that she felt it skim her belly, her hip, and the inside of her thigh.

Her entire body revolted against the intimate intrusion, yet except for the small, negating shake of her head, there was no movement.

Skye woke slowly. Her limbs were slow to respond to the commands of her brain. The pounding in her head was insistent and almost painful. She covered her ears with her palms. The sound was barely muffled.

"You can't avoid me by sleeping the day away. You have to talk to me sometime."

Raising her eyelids the merest fraction, Skye dared to

look at the door. It rattled in its frame with the force of the fist against it, but the chair held it firmly in place. She found a little comfort in learning all the pounding she'd heard wasn't solely inside her head. Rising from bed, her head swimming, Skye reached out to steady herself. She grabbed the bedpost and held on tightly.

"I'm coming," she said weakly. She realized she could have saved her breath. Walker couldn't hear her for all the racket he was making. Was he bent on waking the entire house?

Skye's robe was lying at the foot of the bed. She didn't bother with it because it didn't look warm enough to ward off her bone-deep chill. Instead, she grabbed one corner of the thick comforter and dragged it around her shoulders like a shawl. She was aware that her nightgown was clinging to her skin and that it was faintly damp. Wondering if she was aching for something, Skye touched her forehead with the back of her hand. She felt a little warm but knew it was no real test of her wellness.

Stumbling to the door, Skye kicked away the chair and leaned heavily against it. Walker's pounding hadn't stopped and the entire door vibrated along the length of Skye's body. "What do you want?" she asked. When her voice was barely audible to herself, Skye realized there was nothing for it but to open the door.

She turned the key and twisted the handle. With the door opened a crack, she peered out. "Go away," she said. "You don't have any sense. You'll wake everyone."

At his first glimpse of Skye, Walker's brows furrowed. The gold flecks in his eyes glinted like shards of amber glass. His gaze roamed her face, surveying the damage. "Everyone *is* awake," he said. " 'Breakfast promptly at six-thirty,' you said. Remember?"

"Yes, but— " She interrupted her own objection to look behind her at the clock on the mantel. Her mouth sagged. "It's after seven," she said, astonishment and despair in the revelation. Sufficiently distracted, Skye was unable to stop Walker from shouldering his way into her bedchamber.

He glanced at the chair that had been pushed aside, but made no comment about it. There was no point in telling her it wouldn't have kept him out. His attention was all for Skye. "You look like hell," he said plainly, his eyes taking quick inventory.

Except for the unnaturally high color in her cheeks, her complexion was pasty. Her lips, especially the lower one, looked bruised. She began to worry it between her teeth even as he was studying her. He watched her wince, as if only becoming aware of her lip's tenderness, and raise her hand to her mouth to explore its edge. Without asking permission, Walker placed the backs of three fingers against Skye's forehead. "You're not fevered," he said, shaking his head. "What happened to you? You look— "

"I know," she said, interrupting. "So you've said." Skye clutched the comforter more closely around her. "I must be getting a cold . . . maybe a migraine." In truth, she didn't know. She felt as if she were recovering from a prolonged illness rather than beginning one. Her muscles and bones ached deeply, and the lethargy had traveled to her brain. She could recall feeling this sluggish only when she'd been sick for days.

Skye brushed a strand of flaming hair from her eyes. It immediately fell back again. Giving up, she stared at Walker through it. "I don't think I slept well last night," she told him.

He looked amused. "That would be understating it a bit," he said. Taking her by the shoulders, Walker turned her so that she was facing the bed. He gave her a gentle push. "Go sit down while I build a fire. Perhaps thawing you out will help."

Skye wondered if she imagined some off-color suggestion in his last statement or if it were really there. She shook her head, trying to clear it. She was not usually such a slow top, she thought. "You shouldn't be here," she said fuzzily. The truth of it had only just occurred to her. She *was* a slow top this morning.

Walker was hunkered in front of the fireplace, putting down coals and kindling. "Yes, well," he drawled, "I was elected by the assembly to beard the lioness."

Skye puzzled over that a moment. "I don't think a lioness has a beard, not so you'd notice, anyway."

He chuckled appreciatively, looking back at her over his shoulder. She was absently rubbing her chin. "You're coming around nicely," he said. Walker went back to his work. When he had a fire blazing, he motioned to her to come closer. He nudged a chair toward the flames so she'd be able to feel the heat.

Still huddled in the comforter, Skye sat down. She'd have curled her legs under her, but Walker drew out her bare feet. At the first touch of his hands on her skin, Skye responded violently, kicking out so fast that Walker was nearly pushed into the fire.

He caught himself and held up his hands, not in a surrendering gesture, but to show he intended no harm. It didn't matter what he did, he realized, watching her cautiously. Although Skye returned his stare, her expression was blank. Slowly the dullness melted away, replaced by a wash of confusion. It was seconds later that she finally noticed him, his posture, the raised hands, and it was only then that an embarrassed flush stole across her features and awareness entered her eyes.

"I'm sorry," she said quickly. "I didn't mean—"

He waved aside her apology. "I should have asked permission." He pointed to her feet. Her toes were already curled against the braided hearth rug and she was inching her feet toward the fire. "May I?"

She nodded and steeled herself to be touched again.

Walker's hands were firm, the palms warm. His touch was substantial, not like— Skye's thoughts stopped. Not like what? she wondered. She was aware Walker was watching her again. "I wish you'd go," she said, huddling into the comforter. The fire was warming her on the outside, but the core of her was like ice. "I need to dress."

"You don't look well enough to leave your room today."

Her room was the last place she wanted to stay. "I'll be fine," she said. More firmly she added, "I *am* fine."

Walker wasn't convinced. In spite of that he gave in. "All right. But if you don't look any better in the afternoon, you're coming back here if I have to carry you."

Skye agreed because she believed she'd feel better, not because she'd allow him to carry her anywhere. When he was gone, she got up slowly and shed the comforter. Stripping out of her nightgown made her warmer almost immediately. She felt the fabric and wondered at its dampness. She could only imagine that she had been very warm during the night and promised herself not to lay so big a fire in the future.

Skye put the gown over the back of a chair so it could dry. She poured water from a blue spongeware pitcher into the basin on the washstand. Dipping her fingers into the basin, she touched water to her face and throat. It trickled between her breasts. Her nipples hardened.

She picked up a washcloth and began her ablutions, scrubbing harder than was her normal manner, though she was scarcely aware of it. In the mirror above the vanity Skye caught her reflection. She drew in her breath sharply when she saw how red she'd made her skin. This was no pink, healthy glow that touched her, but a raw, angry color. Dropping the cloth, Skye stepped out of the mirror's path.

She dressed quickly, avoiding more than a cursory glance in the glass on her way out the door. Her glorious hair was scraped back and coiled smoothly at the nape of her neck. She had pinched color into her cheeks. A small amount of rice powder effectively hid the shadows under her eyes. The dress she had chosen was heather gray, tailored to fit her slight figure. Today it made her look like a wraith.

Mrs. Reading was alone in the kitchen when Skye entered. Her place was still set at the table and several small plates covered with cotton napkins were nearby.

"It was kind of you to save something for me," she said, "but I find I'm not very hungry."

The cook didn't look up from her kneading. Her sleeves were rolled up to her elbows and flour sprinkled the backs of her hands. Her forearms and fingers showed considerable strength as she worked the dough, patting and pushing and folding. "Suit yourself," she said indifferently.

Skye poured herself some tea from the pot warming on the stove. She added a dollop of honey and drank slowly, sluicing her throat. The dull thudding in her head had taken on the same rhythm as dough slapping against the breadboard.

"Do you know anything about the ghost?" The words were out before Skye quite realized she was going to ask them.

Although she looked up, Corina didn't break her rhythm. "The ghost?" she asked blankly. "Did I hear you right?"

Skye was tempted to say that she hadn't, but before she could form a reply, the cook was going on.

"Oh, you mean those stories about Hamilton Granville." She shrugged her narrow shoulders. "I don't pay much mind to that sort of thing. I can't be sure I'd sleep a wink if I did." Her eyes narrowed as she made a thorough assessment of Skye's face. "Have you been listening to the stories? Don't tell me that's your problem this morning."

"Goodness no," Skye said quickly, forcing a smile. "No, in fact, I had a hard sleep. Dreamless. I suspect that's why it was difficult to rise this morning. I do apologize. I'm afraid I didn't set a good example."

Corina Reading's expression didn't change. "That'll be for you to fix, won't it?"

Skye finished her tea. No amount of *mea culpa* was going to satisfy Mrs. Reading. Skye only hoped the rest of the staff was not so intractable.

Annie brushed off both of Skye's apologies, one for her late rising and the other for her teasing. "It's not a necessary thing," she said frankly. "I must have seemed a veritable goose, what with my goin' on about that ghost. It serves me right for being so silly. You'll find I don't mind having my nose tweaked from time to time."

"That's very gracious of you," Skye said, "and I promise not to take advantage. Where's Matt?"

"Mr. Caine took him out. He was going to show him the swan pond."

"The swan pond?"

"Through the woods, he said it was. They won't be gone above an hour." She looked momentarily worried. "Do you think it was all right for me to let Matt go? Mr. Caine is the one who suggested it."

"Then I'm certain he hoped you'd take him up on his offer," Skye told her. "How long ago did they leave?"

"You just missed them."

Skye figured she safely had forty-five minutes before their return. "And Mr. Parnell?"

"Up before anyone was stirrin', I understand. He's gone to his workroom again."

"Hank's caring for the animals?" Skye asked just to be certain. "And Rose—"

"Is with her sister and Jenny in the parlor. When

you didn't come down this morning everyone got started just the same." Her voice dropped to a confidential whisper. "The only one who paid your absence much mind was Mrs. Reading and Mr. Caine. *He* seemed worried, but she was stirring trouble."

And you're keeping it stirred, Skye almost told her. She said nothing, believing Annie meant well. "I think I'll see what the twins and Jenny are doing in a little while. Right now I'm going upstairs to start another inventory."

Annie nodded, feeling important because Skye had thought to tell her her whereabouts. She picked up her feather duster and applied herself wholeheartedly to the bookshelves.

Skye started by pacing off the hallway which joined the bedchambers in her wing. She scribbled a few numbers on her pad, then went to her own room to measure its area. Estimating her own foot to be six inches and a natural step to take her about two feet, Skye walked two sides of her room and made her calculations. The dressing room and bathing room added a few more square feet. She wrote everything down with a rough sketch of the layout of the room.

Parnell's bedchamber was larger than her own, but it was a complementary L-shape so that the suites fit together like pieces of a puzzle. A door to the left of his fireplace could be opened into her dressing room. Skye tested the knob as she had on her own side and found the door just as secure. A brief glance around the room didn't reveal a key out in the open. Even if such a key existed, she wasn't of a mind to go rummaging for it just yet. She turned to go and felt something tug on the hem of her dress. Looking down she saw the material had caught on the head of a nail.

Skye pulled it free, then bent down to examine the nail. It was driven into the door frame and bent sideways to act as a latch on the door. Closer examination revealed there were five such nails along the frame, so small that Skye forgave herself for not seeing them immediately. Two were situated near each corner along the length of the jambs and one was in the middle at the top. Skye decided she wouldn't bother looking for a key at any time. One was quite useless unless someone was willing to pry away the nails keeping the door in place.

She laughed softly. The half-formed imaginings that had made the inspection seem important in the first place were without foundation. Making a few notes on her rough sketch, Skye paced off the room. When she was done, she slipped her notepad back in her apron pocket and stuck her pencil behind her ear.

Parnell's room was furnished in much the same manner as her own. The pieces were stained slightly darker and had a more masculine feel to them in their heaviness and lack of ornamentation. A pair of French doors led out to a balcony that was twice the size of hers. It was also separated from her own by a space of more than ten feet.

Skye picked up a few articles of clothing that were scattered on the floor. The things that required washing were slung over her arm. Parnell's wine-red robe she hung in the armoire. His wardrobe was such a large piece of furniture that it couldn't be squeezed into his dressing room. Instead it stood beside the secured door, on the other side of the wall directly opposite her own armoire.

Skye was unaware how much time had passed until she heard the sound of childish laughter. Scooping up a few more pieces of clothing, she headed for the hallway. She collided with Matt as he charged straight for her skirts, intending to hide behind them, or— she realized with a little start— *under* them. She gave a reflexive jerk, coming up on her toes as the boy tried to burrow between her legs.

Walker reached the top step and saw Matthew's tiny feet peeping out from under Skye's gown. "One is moved to envy," he said feelingly, a wicked grin lifting one corner of his mouth.

Certain his next comment was going to be another unflattering comparison of her face to her hair, Skye dropped the armful of clothes and picked up Matt. "Your mama promised me you wouldn't get underfoot," she said, tapping the boy on his nose.

He gave her a sly look that was much older than his years . . . much, *much* older.

Walker came up on them and noticed Matt's sly expression. He laughed. "That's what I was thinking, young man."

"I'm sure his mind isn't as sullied as yours," she said, with some asperity. She ignored Walker's outstretched hands and hefted Matt to make him more comfortable in her arms. "Get the laundry," she said.

Walker caught up to her again in the rear stairwell, his arms loaded with her castoffs. The narrow stairway was not illuminated and the small window at the second-floor landing didn't shed much light by the time they reached the bottom. Skye's steps faltered once, but she caught herself.

"Are you all right?" Walker asked. "This isn't the way to go without a lamp or candle."

She would remember that in the future. "I'm managing just fine, thank you."

Behind her, Walker smiled. He liked the way she prickled at nearly everything he said. Without being told, he took the laundry to the back of the kitchen and dropped it into a large copper kettle. Stopping just long enough at the table to steal a warm cinnamon bun from under Mrs. Reading's nose, Walker caught up to Skye again in the dining room.

"Are you following me?" she asked, setting Matt in a chair. "Don't you have an employer who requires that sort of attention?" She went to the sideboard and opened the middle drawer. She took out a half-dozen spoons and a polishing cloth and put it all in front of Matt. After a brief demonstration on how to clean the spoons, she turned it all over to the little boy. In seconds he was making happy clatter, completely amused by the shiny spoons.

Walker was skeptical. His arms were crossed in front of him, reinforcing his expression. He stopped chewing on the cinnamon roll. "You don't really believe he's going to polish the silver."

The look Skye shot Walker told him how ridiculous his comment was. "What I expect is that he'll be playing while you find his mother and bring her here. She can work in this room and her son can contribute in his own small way." Skye went back to the sideboard, pulled out the entire drawer, and placed it on the table. With another polishing cloth she began to wipe the silverware in earnest.

She looked up at Walker when he didn't move. One of her eyebrows lifted in question.

"In the army," he drawled softly, "the captain generally yelled 'dismissed' when he was done with the troops."

On impulse Skye stuck her tongue out at him.

Watching the warmth run up her face, Walker smiled slowly. "That'll do." He turned smartly on his heel and left the room.

As the day progressed, it was as if the morning had never happened. Skye's headache vanished and her eyes brightened of their own accord. She kept busy with her inventory and by dinner, with the exception of the cellar and certain locked closets, she had cataloged the contents of the first floor.

Skye ate lightly at the evening meal, certain that her problems at rising had had to do with something she'd eaten the night before. The meal that Mrs. Reading served in the kitchen was a scaled-down version of what Parnell and Walker were enjoying in the dining room. Portions that could not easily be prepared in small amounts were available to the staff. Rose and Daisy Farrow ate in shifts between taking out the courses. Annie helped clear trays and store what food she could in the icebox on the back porch.

Skye shared the table with Matt, Jenny, and Hank. She purposely avoided the shellfish and heavy sauces, taking her fill with the clear soups and vegetables. Annie encouraged her to eat more, but Skye found it easy to resist the temptation.

On the way to her room that evening, Skye was stopped as she passed the parlor. Jonathan Parnell and Walker Caine were sitting opposite one another in the large armchairs, smoking cigars. A blue haze wreathed their heads, and Skye couldn't quite mask her dislike for the odor as she was waved inside. She was thankful that her father had put aside his fondness for cigars years ago.

"I take it you have no appreciation for a good cigar," Parnell said.

"Pity," Walker added softly, with an edge of sarcasm. "He had so much hope for you when you showed good taste in wine."

In tandem Skye and Parnell shot him a sour glance. Walker merely blew a smoke ring into the air.

"Pity *him*," Parnell said. "He drank most of his dinner tonight."

Skye didn't comment, though she was surprised to learn that Walker drank to excess. It didn't fit with the kind of man she suspected he might be. "Is there something you wanted, sir?"

"A moment of your time," he said soberly. "Is there something pressing you now?"

She shook her head. "Actually, Mr. Parnell, I would

like a moment with you. I have some questions about the house that you could answer."

He indicated the vacant wing chair. "Won't you sit?"

Skye was going to refuse, but thought better of it. She was learning that sometimes her employer's politeness merely sheathed a command. Pushed, he could insist that she sit and the conversation would be stilted and uncomfortable from then on.

Taking a seat on the edge of the wing chair, Skye folded her hands primly in her lap. The pose was an uneasy one for her. In her own home she rarely sat quietly in one place for long. Now she could hear Mrs. Cavanaugh's admonishments: "You flutter too much. Keep still. Back straight. Don't be so quick to look everyone in the eye. Don't look away too long, though— it gives the impression of furtiveness. No one wants a furtive housekeeper. There's always suspicions about the silverware count." Skye couldn't imagine anyone less furtive than Mrs. Cavanaugh.

"You appear to be miles away," Parnell said, observing Skye's expression. "Where do you go?"

Her efforts to play the part right had only succeeded in her being chided for daydreaming. "I'm sorry," she said. "You were saying . . ."

"Actually, I was waiting to hear what you wanted to say." When she merely looked at him blankly, he prompted, "About the house?"

"Oh, yes. I can't seem to find keys for all the closets. There are two on your wing which don't open and another near Mr. Caine's room. I can't open the one under the stairs, either."

Parnell was thoughtful for a moment. "Do you know, I'm not certain any keys to those closets exist. Did you ask Mrs. Reading?"

"No."

"If she doesn't have the keys, then it's a certainty there's nothing in the closets."

"Well, if they're empty, I'd like to utilize them to reorganize some of the more crowded linen cupboards. And the space under the stairs would make a nice area to hang coats and hats. You have no such place in your entryway."

Parnell appeared not to have realized this before. "Is that so?" he asked, frowning slightly as he pictured the foyer in his mind. "Why, you're right." With a small apologetic smile, he shrugged. "I've never noticed."

"Then I have your permission to reorganize?"

"If you can find the keys," he said. "Not if it means taking doors off their hinges or picking locks. I don't believe it's worth that sort of effort."

"It really wouldn't be hard," Skye began to explain. "I could do it eas—"

"No," he interrupted, with a firmness he hadn't used with her yet. His handsome smile took the edge off the command, but the command itself was very much there. "I'm quite serious about this. If the keys can't be found, then leave the doors as they are. I don't want a lot of fussing over some closets. You may have to be creative with your rearranging."

"Very well," she said, hiding her confusion. She hadn't thought it was an unreasonable request. "I'm sure I shall manage."

"I'm sure you shall," Parnell said gravely. "Was there anything else?"

"No."

"Then it's my turn."

Skye waited expectantly, though not eagerly. She worked hard at avoiding Walker's gaze, though she felt his eyes hard on her. Talking to Parnell was unnerving in Walker's presence. She felt as though she could never completely relax.

"Mrs. Reading mentioned earlier that you were asking questions about our ghost."

There was no possibility that Skye could mask her surprise, and she didn't try. She simply couldn't have imagined that Mrs. Reading would think to pass on an off-handed comment about the Granville ghost. "I believe I merely asked her what she knew."

"That's what she said. But I see I've startled you. Certainly you're welcome to talk about the ghost as you see fit. I wouldn't think to censure your tongue." Parnell drew deeply on his cigar, then let out the smoke slowly. "However, I would suggest that you consider with whom you are broaching the subject. Mrs. Reading rightly believes that Daisy and Rose Farrow are entirely too suggestible when it comes to the tales of Hamilton Granville. Mrs. Givens used to have trouble getting one of them to go anywhere in this house without the other."

"Of course," she said, struggling not to become defensive. "I spoke only to Mrs. Reading, not to the twins."

"I understand that. It's just something for you to consider." He paused, studying Skye's rigid posture. "I thought you might have some questions for me about the ghost."

"I wouldn't presume to take up your time with that nonsense."

Do I detect a note of bravado?" he asked lightly, casting a sideways glance at Walker. "Did you hear it, Mr. Caine?"

Walker stubbed out his cigar and rose to his feet. "I heard it," he said tersely. He went to the fireplace and poked at the flames.

"Is that all, sir?" Skye asked, hoping to be dismissed. If Parnell noticed her anxiousness, he gave no sign. She wondered what was making Walker Caine out of sorts. He seemed as impatient to be gone as she. Perhaps it was the effects of the drink.

"There's a book in the library that will give some

history of the Granville family," he told her. "If you're interested, I suggest you use it as your source. No one here will be quite so reliable in relating the details." His smile was swift. "Now, that's all, Miss Dennehy."

Skye did not enjoy being the object of her employer's amusement. It was doubly difficult to take with Walker observing it all. Mustering her dignity, Skye bade them both good evening.

Skye lay in bed for two hours before she surrendered to the fact that she wasn't going to sleep. Still, she rose reluctantly and sat on the edge of the bed for a few minutes. The clock on the mantel beat a tattoo in her head while it clicked off the passing time. She had already heard Walker and Parnell part ways in the hall as they retired to their own rooms. She knew that Annie had gone to her quarters with her son long before. It was doubtful Mrs. Reading was still up, or at least out of her room.

The realization that she would be alone gave Skye a motive to get out of bed. She put on slippers and wrapped herself in the familiar comfort of her thick cotton robe. It was like a hug around her body. Smiling to herself, Skye gathered the strands of hair that had drifted over her shoulders and let them fall down her back. She plaited her hair quickly in a loose braid that she did not bother to fasten. Tendrils of it were damp from the quick washing she'd given it; if she confined it now it would still be damp in the morning. At least, that was the excuse she gave herself for walking out of her room with her hair unbound.

The bedside lamp she carried gave sufficient light to permit her to use the servants' stairs easily. She hesitated at the bottom, listening for the sound of any other occupant of the kitchen. When only silence was returned, she pushed open the door with confidence.

Skye took the lamp with her to the enclosed back porch, where stoneware jugs of milk had been set to keep cool. The wind sounded louder here, she thought, as she chose one of the smaller containers. Each gust rattled the outside door and made the wooden beams creak overhead. The force of it seemed more than enough to separate the porch from the rest of the house, and Skye quickly backed into the pantry area with her lamp and jug.

She put both on the kitchen table and began looking for a cup. The kitchen was so much the province of Mrs. Reading that Skye had no clear idea where to search. Locating the cup proved easier than finding the cinnamon and sugar among Mrs. Reading's spices and dry goods.

Skye fired up the stove and warmed the milk in a small saucepan. Her eyes kept drifting to the door off the pantry area while she worked. She had managed to resist testing the handle on her way to the porch, and again on the way back, but it was getting more difficult to think of reasons why she shouldn't at least try the entrance to the cellar.

Listening again for sounds that would indicate someone else was up, Skye heard nothing except the fire in the stove and the whisper of milk scalding in the pan. She removed it from the heat and set it aside.

Aware her palms were suddenly damp, Skye wiped them on her robe as she headed for the cellar door. She laid her fingers against the handle and before her resolve failed, she twisted it.

Skye's heart knocked against her chest as she felt the door give. She opened it a crack, listened, then opened it wider. It took a moment for her eyes to adjust to the dark. She considered going back for her lamp and decided against it. She could see well enough to manage the steps without breaking her neck. There was bound to be a lamp in the workroom, she thought.

The steps were smooth, indented slightly in the middle by the numerous trips up and down them over the years. Skye placed one hand on the dank whitewashed wall to steady herself and made each step a cautious one. When she reached the bottom, she simply stood there. There may indeed have been a lamp in Parnell's workroom, but she couldn't see well enough to get there. She had no clear idea which part of the cellar might hold the inventions and which might hold the wine. There was nothing for it but to retrieve her lamp.

She turned just in time to catch the last glimpse of light that was available to her as the door shut. A single gasp, as if it were air that was being denied her, rose from Skye's throat. She scrambled up the stairs and groped for the handle. It only turned fractionally in her hand. The door was already locked.

Skye leaned against it, catching her breath and thinking furiously. It was no accident that had closed the door *and* locked it. Someone meant for her to be found out. It was what kept her from pounding on the door and begging for her freedom. She refused to believe there wasn't another way out.

The darkness of the cellar was oppressive. The damp air was cloying. Skye strained to see as she placed her left hand on one wall and began cautiously to follow its path around the perimeter.

Once, when she was still a child, her father had proposed a visit to a maze garden. Thinking he meant a maize garden, Skye was less than enthusiastic about the Sunday excursion. It wasn't until they arrived and she was confronted by hedgerows taller than her father that she realized there was something about it all that she hadn't understood.

She could still remember listening intently to her father's explanation of the maze, thoroughly intrigued by the lifesized puzzle. Her four sisters had paired off immediately, the twins together, and Mary Francis with Maggie. That left Skye alone. Jay Mac and Moira had planned to accompany her, but she would have none of it. After her sisters disappeared into the maze, Skye followed at a deliberately thoughtful pace.

It took her a while, but she still finished before any of her sisters.

Mary Francis, Mary Michael, Mary Renee, and Mary Margaret all thought Skye had cheated when they discovered how she'd managed the hedgerow maze. Jay Mac thought she was very clever and her mother declared her a genius to anyone who would listen.

All she had done was keep one hand on the hedgerow through every turn and corridor. It brought her to the same end as everyone else.

She used that method now, confident that if she didn't reach an outside entrance, she'd return to her starting point none the worse off.

Skye paid attention to the texture of the path she was following so she could distinguish between the stone wall and the doors that blocked off other areas of the cellar. Though she tried each of the two doors her hand made contact with, neither opened. For her pains she was rewarded with a splinter in her index finger.

Occasionally her feet found obstacles on the floor. She had to go around a pile of wood stacked against one wall and several covered barrels shoved in a corner. She tripped over an empty jar, then had to get down on her hands and knees to find it when it rolled away. Skye could only imagine the mess she was from crawling around on the dirt floor.

She estimated that she had covered just more than half the cellar's perimeter when she came to an opening in the wall and found stairs leading from it. They rose five high, and when she reached the top, she discovered what she was looking for: double wood doors latched on the inside that opened outward to freedom.

"Eureka," she said softly.

She pulled the latch and pushed open the doors. Frigid air swirled in to greet her, but she breathed deeply. Even in the dead of night it was easier for her to see once she was out of the cellar. Starshine and moonlight allowed her to close the doors easily and make her way around the house without fear of falling. She didn't expect the door to the porch to be open, and it wasn't. She paused on the steps, shivering as she determined her options.

She was still thinking when the door was opened behind her. Skye nearly toppled off the steps. It was a hand grabbing the collar of her robe that kept her from falling. Another hand covered her mouth and silenced her surprise.

Remembering the time not long ago when she'd been held in a similar manner, Skye found that her struggle was as instinctive as it was panicked. She clawed at the hand on her mouth and tried to shimmy out of the robe.

"Settle down," Walker said. He lifted, more than dragged, Skye inside, then released her. He didn't give her a moment to catch her breath, forcing her back to the door and placing a stiff arm on either side of her shoulders. When she tried to duck under him, he feinted in the same direction and kept her enclosed. "Don't fight me," he said. "You're in enough trouble already."

Skye was aware of his closeness, of the heat of his body, of warm, sweet breath that touched her face as he spoke. She stared at him mutely.

"What were you doing out there?" he asked.

He was studying her face as if he could see the truth imprinted on her features. It didn't matter to Skye. She believed she had no choice but to lie. "I just stepped out," she said. "The wind . . . it was so loud and I heard . . . I thought I heard something tearing away from the roof." It was difficult to catch her breath when Walker was so near. She wasn't certain she liked sharing the air with him, having him steal the very breath she needed. "I went out . . . out to investigate."

He didn't say anything for a moment, skeptical, measuring her response. "That so?" he asked blandly. She only stared back at him. "All right," he said, dropping one arm. "Get into the kitchen."

Skye hurried past him, straightening the collar of her robe and tightening the sash around her waist. Her milk was still on the stove, a thin film on the surface. Trying to keep her hand steady, she drew it off with a spoon and poured the milk into her cup. She didn't bother adding cinnamon or sugar.

"Drinking it straight?" Walker asked from the doorway.

Skye's hands were wrapped around the cup. She shrugged and started for the servants' stairs.

Walker blocked her way. "Not so fast. Have a seat at the table."

She raised mutinous eyes to him but in the end was forced to look away. She took a seat.

"That's better." Walker pulled out a chair for himself and straddled it. "The roof's all of one piece?" he asked.

For a second Skye didn't know what he was talking about. She wondered if her confusion showed on her face. "The roof's fine," she said, remembering her lie. "At least, so far as I could tell."

"Did you climb up to investigate?"

"What?"

He pointed to Skye's hands. "They're dirty. So's your robe. Your knees, too. That should take a little explaining."

Skye was up to it. "I tripped and fell."

"No grass stains, though."

He didn't miss anything, Skye thought. "I was fortunate, but then, perhaps you've noticed that there's not much grass off the back steps."

"Plenty of frost, though. Your hem's damp, but not your knees. Your hands are dirty, not wet."

"I'm sure I don't know why that is," she said tartly, "but I'd be happy to listen to your explanation, if you have one."

Walker had been waiting for the opportunity. "I'd say you were trying to get into the cellar," he said. "The door leading off the kitchen is locked. You must have thought you could get in from the outside entrance. Those doors, however, lock from the inside, so you didn't have any success. You were careless when you left the porch, though, and the door caught in the latch behind you. Maybe the wind had something to do with it." He was watching her carefully. "Any of that sound about right?"

Swallowing a mouthful of milk, Skye nodded. "The part about the wind and the door."

When she didn't give an inch, Walker's brows rose slightly. "What brought you down here, then?"

Skye's eyes widened dramatically as she feigned complete astonishment. "You mean you figured out all the other with barely any evidence?" she simpered. "While the milk on the stove, the mug on the table, and the cinnamon and sugar weren't enough to help you deduce I couldn't sleep?"

Far from taking offense at her antics, Walker laughed. "Your point's taken." He rested his forearms on the top rail of the chair and looked at Skye intently. "Just so you know, however, I don't believe a word of it. I think you're up to something, Mary Schyler." The use of both her names was deliberate. As far as Walker was concerned, she was more than knee deep in trouble.

Skye yawned abruptly. Her attempt to cover it came too late. "I'm finished with my milk," she said, setting down the cup. "Are you done with your questions?"

Walker didn't acknowledge Skye right away. He was looking at the loosely plaited hair that had fallen over her shoulder. The end of it had unwound and lay thickly against her robe. His fingers itched to touch it, to see if it burned, if the texture was as slippery and cool as a waterfall. His eyes followed the curve of her burnished hair from her breast, to her shoulder, to the angled line of her jaw. She fiddled with a tendril near her ear, drawing it toward her mouth in a nervous movement.

Walker's attention strayed to her lips. The full lower one was drawn in slightly. As he stared her mouth parted fractionally and the tip of her tongue peeped out. His eyes went immediately to hers to gauge her intention in the gesture. She only seemed to become aware of it when his gaze bore into hers. She straightened and dropped the strand of hair she'd been playing with. Her expression was guarded.

Walker shook his head. "You're not just *in* trouble, Mary Schyler," he said softly. "You *are* trouble."

Skye wished he hadn't said it, not in quite that way. She wanted to ask him if he'd been the one to lock her in the cellar, if he'd intended to teach her a lesson. She couldn't, though, not without laying her cards in front of her. Jay Mac had taught her to play poker better than that. Poor hand or not, she had to do what she could with what she had. She pretended not to understand what he'd meant.

After a moment, Walker got up. He went to the narrow pine cupboard by the sink and took out a quarter-filled bottle of Scotch. He found a tumbler and poured himself two fingers of liquor. "Do you want some?" he asked Skye.

She had to stifle another yawn to answer. "No, thank you. The milk is what I needed. I'd like to go to bed now."

"In a moment." He leaned back against the sink counter and sipped his drink. "I noticed yesterday that when Parnell asked if you'd worked for someone other than the Marshalls or the Turners, you managed to beg the question."

"Did I?" she asked smoothly. "I don't recall. Why do you suppose he cared?"

"You'll have to ask him that. I just want your answer now."

"I don't see that it's any of your business, Mr. Caine."

"Did you know Parnell before coming here?"

Skye stood. "I'm not in favor of inquisitions, and I've had enough of this one. Last night I felt that I owed you an apology for my rudeness, but I think we're even now. I'm glad I saved my breath." She skirted the table. "Goodnight, Mr. Caine."

She never suspected he was going to reach for her. In one moment he was standing casually at the sink, and in the next he had her pulled flush to his body. There had been no hint with his eyes or his hands of his intention, just the lightning-quick action that had drawn her close with the sureness of a magnet.

His mouth closed over hers. The kiss was hot and hard and brief.

Skye staggered back when she was released. The sensation of his lips lingered against hers.

"*Now* I think I have something to apologize for," he said.

But he didn't bother. Skye only realized it when she was standing alone in the kitchen.

It was wings again, fluttering lightly against her cheeks. At first it tickled. When it didn't stop, she turned her head to elude it. The fluttering followed. She rubbed her cheek against the pillow when it became unbearable. The tickling sensation merely swept across her lips and touched her other cheek.

She was annoyed now and frustrated further when she couldn't raise an arm to brush it away. Silken threads drifted across her face as if she'd run headlong into a cobweb. She wanted to open her eyes to see if this was indeed the case, but there was no cooperation from either of her lids. A band of the thinnest gauze seemed to hold them in place.

There was a touch on her forehead, then her chin. Her lips felt moist heat close to them. A moan was trapped in her throat as she was robbed of breath. Her mouth was parted by something damp. She couldn't close against it.

The sensation vanished suddenly, then came again, this time at the hollow of her throat. Her heart raced. She arched, trying to force the scream out of her, but there was no sound. Cool air touched her breasts and belly. Something silky snaked across her navel and was dragged across her thigh.

Her breasts felt heavy, the tips hard and aching. She would have almost welcomed a touch there, but none came. There was a hot lick of sensation across her collarbone, then on the inside of her arm.

Her stomach roiled. A thousand spiders crawling across her skin couldn't have caused more revulsion.

Skye twisted. Tears burned her eyes. She whimpered as a weight covered her. Her body was stretched tautly and her legs wouldn't move. Skye's fingers curled into tight fists and her nails bit into her palms. Self-inflicted pain made her lucid, and she began to make the climb toward consciousness. It was then that the voice came. The words were unintelligible, but there was no mistaking the threat in them.

A sob shuddered through Skye. The weight left her body and she seemed to float upward, tensionless. Behind her closed lids darkness shattered into shards of bright white light.

She fell back on the bed even as she fell asleep.

Six

Skye woke much as she had the previous day. This time she knew who to expect at the door.

Walker took one look at her and made his decision. He noticed that she didn't protest when he picked her up. Kicking the door behind him, he carried her straight back to the bed. "Raise your arms," he said. She managed to lift them to a half-mast position. "Your gown is soaked," he told her, tugging at the hem. "You have to get out of it."

"Don't need your help." To her own ears her words sounded slurred and barely intelligible. It was no wonder Walker ignored her.

"Look at me," he said, yanking harder on the fabric. "I'm closing my eyes so I can't see a thing."

Skye stared at his face. She imagined she could see a hint of the gold flecks that highlighted his eyes. "You're peeking."

"Just a little."

She nodded. "That's all right, then."

Walker realized Skye's thinking was as fuzzy as a drunk's. He leaned closer.

Skye's head retracted. "Don't kiss me," she said quickly.

"I wasn't going to." There was no alcohol on her

breath. "Lift," he said, as he worked the nightgown to her hips.

She pushed herself up and felt the nightgown being whisked off her body. He immediately covered her with a quilt, then searched for another gown. Although it didn't take Walker long to find one, Skye's teeth were chattering by the time he returned to the bed. She didn't want to give up the quilt.

"Do what you want," Walker told her, shrugging. "I don't care if you crawl under those blankets naked." His words had the desired effect. She raised her arms and allowed him to slip the nightgown over her head. He helped her get settled under the covers, then sat on the edge of the bed. Skye was struggling to stay awake. To take her temperature, Walker lightly touched her forehead as her eyes closed.

Skye's reaction was immediate and violent. She jerked back and tried to slap at his hand. The blankets co-cooned her, trapping her arms, but she was able to slide out of his reach.

Stunned, Walker let his hand hover in the air a moment. He brought it back to his side slowly. She was staring at him now, her eyes alert and wary. Seconds before, he thought he'd glimpsed terror in their depths.

"You shouldn't touch me," she said weakly. She was out of breath, as if she'd run a great distance, and her heart was still pounding. Skye had a hard time hearing herself above the rush of blood to her ears. "You shouldn't," she repeated. There was uncertainty in her voice, but the plea was urgent.

"Why is that?" Walker asked quietly. Her phasing was odd, he thought. He might not have questioned "Don't touch me," but what she was saying was different. "Why shouldn't I touch you?"

A small vertical line appeared between Skye's brows as they drew together. She freed one of her arms from beneath the blankets and lifted her hand to her temple. She massaged it as she considered the question, puzzled that she had no good answer. "It's not right," she said finally. "I . . . I don't think I like it."

"I kissed you last night."

Skye had been thinking about that, too, wondering what made it different. And it *was* different. She was certain of that. "I didn't want you to do that, either," she said.

But she hadn't been frightened of him then, Walker thought. Or particularly outraged. She hadn't even tried to slap his face. "All right," he said, letting it drop. He rose from the bed. "I'll send Annie up with a tray. I should be able to have the doctor here in a few hours."

Skye pushed herself to a sitting position. "No," she said. "No doctor. I don't need one."

"I'm afraid you don't have a choice. You're the one in bed. I'm the one who's going to ride to Baileyboro."

"Don't," she said. Her look beseeched him. "I really don't— " Her eyes slipped away from Walker's as the door behind him opened. It was Parnell. Mrs. Reading was on his heels.

"I told you he was here," Mrs. Reading was saying as Parnell's first glance went to Walker. "It's not fitting. Rose and Daisy will have it all over the village that you hired a whore."

Skye's breath caught. She looked anxiously at her employer. Parnell's face was impassive and though he spoke to Mrs. Reading, his eyes remained on Walker.

"That was unnecessarily cruel," he said.

Mrs. Reading flushed, but she refused to back down. "Cruel to be kind. She should hear it from one of us before she hears it from one of the townsfolk. This is the second day she's entertained him and it's only her third morning here." She stared hard at Skye, daring her to deny it.

"I'm going for a doctor," Walker said tightly. Without waiting for any comment, he left the room.

Parnell watched him go, then he glanced at Mrs. Reading. "You've said quite enough. Leave us."

Her eyes darted nervously from Skye to her employer. "But—"

Jonathan Parnell simply pointed to the door.

Corina Reading turned sharply on her heel. The hem of her gown swayed at her ankles. "It's no different to those Farrow girls if it's Mr. Caine in here or you," she said.

"Shut the door behind you," Parnell told her. When she was gone, he turned to Skye. "I shall stay only a moment. Mrs. Reading may have been cruel, but her comments bear hearing. However, I do not choose to admonish one employee in the presence of another. You will not entertain Mr. Caine in your bedchamber again under any circumstances. I will have words with him later today."

It didn't appear Skye was expected to respond, and she didn't.

Parnell's face softened a fraction. "You're ill?" he asked, then didn't wait for a reply. "Yes, I can see for myself that something's not quite right."

Some last bit of vanity made Skye lift a hand to her face. She brushed aside loose strands of hair. "I don't know what's wrong," she said. "I didn't mean to disrupt your household." Skye could see that Parnell had been working in the cellar again. His sleeves were rolled up to his elbows, and there were smudges of grease and oil on his forearms. He made no comment about having his work interrupted, but it was there for Skye to see.

"I'm sorry," she said. He was quiet for so long it occurred to Skye that perhaps he meant to dismiss her after all. It hadn't seemed to be his intention when he entered the room, but she couldn't say what he was thinking now. "It won't happen again."

Parnell considered that. "No, I'm sure it won't. You're nothing like Mrs. Reading thinks."

Skye flushed. She wished he had not referred to the cook's comment. It was almost as if he'd wondered about it. She felt more uncomfortable in his presence. "I'd like to be alone now," she said.

He studied her face, his blue eyes dark, almost piercing. "Of course," he said after a moment, his own face clearing. "Someone will sit with you until the doctor arrives."

Skye thought to protest, but held back. It seemed she had no choices. Jonathan Parnell would do as he wanted, just as Walker had. "Thank you," she said instead.

He nodded briefly, then left her.

Annie arrived while Skye was in the last stages of dressing. "What's this?" she asked. "Mr. Parnell told me you were ill and Mr. Caine's gone to fetch a doctor."

"No one's asked me what I want," Skye said. "Here, help me fasten this dress." It buttoned down the back and was almost impossible to secure without the help of a maid. It was not at all practical for a housekeeper, but Skye brought it with her because it was one of her plainest gowns. The purple color was so deep it was almost black, and except for the white cuffs, the dress had no ornamentation. Skye fixed a brooch to the throat of the gown when Annie had finished with the buttons.

Sitting at her vanity, Skye brushed her hair with hard, brisk strokes, then twisted it into a knot. She secured the tail of hair with a tortoiseshell comb and gave her reflection a brief glance. "You can see for yourself that I'm not ill," she said to Annie.

Annie clucked softly with her tongue. "And I know wishful thinking when I hear it. Those aren't roses in your cheeks. It took some hard pinching to put that color there."

Skye's flush was real enough and it pointed to the truth of Annie's words. "Well," she said, "if I wasn't feeling quite the thing earlier, I'm much better now. I don't need people fussing over me."

"Like Mr. Parnell?" Annie asked, raising both brows. A smile edged her mouth. "I can't say as I'd object to that. Or Mr. Caine, for that matter. Could be they're sweet on you."

"Annie," Skye said quellingly. "Please don't say things like that. Someone might take it seriously."

"But I was serious." She caught Skye's severe glance. "Oh, all right. I won't even *think* it, if that's what you want."

Nodding, Skye rose from the vanity.

Annie blocked her path when Skye headed for the door. "Oh, no. You're not leaving this room. It's one thing to get dressed, quite another to leave. I'll not have Mr. Parnell take issue with something I've done."

Skye acquiesced, though not gracefully. "Very well, but don't hover so. I can't bear it."

Annie didn't take the least offense. She pointed Skye in the direction of one of the chairs, stoked the fire, and set about making the bed and straightening the room. It wasn't until she'd finished that she noticed Skye had fallen asleep. "That's just as it should be," she said softly.

Walker hunkered down beside the armchair and touched Skye lightly on the wrist. She didn't stir. He glanced up at the doctor.

"Move her to the bed," Dr. Emmet said. "She's going to have a mighty crick in her neck, sleeping that way."

Gently, cautiously, Walker slipped his arms under

Skye, one beneath her knees and the other at her back. Her head lolled against his shoulder as he carried her to the bed. She murmured something he couldn't make out as he laid her down. There was the faintest smile on her face.

Walker backed away from the bed, but he didn't leave.

Dr. Emmet put his black leather case on the side table and opened it. Without looking up he said, "You have to leave now. I'm not conducting my examination with you here." When Walker hesitated, the doctor glanced up, scowling. He pointed to Annie, who was standing at the foot of the bed. "She can stay. It doesn't appear a stick of dynamite would move her anyway."

"It'll be all right, Mr. Caine," Annie told him. "You just wait in the hall."

Clearly indicating he didn't like it, Walker left and cooled his heels in the corridor. From the muffled sounds inside the room he realized that Skye had awakened. He could imagine her objections without having to hear them. The doctor would have his hands full.

The examination lasted just over twenty minutes. When the doctor entered the hall, Walker pushed away from the door where he'd been leaning. "Well?" he asked.

"Well, nothing," Dr. Emmet said. His brows were thick and wiry and they overhung the low edge of his forehead like snow on a mountain crag. They pulled together in single line as he hefted his case under one arm. "It's not for me to talk to you," he said. "I'll speak with Mr. Parnell. Mrs. Reading was specific about that."

Walker wondered if it might have been different if Corina hadn't met them at the door and announced their employer's very definite wishes regarding Skye Dennehy. "I'll get him for you. You can wait downstairs in the parlor."

Parnell was slow in answering the door to his workroom. Walker had to knock twice and call his name.

"The doctor's finished with Miss Dennehy," he said, when Parnell poked his head out. Parnell's complexion was slightly flushed and his eyes were furtive, as if he'd been caught at something he didn't want to explain. Walker noted these things but didn't comment.

"All right," Parnell said curtly. "I'll be there in a moment." He shut the door in Walker's face.

Walker Caine stared at the closed door, in the exact spot where Jonathan Parnell's face had briefly appeared. Walker's features remained impassive while he entertained certain violent images. The difficulty wasn't in dismissing the scenes that played in his mind's eye, but in not revealing his pleasure in them.

Parnell appeared again within the minute, this time looking calm and in control of himself. Walker followed him to the parlor and waited in the doorway to see if he would be invited to hear what the doctor had to say. He wasn't surprised when he was summarily dismissed. He stepped out and closed the doors just as his employer offered the doctor a drink.

Walker glanced at the main staircase and considered his options. Parnell might never share anything with him regarding Skye's condition. It was doubtful Skye would have much to say. But Annie? Walker smiled to himself. Annie might be very forthcoming.

Walker caught her in the hall just outside of Skye's room. "What are you doing?" she asked suspiciously. "You can't go in there."

"Wouldn't dream of it." His voice clearly suggested he was thinking otherwise.

"Go on with you," Annie said. "I know when my leg's bein' pulled." She thrust the tray she was carrying into his arms. "Let's move on. It wouldn't do to have her know she's being talked about."

"Then you'll tell me what the doctor said."

Annie's expression was pained. "I didn't say that.

Doctor Emmet wouldn't like it, and neither would Miss Dennehy."

Walker touched Annie's elbow and got her to slow her steps, then halt completely. "It's important I know, Annie."

"Please, Mr. Caine, don't make me say."

He hesitated, wanting to press the issue, then decided against it. Annie owed her position in the house to Skye. It wasn't fair to ask her to betray a confidence. "All right," he said. He nudged her with his hand, urging her forward. He didn't follow even when she turned to look at him. "Go on," he told her. "Take the tray to the kitchen."

Walker didn't move until Annie disappeared around a turn in the hallway. He let himself into Skye's room without announcing himself. She was standing at the French doors, staring out. She didn't turn. He wasn't certain that she even knew he was in the room. He used the moment to study her without fear of reprisal.

She had a small elegant frame with a narrow waist and long legs. It had been no effort to lift her or hold her against him. She had strength in her, but it was no match for his. As he watched, she folded her arms in front of her and leaned forward, resting her forehead against the cool glass. He could imagine her shutting her eyes. He wondered what she was thinking.

"What do you want?" she asked tiredly. A small shudder went through her shoulders and down her back. From beneath the cuff of her sleeve she pulled out a handkerchief and touched it to each eye before she turned on him. The scrap of linen was clutched in her left fist. "Never mind, I know you want to see me dismissed. That's the real reason you're here, isn't it?" When he only looked at her blankly, she went on. "Mr. Parnell will let me go if you're caught in here."

"Did he say that?"

"No, but he was very clear that he didn't expect me to *entertain* you again." She sighed, impatient with herself for explaining. "Please leave."

Instead, Walker's fingers twisted the key in the door behind him, locking them in the room. "No one will know I'm here," he said lowly. "I promise." His approach to Skye was almost soundless. She held her ground until he was a few feet away, then she leaned back against the French doors. He stopped. "What did Doctor Emmet say?"

The cornered, nervous look did not leave her eyes. "It's none of your— " He would never leave if she didn't tell him. It was there in his implacable expression, in the set of his shoulders. "He said I showed signs of exhaustion."

"That's all?"

She nodded. "I told you I hadn't been sleeping well."

"You told me you *thought* you hadn't. It's not the same thing at all."

Skye shrugged. Her fingers opened and closed around the handkerchief.

"You're not pregnant?"

"No." Her tone was bitter and angry. "I'm not pregnant. Is that the first conclusion everyone reaches? Or did you put that idea in that doctor's tiny brain? Is that why he insisted on— " She didn't finish. She couldn't finish. The memory alone was humiliating. Discussing it with anyone was painful.

"He examined you?" Walker asked bluntly.

Tears welled. She forgot about the handkerchief and knuckled them away with her right hand. "You shouldn't have brought him," she said, swallowing a sob. The tears could not be restrained. They slipped over her cheeks. Her voice was plaintive. "Do you think I wanted his hands on me?"

Walker hadn't considered that. "I thought I was the only one who couldn't touch you."

Hugging herself, Skye shook her head. She was frightened by what was happening to her and more afraid to admit it to anyone. "Please go, Mr. Caine. I don't want you here. I only need to rest today." She pointed to the bedside table. "The doctor left me something."

Walker glanced at the small brown bottle next to the lamp. "Laudanum?" he asked.

"Yes."

"Be careful with it."

"I know the dangers." The opiates in laudanum were addictive. "My sister told me all about it." Maggie had studied a great deal in preparing for her entrance exam to medical school, and Skye was forced to hear most of what she'd learned at one time or another. "She's going to be— " Skye stopped as she became aware of what she had almost blurted out. She was more tired than she realized. In another moment she would have been talking freely of Maggie's plans to become a doctor. "She's going to be addicted herself someday if she's not careful." *Forgive me, Maggie.*

Walker frowned, but he set the bottle down. "I didn't know you had a sister."

"I don't think I've ever discussed my personal life with you." Skye's full mouth thinned a little. "And I don't think I care to." She was on the verge of pleading with him to leave again when a knock at her door forced the issue. Her panicked eyes flew to his face.

He put a finger to his own lips. He'd been prepared for this possibility when he turned the key in her door. He pointed to the French doors and motioned her to step aside. As soon as she did he opened them and went out onto the balcony. Frigid air slipped into the room before he shut it out.

The knock came at the door again and Skye started backing toward it, unable to take her eyes off Walker on the balcony. He was perfectly visible. Where did he think he could possibly go? She held her breath as he climbed on the balcony rail. Skye knew from her own estimates that it was at least ten feet to Parnell's balcony. With no running start, how did he expect to—

Her chest ached from holding her breath. He leaped. Skye forgot about the door. The only insistent pounding she heard was her own heart. She ran to the French doors and looked out. Walker was hoisting himself over Parnell's stone rail.

"One moment," she said, composing herself. She wiped damp palms on her gown and retucked the handkerchief in her cuff. Skye opened the door to Parnell himself.

"I didn't expect your door to be locked," he said, his eyes quickly going over her.

"Doctor Emmet said I should rest. I thought it would be better if I were undisturbed."

He had the grace to flush. "I apologize. I had only your welfare in mind. The doctor just left. Hank's taking him to town because we couldn't locate Walker." When he spoke, his glance strayed past Skye's shoulder as he tried to scan the room.

Pretending not to notice his intent, Skye casually opened the door wider. Parnell didn't ask to come in, nor did she invite him. She let silence speak for her innocence.

Parnell's attention returned to Skye. "Mrs. Reading will address the rest of staff regarding your illness."

"I'm *not ill.*"

"No, of course not," he said quickly. "I meant to say that she'll simply tell them you need some rest."

"I don't think that speaks very well for me, Mr. Parnell. Are you certain you wouldn't rather give me my notice now?" The question was a challenge, and Parnell seemed a bit taken back by it.

"Give you your notice, Miss Dennehy? Just because you need a day's rest? I don't know what you were used to elsewhere, but that's not how I do things here. I expect you'll be fine tomorrow."

Skye was niggled again by doubts. Were Jonathan Parnell and Jay Mac partners in some scheme, or was Parnell's interest in her genuine? Both things could explain why he was adamant that Walker stay out of her room. Which was true? Perhaps both. Perhaps neither.

She rubbed at the back of her neck, at the sudden building of tension she felt there. "Was there something else, Mr. Parnell?"

He hesitated. "Would it be presumptuous for me to ask you to call me Jon? When we're alone, that is."

"Yes," she said. "It would be presumptuous." Very quietly, but with clear intent, Skye closed the door in his face.

Skye knew it would happen. She slept on and off throughout the morning and afternoon and by evening she was restless. She was also more than a little scared. Restless and scared. One or the other could have put her off sleep until after midnight. Together, Skye thought she would still be awake when the sun came up.

Every lamp in Skye's room was burning. Hank had carried extra wood to her room earlier and now Skye had a fire blazing with no fear that it would die anytime soon. Her half-eaten dinner was on a tray by the door. Annie refused to take it away when she saw Skye hadn't finished it. The dishes were covered, but Skye imagined she could smell them anyway. The odor of baked trout made her queasy. The pot of tea was cold and bitterly strong now. It wouldn't settle on her stomach any better than the first cup she'd poured.

The clock on the mantel ticked off the time with agonizing slowness. Skye watched it more than she cared to. Sometimes she looked out the French doors, even going so far as to stand on the balcony once. It was just after ten o'clock when she pushed her tray into the hall. At eleven she sat at her writing desk to compose a letter. At midnight she tore up the letter and tried her hand at poetry. When she couldn't think of a word to rhyme with "bloodcurdling," she gave it up.

She felt all of five again, excitement and dread mingling in her mind. She could have been in the attic of her summer home, sitting at the windowseat, watching for the ghost. The same sense of anticipation captured her imagination. Fire shadows leaped eerily.

"Ridiculous," she said softly. She lay back on the bed and stared at the ceiling. Skye listened to the clock and counted. It should have made her drowsy. At one o'clock she was still wide awake.

The house was silent when Skye tiptoed down the main staircase. She carried a lamp. Her shadow jumped when she took the last two steps as one. Her first destination this evening wasn't the kitchen, but the library. The room felt unbearably cold when she strayed off the rug onto the hardwood floor. She set down the lamp and tied her robe more tightly. She brushed a bit of dirt from her sleeve, a remnant of the previous night's excursion.

The book took her a while to find. Having researched subjects as diverse as medieval castles and the chemistry of dynamite, Skye knew libraries well enough to know there was little rhyme or reason to the way this one was organized. The history of the Granville family was situated between Darwin's *The Descent of Man* and Mill's *Principles of Political Economy*.

She made a little face as she examined the other titles. "Something my sisters would read," she said softly. "Something they probably *have* read." When Skye wasn't reading to prepare for adventures, her own tastes went to Poe and Hawthorne. She removed the Granville history carefully and slipped it under her arm.

It had never been Skye's plan to return immediately

to her room. The book gave her an excuse to be downstairs. She hardly dared breathe as she padded down the hallway to the kitchen. She stopped several times to make certain no one else in the house was stirring.

The door to the cellar was locked. She twisted it twice, just to be sure. Frustrated, she made the decision to go through the outside entrance. Leaving the book behind but taking the lamp with her, Skye left the back porch. She propped the door open with a jar of beets from the pantry and circled the rear of the house.

The moon and stars were not her companions this evening and she was glad to have the lamp. The wind was bitterly cold. Skye was shaking before she reached the slanted double-door entrance. She bent down and gave one of the door handles a yank, fully expecting it to open for her.

The door didn't budge.

Confused, she tried the other. It didn't move, either. The doors were locked again from the inside. Skye was too cold to stand outside and wonder how it had come to pass, who had found them open and thrown the bolt, or why no one had been confronted about the lapse. At least one person in the house knew she had been in the cellar the night before.

Skye retraced her steps quickly, pushed aside the beet jar, and closed the back door behind her. Giving her feet a little stamp to warm them, Skye locked the door and went back to the kitchen.

Walker Caine was sitting at the table, casually thumbing through the history of the Granvilles. He didn't look up as she stood rooted in the open doorway. "This should make for interesting reading," he said, turning another page.

"That's why I got it," she said weakly.

He glanced up. "I take it you couldn't sleep again."

"That's right."

Walker nodded thoughtfully, his attention still on the book. "And while you were down here you heard something outside."

"Hmm-mmm."

"So you went to investigate."

"Yes."

"You're intrepid, Skye. I'll give you that."

In another place, at another time, Skye would have been thrilled by that evaluation of her character. She was wary, though, of Walker's estimation. Her reply was feeble. "I try."

A faint smile touched his lips. He closed the book in front of him and gave Skye a considering look. "But you're not a very good liar," he said. Walker held up his hand to halt the interruption and protest she was prepared to make. "Come outside with me. I want to show you something."

"I don't think—"

He leveled her with a hard gaze this time. Pleasantness vanished from his voice. "It wasn't an invitation, Skye. It was a command."

Dread clenched her insides. The feeling was so powerful, so real, that Skye drew her arms across her middle. Her eyes followed him warily as he came around the table. He extended his palm and indicated she should precede him.

"Here," he said just as they were about to step outside. "Put this on." He slipped out of the jacket he was wearing over his nightshirt and trousers and handed it to Skye.

"What about you?" she asked. The cotton nightshirt wasn't proof against the cold. "You need something."

Walker gave her an odd look, then pressed the jacket into her hands. "Put this on," he said again.

"I know," she said, sighing. "Not an invitation. A command." As soon as she was in the jacket, she felt his hands at the small of her back pushing her out the door. She stumbled on the last step. "You should have brought the lamp."

"That's what got you into trouble in the first place."

Skye glanced over her shoulder. "What do you mean?"

"This way." Walker pointed to his left. When Skye didn't move quickly enough to suit him, he said, "Give me your hand."

She hesitated a moment, then held it out.

Walker took it, enfolding it in his own. "Are you all right?" He felt the tremor that had gone through her and knew it had nothing to do with the cold. "If you're nodding, I can't see it very well."

"I'm fine," she said. It surprised her that she meant it. The hand covering hers was comforting. Skye didn't understand how that was possible.

"Good. Let's go." Walker pulled Skye along the perimeter of the house until they came to the cellar doors. He dropped her hand. "Notice anything?" he asked her.

Skye looked around. She had no clear idea what he intended her to see, and she was wary of falling into a trap laid by him. "You're not making any sense. I see the entrance. I suppose it leads to the cellar."

"I think you know it does. What else?"

She turned. The dried, frozen limbs of rose bushes bordered the house. She imagined their fragrance in the spring and summer was carried in through open windows. It was the windows themselves that caught her attention next. Skye pointed to the closest one. It was a wide, double-arched window and only the large abandoned ballroom had ones like that. She shook her head, not comprehending the purpose of this trip.

"Higher," Walker said.

Skye tilted her head upward. A small balcony jutted out on the second floor, surrounding a pair of French doors. She frowned as she tried to place the rooms and their occupants. Her face cleared suddenly as the answer was borne home. "That's your room," she said.

"That's right."

"I suppose you can see quite a bit from your balcony."

He nodded. "Quite a bit. In the autumn the trees all along this ridge burn with color. Now that it's winter, I can actually see the river in different places."

Skye didn't appreciate Walker's tormenting. "You know what I meant," she said.

"Why don't you say it?"

She couldn't. It would mean showing her hand. Skye shook her head. Walker was the one who would have to say it. She had to be certain he wasn't bluffing.

"Very well," he said. "You carried that lamp out here and tried to open these doors. I watched you. The doors were locked and you gave up immediately. You'd have been better off not to have carried the lamp. It was the light that drew me to my window in the first place."

"And your point is?" she asked.

Her question gave Walker a start. "My point is that I saw you trying to get into the cellar."

Skye shook her head, remembered he couldn't see her gesture, and said flatly, "No."

"No?"

"What you saw me doing was testing the doors to be certain they were locked. I told you I heard something outside. I went out to investigate. Intrepid, remember? With Mr. Parnell being so adamant that no one except a select few enter the cellar, I thought I'd better check."

"That's your story?"

"That's the truth."

Walker's shoulders were stiff with cold. "There's nothing more that needs to be said out here. Let's go back inside." He didn't offer Skye his assistance, thrusting his hands in his own pockets this time. When they were back in the kitchen, Walker fired up the stove and set water on to boil.

Skye began to remove his jacket. He stopped her. She was very nearly lost in the thing, but her teeth were still chattering. She gave him a grateful look.

Walker leaned against the stove, his arms crossed in front of him. The single dimple that sometimes marked his smile was nowhere in evidence. His features were drawn and the slightly crooked line of his nose was more pronounced. His eyes were narrowed but remote, his gaze going past Skye to some distant point, some distant thought.

"The water's boiling," Skye said for the second time.

"What? Oh." He jerked away from the stove and filled two cups from the kettle. He let the tea steep, removed the strainers, and handed one mug to Skye. "Sugar?" When she nodded, Walker found a spoon and put it on the table next to the sugar bowl. He didn't take a chair, preferring the stove's residual heat. "Do you play much poker, Skye?"

To keep from spewing tea, Skye swallowed hard. She felt the liquid burning all the way to the hollow of her stomach. "It's not a woman's game," she said, just managing not to choke on the words.

"That's a response to a question I didn't ask."

"I've played a little," she admitted. Jay Mac had taught all his daughters to play. Michael was very good at it, Mary Francis even a shade better. Rennie couldn't bluff at all, her face too expressive. Maggie didn't particularly enjoy playing, but she hated to disappoint Jay Mac by sitting out. As for Skye, her abilities were somewhere between Michael's and Rennie's. What she had going for her was luck. It seemed when it was shining on her she could do no wrong. The whole family marveled at it.

Right now Skye felt as if she was at the end of her run.

"I thought perhaps you had," said Walker. He exhaled

slowly, not quite a sigh, more a signal that his patience was at an end. "Look, there's no particular reason you should trust me—at least, I can't think of one—all the same, you'd do better to throw in with me than oppose me."

Skye's puzzlement wasn't entirely feigned. "Throw in with you how?" she asked.

"Your snooping is going to get you hurt. You'd be better off just asking me whatever it is you want to know."

But of course, she couldn't. She sipped her tea.

Walker let the silence sit for a while before he said, "Parnell's life has been threatened."

"You don't think—"

"You?" He shrugged. "I don't really know, do I?"

"But when? You mean, just today he was threatened?"

"No. It started months ago. A few weeks before I was hired. In fact, it's the entire reason for me being here. I was hired to protect him."

Skye frowned. This was an unexpected piece of information. She had supposed that Walker's presence was meant to protect the invention, not the inventor himself. Where was the truth in what her father told her? Did she dare accept everything he said at face value? In that case Jay Mac hadn't known it all. He would never have sent her into any kind of danger. "I'm not certain what you think this has to do with me," she said.

"I thought that much was obvious. If your aim is to hurt him in some way, I won't let you do it."

"Hurt him?" She was dumbfounded. "Hurt Mr. Parnell? You have some very strange ideas. Have you had this conversation with anyone else? Mrs. Reading, for instance? Or the twins?"

"I watch everyone," he said. "But you seem to draw my attention more often."

"I don't suppose you meant to be flattering."

His mouth flattened as he shook his head. Gold shards of light flickered in his eyes.

"I see," she said slowly, setting down her mug.

"I don't think you do." He finished his tea and pushed away from the stove. When he came to the table he didn't pull out a chair, but intentionally towered over Skye. "I've decided you bear watching more closely."

"You're practically living in my pockets now!" Skye's raised voice only hinted at her alarm. She started to rise, but Walker extended his hand and let it hover near her shoulder. She sat back slowly.

"I can't seem to trust you not to wander around the house at night, and I'm not losing more sleep over it."

Skye didn't think she liked where Walker was heading. The only conclusion she could draw was—

"You can share my room, or I can share yours," he said.

She hadn't mistaken his line of thinking. There was small comfort in that. "You're quite insane," she said calmly.

"And quite serious."

"Mr. Parnell won't stand for it. He didn't want you in my room for a moment. He won't allow you to spend the night there."

Walker shrugged. "You can take it up with him in the morning."

Skye was of a mind to take it up with her employer now. Her intention showed clearly on her face.

"All right," said Walker. He stepped back and let her stand. "You go and wake Parnell."

Skye hesitated. He made it sound as if waking Parnell was not a particularly wise decision. She was certain Walker was very deliberate in giving her that impression. She was also fairly sure he was right. "I'll speak to him in the morning."

"As you wish."

"I'm not going to stay in your room," she said.

"Then I'll stay in yours. I told you it was your choice."

"Between Scylla and Charybdis," she uttered, under her breath. Realizing what she'd said, Skye glanced at Walker quickly. It wasn't likely that a housekeeper would reference Homer's *Odyssey*. She wished she'd said something about the devil and the deep blue sea instead. It was a relief that Walker hadn't heard or at least hadn't commented.

He pointed to the servants' stairs. "We'll take those to my room. I need to get some blankets." Walker put the book in Skye's hands and picked up her lamp. "I'll go first."

Skye followed Walker to his room and waited just outside as he collected blankets and a pillow. She half hoped that Mrs. Reading would come out of her own room and surprise them. Skye doubted the cook would have been as reticent to wake Parnell.

In truth, Skye was bothered more than a little by her own reluctance to do so. Walker had called her intrepid, but she was feeling decidedly cowardly. He had just given her a perfect opportunity to get away from him. She could lock herself in her room and be done with his interference— at least for the night. Yet she didn't move.

Skye didn't think her action, or lack of it, could bear much scrutiny. She consciously put it out of her mind. When Walker was finished collecting his things, she followed him to her own room without a word.

He locked the door as soon as they were inside, leaving the key in the hole. "No one has to know I was here," he said. "That will be your decision."

"I can't think of a reason that I'll want to keep this to myself," she said stiffly.

"Just the same," he said indifferently. "Your choice."

Skye placed her book on the nightstand beside the unopened bottle of laudanum. In her absence the fire had been reduced to embers. She stoked the logs and added more wood. Walker had already moved aside a chair and was snapping out one of his blankets on top of the braided rug. It could not possibly be very comfortable for him, but Skye didn't offer to share her bed. She turned back all the lamps except the one at her bedside and removed Walker's jacket.

Holding it out to him she said, "You might need it. It could get cold there."

He placed it on the nearby chair. "Are you going to read?" he asked.

"Will it bother you?" As soon as the words were out Skye flushed, painfully aware it was the sort of question her mother might have posed to her father. It was the kind of question that had a comfortable relationship behind it, something one asked when concern for another was the motive. "No," she said quickly, before he could answer. "I'm going to try to sleep." In an odd way, she thought she'd be able to now. This also did not bear scrutiny.

Skye lifted the glass globe covering the lamp and gently blew on the flame. Except for firelight her bedchamber was dark. She replaced the globe and turned her back on Walker. Skye removed her robe.

"Pleasant dreams," he said.

She couldn't remember having a dream since she'd arrived at the mansion. Skye thought about that as she climbed into bed and pulled the comforter up to her neck. Walker was already lying on the floor in front of the fire. His long frame was silhouetted by the light.

"How did you break your nose?" she asked. She watched the dark outline of his body change shape and knew he was touching the slightly bent bridge, feeling the shape of it. "Were you in a fight?"

"I was in lots of fights," he said. "But I broke my nose falling down a flight of steps."

"Oh."

Although he knew she couldn't see, he smiled. This time his signature single dimple appeared at one corner. "Disappointed?"

"No, of course not." But she was a little disappointed. She had imagined something quite different. A saloon brawl in Dodge City, or a gang fight in the Bowery . . . even an attack in Central Park. Skye drew her knees closer to her chest. It had been a long time since she'd thought of the stranger in the park. She sighed.

"Would you think more of me if I told you I'd been pushed?"

"Hardly," she said primly. Then, more softly, "Were you?"

He chuckled. "No, but I was prepared to make up a story."

Skye thought about that. "You'd like me to think more of you?" she asked.

"Something like that."

There wasn't a good reason to be so attracted to him. Jonathan Parnell had more strikingly handsome features and was more refined, less irritating, probably smarter, definitely wealthier, and . . . possibly the person her father had handpicked for her. The last reason worked strongly in Walker's favor, but Skye was sensible enough to know it did not count as a good reason. Yet the attraction to Walker was there, sensible or not.

Turning more fully on her side, Skye slipped one arm under her pillow and closed her eyes. She had other questions she wanted to ask him. She fell asleep with one of them forming on her lips.

It was the fluttering touch against her cheek that she felt first. Skye wrinkled her nose and turned her head. There was no avoiding the touch. It covered her face, her neck. It was lightly drawn across her breasts. She sucked in her breath as the sensation swept lower across her belly and her thighs. She tried to lift an arm, then her knee. She could only twist from side to side with the movement of her head.

Her lashes lifted a fraction, then closed again as she struggled toward complete consciousness. There was a voice. Words she couldn't quite make out drifted toward her. She strained to hear and her ears failed her just as her arms and legs had.

The voice receded and with it the weights that kept her in place. She raised one arm, then the other. They both dropped limply back to the mattress, her strength depleted by the small movement. Her knee was raised a few inches. Exhaustion shivered through her.

The shutter of darkness lifted suddenly and with its passing Skye woke completely, her eyes opening wide. There was a pressure in her chest, an ache she was desperate to release. She pushed herself to sit up. Her fingers clutched the sheet. Skye opened her mouth.

The thing that was a terrible pressure in her chest, the ache that needed to be released, was Skye's anguished scream.

Walker's drift to consciousness was even slower than Skye's. He couldn't quite contain the groan as he sat up, and pressing both hands to his ears didn't relieve the pounding in his head or the sharp pain in his ears.

It was when he became aware that the things inside his head were also happening outside it that he opened his eyes.

The pounding was coming from the door. The source of the piercing ache in his ears was Skye.

Walker scrambled to his feet, his normally graceful balance challenged by the darkness and the burning sensation at the back of his head. He stumbled once, righted himself by grabbing the back of a chair, and went straight to Skye.

She was sitting on the edge of the bed, her entire body rigid. The wide straps of her nightgown had fallen off her shoulders and the fabric was bunched below her breasts. The hem of the garment rested against her upper thighs. She was virtually naked and insensible to it.

"What's going on in there?" The cry, mingled with the pounding, came from the other side of the door. It was Parnell. It was joined a moment later by Annie Staplehurst's entreaty.

Walker ignored both. He spoke softly to Skye, whispering her name and nothing more. Her scream dissolved into a sob and he absorbed her shudder by taking her into his arms.

"It's all right," he said quietly. "You're all right. It was a dream." He said it because he hoped it was true. More difficult to explain was the ache at the back of his head. Walker released her slowly, afraid his touch would have a reaction opposite to the one he wanted. She was still shaking, her smile bereft of any warmth. "Let me help you," he said.

Skye looked down at herself. Her nakedness frightened her. She didn't remember . . . she glanced sideways at Walker. Outside the room Parnell continued to slam his fist against the door. Skye heard Annie, then Corina Reading. Her screams had awakened everyone. And here was Walker, solicitous and gentle, sitting next to her, telling her it was a dream.

"Did you?" she asked.

"Did I?" He wasn't certain what she was asking.

Skye hooked her index finger around one of her nightgown straps and raised it to her shoulder. With the other hand she pushed at the hem of the cotton gown and covered her thighs. Clothing gave her the courage to pose the question.

"Did you rape me?"

Seven

"Jesus," was what Walker said.

Skye watched him get up slowly and go to the door. He fumbled with the key and opened it. Annie Staple-hurst practically fell into the room. Jonathan Parnell was right behind her. He held a lamp in his left hand and raised it as he entered. His eyes scanned the scene in front of him, missing none of the detail. Skye could only stare at him, knowing what he saw was damning. He would want an explanation, she thought. How could she explain when she didn't understand it herself?

Walker pulled on his trousers and tucked in the tails of his nightshirt. His action was unapologetic, neither hasty nor clumsy. He picked up Skye's robe and carried it to her. "Here, put this on."

The hand she held out trembled. Walker had to press the robe into her grip. He gave her a moment, then helped her into it, lifting her hair out of the way and straightening the collar of the robe.

"Get away from her, Walker," Parnell said. He raised his right hand slowly and drew all eyes to the gun he held. He carefully set the lamp aside, never taking his gaze from Walker. "Take your goddamn hands off her." The weapon was as steady as his voice. "I mean it. Now."

Walker's fingers slipped away from Skye's collar and he raised his hands slowly. His face was expressionless.

He didn't watch the gun in Parnell's hand. He watched Parnell.

Skye could hardly speak for the hard knot in her throat. She forced words out, harsh and raspy, and prayed they made sense. "No . . . please don't . . . it's not— "

Parnell wasn't listening. His hand tightened on the weapon and he jerked it once to indicate where Walker should move. "What did you do to her?" he demanded.

Walker didn't answer. He simply continued to stare at Parnell.

"Say something, damn you."

"You already think you know what I did," he said. "I'd be a fool to talk with a gun pointed at my chest."

Parnell's brows lifted in a slight arch. His look was frank. "You'd be a fool not to."

Skye's legs were shaking as she came to her feet. She held the corner bedpost for support. "For God's sake, put the gun— "

What happened next took only seconds, but in Skye's mind the players moved slowly, as if the air had taken on the density of water. She saw Parnell glance in her direction. Behind him, Annie's head swiveled toward Walker and Mrs. Reading's mouth opened to shout a warning. Walker pivoted on his left foot and faced the mantel. In part of the same motion his right leg struck out, and using the bottom edge of his foot, he delivered a snapping kick to Parnell's hand. Advancing closer in an identically fluid movement, Walker landed a slashing blow with his cupped hand on Parnell's wrist. The weapon spun free of Parnell's numb fingers and thumped loudly against the wall. It skittered across the floor and slammed against the wall without discharging.

Parnell staggered back, clutching his injured wrist. Annie was thrown off balance when Parnell fell into her and Mrs. Reading had to move into the hallway to avoid being crushed against the door jamb.

Walker's long, light stride covered the floor quickly. He calmly picked up the gun and flipped open the barrel. Taking out the bullets, he dropped them into a pocket, then examined the weapon more closely. "This is a short-barrel Colt .45," he said. His tone was emotionless, without inflection. He was not winded or flushed. His posture was casual, relaxed, with no visible sign that anything untoward had just occurred.

Skye watched Walker's long fingers rub the cool blue-gray Colt like Aladdin must have rubbed his lamp. Shock and fascination stirred her. His words were coming to her as if from a great distance. She was remembering another place and time when she had seen a man strike out with equally graceful menace.

Walker's eyes lifted from the Colt to Parnell. There was a question in them. "Men who make their living with guns use this weapon," he said. The four and three-quarter inch barrel was preferred by gunfighters for its ease in handling. It had a maple handle and a cutaway trigger guard that could save a shooter a split second in reaching the trigger. "Not what I'd expect you to have."

Parnell set Annie from him and shook out his injured hand. He didn't respond to Walker's comment and looked at Skye instead. "Are you all right? We all heard you scream."

More than a little numb by what she had witnessed, Skye nodded. "I'm fine."

"Then what the hell was it all about?" he demanded impatiently. His brow was furrowed and he raked his thick hair back with his fingers. He looked at Skye, then at Walker.

It was Walker who spoke. "Let's discuss it privately," he said, his eyes darting to Annie, then to Mrs. Reading.

Parnell nodded. "Very well." He started to indicate that the women should leave when Walker interrupted.

"Downstairs," he said. "We'll talk in the parlor."

Jonathan Parnell's mouth thinned and he let his annoyance clearly show. He had no appreciation for taking orders from his own employee. He was silent about it because Walker's employee status was certainly going to change. His features softened only when he looked at Skye. "Miss Dennehy, do you have anything you wish to say before I listen to Mr. Caine's explanation?"

Walker interrupted again. "She'll join us."

Parnell's jaw clenched and a muscle ticked along his jaw line. "Is that your wish?" he asked Skye after a moment.

She nodded again. "I'd like to change, please."

"Of course. We'll leave you alone." When Walker didn't move, Parnell emphasized what he meant. "*All* of us will leave you alone." He waited by the door until Walker finally moved, then held out his hand for his weapon. Walker dropped it into his open palm. To Skye, Parnell said, "Will fifteen minutes be adequate?"

An eternity would not be adequate. "Yes" was what she said.

"Don't ever countermand me in front of others," Parnell said. The deep-indigo centers of his eyes were hard. The planes and angles of his face were taut with the strength of his anger. His mouth was thin. Tiny white lines were etched at the corners. He was at the sideboard in the parlor pouring a drink, but his attention was all for Walker. He replaced the glass stopper in the decanter. "You overstepped yourself tonight."

Walker Caine didn't expect to be offered a drink and he wasn't going to ask for one. Right now he needed his wits. He stood by the fireplace, facing Parnell across the room. "You pointed a loaded gun at me," he said calmly. "I take exception to that." He didn't look away from Parnell's leveling stare. "There should never be a next time."

Walker's unnamed threat hung in the air. Parnell slowly lifted his glass to his lips, then knocked back a large swallow. He poured another. "I should fire you," he said indifferently.

Walker was only surprised that Parnell hadn't done it yet. "Are you going to?" he asked. There was a certain detached curiosity in his tone, as if it was not his own fate he was questioning. He knew Parnell would take pleasure in getting rid of him. His presence was tolerated, not trusted.

"I haven't decided yet," Parnell said. He moved away from the sideboard and sat in his usual armchair. His eyes scanned the room, taking in the changes precipitated by Skye Dennehy, before settling on Walker again. "I can't fault the work *she's* done here," he said.

Most of the shawls and antimacassars that had covered the furniture had been removed. The ones remaining were brightly colored or gleaming white from a recent washing. The surface of every side table in the parlor had been polished. The ashtrays were empty and the only pile of paper in the room was a small stack of sheet music on the piano. Figurines had been rearranged on the mantel and now had the interesting look of *objets d'art* instead of knickknacks. Even the deep crevices of the ornate portrait frames had been cleaned, giving a whole generation of Granvilles a more flattering appearance. Parnell was impressed by what she had been able to accomplish in a matter of days. Under her direction there was no telling what the staff might be able to do with the house.

"Why don't you tell me what's going on?" Parnell asked. "Did she welcome your advances or did you force her?"

Walker had been expecting this. "There were no advances and there was no rape. Anything she says to the contrary is a lie."

One of Parnell's brows arched. "And will she say something to the contrary?"

"It's always possible," he said. Walker's hand rose to the back of his head and his fingers gently touched the outline of the rising lump. "But I didn't do anything to earn this from her."

Frowning, Parnell motioned Walker closer with the crook of his finger. He felt the knot when Walker bent over and whistled softly. "That's quite a goose egg."

"You should be on *this* end of it," Walker said. He returned to the fireplace and hunkered down, putting another log on the meager flames. Straightening, he added, "In fact, you *should* be on this end of it."

"What are you saying? That I was the intended victim?" His light-colored brows knit and his eyes grew introspective. "But who . . ." Parnell's features cleared. "You don't think that she . . ."

"Who else?" he asked casually. Walker gave Parnell a moment to digest that, not pressing, then he made his points quietly. "The door to the room was locked. You know that yourself when you came upon it. Miss Dennehy and I were the only ones in there. If you believe I didn't clobber myself with a poker— or whatever the hell was used— then you have to believe she did." He smiled faintly, one corner of his mouth rising cynically. "Unless you believe in the Granville ghost."

"Ridiculous."

"Then . . ." Walker prompted.

"Then she's the one who gave you that knot," Parnell said. "But to what purpose?"

Walker shrugged. "To discredit me or get to you. Either would suit her. She has a key for most every room in this house, remember? A locked door doesn't pose much of an obstacle for her. If her aim had been truer she may have done it tonight." Now Walker went to the sideboard and poured himself two fingers of whiskey. He was close enough to the door that he could listen for Skye's approach. "Look, Mr. Parnell, I found her outside this evening poking around. This is the second night she's been up and about."

"Second night? Why didn't you tell—"

"Because I was handling it. That's what you're paying me to do. Did you really want to be distracted from your work?"

"No, but—"

Walker cut off his employer's objection. "When I caught her this evening I decided I couldn't let her out of my sight. I gave her a choice of her room or my own. She chose hers. I took the floor and she had her bed. After she fell asleep I went through her things. There's something you should see." Walker reached in his pocket and pulled out the shells from Parnell's Colt, along with a small notebook. He dropped the shells on the sideboard and gave Parnell the notebook. As his employer flipped through the pages, Walker explained, "You can see for yourself that it's mostly a list of things she wants to do. She's got her inventory of your possessions, notes about restoring some of the rooms, suggestions for fabrics, colors, things like that." He watched Parnell stop thumbing through the pages and concentrate on the drawing in front of him. "Yes, I thought you might find that interesting. I did."

"It looks like my room," Parnell said. "And hers."

"It is. She's noted the dimensions, the furniture arrangements, the distance between the balconies. I wouldn't be surprised if she's memorized it all so she can walk through your room with her eyes closed. You're not safe with her here, Mr. Parnell."

Shaking his head, his lips pressed together in a thin, thoughtful line, Parnell closed the book and handed it back to Walker. "She's a deceitful bitch, then." There was more disappointment in his tone than disgust. "I had hoped . . ." His voice trailed off wistfully and the focus of his eyes became distant and vague. "What do you suggest?"

"Put her out. Let Hank take her to Baileyboro right now. She didn't succeed tonight, but she'll try again."

Parnell hesitated. "I'm not sure I want— "

"What's it going to take to convince you?" asked Walker. "You saw for yourself what— "

Jonathan Parnell held up one hand. "What I saw was a very frightened young woman. I haven't heard what she has to say. Perhaps she clubbed you with a poker for very good reasons. You haven't explained why she was screaming. It was, after all, her screams that drew us to the room."

"Who can say what goes through her mind, but I imagine it was something like this: she realized too late that I wasn't out cold— perhaps I twitched or groaned— but it was enough to make her think twice about coming after me again or risking going after you. Those screams were calculated to bring you running, and you were everything she could have hoped for. Your defense was gallant, and you considered pulling the trigger on me." Parnell looked as if he was still considering it, in spite of Walker's warning. "With me out of the way, you're a clear target. Get rid of her, Mr. Parnell. Neither you nor your invention is safe." His attention was distracted as he heard movement in the hallway and the muted tones of whispering voices. He pointed to the doors, announcing Skye's approach.

Parnell nodded and his voice dropped accordingly. "You're making a good wage," he said. "Perhaps it's time you earned it."

Walker's eyes narrowed. It wasn't what he expected to hear. "What's that supposed to mean?"

Parnell finished his drink and set the tumbler on the table beside him. He got up and began to go toward the parlor pocket doors. "It means she stays for now."

"But—"

"I have a pretty good idea who she's working for," he said. "I need to know if it's true."

"Are you going to share a name with me?"

Parnell shook his head. "Not this name," he said. "Do what you have to do with Miss Dennehy, but I'm not releasing her from her position. Is that clear?"

Walker nodded. Parnell's refusal to speak a name made his implication clear. The person he suspected was very powerful.

"Good," Parnell said, satisfied. "Let's hear what our would-be murderess has to say. After all, you insisted she join us."

"Corina and Annie were there. They'd expect she'd have an opportunity to speak. I couldn't ignore that, but I wanted you to hear me out first."

"And I did. Now, let's hear Miss Dennehy. It should be interesting, don't you think?" He slid open the doors and stepped aside.

Skye's features were perfectly composed as she entered the room. Her face was pale and there was a faintly swollen edge to her eyelids, but those were the only indications that she was under any stress. She had changed into her deep purple day dress and fastened her hair at the nape with an amethyst barrette. A scrap of lace peeked out from under her right cuff. The handkerchief was her small concession to the state of her mind and her uneasiness over the impending interview.

Skye waited to be offered a seat and when she was, chose the stiff wing chair and sat poised on the edge of it, her hands folded primly in her lap. She breathed slowly and evenly, willing herself to remain calm.

Parnell indicated the sideboard. "A glass of sherry?"

"No, thank you," she said. "Nothing for me." Skye kept her eyes on Parnell, studiously avoiding Walker's watchful gaze.

Parnell returned to his chair. "You'll understand if I have some questions," he said.

"Yes, of course."

He nodded. "I anticipated you would breathe some life into this house," he told her, "but tonight's events were something else again. Naturally, I'm concerned by what's happened. Perhaps you should begin at the point where you invited Mr. Caine into your room."

It was difficult not to look at Walker, but Skye managed it. "I did not invite him in. He gave me no choice about it."

"He forced his way in?"

She hesitated. "No, but it wasn't a choice just the same. He has it in his head that I mean you some sort of harm."

"Do you?"

"No!"

"I see," Parnell said slowly. "And Mr. Caine has no reason to suppose that you might."

This time her denial was not vehement. "No . . . that is, he thinks he has reason." Skye explained the situation to Parnell, using the same excuses for being out of her room that she had used with Walker. Parnell gave no indication whether he believed her. "And that's why Mr. Caine thought he had cause to be in my room."

"And in your bed?" Parnell asked.

His question made Skye feel tawdry. This time she did seek out Walker. She anticipated something in his face, in his manner, would tell her what she was supposed to say. There was nothing. Everything about him, his posture, the line of his mouth, the expression in his eyes, was carefully neutral. Her glance rested again on Parnell. "I don't know what happened in my room tonight," she said quietly. "Someone . . . *something* . . . was touching→"

"Something?" asked Parnell. "What is that supposed to mean, Miss Dennehy?"

Skye didn't have an acceptable answer for herself. What she was thinking she couldn't share. Unconsciously her eyes strayed to the portraits on the far wall.

Parnell watched her. "You're not going to tell me it was the ghost, are you? I think Mr. Caine anticipated you might offer that reasoning."

"I didn't say that." But she had been thinking it and both men knew she had. Her chin came up. "I suspect it was a nightmare and nothing more. It seemed very real. That's the only excuse I'm prepared to offer for my behavior."

"A nightmare," he said.

"Yes," she repeated firmly. She challenged him. "Am I dismissed, Mr. Parnell?"

"Mr. Caine thinks I should dismiss you. What do you think, Miss Dennehy?"

"I think it only matters what *you* think."

"Just so." His head turned in Walker's direction. "You'd do well to remember that, too." He stood. "Do you want to leave, Miss Dennehy? I should think tonight's experience might send you packing of your own accord. No one would think less of you."

It simply wasn't a consideration. No one thought much of her now. "One doesn't give up a position because of a bad dream, Mr. Parnell." Skye felt Parnell's thorough assessment as his dark blue eyes roamed over her. It was all she could do to sit still for it. The sensation was one of being physically touched, as if fingers were gliding over her face, her shoulders, along her arms. She knew he would find no evidence that she'd been hurt, nothing he could lay at Walker Caine's door. There was simply nothing to be found. But in spite of what she maintained in front of Parnell and Walker, Skye knew something had been done to her. It had *not* been a dream.

Upon being given her leave by Parnell, Skye headed for her room. She was almost to the top of the stairs when she heard the doors below her open and close again. Sensing Walker was going to follow her, Skye increased her pace. She wasn't quick enough to prevent him from shouldering his way through the door before she could close it.

Skye immediately put space between herself and Walker. Her arms came across her middle. She hugged herself protectively. "What do you want?"

"You."

She flushed. Her eyes darted away, embarrassed by the frank look in his. "It wasn't a dream," she said quietly. She hadn't known she was going to say the words until they were out.

His features remained expressionless. "Come with me," he said. "You'll spend the rest of the night in my room."

Skye's head came up. "No. I won't do that."

"You don't have any choice. None."

"Mr. Parnell didn't say—"

"Mr. Parnell is allowing me to handle this." He stepped aside and indicated the door. "You can ask him if you wish. Now, before he returns to bed." When she didn't move immediately, he said, "Good. You know I'm telling you the truth." He pointed to her nightshift and her robe. "Collect your things and come with me." He picked up his blankets and pillow from the floor. "If you don't like it, you can always quit."

"I can't afford to do that." It was true, she thought, but not in the way he would think. Skye would always count it as a failure if she left the Granville house now.

He shrugged. "Then you'll have to learn to make the best of these circumstances."

Skye picked up her nightgown. "Allow me to change here." She had a dressing room where she could have some privacy. Walker's room had none.

Walker merely pointed toward the door.

Skye's mouth flattened. She yanked her robe off the back of a chair, picked up a few items from her vanity, and all but marched out of the room. "I haven't done anything to warrant this treatment," she said.

"I'm making certain it remains that way."

"You're treating me like a criminal."

"Consider yourself fortunate, then," he said. "I've a mind to treat you like a whore."

Skye sucked in her breath. "I'll kill you if you lay a hand on me," she said through clenched teeth.

They had arrived at Walker's room. In deliberate defiance of her threat, he opened the door, put his hand on the small of her back, and shoved. Skye was propelled into the room. She spun on him, her expression feral. "Parnell already thinks you tried once tonight," he told her.

That calm announcement stopped Skye. Instead of dropping the things she held to strike him, she gripped them tighter. "What do you mean?"

Walker approached her. Prying the things loose from her clenched fists, he tossed them on a chair. Without giving her time to react, Walker's fingers enclosed Skye's wrist and he raised her hand to the back of his head. "This," he said. "Feel it."

Skye's fingers trembled as she explored the raised edge of the bump. There was blood on the tips of her fingers when Walker allowed her to withdraw. She stared at her hand, then at Walker. Her voice was a husky whisper. "I didn't do that." The denial wasn't as firm as she might have wished. Her next words were barely audible, but clearly framed as a question. "Did I?"

Walker felt her question as a real physical blow, but it registered on his face as a mere blink. What exactly had happened to her tonight? "Don't you know?"

Skye's face went from pale to ashen. Shadows deepened her green eyes and, to her horror, tears welled. She did not want to be vulnerable in front of this man. She bit her lower lip and concentrated on the pain instead of on her confusion. The horrible truth was, she *didn't* know.

Walker didn't pose the question again. He didn't need to hear her answer to understand her confusion. "Change your clothes," he said, plucking at his suspenders and slipping them off his shoulders. "Unless you want to sleep in your dress."

The tears dried in her eyes. She gave a short nod and turned away. The buttons were difficult, and without Annie to help, Skye struggled. Walker brushed aside her hands and began the task. Skye stiffened, but she held her place and said nothing. He was quick, impersonal, but each time his knuckle brushed her skin, Skye felt her breath catch. He finished without a word and stepped back. The silence in the room was powerful.

Walker's hands remained at his side as Skye removed her gown. Her head was bowed, the back of her neck exposed. There was nothing provocative in her action, no intended tease, yet Walker felt a rush of desire that made it impossible for him to look away.

Clasped in the loose barrette, her flaming hair had fallen over one shoulder. He could have reached for it, clutched it, and drawn her back against him. He'd felt her against him before, known how her contours would fit the angles of his own body. She wasn't entirely afraid of him, not as he expected her to be, not as he *wanted* her to be. It was probably more accurate that she was afraid of herself.

Skye stepped out of the gown and reached for her nightshift. Still modestly covered by her chemise and one petticoat, she drew it over her head. She wished Walker would say something. Without turning around, she knew he was watching her. The strength of his stare was like hands on her body. She shuddered.

The movement challenged the silence. Swearing softly, Walker stepped backward, away from Skye, and removed his trousers. He turned back the covers on the bed, then poured a small amount of water into the basin on the washstand and began to attend to his head.

Reaching under her nightgown, Skye managed to remove her chemise and petticoat without showing any more flesh than she already had. Rather more satisfied, she sat in a chair to take off her shoes and stockings. She picked at the laces, watching Walker. "You may need a stitch," she said.

"I don't think so."

"I've done it before," she added. "Stitching, I mean."

The glance he shot her was patently skeptical.

"Well, I've watched my sister do it. It didn't look so hard."

"No, thanks." Walker washed the knot on his head gingerly, then explored with his fingers, wincing as he touched a particularly tender spot. "I'll survive this injury better than I'd survive your attentions to it." He wrung out the washcloth and tossed it to her. "Your fingers," he said. "You have my blood on them."

There was only a small stain, barely visible now. Skye washed it away and carried the cloth back to the basin. "I suppose since this is your room, you'll be wanting the bed."

"That's right," he said frankly. "And I'll want you in it with me."

It was the knowledge that Walker wouldn't want her in his bed that had helped Skye remain calm. Realizing it hadn't been knowledge at all, but only an assumption, Skye's vision blurred at the edges. She grabbed the corner of the washstand.

"Are you going to faint?"

"No." Her weak reply didn't convince her. She understood why Walker simply picked her up and laid her on the bed. He stood over her a moment, studying her still and wary face before he pulled up the covers. Skye's eyes followed Walker as he rounded the bed and climbed in from the other side. She continued to stare even after he blew out the bedside lamp.

Walker punched at his pillow until it was the shape he wanted. He stretched out, turning to face Skye, his arm supporting the pillow and his head. "You have to sleep sometime," he said.

Skye said nothing for a long moment. "Is that when you'll do it?" she asked finally.

"Do it?"

"Touch me . . ."

"Rape you, you mean." He edged closer to her. "That's the second time tonight you've said something like that to me. Is that what you think I want to do?"

"I don't know." Her voice was small, choked. His face was close to hers now. She could feel his breath on her skin. There was the faint smell of whiskey and she remembered the drink he'd been holding in the parlor. "Why am I here, then? Who are you really protecting? Parnell? Yourself?"

"Don't you know?" he asked softly. "I'm protecting you."

She had a host of things she wanted to say, and they all remained unspoken as Walker's mouth touched hers.

His lips were firm and warm. The pressure was gentle—insistent, but not invading. Skye knew she could pull back at any time. He didn't touch her with his hands. His leg didn't move to hold her captive. Yet she didn't withdraw, even when his mouth parted her own and there was the moist heat of his tongue along the edge of her lips. Her heart raced. Her breathing quickened. There could be more to this kiss, she knew, and longing warred with disturbing images inside her head.

Walker sensed her reluctance before Skye knew it herself. He raised his head. "Go to sleep," he said. There was a tiny sigh from her, a small sound of disappointment that she couldn't quite contain. He smiled. "You can't have it both ways, Mary Schyler. Either you trust me or you don't . . . either you want me or you don't. You have to be sure."

She couldn't think of anything to say to that. She was sharing a bed with a man she hardly knew and she barely knew why. Skye had never imagined that desire might not be a straightforward emotion, that the peculiar hunger she associated with it would not come on suddenly, but in small twinges that made her uneasy. She had never imagined that it could sneak up behind her, hover, then disappear, leaving her unsettled and confused.

Skye's adventuring spirit could have accepted being blindsided by an onslaught of passion. She was prepared to be a fool for love.

This was different.

Walker Caine only wanted her. She hadn't expected to want a man like that. There would be no grand passion to blame, no false promises to lead her astray. There was only an emptiness aching to be filled when he was around.

It was still dark outside when Skye woke. Shards of sleet made a steady scratching sound as they hit the windowpanes, and the French doors groaned when the wind whipped across the balcony. The rising storm brought the house to life. Boards creaked as if bracing

themselves. The gutters rattled. An eddy of air whistled
in the chimney flue. Skye was more comforted than
disturbed by the storm. She turned on her side and
drew in her sprawled limbs, burrowing into the mattress
and blankets. A sleepy, contented smile marked her
face. She closed her eyes.

And opened them wide an instant later when she
realized where she was. Walker wasn't in bed any
longer. A moment ago her body had been stretched out
to command most of the bed. She had all the blankets,
but the pillow she was hugging to her chest had
Walker's scent on it.

Slowly Skye turned again, this time facing the fireplace. He was almost a silhouette against the flames, a
dark apparition except at the edges, where orange light
burnished his smooth skin. He was standing at a right
angle to the mantel and the smooth line of his shoulder,
chest, and arm clearly showed he was naked to the waist.

Fascinated by his deliberate stillness and the purposeful stance of his lean body, Skye watched through the fan
of her lashes as Walker inhaled fully and raised his arms
to chest height. He exhaled slowly, moving his arms down
to his thighs in a fluid motion while bending his knees
slightly. The splendid line of his back remained straight.
He pivoted then, facing south and placing his weight
lightly on his right foot. His hands moved with conscious
gracefulness around an invisible wheel. Eventually his left
hand fell away from the imaginary rim, palm back. When
Walker's right hand reached the top of the wheel he raised
it forward, as if in gentle greeting to the wind, keeping
his palm toward his face. In the same motion his right leg
was lifted and he stepped forward, shifting his weight in
that direction.

Skye's breathing was light and shallow. Her eyes were
filled with Walker's beautiful form as he stretched and
shifted. His arms were in continuous choreographed

motion. The movements were spare and fluid, curling and rounded, and they all seemed to serve some purpose or illustrate some thought in his mind's eye. Firelight was reflected in the thin sheen of perspiration that touched his skin, proof there was exertion in making each movement appear effortless.

It was a long time before Skye sensed Walker was bringing it to a close. His body was facing east again and his hands flowed in outward circles. He raised them to his forehead, palms out, then continued the movement outward in a sweeping circle before bringing them to his chest, crossed this time, then dropping them gently to his thighs. There was the slightest pause before Walker drew his arms inward and raised his hands to chest height, his wrists relaxed. Slowly he lowered his hands back to his thighs.

"It's called the Great Circle," he said after a moment. He padded softly to the washstand and poured fresh water into the basin.

"You knew I was watching?"

"Only in the end. Tai-Chi demands concentration. It's difficult to be aware of someone else."

Skye pushed herself upright. The strap of her nightgown slipped over one shoulder. Before she could bring it up, Walker was leaning toward her and hooking it with his index finger. The back of his knuckle lightly brushed her skin. He withdrew immediately, taking up the washcloth, dipping it in the water, then running it over his face, arms, and chest. He glanced in Skye's direction once and when she realized she was staring she turned away, embarrassed.

Tai-Chi?" she asked. As if her flushed face were not evidence enough that she was flustered, the pitch of her voice was a bit too high. Skye wanted to pull the covers over her head. She forced herself to brazen it out. "I thought you said it was the Great Circle."

"It's just a way of practicing Tai-Chi. If you were watching for a while, then you know that some of the movements are repeated."

She had been watching from the very beginning, but she didn't tell him that. "It's lovely," she said, a shade wistfully. Each gesture had been sweeping, yet gentle. Walker had moved slowly, as if through water, dipping and floating. "You've been doing it for a very long time, haven't you?"

"Years."

"Tai-Chi," she said again, testing the unfamiliar words.

"It's Chinese."

"I thought it might be. Where did you learn it?"

"From a master."

That wasn't the answer Skye had expected to hear. "I meant, where did—"

"You're asking a lot of questions," Walker pointed out. The observation silenced Skye for a few seconds.

"You use it to fight," she said.

Walker smiled to himself. He finished with the washcloth, wrung it out, and laid it over the edge of the basin. His robe was lying at the foot of the bed. He picked it up, shrugged into it, and stretched out in the chair that angled away from the fireplace.

"I recognized the movements," Skye went on. She pushed a pillow behind the small of her back and raised her knees, curving her arms around them as she drew them close to her chest. Although she could hear the ticking of the clock, she couldn't make out the time. She couldn't imagine herself falling asleep again, even if it were only the middle of the night. "When you knocked the gun from Mr. Parnell's hand it was the same."

"Was it?"

"Faster," she said. "Although it didn't seem so then.

I remember thinking it was as if you were moving through water. I noticed it again just now."

"You're very observant," he said. His brown-and-gold-flecked eyes regarded her frankly. She was pressed against the headboard, curled in the cocoon of her own cotton nightshift. Her eyelids still had a heavy, hooded look to them, sleepy and sensual. Her bright hair hung loosely about her shoulders. The line of her lower lip was full and faintly damp where she had touched it with the tip of her tongue. In that moment she was a temptress. In the next, when she drew in that lip and worried it gently, she was an innocent.

Two sides of the same coin, he thought, shifting in his chair. He pulled at the sides of his robe, covering the smooth breadth of his chest and belted it.

"I *am* observant," she said. "And curious. And intrepid."

He smiled again. "All the things that get you into trouble, Mary Schyler."

Staring at her hands which were folded on her knees, Skye sighed. "I suppose so." She looked at him suddenly, her expression forthright. "Are you really protecting me?" she asked.

"Yes."

A small vertical line appeared between her feathered brows as she considered his answer and weighed the truthfulness. "Did someone ask you to?"

Now Walker frowned. "Ask me to?"

"Yes, were you asked to protect me? Perhaps even hired."

It was a very odd question for a housekeeper to pose, and Walker filed it away instead of taking issue with it now. "No one's asked me and no one's offered me any money for it. If ever there was someone who needed a keeper, it's you."

Her chin came up. "That's insulting."

"That's the truth."

Skye ducked her head again, resting her chin on knees. She supposed she hadn't given him much reason to think otherwise. "I know who you are," she said after a while.

"What?"

She was aware that Walker's relaxed posture was more pretense than real. It was his very stillness that gave him away. She didn't have to see his eyes to know that they were sharper now, the gold flecks splinters of light. "I know who you are," she repeated. "Or perhaps it's more accurate to say that we've met before."

"Is that right?"

She nodded, sparing him a glance. "I doubt that you'd remember," she said. To herself she could admit that she would never forget. "You had other things on your mind that night."

Walker leaned forward in his chair and rested his elbows against his knees. Intrigued by the notion that he had made Skye's acquaintance before, he studied her face hard. The smile that edged her mouth had taken a decidedly impish turn. The slant of her eyes could only be described as mischievous. The light color stealing into her cheeks was a telltale sign that she was uncomfortable with his scrutiny. She pulled her hair to one side and twisted it in a single thick braid to keep her hands busy.

He wouldn't have forgotten that face, he thought. Not those clear green eyes, not the fiery hair. If she couldn't strictly be called beautiful, she was, at the very least, arresting. He couldn't imagine the situation where he might not have noticed her. Whether inadvertently or by design, she drew attention to herself. He clearly remembered her waiting in the foyer for her interview, leaning over the bench, her bustle and her behind pointed in the air.

She drew attention to herself, he thought again, even if it wasn't to her face.

"Why are you looking at me like that?" she asked. She

rubbed the tip of her nose self-consciously. "Do I have a— "

"It's nothing," he said. "My mind went off in an entirely different direction for a moment." He held up his hands briefly. "I'm afraid you have the advantage. I don't recall seeing you before."

"You didn't really see me."

He frowned. "But we met?"

She nodded. "We spoke."

"It's a riddle," he said, coming to his feet. "And I'm afraid I don't know the answer."

The lilting cadence of her mother's Irish accents came out as Skye responded. "Sure, and you're not givin' up so quickly, are you? It can't be that much of a quizzle for a smart man like yourself."

For just a second Walker felt himself rooted to the floor. Had she noticed? "I must not be as smart as you think. Nothing's coming to mind."

Skye was disappointed. Either he didn't remember or he was pretending not to. "It's all right," she said. It was impossible for her voice not to indicate that the opposite was true.

"Are you going to tell me where it was?" he asked.

She shook her head. "It's not important." Again the lie was in her voice.

"Perhaps you've mistaken me for someone else."

"Perhaps I have," she agreed softly. But she hadn't. She was certain of it.

Walker approached the bed. He sat down on the edge near where she was curled and contemplative. He placed one hand over hers. She watched him, but she didn't shy away from his touch. "Trust should be mutual," he said.

Her eyes were solemn. "I've always thought so."

His slow exhalation had the sound of resignation in it. He withdrew his hand, his decision made. "It was in the park," he said. "Central Park. You were hiding along one of the paths, in the pines. You called out to your friends to give me time to get away."

"They weren't my friends."

"I didn't go far. They knew you."

Skye wondered what he had heard. She remembered they had kept walking, so unless he had trailed them, she and the others would have been out of earshot quickly. "And I knew them," she said. "But except for Daniel, they weren't my friends."

The distinction seemed important to her, and Walker let it pass.

"Why didn't you want to tell me that you remembered?" Skye asked.

"I have more practice keeping secrets than sharing them."

"I can keep secrets, too."

"You'll have to." His tone was flat. His eyes were serious. He leaned toward her. "Otherwise you'll be dead."

A slip of air passed between Skye's parted lips. The centers of her eyes darkened, widened. He was going to kiss her, and this time she welcomed it.

His mouth moved gently over hers, sipping, tasting. Skye's hands unfolded on her knees and lifted to the level of Walker's shoulders. They hovered there, fluttered, then alighted. She gripped the lapels of his robe between her thumbs and forefingers. The fabric was soft. The warmth was Walker's heat.

The damp edge of his tongue touched her mouth. She opened to it. Her body unfolded beside his as he stretched out on the bed. They were on their sides, mouths cleaving. He explored her mouth, the fullness of her lower lip, the peaked curves of her upper one. He kissed the corner of her mouth and traced the edge of her jaw. He nuzzled her ear and his teeth caught her lobe and tugged. His fingers threaded in her hair, tangling in the silken flames. The fragrance of her drew him closer. There would be a tiny mark on her skin later where he sipped at the curve of her neck.

He felt the pulse in her temple against his mouth, the thrumming of her heart in the sensitive cord of her throat. She made a tiny sound of wanting when his lips traced the rounded neckline of her gown. Where his tongue dampened it, it clung to her skin. He nudged it aside and kissed her. She was warm, supple. The entire length of her body was pliant.

He palmed the inward curves of her waist and twisted until he was under her. Skye's slight weight pinned him to the mattress.

She raised her head a fraction, breaking the kiss. Walker's hands stilled on her waist. "What is it?" he asked. The grip of his hands was warm and solid.

"I thought I would be afraid," she whispered. "But I'm not."

"Good," he said. "Because I'm terrified."

His lie made her smile and the firelight gave it warmth. It washed over Walker. Skye bent her head and this time it was she who initiated the kiss. Her nose nudged his as she found the comfortable slant. She pressed her lips against his. They shared the same breath. At the small of her back his thumbs brushed back and forth against the fabric of her nightgown. She could feel the rubbing pressure on her skin and knew an urgency to thrust herself against him. The hard, rigid length of him was cradled by her thighs. It was the most natural thing in the world to deepen the kiss and accept the soft groan at the back of his throat.

Walker tugged at Skye's nightgown, raising the hem past her calves, the backs of her knees, her thighs. The rise of the fabric, the flimsy, insubstantial brush of it against her skin, caused Skye to shudder. Her short gasp was unlike Walker's, tinged with alarm, not desire. She raised her head and pushed at his shoulders in the same motion, twisting away from him with her entire body.

Walker made no attempt to pursue her. His breathing was short and ragged. The struggle was to steady it. He raked his hair with his fingers and exhaled slowly. Skye was sitting up on the edge of the bed, her arms hugging her midriff and her shoulders hunched.

"This was a bad idea," he said finally. His voice was husky, gritty with his efforts at denial. "I shouldn't have—"

"No," she said quickly, her own voice raspy. "It's not your fault." She straightened and pressed her fists against her middle. It helped her take a breath. "It's something about me. Something that's wrong."

Wondering if she could put it into words, Walker waited for her to tell him. He let the silence stretch between them for so long that he was certain she wouldn't explain herself. He was ready to say she didn't have to when she turned her head to look at him. Her warring thoughts were etched in the tiny lines at the corners of her eyes and mouth. She pressed again on her middle with her fists and the words spilled out.

"Do you believe in ghosts?"

Eight

Walker pushed himself up so he could rest on his elbows. He didn't ask Skye if she was serious. He could see that she was. "Ghosts," he said flatly. "You're asking about ghosts."

She was earnest. "Yes. Do you think it's possible?"

He hedged. "Anything's possible."

Skye nearly removed the fist clenched against her own midriff and plunged it into his. "Don't do that. Don't humor me." She let her feet slide off the bed rail and stood. When she picked up her robe, she was near enough to the mantel clock to read the time. It was almost six o'clock, time for her to be up anyway. "I'm going back to my room to get ready. There's no reason for others to know I spent the night here."

Walker got up. He lighted the bedside lamp. "Parnell already knows," he reminded her. "And Corina will find out from him. I suspect it will be common knowledge among the staff by the end of breakfast. Besides, I'm not letting you out of my sight. I still have to protect Parnell."

That stopped Skye. "I thought you were protecting me."

"I am."

"*And* yourself, no doubt."

His grin appeared as he came to his feet. The single dimple marked one corner of his unrepentant smile.

"That's right." He cornered her at the washstand and placed one arm on either side of her. His smile faded as quickly as it had come.

Startled, Skye braced her shoulders defensively. She raised her chin. He wasn't touching her anywhere, but she was as aware of him as she had been when her body had been pressed to his.

"Now, suppose you tell me why you asked about ghosts."

Skye's mouth flattened.

"Don't," he said, shaking his head. "Don't go tight-lipped now. You raised the question. You're the one who leaped out of our bed."

Our bed. Skye blinked hugely, dumbstruck by his phrasing. Walker Caine took a lot of liberties.

"Well?"

"I trusted you," she said, on a thread of sound.

His eyes locked on her accusing ones. "And you still can. I haven't lied to you."

"You haven't told me the entire truth, either."

"Fair enough."

She hadn't expected him to admit it so easily. "Are you going to?"

"I don't think so."

"And you still expect me to trust you?"

"Your safety depends on it. I can't say it any plainer than that." He searched her features and knew the moment she resigned herself to accepting his words at face value. "Now tell me why you asked about ghosts."

It didn't seem to matter that he hadn't answered her question. He was determined to get an answer to his own. "I asked because there was one in my room last night." She waited for him to laugh. When his expression didn't change, she continued. "And I think it's happened before."

"What makes you think that?"

Skye struggled to find the right words. Her efforts were inadequate to her own ears. "It seemed vaguely familiar," she said. "I have this . . . *sense*— I don't know any other way to say it— that something was touching me. Last night the feeling was stronger."

Walker removed his arms from either side of Skye and took a step backward. He thought she was probably unaware of the relief that shaded her eyes almost immediately. He considered her actions in their bed a few minutes earlier and then he considered his own. He couldn't have said he understood, but an idea was forming in his head. "Tell me about last night," he said. "Tell me what you can remember."

Skye glanced at the clock again. She needed to get ready, yet she was reluctant to return to her own room. She turned her back on Walker and began washing at the basin. Behind her, she felt him return to the bed, where he sat on the edge. "Last night the feeling was stronger," she explained. "If I could have just opened my eyes a moment sooner I would have seen him."

"Him?"

The washcloth was cool against Skye's hot face. It would have been more comfortable to stay buried in it than answer Walker's question. She let it slip away and wrung it out. "It's a he," she said softly. She could almost feel his skepticism and she shrugged. "I just know."

Walker didn't argue. "Why didn't you open your eyes?"

"I couldn't." Skye picked up her brush and began pulling it through her thick hair. "It's true I was afraid, but that isn't why I didn't look. I *didn't* because I *couldn't.*"

"There was something over your eyes?"

The brushing stopped for a beat. Skye turned toward Walker, her eyes distant with thought. "No," she said. "It wasn't like that. They were just so heavy I couldn't lift them. I tried. I know I tried." She resumed brushing her hair and looked at Walker. "It sounds mad, doesn't it?"

Walker was reserving judgment. "Tell me about the touching."

Skye would have turned from him again, but his eyes held hers and she found herself unable to look away. Her voice was only a thread of sound. "It's soft. Feathery. Fluttering. Like butterfly wings. It beats against my skin sometimes. Sometimes it just slides over me. It's barely a touch at all." She forced herself to tell him all of it. "Last night . . . he touched me everywhere."

Walker reached out and took the brush from Skye's nerveless fingers. He tossed it to the foot of the bed. His fingers caught the sleeve of her robe and he tugged, pulling her between his open legs. He grasped one of her hands in each of his. Sitting on the edge of the bed as he was, Walker was the one who had to raise his face to Skye. His brown-and-gold-flecked eyes searched her features. His voice didn't hint at the anxiety he felt. "Do you believe it wasn't me?" he asked her.

She didn't hesitate. "I *know* it wasn't you," she said. "I couldn't have— " Her eyes drifted to the pillows lying side by side on the bed. "I couldn't have . . ." She trailed off, unable to find the right words.

"You didn't," he reminded her gently. "We exchanged kisses. Nothing else happened."

She knew her face was burning. Walker's stare was frank and unembarrassed. His thumbs were rubbing the backs of her hands. Those kisses, she thought, those kisses were different than anything she had experienced. Which meant they were not like Daniel's and nothing like the ghost's. She would have felt foolish telling Walker that. Instead, her voice just a whisper, she said, "I couldn't even have slept beside you."

Walker could have told her that for most of the night she *had* been alone. He found it much more difficult to sleep than she had. After tossing and turning for the better part of an hour, he'd left the room briefly. On his return Walker had moved to the chair beside the fireplace. He imagined it wouldn't be so different this evening. "You know I'm not going to hurt you," he said.

Skye thought he probably would, but not in any physical way. "I know," she said.

"All right." Walker's thumbs stopped massaging her hands. "Let me change my clothes, then we'll go to your room so you can get ready. Sometime today you'll have to move your things in here."

"But—"

He shook his head, cutting her off. "In here," he repeated. "This is where I want you."

Throughout the morning Walker's voice would intrude on Skye's thoughts. *"This is where I want you."* At different times she caught herself staring at him as her mind wandered from her work. He seemed oblivious to her confusion, treating her impersonally but politely in front of the rest of the staff and even coolly when Parnell was around. He seemed equally oblivious to the looks they received from the others. Skye wished it could be the same for her.

Annie watched her with concern. Corina Reading's expression was smug. The twins exchanged giggly glances with each other and Jenny Adams's mouth was drawn in a line of tart disapproval. Hank avoided making eye contact at all, while Parnell's stare bore right through her.

Although Parnell was the only one who should have known, no one asked her how she had acquired Walker Caine for a shadow. Skye imagined that they had heard some version of the truth from Mrs. Reading, just as Walker had thought they would.

Skye's duties took her all through the house, and

Walker, while not quite dogging her footsteps, was always there when she turned. He made himself available to assist her, stripping linens from beds, moving furniture, reorganizing books, but by afternoon Skye was ready to scream in frustration. At lunch she made a point to sit at the far end of the dining room table just to get away from him.

Skye pushed food around on her plate for a while. "What exactly is it you suppose I'll do?" she asked, exasperated. "Mr. Parnell's been in his workroom most of the morning. Why don't you spend time with him?"

Walker pretended to consider that a moment. "You have prettier eyes."

Skye scowled and pointed her fork at him. "Don't flatter me. I'm prepared to plot *your* murder."

"I'm surprised you haven't already."

Simultaneously they looked toward the door. It was Parnell who had spoken. His eyes darted from one to the other, then he pointed to Walker with his forefinger and made an exiting gesture with his thumb. "I want to speak to Miss Dennehy alone," he said.

Walker didn't move immediately, considering his options. In the end he realized he had no choice. His position in the house was precarious at best. Parnell was merely suffering his presence until he made up his own mind about the threat Skye Dennehy posed. Walker pushed away from the table. "I'll be in the hall, if you need me," he said.

"Go further than that," Parnell said flatly. "I want a *private* conversation."

"Very well." Walker didn't look at Skye as he left the room, but he imagined she had changed her mind about not wanting him around any longer.

Parnell waited until the doors had been closed behind him and he heard Walker's steps receding in the hallway. He chose the chair at a right angle to Skye and sat down. "Please," he said amiably. "Finish your meal. I ate earlier. When I'm working, my schedule doesn't seem to fit with anyone else's."

"I've noticed that." She didn't think her food would taste any better than sawdust, but she gamely lifted her fork. Her eyes dropped to Parnell's lean fingers and tapered nails, wondering what it was about his hands that disturbed her. "How can I help you?"

Parnell's smile formed slowly. "Actually, I thought I might help you. If you're tired of Walker's company, that is."

Skye scarcely knew what to say. "He's hardly been a companion. More of a thorn in my side."

"Then spend the rest of the day with me," he said.

It was difficult not to keep her astonishment in check. "But— "

Parnell's expression became earnest. "I'd like you to see what I've been working on."

Now Skye's eyes widened and her disbelief was plain. "You're talking about your workroom?" she asked. "You'd let me see it?"

"That's why you're here, isn't it?"

It was all Skye could do not to nod dumbly. She caught herself and managed to ask calmly, "What do you mean?" She watched a shadow cross his features. Had it been disappointment she'd glimpsed there? "I'm here because you advertised for a housekeeper."

"Yes," he said finally. "Yes, you are." He stood. "But you'd like to see my invention."

"If you're still making the offer," she said. "Frankly, I'd be fascinated."

The smile that returned to his mouth was cynical where it touched his eyes. "Really, Miss Dennehy? What do you know about four-stroke internal combustion engines?"

"Not a thing."

He nodded, satisfied with her response. "At least you

can admit that much." He held out his elbow and this
time would accept nothing less than Skye taking it.

With a reluctance she was careful not to show, Skye
slipped her arm through Parnell's. The only people in
the kitchen when they walked through were Corina Reading and Walker Caine. They were talking quietly at the
sink while Corina stacked plates. They both looked up
and fell silent when Parnell and Skye entered.

"I'm taking Miss Dennehy to the workroom," Parnell
said. "I imagine we'll be a while."

Skye expected someone to object. Mrs. Reading
looked as if she might, but something made her hold
her tongue. Walker merely shrugged.

Parnell carried a lamp and preceded Skye down the
stairs. The cellar was not so foreboding as it had been
on the only other occasion she'd had to visit it. The
rough stone walls were whitewashed, which, with the
addition of the lamplight, made the area seem less oppressive. There was still the clutter of barrels and jars
and papers against the walls, but the path to the workroom was easy to negotiate now.

Looking around, Skye realized that neither of the
doors she'd found while trying to escape the cellar led
to Parnell's workroom. One was probably the wine cellar
and the other might have been for fruits, vegetables,
and canned goods. Parnell's workroom was on the side
of the cellar she hadn't explored. The door to it was
heavy, reinforced with a thin sheet of steel. A metal bar
was drawn across it and locked into place. Walker removed the key from his pocket and turned it in the
padlock. He raised the bar, pulled on the door, and
ushered Skye inside.

Watching Skye's face, Parnell said, "It's not quite
what you expected, is it?"

Short of the table in the middle of the room, it was
nothing like what she'd imagined. A narrow workbench

ran along the perimeter of the room. There were a few tools lying on the top, but nothing that wasn't familiar to her. The floor of the workroom was relatively clean. A small pile of metal shavings had been swept under the table. Her attention no sooner stopped on the pile than Parnell was gathering it up, not with a dustpan and broom, but with a magnet.

"Clever," she said, as he deposited the magnet on the bench.

"Easier than the conventional method."

"I don't suppose it works on dust."

He shook his head.

"Pity." She walked to the table. In the middle of it was an iron and steel contraption she thought must be the engine. It didn't look like much of anything to her. She couldn't identify a front or back, or determine which was up or down. There were pieces that had a squat cylindrical appearance lying on top of the table. An odd-shaped piece of metal protruded from the middle of them like the clapper of a bell. A pool of thick oil had gathered in a depression in the wood. "Is this your invention?" she asked.

"That's it."

"Does it work?"

"Not yet."

"Hmmm." She wondered how he would know. There didn't seem to be many moving parts. "What are those?" she asked, pointing to the cylinders.

"Pistons."

That made everything clear. "They're part of it?"

He nodded.

"What is it you do all day?" she asked.

"Sometimes I sit and think," he said, shrugging lightly. "And sometimes I just sit."

Skye smiled because it was expected of her. He had said it with a smoothness born of practice. She realized Parnell wasn't predisposed to make many explanations

about his work. For some reason he had simply wanted
her to see it. She looked around casually again, trying
to memorize everything she was seeing. There was no
chance she was ever going to steal this greasy black
monstrosity for her father. Did Jay Mac think it would
fit in her valise? Her only hope was to commit the look
of the thing to her mind. "What's that?" she asked,
pointing to the large glass jugs on the floor. They were
filled with a very light amber liquid that looked to be
no thicker than water.

"Fuel."

"I see," she said. "It doesn't smell very good, does
it? Worse than kerosene."

"It's very much like kerosene," he told her. "Highly
flammable. Not something to be careless with, I assure
you." Parnell leaned against the door while Skye walked
around the table, viewing his invention from all angles.
"You're inspecting it like a piece in a museum," he said,
watching her.

"I don't know quite any other way to look at it," she
said frankly. A little sheepishly she added, "It's not as
interesting as I thought it might be." She risked a
glance at Parnell to see if he was offended. Far from
it, he was smiling at her.

"You have a disarming sort of charm, Miss Dennehy,"
he said.

Skye's attention was back on the engine. For no reason
she understood goosebumps suddenly rose on her flesh.
She was wary. Something had shifted in the room. Was it
only the conversation, or her perspective? She quelled the
urge to shiver by crossing her arms in front of her.

"Is that what Mr. Caine finds so attractive?" he asked.

"I wouldn't know."

"You mean he hasn't said?"

Skye looked at Parnell straight on. "This is hardly ap-
propriate to discuss. You're making me uncomfortable."

Unabashed, he returned her stare. One of his brows lifted slowly. "You like Mr. Caine, don't you?" He didn't wait for her to answer. "Never mind. The truth is there in your eyes. He must know it as well."

Skye's palms were damp. "I'd like to go up now," she said with a calm she didn't feel.

"In a moment." He pulled the door into place as he moved away from it. Curiosity was evident in his eyes as he set the lamp on the table. "Why, Miss Dennehy," he said. "I believe I've frightened you."

"I said you're making me uncomfortable." She backed toward the bordering workbench as Parnell came around the table. "What is it you want?"

"The same thing you're giving Mr. Caine," he said. His tone was matter of fact. "I saw you first. I *wanted* you first. You must have known when I hired you how I intended it to be. It really isn't right that Walker's taken you for himself. Not in my house, not under my very nose."

Skye's thoughts were muddling as Parnell came closer. Her voice was a strained whisper. "Don't you think I'm trying to kill you?"

"Are you?"

"If you come any closer I might."

His blue eyes were cool as they searched her face. "I'll take my chances." Skye feinted to the left to dodge his outstretched arms. Parnell was too quick for her. He grabbed her wrists, hauled them up behind her back and pushed her against the workbench. The small of her back was pressed to the sharp edge of the bench. Pain caused her to gasp. Her parted mouth was all the invitation he needed. His lips were hard on hers, the slant of his mouth angry. His teeth ground in her as he forced his tongue into her mouth.

Skye struggled, striking out with her legs. Her skirts trapped her. She couldn't raise a knee with any force.

She tried to retract her head but he bent her farther, painfully, following her movement with his head. Skye had only one tactic left. She went limp.

Parnell didn't react immediately. His mouth remained insistent on hers as if he could resurrect a response. When there was none he lifted his head slowly. His grip on her wrists lessened as he straightened. Her face was pale. He could see faint blue lines against the skin of her eyelids. In contrast to her ashen skin her mouth was suffused with color. He stared at it.

Skye wrenched away from him and surprise made his response slow. Her hip caught the corner of the table as she lurched past it. The lamp teetered on the edge. Parnell shouted at her to catch it. Skye could hardly take in what he was saying, but the urgency of his message caught her attention. She reached out, her arms flailing, and caught the lamp halfway in its fall to the floor.

She was breathing hard as she held it to her middle and secured the fragile glass globe. The flame flickered wildly, then was steady. During her struggle one of the fuel jugs had been kicked over. It hadn't broken, but the stopper was loose now. Droplets of liquid were pooling on the floor.

Skye looked at Parnell. She understood his urgency. His eyes were darting between the upended jug and the lamp she held. Skye seized her advantage and with complete presence of mind she smiled at Jonathan Parnell. It was a smile that was as cool as it was cruel.

"I suppose this answers your question about my intentions, doesn't it?" She lifted the glass globe slowly, exposing the flame. Keeping her eyes on Parnell, Skye backed toward the door. "I wonder if your invention will survive the fire," she said idly. "I know you won't."

Parnell didn't blink.

Skye thought he must have ice in his veins. "Do you think I won't do it?" she asked, raising the lamp.

The answer came from behind her. "I think Mr. Parnell's counting on me," Walker said.

Skye's hands shook.

"Easy, Skye. You don't want to make a mistake now." His arms came around her and he took the lamp and globe. Instead of replacing the globe to secure the flame, he blew it out. The workroom and the cellar beyond were dark again. "I'm sure you can find your way, Mr. Parnell. I'm taking Skye with me." Walker set the lamp on the floor and yanked Skye out of the room. He all but pushed her up the stairs to the kitchen. Without pausing, he showed her the servants' stairs. She had to raise her skirts to go as fast as he wanted. When they reached the second floor, he pointed her to his room. "Get in there."

"It's not what it seems," she said hurriedly. "You don't— "

"Get in there." He gritted the words, his lips unmoving. "Or I might just kill you before Parnell does."

He looked as if he would do it, too. Skye couldn't recall seeing anyone as angry as Walker Caine. If only she could explain. He didn't understand what had happened in the workroom. He wouldn't be so quick to condemn her if he had.

Walker placed his hand between Skye's shoulder blades and pushed. She stumbled into the room. He closed the door behind her and locked it. Almost immediately she began pounding. He waited for a pause. "You'll be safe in there." Then he walked away to find Parnell.

He found his employer in the parlor, searching for the gun he'd left there the night before. Mrs. Reading was helping him. "I took it," Walker told him. "I came downstairs after everyone was sleeping and put it away. I'm not telling you where it is."

Parnell's eyes were like ice chips when he turned on Walker. "That bitch was going to kill me," he said.

"I warned you." He pointed to Mrs. Reading, who

hadn't stopped her search. "Get out of here, Corina. Your loyalty's admirable, but it is misplaced in this case."

She didn't respond to Walker's order, but to Parnell's curt nod. On her way out of the room she said angrily under her breath, "What do you know about misplaced loyalty?"

He didn't respond, though he imagined his answer would surprise her. He knew quite a bit. "What were you thinking, taking her down there?"

Parnell drew in his breath, calming himself. "I thought you were lying about her," he said. "I thought you only wanted her for yourself."

Walker swore softly. "So you set her up to force her hand?" he asked, incredulous. "It was an elaborate test? You may be some sort of genius in your workroom, Mr. Parnell, but you don't know what you're doing out of it. Leave Skye Dennehy to me." He paused. "Unless you want her out of here. I'm still offering to pack her up and take her back to Baileyboro. Hell, I'll take her all the way back to New York, if you'd like." Walker didn't expect Parnell to consider it, but he did.

"I have a better idea," Parnell said after a moment. "Let her think she's dismissed. I'm interested in where she goes and what she does."

"And then?"

"Return her here, of course. There will be questions to answer."

Walker shook his head. "Just let her go, Mr. Parnell. Who's going to watch your back if I'm following her?"

"With her out of the way, there's no need to watch my back." He went to the sideboard. "My mind's made up about this, Walker. If you won't do it, I'll find someone who will." He let Walker see his resolve. "You know I will. I found you."

"All right," Walker said finally. "She leaves in the morning. I'll take her to Baileyboro and follow her after that. You know there's a chance she won't return with me."

"Then don't return."

Walker would have liked to set Parnell on his ass. He walked out of the room instead.

Walker turned the key in the door. He thought he might find Skye prone on the bed, exhausted from crying. He was wrong. She was sitting up at his small writing table. It was obvious from her posture that she had been working there. A scrap of paper peeked out from her apron pocket. She had splashed a droplet of ink on the desk in her hurry to stopper the well. And then there was the faintly guilty look in her eyes.

"He's dismissed you," he said. Stepping into the room, Walker locked the door behind him.

She nodded.

"You're not surprised."

Skye's tone was philosophical. "He could hardly do otherwise, could he? He thinks I was going to kill him."

"And you weren't?" he asked drily.

"No," she said. "I wasn't." She stood, smoothing the fabric of her gray gown over her midriff. "What I was going to do— what I did, actually— was scare the hell out of him."

"You're pleased with yourself."

Skye's eyes flashed and narrowed. "The bastard deserved it."

"That *bastard* went looking for his gun."

Some of her fierceness faded. She could only stare at Walker. He was still clearly furious with her. "Did he find it?" she asked.

"Not for lack of trying. I hid it earlier."

Her response was flippant. "It looks as if you've protected us all again. I hope he's paying you well. You seem to be able to anticipate all sorts of situations." Skye's eyes dropped to Walker's side. His right hand was clenching and unclenching. Realizing that he would have liked to put that hand around her throat, she swallowed hard.

There was some small satisfaction in seeing Skye grow uneasy. "Why did you go with Parnell?" he asked.

"I wanted to see his invention. I didn't initiate it. He made the offer."

"And didn't that seem suspicious to you?"

"I don't know . . . yes . . . I suppose so. I wasn't thinking about that." Not clearly, anyway.

"God, you really do need a keeper."

"No one's hiring you for the job," she snapped.

Walker raked back his thick, tawny hair where it had fallen forward. The brief pause helped him gather his thoughts and cool his temper. "What happened down there?" he asked tightly.

Skye feigned surprise. "Oh, you mean something might have prompted me to threaten to set him on fire?" she simpered.

The gold flecks in Walker's eyes flashed. Gritting his teeth, he gripped Skye's elbow and yanked her toward the bed. He sat her down hard, then stood over her. "Tell me what happened."

Skye had to raise her face to look at him. "He made advances."

"What does that mean?"

She gave him a sour, disbelieving look. "You know perfectly— "

"I'm asking you."

"He kissed me."

Walker waited for Skye to say more. "And?" he prompted, drawing out the single word when she remained silent.

Skye's green eyes darkened. The narrowed look was both stubborn and defiant. "And I didn't want him to."

Walker exhaled slowly. "That's all I had to know," he said quietly. He sat beside her. "Are you all right?"

Staring at her hands in her lap, she nodded. "I was able to get away from him. Did Mr. Parnell tell you I welcomed his advances?"

"No. He didn't tell me anything like that." What Parnell had done hardly fit the category of setting Skye up.

She turned her face to look at him, her expression anxious. "You believe me?"

"Yes," he said.

Skye saw the truth of it in his face. It was important that he didn't doubt her now, not about this.

Walker took Skye's hands and raised them from her lap. He turned them over, examining the wrists. The skin around her small bones was still red. "Did he do this?" he asked.

She looked down at herself. By tomorrow she would have a bracelet of bruises on each wrist. "I suppose he did." It had all happened so quickly. She hadn't had time to think of what was being done, only that it was being done to her. Closing her eyes, she thought about it now. She could see herself being bent painfully backward over the workbench, her arms jerked hard behind her. He had forced her down so that her own weight pinned her arms. His mouth was a weight on her, too. Mashing against her lips, her teeth, her tongue.

Skye shuddered.

Walker was watching her. She was not so unmoved by the experience as she would have had him believe. He let go of her hands and cupped the side of her face with his palm. Her eyes opened. For a moment she simply looked at him blankly. When her eyes focused she gave him a weak smile. His fingers drifted over her face lightly. He touched the arch of her cheek, her temple. He let the tips follow the curve of her jaw and his thumb passed back and forth across her lower lip.

The touch was gentle and sweet. In the dark of night, in her own room, Skye might have been repelled by the very lightness of it. But this was afternoon. Pale winter sunshine filtered in the French doors and cast a long rectangle of light on the hardwood floor. She could see the man touching her was Walker and there was nothing insubstantial or otherworldly about the tautly carved edges of his face or the slightly crooked line of his nose. The centers of his eyes were darkening as he searched her face. There was desire there . . . and a question.

Skye leaned into him. She rubbed her cheek against his palm, turning into his caress. His head lowered a fraction. Her own hands lifted and slipped behind his neck. Her fingers threaded in the hair at his nape. She raised her face and urged him forward with her fingertips. The air fairly hummed between them.

Walker's mouth fit itself to hers. There was a hard and heady hunger sustaining the kiss. His lips moved over hers insistently, greedy for the taste of her. His tongue pressed for entry. It wasn't enough to touch the corner of her mouth or trace the line of her lips.

Skye's hands slipped from Walker's neck to his shoulders. At his sweetly urgent stroking, her mouth parted wider. The kiss deepened. She answered it, thrusting against him, not only with her tongue but with all of her body. The intimacy of the kiss was being repeated all along her length. She felt herself falling backward, cradled first by Walker's arms, then by the bed. He followed her and she took his weight onto herself. For a moment his chest was flush to her breasts and it was her flesh that yielded. She knew the hard length of his legs by the separation of hers and the broadness of his back when her arms clutched him close.

He shifted, twisting so they lay stretched across the bed. His hard, deep kiss had become a dozen swiftly pressing ones. She felt the imprint of his mouth on her eyes, her cheek, at the base of her throat. His tongue found the sensitive spot just behind her ear. His touch there made her body arch and her fingertips whiten against his shirt.

Walker had no patience for buttons. He tore at the ones at Skye's back. He pushed the loosened neckline over her shoulders, along with the straps of her chemise. His hand slipped beneath her bodice. She flinched, not from the intimacy of his touch, but from the heat. Still, he paused and looked at her. She didn't avert her eyes. He held her racing heartbeat in his palm and the edge of his hand cupped her breast. She turned slightly so that the heart of his palm only held her breast. His thumb passed lightly across her nipple and when Skye's breath caught he bent his head and kissed her again, giving her the breath she had lost in that moment.

It felt good. His weight. His mouth. The shape of his hand against her skin. Pleasure hummed through Skye. She tugged at tails of Walker's shirt, pulling them free of his trousers. Her hands slid under the material and stroked his skin. His flesh retracted under her sweeping touch. He sat up long enough to rid himself of his shirt. It sailed over the edge of the bed as she was reaching for him again.

Walker pushed the edge of her bodice below her breasts. Where his thumb had grazed her nipple, the nub was like a hard pink pebble. He bent. His mouth closed over the tip, worrying it gently between his teeth. He felt the shudder that rippled through her as if he had tugged on ribbons of pure sensation. Her fingertips trailed upward along his spine. He raised his head. She tried to say something but the words never came as he gave equal attention to her other breast. Her fingers tightened in the curling ends of his hair at his nape.

He laid a trail of kisses between her breasts. They went upward, ending at the curve of her neck. He sipped her skin. When she moved under him her thigh was pressed to his groin. Of their own accord his hips thrust against her.

"Sweet Jesus," he groaned. Her skin seemed to vibrate against the moist heat of his mouth. He raised his head a fraction. Skye was watching him, her eyes dark and wide, alert with passion rather than sleepy with it. There was a certain willfulness in her desire. Her sensual maturity had not quite outstripped her innocence. She wasn't challenging him, he thought, she was daring herself.

Skye sensed his hesitation. She raised her face and touched her mouth to his. Her lips moved over his mouth in the manner he had taught her. Her tongue traced the edges and slipped along his upper lip. She let his shudder pass into her and the weight of him cocooned her again. They engaged in a sweet battle where his mouth was a formidable weapon and her hands were no shield at all.

Her gown was pushed to her hips, then lower, past her thighs, her knees, until it was sliding over the edge of the bed. Her chemise gathered at her waist. Her petticoats were already a tangle about her legs, hiked up to the level of her knees. Her calves lay bare and smooth against the bedcovers. She raised one leg and wound it around his, stretching with feline grace to feel more of him against her. He groaned softly as her palms stroked his back and arms. Her fingers edged along his waistband and sometimes dipped beneath it. His skin burned where she touched him.

Walker rolled away from Skye and made short order of his clothes. He made no attempt to hide his arousal but turned toward her, unashamed by his body's response.

Skye's flush covered her entire body but it never occurred to her to look away. In truth she was fascinated, frightened, and a little awed. "Oh my," she said softly. She glanced at Walker's taut features, the creases at the corners of his eyes, the muscle working in his jaw, and asked worriedly, "Does it hurt?"

He stared at her a moment, a little amazed himself. A wicked grin slowly transformed his features as he bent over her. "More than you know," he fairly growled. Kissing her full on the mouth, his hands finished with her undergarments until they were both splendidly naked.

Skye's hands trailed to the small of his back, then over his buttocks. The texture of his skin delighted her. She kissed his shoulder and she moved lower. Her fingernail flicked his flat nipple. Her tongue aroused it. Whatever happened in this bed, she thought, was not simply being done to her. She was doing it, too. The power of it was heady.

Walker's hand traveled over the length of her thigh. The caress was insistent and a shiver of desire coursed through Skye. His mouth covered hers while his fingers teased the underside of her raised knee. He drew them across the back of the thigh, then the soft inner side. Her lips parted. Her legs parted. He touched her intimately, his fingers making a gentle exploration. She was tense now, but not resistant. When he lifted his head to watch her she drew a ragged breath.

The response of her body surprised her. She was warm and wet where he touched her. Her hands fell away from the back of his neck and curled in the covers beneath her. His hand was between her legs, but he was watching her. She couldn't look anywhere but at him, feel anything but the heat. It was growing white-hot just beneath his fingers and there was a certain way he would touch her that would make sparks skitter along the surface of her skin. She drew in her lower lip as she sipped her next breath. Sensation started to coil in her. She lifted her hips slightly, pushing with her heels against the mattress. Her fingers tightened. Her eyes fluttered closed.

He nudged her mouth, kissing her softly. "Open them

for me," he said against her lips. She raised her lids. Her legs parted more. He was satisfied with both responses. "You're so beautiful," he whispered. He eased a finger inside her. She was tight but accepting. Kissing her again, thoroughly and deeply, he removed his hand. Walker changed his position, parting her thighs wider with his knees. His hands slipped under her bottom and lifted her. Her eyes had dropped away from his and she was watching their bodies now. She reached out but her arms fell away uselessly and her fingers curled into the covers again as he entered her this time.

Pain, not passion, darkened her eyes now. He held his entry and gave her time to adjust before he moved again. He leaned forward and pushed into her with a single hard thrust. She would have cried out save for the mouth that covered hers. Her body trembled beneath his. She struck at his shoulders. He quieted her with gentle words. His breath was sweet and soft against her skin. His mouth nudged her ear and he kissed the tears that spiked her lashes.

He held himself very still and denial etched lines in his face. He felt Skye relax under him, and even shift slightly to accommodate him. Her eyes were still faintly accusing.

"You hurt me," she whispered.

"I know," he said. "I'm sorry. It won't happen again."

Skye's eyes clouded. What wouldn't happen again? The pain or the pleasure? She was on the verge of asking him when he began kissing the side of her neck. Her breasts seemed to swell against his chest. He was moving in her with slow, deliberate thrusts, and her hips were rising to meet him separate of any thought she had to the contrary.

The spiral of pleasure was rising from the exact point where it had stopped. The initial rush of it was intense, and it only increased from there. The driving of his body was rhythmic, and Skye was captured by the seductive cadence, even her breathing was rising and falling in the same arc of desire.

She held his shoulders, his upper arms, then ran her hands along his torso. She held him to her. Her neck arched. He kissed the hollow of it and the underside of her chin. Her thighs pressed the sides of his buttocks. She found purchase in the mattress and pushed herself against him.

He rocked her. She cradled him. There were moments when she thought she could not bear the pleasure and others when she could not bear it to end. Sensation rose swiftly and powerfully, and at the very apex of it, she cried out. He thrust into her harder, then more rapidly, pushing himself over the same edge where he had driven her. She watched his face as pleasure twisted it, then she shared his shudder and accepted his seed.

Skye's body fell quiet slowly. Her muscles released tension by degrees and they trembled again when he eased himself out of her. She was reluctant to let him go but did nothing except let her fingers drift across his shoulder as he rolled away.

Walker turned on his side. The angle of the sun had changed and now light slanted across the edge of their bed. The curve of Skye's shoulder was caressed by it. Where it touched her hair the color looked bright enough to burn her skin. Fascinated, he wound and unwound the lock around his finger. He bent his head and kissed her on the mouth. Her lips were pliant and soft. The kiss lingered.

"Mmmm," was all she said, when he withdrew.

Walker smiled. Her eyelids were heavy and her full mouth had a sleepy, pouting look to it. He reached around her and pulled part of the coverlet across her thighs and midriff. Her eyes closed completely and she stirred without energy. He rolled off the far side of the bed, then wrapped the rest of the coverlet around her. The last glimpse of her breasts actually made him sigh.

Walker chuckled under his breath. The last time he'd been moved to sigh at the sight of a bosom was fifteen years ago. On that occasion he had surprised the daughter of the ambassador to China by letting the stableboy sample her not inconsiderable charms. He'd sampled them himself much later in life and had not been so impressed on his second viewing.

Walker gathered up his clothes as he rounded the bed. He washed at the basin before he dressed. His eyes kept wandering to Skye. He hardly knew a thing about her, except that she wasn't a housekeeper. She knew even less about him. For what had just taken place in his bed hadn't seemed to matter. It had never bothered Walker before. He wished it didn't now.

He picked up Skye's clothes and laid them over the back of a chair. The paper she'd been writing on before he'd come into the room fell out of her apron pocket. He couldn't believe he had forgotten about it. Walker saw it as another sign he was in too deep.

Hunkering down, he retrieved the paper. It had been folded carelessly into quarters. He opened it and stared . . . and whistled softly. Based on his own very limited contact with Parnell's invention, he found Skye's drawing to have a high degree of accuracy. He wondered how much she really knew about engines. Had she only drawn it from memory, or did she understand its workings? He looked over his shoulder at the bed. She was still sleeping, her back to him.

Walker absently folded the paper and stuffed it back in her pocket. He stood and rested his hip on the edge of the writing table. Which of Parnell's investors did she work for? he wondered. How many were there that he didn't know about? The kind of business arrangement Parnell had was more scam than scheme. It was no wonder he wanted a gun as quick to fire as the Colt he'd carried the other day.

Walker left the desk and went to his wardrobe. Parnell's gun was still where he had hidden it. He supposed it would be safe enough there. Tomorrow he would take it with him. Parnell and Mrs. Reading could search all they wanted, but the gun was leaving the house. He didn't relish the thought of Parnell pointing it at him again. He hadn't thought it would come to killing the inventor, but it might, if that happened. His warning hadn't been an idle one.

He stepped away from the wardrobe and shut the door carefully.

"You don't have to be so quiet," Skye said. "I'm awake." Her eyes were still closed and her voice was just a sleepy whisper, but she had made the effort to turn on her side toward him.

Walker smiled. "Go back to sleep. I'm leaving."

"Hmm-mmm."

Her murmur drew him to the bed. He sat on the edge and placed a hand on her bare shoulder. His thumb stroked her skin. "I'll have dinner brought up to you. Don't worry. I'll send Annie with it."

She rolled on her back and raised her eyelids to half mast. The back of her hand touched her forehead as she brushed aside a strand of hair. "Do you have to go?" she asked.

He nodded. "I've spent too much time here already."

She surprised herself by blushing, but she welcomed the kiss she got in response. "Will the lock keep Parnell out?" she asked, when he sat up.

"This one will. There's no duplicate key for this room. Or rather, there is, but I have both." He patted his trouser pocket. "And no, you're not getting one."

Skye had no desire to be locked in, but the alternative worried her more. "Will you bring me something to read?" she asked. "I never had time to move my things in here today. Now, it seems a useless exercise. Will you get the book I took from Parnell's library?"

"The one on the Granville family?"

"Yes. I don't suppose I'm going to learn anything else about the ghost firsthand. I may as well learn something about him in his corporeal life."

Walker laughed. "You're quite serious about this ghost, aren't you?"

"Until I can prove otherwise," she said, unmoved by his amusement. "There's something to be said for entertaining *all* possibilities."

"I'll try to remember that," he said drily.

She raised herself on her elbows. The coverlet slid a few inches over her chest and rested on the outer curve of her breasts. "I suppose you have an explanation for how you got that knot at the back of your head?"

Walker barely heard the question. He found himself utterly fascinated that the coverlet could hover *just so* on Skye's breasts, rising and falling with each breath, but not sliding even a fraction of an inch lower.

Amused and disarmed by his boyish grin, Skye looked down at herself. "I wore a ballgown with a bodice like this once to the Astors'," she said, without thinking. "It was emerald satin and had more flounces on it than a dance hall girl's petticoat. Of course it had stays in it to hold it up. And I wore a corset that made it impossible to draw a breath." She pointed to the swell of her breasts and the line of the coverlet. "What's keeping this up is anyone's guess."

Skye looked up at Walker, her smile full of feigned innocence, her eyes filled with flirty guile.

He wasn't smiling in return. "Just who the hell are you?"

Nine

"What do you mean?" Skye asked.

"Emerald satin ballgowns," he said. "How is it that you had one of those and ended up working for Jonathan Parnell?" He had known she wasn't a housekeeper, but he hadn't fully considered what her background might be. Somebody's mistress? No, that was something he was sure she wasn't, at least until now.

Skye didn't so much as blink. "The dress was a hand-me-down," she said. It was perfectly true. Her mother had never been of a mind to settle all her daughters in new gowns each season. The emerald one with the wicked bodice had belonged to Rennie.

"But you wore it to the Astors'," he pointed out. "Invitations there aren't given to just anyone."

"I'm *not* just anyone," she retorted. "This was a benefit for Jennings Memorial, and Dr. Turner and his wife insisted I accompany them." The benefit was a true enough event, but it wasn't when she had worn the emerald gown, and it hadn't been to raise money for the hospital. She couldn't even remember if she'd seen Scott and Susan Turner there. Skye was rather chagrined to realize what a facile liar she had become. "There were many people there who wouldn't have been in the Astor home otherwise. Dr. Turner managed to put almost fifty patients on the invitation list, some of them indigents from the Bowery and Paradise Square. The whole thing caused quite a fuss, but it raised money."

Walker was watching her closely. Things had a way of rolling glibly off her tongue. "I think there's a bit of the blarney about you, Mary Schyler."

More than a bit. Anyone in her family could have told him. She managed to look properly affronted, but then he was kissing her and she realized he didn't really care who she was. He just liked her. The thought warmed her. Her arms stole around his back and the coverlet finally slipped over her breasts.

It took a visible effort on Walker's part to draw away. He looked down at the fallen coverlet that she was in no hurry to raise. If not for the heat in her cheeks, he could almost accuse her of being brazen. "It *would* fall now," he said, sighing.

"Everyone's talking about it," Annie said. She cleared a place on Skye's bedside table and set the dinner tray down. Matt was trying to climb onto the bed where Skye was sitting. Annie was prepared to scold him when Skye put her book aside and hauled Matt over the edge.

"He's all right," she said, pulling him into her lap. Skye was sitting crosslegged at the head of the bed, a pillow at the small of her back. She played pat-a-cake with him while she talked. "I imagine they're glad to see me go."

Annie shook her head and her mouth flattened. "That's not true at all."

Skye's glance was skeptical.

"Well, perhaps Mrs. Reading feels that way. But the twins are going to miss you, and Hank says you were good for the place. Jenny's keeping her counsel, but she's not mean-spirited. I know I'm sorry that Mr. Parnell's dismissed you."

"I can't say that I'm sorry," Skye said truthfully. "But all the same, I'm going to miss you. Have you been asked to take the position as housekeeper?"

She nodded, fiddling with the covered dishes on the tray. It wouldn't have been proper to show too much pleasure. After all, her new position had come at Skye's expense. "He spoke to me before dinner. Mrs. Reading made the announcement to the others."

"I'm happy for you," Skye said sincerely. "You'll do fine."

Annie's dour expression lightened. "Thank you. That means a lot to me. I wouldn't have this opportunity if it weren't for you."

Skye waved her gratitude aside. She rested her chin on the crown of Matthew's blond head. "You know, Annie," she said casually, "I was wondering about last night."

"Hmmm?" She laid out the silverware on the tray.

"You were so prompt in responding to my cry. I don't think I expressed my appreciation."

"I don't expect any thanks," said Annie. "I didn't really do anything."

"But you came. I'm a little surprised you heard me. I wouldn't have thought could have been heard above stairs. I hope I didn't frighten Matt here."

"Oh, no," she said, shaking her head. "Matt slept through the whole thing. I probably would have, too, if I hadn't been up already. I was coming down the hall on my way to the kitchen when I heard you scream. I don't mind saying I nearly lost my heart in that moment. It came as near to jumpin' out of my chest as it ever has."

"So you were in the hall, then."

Annie's voice dropped to a whisper. "You know I

can't abide those back stairs. It's all I can do to use them to get to the third floor. I've a fearful imagination when it comes to things like ghosts."

Skye made a wry face and pointed to the book beside her. "I'm beginning to think it's the same for me." She let Matthew grab her hand and pull it back into the pat-a-cake ritual. "You must have been on your way downstairs."

Annie nodded. "I was." The corners of her mouth drooped a fraction lower. "But what makes you think so?"

"You weren't carrying anything from the kitchen."

"I could have had myself a cup of tea there," she pointed out.

"You could have," she agreed. "But I can't imagine that you'd want to sit alone downstairs when you could be back with your son."

Annie admitted it was the very thing that had gone through her mind. "You've very observant," she said. "I noticed that about you from the very first." She extended her hands to her son.

Skye gave Matt a small boost to help him reach his mother's outstretched arms. "Then you're observant as well. I suppose it's all part and parcel of being a good housekeeper."

Annie picked up Matt and rested his small squirming body on her hip. "That's true enough," she said. "And I aim to be a good one."

Once Annie and Matthew were gone, Skye pulled the dinner tray onto her lap and ate while she read. The history of the Granvilles was infinitely more interesting than any of the fare Mrs. Reading had prepared for her. It wasn't long before Skye pushed aside her meal and concentrated on the book.

The Granville family could trace its origins to an arranged marriage between Lady Jane Suffolk and Ed-

ward Granville. Something was made of Lady Jane's
lineage, but little was noted about Edward Granville's
birth and parentage. Skye could guess at the reasons
for that. Still, it was the introduction of the Granville
name, and some mention had to be made of it.

The most significant early event for the family was
Edward's participation in the voyages to the New World.
He sailed with Raleigh until the Queen had Raleigh
beheaded and then, knowing the risks of displeasing
the Queen, he accepted an appointment as commander
of his own vessels. Far from displeasing the Queen, Edward Granville had distinguished himself with his service. He amassed treasure for the Queen and a small
fortune for himself by raiding the coffers of Spanish
galleons. As a reward he was given land in America.

Edward Granville never made much use of the property during his lifetime. Apparently he preferred pirat-
ing to planting and visited his property on only two
occasions. It was on the second voyage that his treas-
ure-laden ship was attacked by raiders on the Hudson.
He lost a fortune, his ship, and nearly his life. He never
returned to America's shores again.

It was left to his youngest son, who, with no other
prospects, claimed the land for himself. Robert was un-
married when he went to America, but once he was
established, he sent home for an English bride. Skye
imagined the young settler exaggerated both his good
fortune and his consequence. He managed to make a
match that he could not have made if he had remained
in London. His bride, Lady Emma Cordery, was the
daughter of the Earl of Whitested. She could have had
her pick of suitors, but she chose the youngest son of
a bastard privateer. It was unclear if the earl actually
supported the match or whether Lady Emma had de-
fied him to take her place beside Robert Granville. It
was also unclear if Robert and Emma had known each

other before their wedding. The family historians seemed to be reluctant to put some things in writing.

What followed was an account of their years together. They faced disputes over their land from the Dutch and the Indians, droughts that killed the crops, floods that ended the droughts. Lady Emma proved to be no hothouse flower, bearing Robert eight children, five of whom lived well into adulthood and had children of their own.

The history expanded there, but in detailing each of the descendants' lives, there was mentioned the tantalizing notion that Edward Granville's lost ship had never been relieved of its treasure.

Walker was not particularly quiet when he entered the room, but Skye didn't give any indication that she was aware of his presence. Struck by her concentration, he leaned back against the door and took advantage of the moment.

Skye was lying on her stomach, her head propped on her elbows. Her unbound hair fell across her shoulders and curtained a portion of her face. She had turned completely around on the bed and was now pointed toward the foot of it. With the tangled bedclothes as indicators, Walker could see that in the last several hours she had been sprawled in all possible directions.

One of Skye's legs was bent at the knee, with her bare calf and foot raised toward the ceiling. She rotated her ankle in small circles as she read. Sometimes she would simply let her calf drop back to the mattress, where it would rebound to its starting point and her small foot would begin the circles again. The hem of her gown was bunched up at her knees and there was more petticoat showing than dress fabric. The stiff collar must have been uncomfortable, because she had undone the buttons. Walker found the tiny glimpse of the hollow of her throat as enticing as the bare length of her legs.

It was that glimpse of skin and his reaction to it that

reminded Walker that Mary Schyler Dennehy wasn't so young as her posture made her seem, or at least so innocent. It occurred to him that he didn't even know how old she was. Walker was more disturbed by the fact that it bothered him than by the fact that he didn't know.

As he pushed away from the door, it clicked into place behind him. It was that small sound that captured Skye's attention. She looked up, blinked owlishly, and said the first thing that came to her mind: "You're scowling."

He made a low sound that could have been agreement or surprise.

Skye shrugged, changed her position, and went back to reading. It took her only a few moments to become immersed in the Granville account again. She was oblivious to Walker as he added logs to the fire and poked around the flames. She didn't see him remove his jacket or hang it up in the armoire. She wasn't aware he had stepped out on the balcony until she felt a draft on her legs as the doors opened and closed. Her first instinct was to cover up, not to join him, but the tangle of blankets thwarted her efforts.

Skye closed the book and rolled on her side. It was too dark outside to see what he was doing. The glass panes merely reflected back the interior of the room. Sitting up, Skye pushed off the edge of the bed and padded softly to the French doors.

"Go back," he told her, when she stepped outside. He was sitting on the edge of the railing, his arms across his chest and his legs stretched out before him. Wind ruffled hair at his nape. "It's too cold out here."

"For you as well as me," she said. Her teeth had begun to chatter, and the cold balcony floor was like ice on her bare feet. She did a little dance, shifting her weight from one foot to the other to keep warm.

"For God's sake," he said. "You don't have any shoes on."

"Or stockings, either," she said, hugging herself. "But then, you don't have—"

He opened the door with one hand, scooped Skye up with the other, and deposited her inside.

"A coat on," she finished lamely.

"And that's just the way I wanted it," he told her. A swim in the Hudson would have suited him better. He pushed her toward the bed. "Hop back in there before your feet freeze to the floor."

Skye didn't have to be encouraged twice. She fairly dived into the bed. She thrust her feet under the mound of bedclothes and rubbed them back and forth against the mattress. "Why did you go out there?" she asked.

Walker turned the chair by the fire so it faced the bed. He sat down. "It's not important."

Disappointed, she didn't look at him. Did he think she couldn't understand or did he just not want her to know? Either way, it seemed something of an insult. "I've been reading," she said, changing the subject.

"I noticed. You were absorbed when I came in."

"Absorbed?" she asked, puzzled. The small vertical line between her brows deepened as she considered this. She remembered looking up as soon as she heard him. When she glanced at Walker, he was smiling faintly.

"I was here a minute, maybe two, before you noticed me."

Skye wasn't certain she liked that. "You should have made yourself known," she said.

"I wasn't hiding."

That was true enough. She also remembered he'd been scowling when she'd looked up. She hadn't considered until now that his mood could have been related to something she'd done. Skye looked at him more closely, but his features revealed little about the nature

Get 4 FREE Books!

We created our convenient Home Subscription Service so you'll be sure to have the hottest new romances delivered each month right to your doorstep—usually before they are available in book stores. Just to show you how convenient the Zebra Home Subscription Service is, we would like to send you 4 FREE Kensington Choice Historical Romances. The books are worth up to $24.96, but you only pay $1.99 for shipping and handling. There's no obligation to buy additional books—ever!

Save Up To 30% With Home Delivery!

Accept your FREE books and each month we'll deliver 4 brand new titles as soon as they are published. They'll be yours to examine FREE for 10 days. Then if you decide to keep the books, you'll pay the preferred subscriber's price (up to 30% off the cover price!), plus shipping and handling. Remember, you are under no obligation to buy any of these books at any time! If you are not delighted with them, simply return them and owe nothing. But if you enjoy Kensington Choice Historical Romances as much as we think you will, pay the special preferred subscriber rate and save over $8.00 off the cover price!

PLACE
STAMP
HERE

KENSINGTON CHOICE
Zebra Home Subscription Service, Inc.
P.O. Box 5214
Clifton NJ 07015-5214

of his thoughts. Even his smile had faded. "What did you do with your day?"

Walker removed the studs from his cuffs and carefully rolled his shirtsleeves to his elbows. "I delivered some letters to the post in Baileyboro for Mr. Parnell."

Her brows rose a fraction. "You left me alone here?"

"I didn't have much choice. I told you I had the only keys to this room. You were safe."

"I didn't think I wasn't safe," she said, a trifle stiffly. "I can take care of myself. I'm just surprised you thought so."

He didn't try to humor her. "I also asked Hank to keep an eye on things. Parnell knew it, too."

Knowing that it was a predictable response didn't stop Skye from bristling. Her back stiffened, her shoulders straightened, and her eyes flashed as she prepared to challenge him. None of it had the desired effect. Instead of putting Walker in his place, it drew him right out of his chair. His long-legged rolling stride covered the distance to the bed in the space of a heartbeat. Skye raised her face, but the defiance vanished from her posture and the expression in her eyes softened.

Walker grasped her upper arms and pulled her to a kneeling position. He bent his head and kissed her. Skye offered no resistance. Her lips were soft and pliant, returning the fullness of his kiss measure for measure. Her hands had fallen naturally against his chest and now they stole higher and clasped him at the back of the neck. Her fingers tugged on the tawny strands of hair at his nape and the kiss hardened as if she'd pulled on some responsive cord. She murmured her pleasure against his mouth as he lowered her to the mattress.

Walker pushed aside the mound of blankets. Most of them fell on the floor as his body covered Skye's. She arched against him. The sole of her foot rubbed along the length of his calf. Her hands left his hair and slipped between their bodies again, this time at the level of his waist. Skye's fingers drew out Walker's shirttails until she could slide her hands under the fabric and rest her palms against his skin.

He pushed at her gown, raising it to her thighs. The petticoats bunched and Skye moaned softly, sharing his urgency when he tugged at her drawers. She lifted her hips and then she could feel the heat of his hand on her inner thigh, on her bare flesh. He was pulling at his own clothes then and she was undoing buttons on her bodice. Her breasts were laid open to him, the nipples hard and aching. His mouth closed over one. Skye cried out with the fierce pleasure of it. Her thighs parted, and when he raised his head to look at her, she nodded once and drew her palms along his arms as he came into her.

He watched her closely, saw her draw in her lower lip as he settled against her. He knew he should withdraw, pleasure her in another way, but he wanted her now, like this, and he didn't think he had the strength to be anything but selfish in taking his own pleasure. He held himself still as long as he was able. She gripped him so tightly, so smoothly, and so much without seeming to be aware of it, that she contracted around him. He raised his hips and thrust into her again. He heard her breath catch, felt the tips of her fingers press into his back, and he willed her to look at him and tell him it was no more than she could bear.

She knew what he needed to hear. "It's all right," she said, on a thread of sound. "I want this."

Walker realized he was incapable of protecting Skye from her own willfulness. His mouth lowered over hers and engaged her tongue in the same intimate dance as their bodies. He felt her rise up to meet him, arching into his thrust and giving to him what he could not give to her. She held him tightly, and when pleasure shuddered through him, she continued to hold him though he was certain she had known none of it herself.

His breathing was still ragged when he moved away from her and sat up. He was surprised that she seemed reluctant to let him go. Walker righted his trousers, made a haphazard attempt to tuck in his shirttail, then slid off the bed.

He ran a hand through his hair as he turned to look back at her. Skye was sitting up. She had already pushed her gown modestly around her curled legs and was fastening a few buttons on her bodice.

"I'm sorry." They said the words simultaneously, then frowned at each other. "Why are you sorry?" Again the words were spoken at the same time. They both opened their mouths to answer, then closed them abruptly. Neither of them spoke for a moment.

Walker was able to draw out the silence longer than Skye. She pulled on a pillow and hugged in front of her, using it like a shield. Her nervous fingers plucked one corner. "I *did* want to," she said quietly, not looking at him now. She added quickly, "So don't think that I didn't." She risked a glance at him. "But I don't think I'm very good at it. So . . . that's what I'm sorry about. I'm not sure I'll be wanting to do it with you anymore." She looked at him frankly now, her embarrassment fading in light of her admission, and thought that confession was probably good for the soul. "Do you know I haven't the faintest idea what to call it?" she said. "I mean, making love is a bit presumptuous— not the act, though I'm sure it can be presumptuous also— but I was referring to the phrasing. And the other descriptive words I know are either scientific or vulgar. That doesn't make it easy to discuss, does it?"

Walker simply stared at her, fascinated.

"Obviously it doesn't," she said, "or you would have something to say yourself."

Still staring at her, Walker sat down slowly.

Skye rubbed her nose with her fingertips. "You're doing it again," she said. "Staring at me. Do I have something on my nose?"

He shook his head.

A strand of hair had fallen across Skye's forehead. Exasperated, she blew it out of the way. "Well, what *is* it?"

Walker felt poleaxed by emotion. He could have bent double with the power of it and still not have relieved the stunning pressure in his chest. He had never struggled harder to hide his hand. "You," he said finally. The single word was lightly said, almost tossed out, with none of the intensity he felt framing it. "Just you."

Skye considered again that she must seem very young to him, what with her mouth running ahead of her thoughts. She sank back a little and hugged the pillow tighter.

"You make me forget that you're not so experienced as you would have me believe," he said.

Skye didn't blush. She flamed. It was all she could do not to press her hands to her cheeks.

"I know you wanted to make love," he said. Unlike Skye, Walker didn't digress on the appropriateness of the word. He could have told her it fit perfectly for what he had had in mind. "I should have thought that you might not be ready. You were still tender from this morning, and I shouldn't have pressed. I didn't mean to hurt you. That's why I said I was sorry— not because you did something wrong." He raised one eyebrow and gave her a lopsided, self-effacing smile. "You should expect less of yourself, Skye Dennehy, and a little more of me."

"Oh," she said softly, blinking once as if coming out of a trance. Her cheeks were still warm but the color was fading nicely. Her grip on the pillow loosened a little. "The beginning is always very good."

"The beginning," he repeated drily.

"The kissing."

"Aaah," he said. "You like the kissing."

She nodded. "And the touching."

He considered that. "You've changed your mind. It wasn't always that way."

"I know." She frowned, puzzled by the revelation herself. "Perhaps it's because I'm touching you, too."

Thinking about it made Walker shift uncomfortably in his chair. It was sublime torture to be halfway across the room from her and listen to her talk about what she had done to him. He could feel her hands on his skin, the hard muscles of his abdomen retracting as her exploring fingers dipped below his trousers. He forced himself to meet her eyes and not watch the absent, idle movements of her hands on the pillow. "Perhaps," he said.

Skye's hands stilled a moment. "Not long before I came here, in fact, the same night we had our encounter in the park, a man— a robber— broke into my home. He tied me up while he searched for some things, and before he released me, he knelt beside me on the couch and . . . and touched me. His fingers were very light on my face, thén my neck . . . my breasts."

Skye's voice was just a whisper now and Walker was straining to hear her. She shivered. "I was blindfolded and gagged. And with no way to see, I didn't know where his touch would come next. In my room the other night, it was like that again. I don't know reality from the memory anymore. I don't understand about the touching, but it seems different with you." With visible effort she drew herself out of her reverie. She wondered if she should have told Walker at all.

Walker correctly read the question in her eyes. "You should have told me about it before now." But even he didn't know when would have been a good time. To hide some of his confusion and work off some of his anger, Walker got up and stirred the flames. After he had added more firewood, he went to the armoire and took out Skye's nightgown. He handed it to her, then went about preparing for bed himself. "I would have understood your fear better." At least, he hoped he would have. It wouldn't have stopped him from wanting her. Or probably from taking her. But he would have liked to have known. "I can understand an intruder better than a ghost."

Skye shrugged into her nightgown, and as she had the night before, removed her clothes from under cover of it.

Walker noted her actions and smiled to himself. It was a bit like closing the stable door after the horses were out, but he didn't raise the issue. Skye wasn't looking too pleased by his comment about the ghost. He turned back the lamp and picked up the fallen covers, snapping them smartly across the bed. Skye helped make the bed from inside it, tucking the covers between the mattress and frame. When they were finished, she raised one corner and invited Walker to slip between the blankets and sheet. She lay on her back while he rolled on his side and raised himself up on one elbow.

Firelight touched her profile. He wanted to run his index finger along the bridge of her nose, pass it lightly across her lips. He refrained. "Tell me about the intruder," he said instead.

"There's not much to tell."

"You said he broke into your home. Where was that?"

Skye hadn't realized she'd made that slip. She rectified it now. "I meant the Marshalls. That was my home then."

Walker simply accepted the information. "How did you happen to run into him? Or did he run into you?"

"I ran into him," she said. "It was after midnight. I heard a noise and went to investigate."

Walker had no difficulty believing that. "It didn't occur to you to wake someone?"

"No," she said simply. "It didn't occur to me. It could have been anything."

Walker could hear the edge of anger in her voice. She didn't like defending herself to him. He brushed a lock of hair from her temple with his knuckle. "But it wasn't anything," he said. "I don't like to think I might never have met you." She glanced sideways at him, passing judgment on his sincerity. When he saw that she was guarded but somewhat mollified, he asked, "How did you get away?"

"He let me go. He never found what he was looking for there. I think he decided it would be in my— in Mr. Marshall's offices."

"Then he wasn't looking to steal the silver or Mrs. Marshall's jewelry."

"Heavens, no. He was rifling through Mr. Marshall's desk when I came around. I could hear him going through the papers."

A muscle worked in Walker's jaw. "When you came around?" he repeated.

She nodded. "There was a struggle initially. Not much of one, though. He got the knife almost immediately, and when he clamped a hand over my mouth, I just couldn't breathe. I wasn't smart enough then to pretend to faint, like I did today with Parnell. That night I actually fainted."

Walker leaned over her. "Knife?" he asked.

"You don't think I'd go to investigate a noise empty-handed," she said. "It could have been anything."

He shook his head and silently gave thanks to her overworked, underappreciated guardian angel. "You used that same argument to explain why you hadn't wakened anyone," he told her drily. "I don't think you can use it twice."

A slight smile hovered on her lips. "Is that a rule?"

He remembered she liked the kissing, and he very much wanted to do it. Walker pressed his mouth to hers and let it linger just a fraction too long to be a peck. "It should be," he said. He wanted to hear more of her story. "What happened when he let you go?"

"He only untied my hands. I suppose I should have pulled the blindfold off or taken away the gag to scream, but I wasn't thinking about either of those things. All I could think about was wanting to hurt him for taking those liberties with me. I drew back my hand and slapped his face. I don't think he was expecting it, because I found my mark."

Walker heard the satisfaction in her voice. "I could teach you to do a little more damage with the flat of your hand," he said, "than simply deliver a slap."

Skye remembered the blows he had struck to the men in the park and how he had disarmed Parnell. "You'd teach me that?" she asked.

He nodded.

"When?"

The question caught him off guard. "Someday."

She turned her head a little toward him, wondering if he meant it. It didn't matter. Skye had sworn to herself she wouldn't ask for anything beyond the hours they had remaining. His agreement to teach her "some day" held the promise of a future, or perhaps it meant nothing at all. "I'd like to learn," was what she said.

He imagined her completing Tai-Chi's Great Circle. She would be graceful, every gesture flowing into the next, her body lithe and supple. In the beginning she would want to rush the movements, hurrying to Touch the South Wind or Take the Blossom. She would have to cultivate patience and let her spirit flow in harmony with her surroundings, rather than in opposition to it. And in the end, she would be the stronger for it. "Someday," he said again.

Walker's hand rested lightly on her shoulder. His thumb massaged the curve of her arm. "Did the intruder ever come back?" he asked.

She wished he would kiss her again. "Not that I know of," she said. "Not while I was there."

"Did it have something to do with why you left the Marshalls'?"

"Some," she said. Her mouth flattened a little and signaled her refusal to answer more questions. It wasn't fair, she thought, that he was able to ask so many and she could barely get one in edgewise. "What time do I leave tomorrow?"

"The train leaves at ten. That's something else I did in Baileyboro today." When she looked at him questioningly, he explained, "Purchased your ticket." He didn't add that he had bought a fare for himself. Her seat was with the other passengers. He had had to make special arrangements to ride in the mail car. He couldn't risk her moving through the cars and running into him.

"Then I owe you some money," she said.

"No. Parnell paid for it."

Under the circumstances, it was the very least he could have done, Skye thought. She was silent, considering what her father would say when she arrived on the doorstep. He would be pleased about the engine, of course, and probably surprised that she had accomplished the thing so swiftly. He would be disappointed that she didn't have it with her and perhaps even a little frustrated that her success had not been at the price of sheer boredom. She sighed. There was no predicting Jay Mac's response. When he discovered she was not returning to school, he was likely to consider his grand scheme one of his few personal failures. He wouldn't thank her for that.

Walker watched the play of emotions on Skye's face. "What is it?" he asked, wondering at her troubled expression.

"Hmmm?"

He repeated his question.

"Just thinking," she said, shrugging a little. "Just because you've lived in my pockets doesn't mean I'll let you live in my thoughts."

He knew what she meant, but there was a deeper meaning to her words that she wasn't denying, either. It was as if she was planning intentionally to wipe him from her memory. Was he so forgettable, or would she have to work at it?

Walker's fingers shifted from the curve of her arm to her collarbone. Tugging at the fabric of her gown, he was able to pull it aside to sweep his fingertips along her bare skin. He felt her small shiver and recognized it wasn't one of pleasure. "Does this bother you?" he asked.

It did. "A little," she said.

Walker's fingers stopped their light trailing across her skin. Twisting away he lighted the lamp at their bedside. When he returned he laid the back of his hand against her cheek. His caress was soft, barely a touch at all, and he watched Skye's reaction. She turned into him like a kitten. He didn't have to ask if the light made it better for her. His answer came in the way she responded to his touch.

His knuckles brushed the line of her jaw, the underside of her chin, and dipped to the base of her throat. He bent his head, his mouth hovering just above hers, but when he kissed her, it wasn't on the lips. She made a small sound of distress and desire as he ducked his head and touched her neck with his mouth, just below her ear. The heady fragrance of her hair mixed with the fragrance of her skin.

His lips trailed along her throat, rested in the curve, and sipped gently, tasting and teasing. Her fingers moved restlessly through his hair, hesitating only once as his attention shifted lower.

At the open collar of her nightgown, Walker tracked kisses between her breasts. He didn't work the gown off her shoulders to kiss her breasts. When his mouth closed over her nipple, it was through the fabric, his tongue laving a damp circle over the rose tip and the material causing its own unique sensation of pleasure against her skin. She moved restlessly under him, impatient for the suck of his mouth on her other breast. Her fingers curled harder in his hair and her breath caught when his lips closed over the distended rosebud.

The bedclothes tangled in their legs again and were pushed aside. She rubbed her leg along the length of his and he laid his hands on her hips, raising her nightgown while his mouth moved to the underside of her breast. He paused there briefly, then moved lower still, trailing down across her abdomen, making a small indentation in the fabric of her gown at her navel. Her flat belly contracted in anticipation of his touch. Her fingers drifted from his hair to her sides and caught the sheet beneath her, twisting it hard when he laid his mouth on the soft, sensitive flesh of her inner thigh.

He raised his head as he felt sensation jolt her. "Open for me, Skye." She was tense and tight and not sure she wanted him to do this thing to her. Watching her, gauging her reaction, he stroked her thigh with soft, sweet insistence. "Open for me," he said again. He raised himself up and kissed her breast, then her throat. His hand slipped between her thighs as his mouth brushed her lips. "Open."

Her mouth parted and she accepted his kiss. Her legs

parted and she accepted the caress of his fingers. And later she accepted the caress of his mouth, the stroking of his tongue, and the pleasure that came with this new intimacy.

He held her while she shuddered in his arms, liking the flush that stole across her skin and the dark, sleepy arousal that widened the centers of her eyes. When she was aware that he was staring at her, she turned away and pushed down her nightgown, embarrassed by her abandon, a bit shamed that she had let him do the things he had. He touched her chin and drew her face back to him. "You didn't do anything wrong," he said, lifting the blankets over them.

The expression in her green eyes was anxious. She worried her lower lip wondering how to explain it to him. "I'm not certain I should enjoy it quite so much," she finally blurted out. "And I have no idea what to call it."

He blinked. After a moment, repressed laughter became a pressure in his chest and a wide, wicked smile deepened his single dimple. He kissed her hard on the mouth. "It's part of making love, and you can call it that." He laid his mouth near her ear. "Or you can call it this." He whispered in her ear, then raised his head to watch her expression. She was screwing up her face with a charming lack of guile.

"I can't say I like the sound of that," she said.

"I didn't think you would," he said gravely. "I simply offered it as an alternative."

Skye knew he was laughing at her, but she found she didn't mind. She had never taken herself quite so seriously as Mary Michael or Mary Renee. She was also more likely to see the humor in everyday situations than either Mary Margaret or Mary Francis.

"What are you thinking?"

Skye wondered why he asked. Then she realized she was smiling. "About my sisters," she said.

"Sisters," he repeated. "Perhaps I should be worried about your brothers. Do you have any of those?"

"No. And that's the last thing I'm telling you." She snuggled against him, curving her body to his. "Besides, you should be *very* worried about what the Marys will do to you." She brought his arm around her waist and held it there. Skye closed her eyes.

The Marys. He wondered what she meant by that.

In the morning, Walker left Skye alone while she prepared to leave. Annie brought her breakfast, but most of it remained uneaten on the tray. The ache in Skye's throat made it difficult to swallow, and the knot in her stomach, like a fist clenched around her middle, made her think she couldn't have held food down anyway.

No one else came to see her, not that Skye expected it. She was rather surprised Walker had entrusted Annie with the key to their room. She doubted he was going to give it to anyone else.

It was while Skye was packing that she missed her small notepad. It wasn't so important, she thought, because it had only information about the house. She'd never really had time to explore the way she wanted to, or complete her drawings. Once Walker had become her shadow, she hadn't even given much thought to proving or disproving her theory about the house's peculiar design. But it bothered her that she couldn't find the pad. She couldn't recall keeping it anywhere but in the pockets of her aprons, and she had only two of those.

After checking both, Skye made a thorough search of all her gowns. She ran her hand along the bottom of her valise and her trunk, thinking it might have fallen in a rip in the liner. The last time she remembered

having it she had still been staying in the other bedroom. If it was anywhere, it was still in there.

In spite of that, Skye looked under the bed, in the
dresser, beneath the hearth rug, and in Walker's armoire. That was how she found Parnell's gun. The Colt
was lying at the back of the wardrobe and Skye's fingers
froze when she touched the cool blue-gray steel. She
pulled it out cautiously and checked to see if it was
loaded. It wasn't.

Releasing a breath she hadn't known she was holding,
Skye began to put it back. She stopped halfway, drew
her hand out again, and placed the gun at the bottom
of her valise. She had no particular use for the Colt.
Her own preference was a five-shot Remington .22, but
removing the Colt from the Granville mansion seemed
a better idea than leaving it behind.

Skye's sketch of the engine was in the pocket where
she remembered leaving it. She stopped worrying about
the notepad, thankful she hadn't lost what was truly
important, and unfolded the paper with her picture. It
still didn't look like much of anything, but her father
had men working for him who might understand what
she had drawn. Her sister Rennie would probably be
able to figure it out.

Skye refolded the paper and noticed now that it
closed neatly along creased lines. Staring at it, she
frowned. She thought back, trying to recall the circumstances of drawing it. Skye rose from her kneeling position in front of the wardrobe and sat at Walker's desk.
She took out another piece of paper and went through
the motions of sketching on it. Her head jerked up as
she remembered Walker's approach, his hand on the
door, and the sound of the key in the lock. She grabbed
the paper and thrust it hastily into her pocket.

Skye looked down at her hands. The paper wasn't
folded like the one she had found. She had been in too

much of a hurry to crease it neatly. She looked at her drawing again. It was her sketch, her writing. That, at least, wasn't different.

The only conclusion Skye could reach was that someone else had seen it. Someone else had folded it and put it back in her pocket.

Walker Caine was that person. He had to be.

Skye wondered how concerned she should be that Walker had seen her work. He hadn't thought it was important enough to take away from her; on the other hand, she didn't know who else he might have shown it to, or if he had copied it himself. If Parnell had entertained any doubts about sending Skye away, the sketch would have tipped the scales against her.

Skye placed the sketch in the bottom of her trunk beside the gun. She replaced her folded clothing in the trunk and closed the lid. Skye was finishing with her valise when Walker came in. The mantel clock had just struck nine.

"We should be going," he told her.

Skye nodded, glancing around the room for anything she might have missed. Her hairbrush was still on Walker's dresser. She picked it up by the ebony handle and dropped it into her valise. The top of his dresser looked strangely bare without her pots of cream and scents and powders.

"That's it, then," he said after a moment.

"That's it." She felt awkward. She smoothed the folds of her dove-gray day dress.

Walker's weight shifted from one foot to the other. "You take the valise," he told her. "Hank's outside with the carriage. Send him up to help me with this trunk."

"All right." She picked up the valise. He handed her her coat, hat, and muff. Skye found she couldn't meet Walker's eyes as she hurried out of the room. She was fighting the urge to cry.

Skye had composed herself by the time Walker joined her in the carriage. It swayed as he climbed in and took the seat opposite her. A moment later she heard Hank command the horses, and then they were under way.

Skye stared out the carriage window. The glare of cold winter sunlight made her squint. It helped her keep tears in check.

"Where are you going to go?" Walker asked.

She had been dreading this moment. It was a double-edged sword. His question proved that he cared something for her, perhaps that he would even want to find her someday, and she had no choice but to lie to him. "It won't take me long to find another position," she said. "I have a little money. I'll probably stay at the St. Mark's."

"A hotel?" he asked. "Not with your sisters?"

"No, not with my sisters."

"Won't they take you in?"

"They would, but I won't ask them. There are some things I need to do on my own."

Walker felt her closing the subject on her family and he still hadn't learned enough to suit him. They rode in silence for more than a mile. "Don't you have anything you want to ask me?"

A dozen questions and not one that she would give a voice to. She shook her head.

He frowned. "Is it so hard for you to ask something of someone else?"

"Not so hard," she said. "But I promised myself I wouldn't and I won't." It was all part of being an adventuress. She had to be able to walk away.

Walker knew that he was going to see her again, and he knew how soon, but she didn't know that. Her stubborn streak was infuriating. "What if there's a child, Skye? Had you thought about that?"

She stopped staring out the window and turned to

look at him. "I'm a bastard," she said. "Of course I thought of it."

"And?"

"And what?" she asked. "I don't know what you want me to say. I knew the possible consequences of lying with you." Of lying *to* you, she could have added. "I chose to do it anyway."

"So did I. If there's a child, I want to know about it."

"So you can do what? Give me money? Marry me? Set me up in a little apartment? Or maybe you just want to keep track of your bastards."

He flinched a little at her cold analysis. "I don't have any children," he told her. "And I don't intend to have any bastards."

"Then it's a good thing I'm not having your child, because I wouldn't have your name."

Walker managed to hold onto the threads of his temper. "This is ridiculous," he said under his breath. "It will be weeks before you know one way or the other." He looked at her sharply. "Won't it?"

She shrugged. "I'll know when I know. It doesn't have to be your concern."

"Where do you get these ideas?" he asked. "Why would you think I wouldn't want to know?"

"The point is, I don't know what you think. I don't know much about you, and you haven't done anything to encourage me to find out." She paused, waiting to see if he would tell her something now. "In fact, you've done quite the opposite."

Knowing that she was right didn't make it any easier to take. "I told you before I was more used to keeping secrets than sharing them."

"And I accepted that," she said calmly, quietly. "Now it's for you to accept that I may want to keep some secrets of my own."

He didn't like it, but there was nothing he could do

about it. Baileyboro came into view as the carriage rounded the last curve in the rutted road. The train station was at the far end of the village and out of Walker's line of sight. He suspected there would only be one or two people waiting on the platform. Most of the traffic for the line came from the north at Albany and south from the city. Baileyboro was an insignificant stop on the route but vital to the villagers.

Walker handed Skye her ticket. Parnell had told him to give Skye his compliments, but Walker hadn't relayed the message. He tried to put himself in Skye's place and wondered if uncertainty would have driven him to press an argument the way she had done. Did it make parting easier for her?

Hank Ryder opened the carriage door and put out his hand to Skye. "Sorry it's come to this," he told her as he helped her down. "Didn't think you were given a fair shake."

"Thank you, Hank." She smiled. "I'd like one now, though."

At first he didn't understand what she meant, then he felt her squeezing his hand. He chuckled, showing this wide, gap-toothed grin and pumped her hand enthusiastically.

"When you're finished . . ." Walker said drily, not bothering to complete his sentence.

Hank flushed and removed his hand. Skye pressed her own into the muff she carried and hurried toward the platform. The wind was strong enough to make whitecaps on the river. Chunks of ice dotted the surface and were trapped by outcroppings of rock. As they traveled along the river's edge, the view from the train would be bleak. It would fit Skye's mood perfectly.

Walker joined her on the platform with her baggage while Hank returned to wait at the carriage. In the distance Skye heard the approach of the train. She continued to stare at the river, but Walker turned to look down the tracks. His eyes lingered on Skye's stoic profile instead.

"I didn't want to argue with you," he said.

"I know."

Sunlight glinted in her red hair. The wind ruffled the fringe of fur on her hat and the fringe of hair on her forehead. She wouldn't look at him. He wondered if she couldn't.

They both stepped back as the train pulled up to the platform. Smoke and cinders clouded the air. A few minutes later Skye's bag and trunk were taken by a porter. It was only then that she turned to Walker. Not knowing what else to do, she held out her hand.

Walker stared at it, then slowly shook his head. His eyes signaled his intent and he gave her time to pull away. She merely raised her face and offered up her mouth. He kissed her long and hard and deep, and when he released her, they were both shaken by the strength of it.

"Goodbye, Mary Schyler," he said softly.

She didn't speak, turning instead toward the porter who was waiting at the door to her car.

Walker watched her board and saw her take her seat next to a window on the far side of the car. She wouldn't look in his direction, and then someone took a seat on the bench nearest him and blocked Skye from his view.

He hesitated a moment longer, then headed for the carriage to get his things. Riding in the mail car didn't promise to be a very comfortable trip. Knowing he would see Skye at the other end, even if she wouldn't see him, was the only thing that made the prospect bearable.

Ten

She wasn't there.

Walker had disembarked as soon the train had arrived in Central Station. The platforms were crowded, as they always were, but Walker situated himself on a bench where he could see all the activity. Anonymous faces didn't escape his attention now. He noticed the young mothers with their children in tow, the harried businessmen adjusting their identical derbies with identical gestures. He watched a woman being pulled along the platform's edge by a pair of small dogs. A flower vendor tried to entice all of them to buy her wares. No one he didn't see got off Northeast Rail's no. 49 engine or its cars.

And Skye wasn't there.

Walker couldn't believe it. Had he given his intention away in some manner so that she could deliberately thwart him, or had he made some greenhorn mistake that allowed her to go by unnoticed?

He was traveling light and was thankful he'd had the foresight to do that much right. He tossed his valise to a porter and asked for it to be checked at the ticket counter. He'd worry about getting it back later.

Boarding the first car, Walker worked his way through the train, checking the aisles and under the seats. The train was virtually empty. There were only a few stops south of the city before the train would return to the station and go north again. Each of the four passenger cars had less than a half-dozen people in it. None of the faces belonged to Skye Dennehy.

The conductor caught up with Walker as he finished surveying the last car. "Here now, what do you think you're doing?" he asked. He had gray hair, and thick, wiry sideburns filled out his sunken cheeks. His black cap was perched on his head and he had drawn himself up to his full height of five foot seven to confront Walker. "If you're riding with this line, you'll have to purchase a ticket."

"I'm getting off here," Walker said. "And I'm looking for someone. She had a ticket for this car. She got on at Baileyboro."

The conductor nodded. "I know just who you mean," he said. "Lovely young lady with red hair."

Walker let his hopes rise. "Did you see her get off?"

"Of course I did." He rubbed his chin with his thumb and forefinger. "Wouldn't count myself much service to Jay Mac Worth if I didn't notice things like that. She left the train at West Point."

Walker swore softly. "But West Point was only a few stops south of Baileyboro."

"As far as I know, it still is," the conductor said. "And that's where she got off."

"Her baggage?"

"Went with her, I imagine. That's the usual way."

Walker didn't acknowledge the conductor's amusement. He couldn't believe he had been so short sighted as not to have anticipated this outcome. He should have observed the disembarking of all the passengers at every stop. "West Point," he muttered. "Damn." He thrust his hand in his pocket and pulled out some bills. "That's where I want to go."

The conductor pointed to the exit and beyond that

to the station ticket counter. "You'll have to go there first."

Walker looked at the line of people waiting for tickets. "How long do I have?"

"This train leaves in ten minutes, but you could wait until the return trip. Number 49's coming back this way in two hours, then we'll be going north."

He nodded. He was hungry and angry, and one was feeding the other. "All right," he said. "I'll take the return ticket."

The conductor watched him go. When he saw Walker was in line, he went to the door opposite the exit and opened it. Skye was standing on the tracks below, out of sight of the station's platform.

"He came looking for you," he told her. "Just like you said he would."

Her eyes were anxious. "What did you tell him, Mr. Pennybacker?"

"That you got off at West Point."

"Did he believe you?"

"Must have. He's buying a ticket to go there now." He scratched his chin thoughtfully. "Are you in some kind of trouble, Miss Dennehy? The kind of trouble I should report to your father?"

There were definitely drawbacks to traveling with Northeast Rail. While her acquaintance with Mr. Pennybacker permitted her to elude Walker, the conductor was not going to ignore his responsibilities to John MacKenzie Worth.

"My father doesn't need to know anything about this," she said. "And he won't thank you for telling him. He'll probably kill the messenger."

Mr. Pennybacker was skeptical. "I'll want to think about that," he said. "You'd better see to your baggage now. He asked about it. Might be that he'll even check to see if it got off the train with you."

Skye's shoulders sagged. She hadn't considered that. "Will you help me?" she asked. While he was hesitating, Skye went on, "Find someone to deliver my things to the Worth Building without alerting Mr. Caine. You can do that, can't you, Mr. Pennybacker?"

"I can do it," he said. "Can't say if it's a good thing to do." All the childhood pranks Skye and her sisters had perpetrated on the conductors and porters and engineers and brakemen of Northeast Rail were being contemplated now.

Divining Mr. Pennybacker's thoughts, Skye said, "I'm not eleven any longer. Anyway, it was Rennie who put me up to climbing on the roof of the caboose." She didn't add the train had been moving at the time or that Rennie's dare had been for her to walk the length of the train from caboose to engine. Mr. Pennybacker obviously remembered the incident with enough clarity to question her common sense now. "Please?" she asked.

He rubbed his chin again. "All right. I'll take care of it. Now, you'd best get moving." He pointed across the tracks to a door only used by station workmen and rail employees. "Take that exit. He won't see you if you stay on the rail side. And be careful not to fall on the tracks."

Skye's smile was grateful as she hurried away. "You won't regret this, Mr. Pennybacker," she called over her shoulder.

Watching Skye almost trip over the rail ties in her haste, Mr. Pennybacker shook his head and adjusted his cap. "I already do, Mary Schyler."

The Worth Building was on Broadway near Ann Street, not far from the white marble palace that was home to the New York *Herald* and the dark monolith that housed the *Chronicle*. The location of the Worth Building so close to Publishers' Square was no accident. John MacKenzie

Worth knew the power publishers wielded in the city. It was better knowing what they were up to than pretending their editorials and pointed political drawings had no influence with the public. As one of the robber barons, along with Vanderbilt and Gould and Rockefeller, Jay Mac found his railroad enterprise was the target of some new legislation or investigation with infuriating regularity. The *Herald* and the *Chronicle* invariably knew about it first. Jay Mac read the accounts while the ink was still wet and the paper still warm.

He lowered the paper he was reading now and swiveled in his burgundy leather chair. He faced the door from across the wide expanse of a massive mahogany desk. Had Jay Mac glanced down, his own face would have been reflected in the polished surface. He would have seen he was scowling. The expression was there in part because of what he had been reading in the *Chronicle*. It had deepened when he'd heard the commotion outside his office.

His normally unflappable, if rather supercilious, secretary seemed to be unable to handle the current situation. Jay Mac folded the paper neatly and dropped it on his desk. He was about to get up when he recognized the other voice arguing with his secretary.

Jay Mac's deep tones carried easily to the anteroom. "I'll see her," he called. The door to his office opened almost immediately. It was his secretary's head that appeared in the crack. Jay Mac could sympathize with Wilson's decidedly frazzled look. "She's like the tide, Wilson. You can't hold her back. Show her in."

Jay Mac's offices were on the third floor and Skye had vaulted the stairs two at a time. She was only just regaining her breath when Wilson ushered her inside. Skye wrinkled her nose. "Could that man be any more officious?" she asked her father, after the door was closed behind her.

"He's doing what I pay him to do."

Skye's hat was slightly askew. She removed it and her coat and dropped them both in one of the chairs that was situated in front of Jay Mac's desk. "And what exactly is that?" she asked.

"He protects me."

"From your own daughters?"

"No one else's daughters give me any trouble."

Skye laughed. "Shall I fix you something to drink?" She pointed to the small sideboard in Jay Mac's office that held a selection of liquor.

"Will I need it?" He leaned back in his chair. Even after years of not smoking, the leather still held the faint aroma of cigars. He breathed deeply now, but didn't consider reaching for the teakwood box on the corner of his desk. The Havanas inside were for special guests. In this case he didn't count his daughter among them.

In response to her father's question, Skye shrugged. She poured a small sherry for herself. "You can't imagine how cold it is outside," she said. "I couldn't get a hansom at the station. Every one of them was occupied. I had to walk almost the entire way."

Jay Mac considered his daughter's trek from the station at twilight with no companion. He didn't like to think he was old-fashioned, but there were certain conventions he still thought should be observed. It was a miracle in his mind that Skye hadn't been taken for a prostitute and been accosted. "I think I'll have that drink, after all," he said. He could justify that it was the end of his workday . . . at least, his office workday. The leather satchel under his desk was filled with documents, requests, and proposals he had not had an opportunity to scan. He had actually been looking forward to sitting in his study this evening, reviewing the papers while Moira read or did needlework. His wife's presence alone would lighten the load.

Looking at Skye, Jay Mac adjusted his spectacles. "Make it a double."

She smiled and added an extra splash of Scotch to her father's glass, then put the drink on his desk and bent to kiss his cheek. She looked at his face. "Better," she said approvingly.

"Better?"

"You were scowling. It wasn't a very warm welcome."

Jay Mac's complexion reddened with embarrassment. He pointed to the folded paper. "Residual scowl," he said. "It wasn't meant for you."

That eased her mind. She sipped her sherry while she flipped over the paper. "Hmmm. The *Chronicle*. And Logan Marshall's a friend."

Jay Mac grunted. "He's your sister's friend. I wanted Mary Michael to work for the *Herald*, remember?"

"Still, he's always been fair with you."

That was true. Jay Mac could generally count on the *Chronicle* to be even-handed in its reporting. He removed his spectacles, rubbed the bridge of his nose, then replaced them. "Look at the editorial page."

Skye set down her glass and opened the paper. Logan Marshall's editorial was a scathing piece on the mayor's latest political blunder. She scanned the columns, looking for some mention of her father.

Watching her, Jay Mac pointed to the lower corner of the page. "There," he said. "The drawing."

The cartoon had nothing to do with Marshall's piece on the mayor. This was a separate issue. The artist's sketch included caricatures of Jay Mac, Andrew Carnegie, and J. P. Morgan. They were standing over an anonymous everyman who was tied to the tracks. The man's hat was labeled LABOR. In the background, an engine with Northeast Rail's markings was running full-tilt toward the hapless man.

"It's not very flattering, is it?" Skye said. Then, just

to tweak her father, she added, "I don't think the artist should have emphasized your nose that way. It's not your most outstanding feature." She refolded the paper, dropped it on the desk, and smiled innocently.

"I should have known better than to expect sympathy from you," he said. "You probably agree with the artist's estimation of my character."

"More than his caricature."

Jay Mac snorted.

Skye was sympathetic now. Her father had been painted with the same brush as Carnegie and Morgan, and it wasn't setting well with him. John MacKenzie Worth liked to think he was very much his own person and dealt fairly with the workers in his employ. "Have there been noises about a strike?" she asked.

"There are always noises," he told her. "Rennie and Jarret have had to deal with the threat of one in California."

"Did Morgan offer to finance you if the workers walk?"

Jay Mac nodded. "He'd own Northeast Rail if it came to that."

Skye could imagine Carnegie's advice. His response to striking steelworkers was to hire Pinkerton thugs. "You've been talking to both men?" she asked.

"Yes. Apparently someone at the *Chronicle* found out. The artist leaped to his own conclusions." He sighed. "There's no point in talking to Marshall about it. In general, there's no public support for striking workers. This sort of thing has to die its own death. Denial only makes me look guilty." He raised his drink and considered his daughter over the rim of his tumbler. "And what about you, Mary Schyler? Are you in trouble?"

Skye dropped into the chair across from his desk and grinned with disarming frankness. "Denial only makes me look guilty."

Jay Mac was hard pressed not to laugh. He swallowed some of his Scotch instead. "What's happened?"

"I was dismissed." She leaned forward, concerned, as her father choked on his drink. "Are you all right?"

He held up a hand and indicated she shouldn't get up. "I will be," he managed to get out, before coughing again. The spasm lasted a few seconds. When he was quite certain he was in control, he sipped his drink and eased the rawness in his throat. "I confess this is the one outcome I didn't anticipate, Skye. I thought you'd make a better show of it. It hasn't been a week." He shook his head, more in disappointment than disapproval. "Does your mother know?"

"I came directly here. I thought I should explain it to you first." She hesitated. "You do want to know, don't you?"

Jay Mac didn't necessarily agree with his daughters, but he had learned to hear them out. He realized he had been dangerously close to drawing his own conclusions about Skye's dismissal. "I want to know," he said.

Skye watched her father closely, gauging his reaction. "Jonathan Parnell made advances, and I demurred."

It would have been enough of an explanation for most fathers, but they weren't Skye's father. "Define 'demurred,' " he said.

"I held an open flame over some engine fuel and threatened to burn him alive."

Jay Mac nodded solemnly. "That's the definition that came to *my* mind."

"Mr. Parnell didn't think we would suit after that," she said gravely. "Frankly, neither did I." She could not divine the look in her father's eyes. "So I came home. Are you very put out with me?"

"Only that you didn't allow me the privilege of defending your honor myself."

"Then you didn't have it in your mind for me perhaps to become infatuated with Mr. Parnell?" Skye did not think her father was a good enough actor to feign such realistic surprise. "You didn't hope there'd be a proposal of some kind?" she asked.

Jay Mac cleared his throat gruffly. "It sounds as if there *was* a proposal," he said. "And not the sort that's to my liking."

"You know what I meant," she said. "A marriage proposal."

"What makes you think I'd entertain that notion?"

Skye ticked off her reasons on three fingers. "Mary Michael. Mary Renee. Mary Margaret. You'd have schemed for Mary Francis, but the Lord got her first." Her smile took the sting from her words.

He blustered a little but in the end conceded her point. "But I wasn't thinking about Jonathan Parnell and you."

Skye realized she believed him. "I'm glad. He and I would never have suited. I wasn't certain if you'd have realized it." She shook her head, clearing it of distasteful thoughts regarding her former employer. "We can leave for home as soon as my luggage arrives," she said.

"You had it delivered here?" he asked. "Skye? Are you certain you're quite all right?" In spite of her overt efforts to indicate otherwise there was something faintly anxious about Skye's demeanor. Jay Mac couldn't pinpoint the thing that made him wary. Her eyes were clear and calm. The set of her shoulders was relaxed. Her smile was disingenuous. Perhaps it was only that in the circumstances she shouldn't have appeared to have so few concerns, or perhaps it was only that her actions were peculiar. "Why would you have your things brought here?"

"Because the thing I wanted you to see is in my trunk," she said. It was the truth as far as it went. She hadn't decided what she wanted to tell her father about Walker Caine. She didn't know what she thought about his behavior herself. "No, it's not the engine," she added quickly. "I don't know what made you believe I could actually steal it."

"I don't think I used the word 'steal.' "

"Call it what you will, I couldn't have got it out of there on my own. It's much too big and heavy."

"Then you've seen it." Excitement edged his voice. "It really exists?"

She nodded. "It exists. Parnell invited me to see it." She didn't add that it had been the inventor's notion of foreplay. Skye could be frank with Jay Mac only to a certain point. "I sketched it as best I could. I thought perhaps someone here would know what to make of it."

Jay Mac's comment was cut off by his secretary's interruption. "What is it, Wilson?"

The secretary remained on the threshold of the office, barring entry to the two men who stood behind him. "These men are insisting Miss Dennehy wanted her trunk and valise delivered here."

In all the years she had known him, Skye didn't think that Wilson had ever called her anything but Miss Dennehy. His formality was absurd, but she had become used to it. "I did insist, Mr. Wilson. Have them bring my things in here."

The men lumbered in with the trunk and Skye tipped them. They were uncomfortable accepting a gratuity in front of the owner of the line until Jay Mac himself assured them it was fine. "Better it comes out of her pocket than mine," he told them. They grinned in unison, pocketed their money, and were herded out by Wilson. "That *was* your money, wasn't it?" Jay Mac asked.

"Honest wages," she said, kneeling in front of the trunk. She pushed back a lock of hair that had fallen across her cheek and tucked it behind her ear. "I was paid for my few days of work." Actually, she had been overpaid. She had supposed the extra money was meant to silence her. She had considered leaving it behind, but thought of a better use for it.

Skye opened the trunk and rooted around inside. Her hand came across Parnell's Colt first and she let it remain where it lay. Her father wouldn't necessarily thank her for telling him about it. She gave him her folded sketch instead.

Jay Mac opened it carefully. He studied it for a long time before he said, "This is very interesting, Skye."

Walker Caine was tired. It was dusk by the time he reached West Point. It hadn't taken him very long to realize that he had been lied to by Mr. Pennybacker. No one working at the small station recalled any woman of Skye Dennehy's description disembarking earlier in the day. Walker found it difficult to believe that Skye's flame-red hair wouldn't have aroused some notice. By the time Walker had finished asking his questions, No. 49 had already left for points north. He was forced to cool his heels for over three hours before another train arrived. He purchased a ticket back to the city, certain now that he had given up too easily.

"You look like hell."

Walker stirred in the stiff wooden chair he occupied and opened one eye. Logan Marshall was standing over him, holding a cup of coffee in his hands. "I don't suppose that's for me," he said.

"Not a chance." Logan turned to his secretary. "Bring Mr. Caine a cup, please. We'll be in my office." He turned the handle on his door. "Coming?"

Walker tipped his chair back on all four legs. "Right behind you." He stood, stretched, held back a groan. His muscles ached. There was a crick in his neck. He rubbed it as he followed the publisher into his office.

Looking around, he was comforted to see that some
things didn't change.

Logan Marshall's inner sanctum was proof that dis-
organization could be planned. Floor-to-ceiling book-
cases on either side of the room were stacked with
folders, documents, manuals, and the occasional book.
Photography equipment leaned in one corner. The surface of his desk was littered with notes and a wooden
tray was overflowing with copy to read. The competi-
tion's newspapers had already been delivered and were
stacked on the floor beside the door. When Walker
picked up some papers that were on the chair where
he intended to sit, Logan stopped him.

"Let me see those," the publisher said.

Walker held them up to Logan to scan.

"They go in the bookcase on your right," he said.
"Third shelf down."

Walker put them away. He stepped over a stack of
books on his way back to his chair. "I know a housekeeper who could make short work of this room."

"Only one?" Logan asked. He held up his hand. "Don't
mention any names. Simply knowing she's out there
frightens me. I like this office just the way it is." He sat
behind his desk as Walker's coffee arrived. He watched
as it was taken gratefully. "No interruptions," he told his
secretary. When Samuel Carson had left, Logan gave his
full attention to Walker. "Sam says he found you waiting
in the lobby when he came to work this morning."

"It was the middle of the night when I got here,"
Walker admitted.

Logan sipped his coffee. His eyes were a cool pewter
gray and their expression was shuttered now. His handsome face had a hard cast that made him look older when
he was a younger man and younger now that he had
reached his fortieth year. His dark hair was still high-

lighted by threads of copper with no sign of going to gray. "It's been . . . what? . . . two, maybe three years?"

"Almost four."

"God," he said feelingly. "How old were you then? Twenty-seven? Twenty-eight?"

Walker smiled. Logan had never inquired about his age. It was enough for the publisher to know that Walker came highly recommended. "I was twenty-four. But if it will make you feel any better, sir, I feel about ninety-four right now."

Logan rolled his eyes. "What will make me feel better is if you never call me 'sir' again."

"Very well. How is Mrs. Marshall?"

"Katy's fine. We're expecting another child in June."

"Congratulations."

Logan nodded briefly in acceptance. "I doubt you've come about anything related to either Katy or myself," he said. "And you still look like hell, so what can I do for you?"

"Actually, I've come about a housekeeper," he said.

Logan blinked and glanced around his office. "You were serious?"

"In a way. The woman I'm interested in says she used to work for you. I'm wondering if that's true."

Logan's coolly colored eyes narrowed now and he leaned back in his chair. "It's against my better judgment to tell you anything, but you'll have to at least give me her name."

"Mary Schyler Dennehy."

The publisher's features remained unchanged. "I see," he said. "And what would your interest in her be?"

"I'd rather not say."

"You'll have to. I'm feeling rather protective about Miss Dennehy."

"Then you know her."

"Yes."

Walker considered that. "Is she staying with you?"

"You'll have to tell me something more than you have to get an answer to that question."

"You're familiar with Jonathan Parnell?" Walker asked.

"I know *of* him. He's an inventor, isn't he?"

Walker knew Logan Marshall had the answer to that. For some reason the publisher was reluctant to give much away. Did he really feel *that* protective toward Skye, or was it something else entirely? "Do you have dealings with him?" he asked. "Business dealings?"

Logan didn't answer immediately. Finally, reluctantly, he said, "I've considered investigating him for the paper."

Walker swore softly. "Considered an investigation, or started one?"

"Preliminary is under way."

"Does she work for you?"

For a moment Logan didn't understand. "You're referring to Miss Dennehy?"

Walker nodded. "That's right. Does she work for you at the paper? I think you've hired women before as reporters. I know she isn't a housekeeper."

"The *Chronicle* had a woman reporter," he said. "Just one."

"Not Skye?"

"No," he said carefully, evenly. "Not Skye."

Walker closed his eyes and rubbed the lids, wondering what he could tell Marshall, what bargain he could strike. While he was thinking, Logan raised his own question.

"What does Parnell have to do with Miss Dennehy?"

That was easy to answer. "She worked for him."

"As a housekeeper," Logan said. His tone was flatly disbelieving.

"It's the truth." He paused, considering his words carefully. "He's a dangerous man, Mr. Marshall, but

I'm supposing you have some sense of that already. To say he's unscrupulous is inadequate. He's amoral."

Logan leaned forward and rested his coffee cup on the desk. Both his hands were still wrapped around it. "Jesus," he said softly. "What goes through her father's mind sometimes, I'll never understand. If I had any idea that's where she was going, I wouldn't have agreed to make the recommendation. He didn't tell me where she was taking the position. I asked. He hedged."

"Who?" asked Walker. "Who didn't tell what?"

"Her father." Logan sighed. "I don't suppose I can judge him too harshly. Not when I have a daughter of my own fast becoming a young woman. I tell you, Walker, men have no business having daughters."

Walker would have laughed if Logan Marshall hadn't seemed so perfectly serious about the matter.

Logan saw that Walker was at a loss as to how to respond. He waved any comment aside. "You can't understand until you have a little girl of your own. He has five."

Now Walker remembered something Skye had told him. "The Marys," he said.

"That's right. Then you *do* know."

Walker wasn't certain what he knew. He started to say as much, but Logan had put aside his coffee cup and was picking up yesterday's afternoon edition of the *Chronicle*. He wet his thumb and quickly flicked through the pages until he found what he wanted.

"Here it is," Logan said. He snapped open the paper and folded it quickly to highlight what he thought would be of interest to Walker Caine. He passed the paper over. "The drawing."

Walker looked at it then back at Logan. "I don't think I understand."

"Only because you don't want to."

* * *

Her first morning back, Skye had breakfast in bed. "Don't get used to it," Mrs. Cavanaugh said briskly. "This wasn't my idea. Your mother, God bless her, thinks you've been through a terrible ordeal. Sure, and what does she think *I* do around here, is what I should be asking her. You were that man's housekeeper all of a week. I've been doing it forty years."

Skye was sympathetic. "Sit here, then," she said. "You can have my breakfast and you can have it in my bed. This wasn't my idea either."

The housekeeper pretended to consider it. Finally she shook her head. "I already had my breakfast." Although she huffed on her way out of the room, Skye's gesture had mollified her.

After eating, Skye luxuriated in a hot bath. Her hair was piled high on her head and the steamy fragrance of lavender salts perfumed her skin. She let her head rest against a folded towel on the rim of the tub and enjoyed the solitude. After yesterday's revelations, her father's questions, her mother's fretting upon her arrival at home, it seemed to Skye that she deserved this time alone.

Until now, she'd had little time to think about Walker Caine. At this moment she could think of no one else.

Skye believed her thoughts would have taken a more pleasant turn if he hadn't followed her from Baileyboro. It was only chance that she had been given the opportunity to see him. At the last possible second she had decided to tell Walker about taking Parnell's gun. Leaving her seat, Skye had gone to the rail car's exit and looked up and down the platform for Walker. She'd seen him at the carriage, talking to Hank. He was carrying a valise.

At first Skye thought the valise must be hers and that she had forgotten it. She had almost called out to him. It was the slightest hesitation on her part that permitted her to learn the truth. Walker turned, valise in hand, and instead of approaching her car, disappeared into one closer to the front of the train. Skye waited to see if he would get off again, but he never did.

Skye considered it was her great good fortune to be riding Northeast Rail. No other line would have accommodated her questions and her requests. Once she knew about Walker, it hadn't taken her long to find out that he was riding in the mail car or that his destination was the city. She almost felt sorry for him because he didn't understand her advantage in his cat-and-mouse game.

"But not sorry enough to give myself away," she said, thinking aloud. The sound of her own voice startled her. Skye sat up in the tub and laughed a little uneasily, looking around to make certain no one had heard her. When she saw that she was still quite alone, Skye relaxed. She picked up the sponge and squeezed water onto her shoulders and between her breasts. She let her head fall back and dripped water along the curve of her throat. Closing her eyes again, she thought of Walker.

She wondered if he would always be so easy to bring to mind or if the image of him would fade in time or blur at the edges. The picture she had of him now was so clear he could have been standing beside her. There would be a slightly wicked smile on his face and perhaps a hint of his single dimple at the corner. His brown-and-gold-flecked eyes would be darkening in the center, but the look would still be intense. He would watch her with frank appreciation, unashamed that he enjoyed looking. His glance was like a physical touch and Skye could feel it on her mouth, her shoulders, then on her breasts. His smile would deepen because she would flush and try to blame it on the steam rising from the water. Walker would know better. He always did.

He'd probably drop down beside the tub. His thick, tawny hair would fall forward across his brow. He would rake it back with his fingers in an absent gesture. One of his hands would touch the rim of the tub. His fingertips would flick at the water, creating ripples on the surface that expanded in ever widening circles. A droplet of water would glisten on her breast. He would touch it. They would both watch the path his fingertip took on her skin, following it as it dipped below the water until it disappeared under the curve of her breast. His thumb would pass across her nipple.

He would chuckle then, a low, deep, raspy sound that would rise from the back of his throat. His hands would move to the collar of his own shirt. Skye could feel herself staring in astonishment as he unfastened the buttons and removed it. He stood up long enough to remove the rest of his clothes and when he was splendidly, gloriously naked, he dropped into the tub with her.

Water sloshed over the edges and puddled on the braided rug. "There isn't room for you in here," she said.

"Who are you talking to?" Moira called from Skye's bedchamber. "Did you say something to me?" She poked her head around the corner of Skye's dressing room. "I came in to show you some scarves I bought yesterday. I could use your opinion." Seeing Skye's flushed face, she frowned. "Are you certain you're all right, Skye? Perhaps I should send Mr. Cavanaugh for Dr. Turner."

"I'm fine, Mama. I was just talking to myself. I didn't hear you come in." Skye sighed as her mother accepted her explanation and ducked out of the doorway again. It was a timely interruption anyway, she told herself. The erotic drama that had been playing in her mind was certain to have left her unsatisfied. She looked down at herself, her raised knees, her elbows barely contained by the tub. "There wasn't room for both of us in here anyway," she muttered.

"You're going to have to speak up," Moira called.

"Sorry." Skye picked up a towel and stood up, wrapping it around her. She dried quickly and slipped into her robe. Padding barefoot into the other room, Skye cinched the belt. Her mother had placed a half-dozen scarves lengthwise on the bed and was standing back, examining the bright array with a critical eye. "You bought all these yesterday?"

Moira nodded. Her smile was a trifle guilty. "I didn't know what to do with myself. Your father was at work and you were gone and nothing seemed to interest me. So I went to A. T. Stewart's and shopped. I think I'm relieved that it didn't make me feel any better. It could have been quite expensive for your father."

"Papa enjoys spending money on you," Skye said.

"That may be true, but six scarves seems excessive to me. At least, today it does. Help me decide which to keep and we'll take the others back to the store."

"I have a better idea. Let's take them all to Mary Francis and then we'll pick out a special new one at Stewart's."

Moira was a little doubtful. "Give them *all* away?"

"Mama, don't be mean-spirited. Mary Francis's charity can use them more."

Moira sighed, understanding. "You don't like any of them, do you?"

It was difficult to be diplomatic when your mother pinned you right to the wall. "They're beautiful," Skye said, "but I don't think they flatter your hair."

Moira considered this, picking up one of the scarves and laying it across her neck. She studied her reflection in the mirror. "I believe you're right."

"Then we'll go see Mary Francis?"

"We'll take her to lunch."

Little Sisters of the Poor was charged with the care of the indigent and needy in Queens. Moira and Skye found Mary Francis working in the hospital kitchen, preparing trays for the patients. They pitched right in, slicing warm loaves of bread and dipping chicken broth into small soup bowls.

"So housekeeping wasn't to your liking?" Mary Francis asked drily. Her beautiful features were framed by the stark black and white of her cornet and wimple. The stiff material didn't prevent her from getting her tongue firmly in her cheek.

"Actually, I discovered I had a flair for it," Skye answered. "What I didn't like was my employer's groping. And don't bother threatening to break his knees for me. I already took care of him."

"Really? How?"

Skye told her.

"That's quite impressive."

Moira clucked her tongue in admonishment as all three of the nuns who were working with Mary Francis had stopped to listen. She sensed, rather than saw, their keen interest. "You shouldn't encourage her, Mary. It's not seemly, and I'm not listening to another word." She pushed the cart loaded with trays toward the kitchen door. "I'll take this around to the rooms."

"Poor Mama," Mary Francis said. "She doesn't know what to make of us sometimes." She looked pointedly at her fellow Sisters of Charity, who quickly went back to their work. Mary Francis touched Skye's elbow. "Come on, there's a little room in the back where we can talk privately." She took off her apron and hung it on a peg by the door. The room where she led Skye only had one chair and a table littered with papers. Mary Francis let Skye have the chair and swept aside the papers so she could sit on the tabletop. "Menus," she said, explaining the papers. "And butcher and greengrocer bills. There never seems to be enough money."

"I have some of my wages left," Skye told her. "It isn't much, but I'd rather you had it." She opened her beaded reticule, extracted a small change purse, and handed her sister some bills and coins. "If I had lasted longer, I could have actually paid off the greengrocer."

"It seems to me you did the right thing, leaving when you did." She put the money on the stack of bills. She studied her youngest sister frankly. "We don't have much time. Tell me why you've come. Donating the scarves was a very nice gesture, but it could have waited."

"How did you—" There was no sense in finishing the question. It didn't matter how Mary Francis knew; she just did. "I've met someone," Skye said, after a moment. "His name is Walker Caine."

The story came out haltingly in the beginning and breathlessly at the end. In between were Mary Francis's thoughtful questions to bridge the gaps in Skye's account.

Mary Francis was silent for a long time after Skye finished. "Are you going to tell him about the baby?"

The question startled Skye. "He asked me that, too. I can't think that far ahead. I don't even know if I'm carrying a child."

Mary Francis had dark red eyebrows. One of them lifted now as she gave her sister an arch look. "There's a family history to consider here," she reminded Skye. "Michael and Maggie and even our own mother. Fertility doesn't seem to be a problem with Dennehy women. I don't think you can count on being slow to start, like Rennie. I imagine she's the exception. Had I made a different choice, I'd probably have half a dozen children by now."

All but groaning, Skye crossed her forearms on the table and laid her head against them. She felt Mary Francis lightly stroke the back of her hair. Her voice was muffled. "I don't think I wanted to hear this," she said.

"I know."

"Maybe it won't come to pass."

"Maybe it won't."

Tilting her head, Skye examined her sister with a single eye. "You could be more optimistic."

Mary Francis shrugged, but her touch continued to soothe. "What is, is," she said gently. "Just don't think you have to handle it all alone."

"You'd think I'd have learned from their mistakes."

"It's hard to know if they made mistakes. Mama has Jay Mac and she's had him for the better part of her lifetime. Which one of us do you think was a mistake?"

"Rennie," Skye said immediately.

Mary Francis smiled. "Do you think Michael regrets Madison's birth or that Maggie regrets Meredith's? And what about the love they found with Ethan and Connor? I imagine there were times when they thought they were making a mistake, but now, who's to say?"

Skye raised her head and looked at her sister with interest. Mary Francis sounded almost wistful. "What about your choice? Do you ever regret it?"

Mary Francis's hands went to her rosary. Her long, graceful fingers slipped over the cool ivory beads. "We're talking about *your* choices," she said.

Skye allowed her sister to avoid answering the question, in part because she wasn't certain she wanted to know the answer. Mary Francis had always seemed so strong, so certain in her opinions, in her decisions. Knowing that she was struggling had the power to rock Skye. It was humbling to realize how little independence she actually exercised. "I'll talk to you before I make a decision one way or the other."

"I don't have your answers, Skye."

"But you'll hear me out and I'll be able to hear myself. I couldn't think clearly at all around Walker."

"Is that a good sign or a bad one? I'm never quite sure."

Skye could hear the amusement in her sister's voice. "It doesn't seem very funny to me."

Mary Francis never found it easy to be contrite, but seeing Skye's distress, she did her best now. "Of course it's not funny. I only wish I could be more help. Are you going to see Walker again?"

"I don't know. I suppose it's up to me. I know how to find him, but he can't reach me."

"You made certain that was the case."

She nodded. "I had to. I still don't know why he was following me. I'm fairly certain it was prompted by his work for Parnell more than a desire to know where he could find me."

"He's something of a mystery, isn't he?"

"Yes. I don't know very much about him. He's always had the advantage there."

"Did he press his advantage unscrupulously?"

"No. Quite the opposite."

"Then perhaps he followed you from Baileyboro to protect you."

"From what? Parnell remained behind. He was the only danger."

"Are you certain?" Mary Francis asked. "What about the ghost?"

"That's not amusing, either. I blame Rennie and Maggie and Michael and you—"

"Me?"

"Yes, you. All of you had some part in those horrible ghost stories when I was a child. It was cruel. I can't help but think that that experience made me more willing to suppose I was being accosted by Hamilton Granville's ghost."

"Are you saying now that it didn't happen that way?"

"Mary Francis, please. Don't pretend you accepted that part of my story. I'm saying now that I don't even know if it happened at all. You can't imagine how real it seemed at the time and how unreal it seems to me at this moment.

I didn't have the slightest difficulty sleeping last night and I don't expect I'll have trouble tonight."

"You think Rennie and I put the idea in your head all those years ago?"

"Michael and Maggie, too. You all planted the seed. Some of you fertilized it a little better than others, but you all had a part." She let herself enjoy Mary's stricken face for a moment. "Oh, don't take it too badly. I'm plotting real revenge when you least expect it."

"Well, *that* eases my mind," Mary Francis said drily. "I won't even warn the others."

"Good. They don't deserve a warning." Her smile contradicted her words. She stood. "I suppose we should find Mama."

Mary Francis slipped off the table and wrapped her arms around her sister. "I'll support you, Skye, in whatever decision you make. And I'll pray it will be the right decision for you."

Skye returned the hug, then let her hands slip along Mary's forearms until she was holding her sister's hands. Her eyes searched Mary's features. "And I'll do the same for you," she said. "I want to say that now in case I don't have the chance again. We all lean on you so much, Mary, perhaps it isn't fair. Who do you lean on?"

Mary Francis's answer was profoundly simple. "God."

Skye and Moira had their fill of shopping by the time they returned home. Mr. Cavanaugh required two trips to the carriage to bring everything inside and there were still items that Stewart's would be delivering in the morning.

"I think your father's already home," Moira said. She was looking at the closed study door. Generally, it was kept open when the room wasn't occupied. She hesitated on the stairs and glanced back at the grandfather clock in the foyer. It was just after six, but that was early for Jay Mac. "Odd. He usually attends the city meeting tonight." She shrugged. "Perhaps he sent someone in his place. See if he wants to eat early, Skye, and then ask Mrs. Cavanaugh if she can accommodate him. I just want to freshen up a bit." She smiled and confided, "I like to look nice for your father."

Skye grinned as her mother blushed at her own admission. Even after all these years, she thought wonderingly. She watched Moira climb the stairs. Her mother was humming to herself. Mary Francis was right to think that perhaps there hadn't been so many mistakes, after all. If the Dennehy women sometimes put the carriage before the marriage, at least they loved wisely and well. Surely there was something to be said for that.

Skye found she was humming as she opened the door to her father's study. Jay Mac was sitting behind his desk. He was leaning back in his chair and wiping his spectacles with a monogrammed handkerchief. Skye recognized her own embroidery work. Her heart swelled. She had done that handkerchief and five others as a Christmas present ten years ago. She had had no idea until now that Jay Mac still carried them.

Her smile was brilliant as she fully entered the room. "Papa," she said in greeting. "How good it is that— "

Jay Mac was getting to his feet. So was someone seated in the wing chair in front of his desk. Skye felt as if the breath was being squeezed from her lungs. Her father's voice was coming to her from a long way off. She had to strain to hear the words, concentrate to understand them.

"Mary Schyler," Jay Mac was saying. "This is Mr. Walker Caine. He says you're already acquainted. Is that true?"

Eleven

She stared at Walker. Her legs were unsteady. Skye found she was thinking more about sitting down than about answering her father's question. "We've met," she said. It surprised her that her voice could capture such cool, neutral tones. Her palms were sweating and she suspected there was a bead of moisture on her brow and upper lip. She was melting, but composed about it. The realization that she could simultaneously accommodate both elements brought her close to hysterical laughter.

"Sit down, Mary Schyler," Jay Mac said. He pointed to the chair beside Walker's.

Skye stayed her ground. "Mama would like to know if you want to eat dinner early. I'm supposed to give Mrs. Cavanaugh instructions."

"It can wait." He hadn't raised his voice, but there was an edge to his tone.

Skye was better at defying her father when she wasn't sharing a room with him. She didn't want to embarrass him in front of Walker by ignoring his order, but then, neither did she want to be embarrassed. It was Walker himself who came to her aid.

"Perhaps it would help if she relayed the instructions now," he said, "to save us an interruption later."

Skye looked at her father, wondering if he would back her into a corner or allow her a graceful exit. She drew in her breath, the lightheadedness fading as he nodded shortly. She needed only a few moments to compose herself. "Will you want to eat early?" she asked.

"No. The usual time will be fine. And tell Mrs. Cavanaugh that Mr. Caine will be joining us."

Skye had been afraid that that would be the case. She didn't show her displeasure until she was on the other side of the door. That's when tears gathered in her eyes. *What was he doing here? How had he found her?* It wasn't fair. The next meeting should have been on *her* terms.

Mrs. Cavanaugh took the news of a guest for dinner in stride. Skye went to her mother's room to give her the same information.

"Who is he?" Moira wanted to know.

"Just a man I met while I was working at the Granville place."

"And he's come here?"

Skye nodded, unaware that she was blinking back tears.

Moira rose from her vanity and came to Skye's side. She drew her daughter over to the bed and urged her to sit down. "What's this about, Skye? What haven't you told me?"

It was what she hadn't told either of her parents. "I need to go back downstairs," she said, begging the question. "Jay Mac wants to talk to me."

"Are you in some kind of trouble?"

"No," she said. "No, I'm not."

Moira looked at her daughter hard, searching a face that was as familiar to her as her own. She patted Skye's hand. "All right. Talk to your father. Don't let him bully you. This was his idea, after all. Perhaps he needs to be reminded of that."

Skye couldn't remember ever receiving advice from her mother on how to deal with her father. Moira's interference, if she chose to interfere at all, was much more subtle than what had just occurred. Most often Skye suspected that Moira simply told Jay Mac what she thought. She certainly wasn't in the habit of using her daughters to relate what was on her mind.

Skye leaned toward her mother and kissed her cheek. "Thank you, Mama. You always know just the right thing to say."

The second time she entered her father's study, it was Skye who was prepared with a question.

"I was correct about your motives, wasn't I?" she asked Jay Mac. "I simply mistook the target."

Jay Mac frowned. Creases deepened along his broad forehead. "You'll have to explain yourself, Skye. I'm afraid I didn't understand a word of it."

Instead Skye turned to Walker. "Please, sit down." She took a seat herself. "I don't blame you," she said. "Jay Mac can be extremely persuasive. It's not so difficult when one has millions to pad the argument."

"Mary Schyler," Jay Mac said warningly. "I think you should stop. If you're heading where I think you are, I'm going to let you hang on that limb all by yourself."

Walker held up his hand. "Oh, no, please let her go on. This is absolutely fascinating."

What Walker said gave Skye reason to pause. The way he said it, with that dry intonation that was at once amused and patronizing, prompted her to plunge ahead. "Jay Mac's paid other men, you know. Not for me, at least, not that I know of, not before now. Jarret Sullivan was given ten thousand dollars to stop Rennie's wedding and take her for himself. Maggie was sold for the deed to a Colorado ranch. My father's bound to feel generous if you can take me off his hands, so I hope you held out for something valuable. After all, I'm the last Mary."

"The last Mary?" Walker asked.

Skye held up one hand and ticked off the names on her fingers. "Mary Francis. Mary Michael. Mary Renee. Mary Margaret. And me."

"Mary Schyler," he said.

"Yes."

Regarding her with interest, Walker shook his head slowly. "Mary Schyler," he said again. This time when he invoked her name, he let her know she was in trouble. "What's it like out on that limb?"

Skye's eyes darted uncertainly between Walker and her father. "I don't know what you mean," she bluffed.

Jay Mac leaned back in his leather chair. "Let her get out a little further," he said to Walker.

"I don't think this is very amusing," she told Jay Mac. "You paid him, didn't you?"

Jay Mac's hands were folded and he tapped his thumbs together in an absent gesture. "I paid him." It wasn't a statement so much as a question.

Exasperated, Skye asked, "Did you or didn't you?"

It was Walker who interjected with a question of his own. "What is it exactly that I'm supposed to have been paid for?"

"To show an interest in me."

Walker's brows rose and his head tilted to one side as he considered this. "There's money in that?"

She gave him a sour look before she turned her attention back to Jay Mac. "Once I agreed to go to Baileyboro, you hired Mr. Caine to make certain no ill befell me."

"I have to tell you, Skye," Jay Mac said, "that I'm wishing I had hired him. You need a keeper."

Out of the corner of her eye Skye saw Walker's smug smile. "It's been said before," she admitted. Her comment only made her father look to Walker with new respect.

"Is that right?" Jay Mac asked Walker.

"Yes, sir."

"Are you volunteering?"

Walker pretended to think it over. He studied Skye's flushed cheeks, her angry eyes. She hated that they were talking about her as if she wasn't in the room. "I might have volunteered earlier, Mr. Worth, but since I learned there's money in it, I can't say that taking the job without compensation interests me."

Jay Mac approved of that answer. His smile broadened.

Skye stood. It was difficult to talk through the ache in her throat. "I'll let the two of you work out the details," she said stiffly. She turned and headed for the door.

Her father came to his feet. One of his arms extended over the desk as he tried to stop her. "Skye. Wait."

She didn't turn back.

The study was silent for a long moment after she was gone. Jay Mac sat down slowly. He stared at the closed door, sighed, and shook his head. "Perhaps we left her out on that limb a little too long."

Walker wasn't so sure. "Perhaps," he said, noncommittal.

"Are you going to go after her?"

"I'm thinking about it." He got to his feet. "Trouble is, I haven't decided what I want to do once I get her."

Jay Mac watched him go. "I know just how you feel," he said softly. The door closed and Jay Mac leaned back in his chair. The back of his head rested heavily against the soft leather. His hands curved around the arms of the chair. His legs were stretched out under the desk. He remained in just that posture, reflecting on the discussion that had taken place, until the door opened again. This time it was Moira who intruded on his privacy.

She looked around, saw he was quite alone, and entered. "I've met the most interesting man," she said. "He was in the hallway just now, looking for Skye."

"You gave him directions, I hope."

"I did. Though I'm not certain that I should have. He seemed rather angry."

"He is. Skye accused him of taking money from me to show an interest in her."

Moira's lilting brogue softened her words. "Did she now? Is it true?"

"I suspect he has an interest her. He followed her from Baileyboro, didn't he?"

"Don't be deliberately obtuse, Jay Mac. Did you give the man money?"

Jay Mac gave his wife his full attention now. "Before today, I never met the man."

"Which doesn't precisely answer my question."

Wounded, he looked at her sharply. "I don't think I'm flattered by your doubt."

Moira skirted the desk and came to stand at his side. She dropped a kiss on his forehead to banish the hurt. "I didn't intend to flatter you, dear. I just want to know if Skye's suspicions are right. In her place, I'd harbor the same ones."

"I never offered Mr. Caine anything," he said after a moment. "No money. No property. I certainly didn't offer him *your daughter.*"

Moira smiled gently. Skye must have pricked his pride a little if he was referring to her in that manner. "I'm very glad to hear it, Jay Mac." She picked up one of his hands and squeezed. "Very glad."

Skye was flagging a hansom cab on Broadway when Walker caught up to her. Ignoring him completely, Skye began to climb in when the driver stopped. Walker simply took her by the waist, lifted, and set her on the sidewalk. "We won't be needing your services," he told the driver.

"*We* won't," Skye said, twisting to get away from him. "*I* will."

The driver tipped his hat to get a better perspective on the situation. From his vantage point the woman appeared to be struggling, but the man was completely at ease in restraining her. The driver had long since stopped being surprised by what he saw on his route. The better addresses were no guarantee of better manners. "She a runaway?" he asked.

"Something like that," Walker said.

Skye glared at the driver. "Can't you see that he's abducting me?"

The driver considered that. "Seems to me like you're the one wanting to go places," he said.

Skye brought the heel of her shoe down sharply on Walker's instep. His grip loosened enough for her to pull out of it. She waved the cab away and started down the street.

"We appear to be walking." He was grinning as he tipped the driver for his trouble and followed Skye.

She set a brisk pace, but she had no hope of outdistancing him. His lithe, rolling walk brought him to her side before they'd reached the end of the block. Instead of crossing the street, she turned at the corner. Facing the wind now, she ducked her bare head. Her hair was ruffled at the temples and crown. Strands of it fell across her forehead and cheeks like leaping flames. Stopping abruptly, she pushed it back impatiently and raised her face to Walker.

"Say what you have to say," she told him. "Then leave me alone."

"I'm not sure I have anything to say to you. I thought I would give you an opportunity to apologize."

Genuinely surprised, Skye blinked. "Apologize?"

He nodded. Wind whipped through his hair. He took time now to button his coat. When he was done, he thrust his hands in his pockets. It was too cold to stand in one place. He began walking and was careful not to show his amusement when Skye followed him.

"Apologize?" she asked breathlessly. "Why ever should I do that? I didn't invite you here. That was my father's doing."

"No," he said coldly, "it wasn't. My being here has nothing to do with your father. If you doubt that, then take it up with him. Apparently he's given you reason to think the worst; I wasn't aware that I had."

"Then why were you talking to Jay Mac? Why didn't you ask directly for me?"

"I did. You weren't home when I got there, remember? I was shown to the parlor first. Your housekeeper must have mentioned my presence to your father and he invited me into his study. I wasn't in there very long before you came in. Your father and I exchanged a few pleasantries."

"Jay Mac doesn't exchange pleasantries," she told him flatly. "He sizes people up."

"I was trying to be polite about the experience."

A faint smile edged Skye's mouth. "There's no need for that. I've seen my father cut people to shreds with a single look." She glanced at him. "You don't seem the worse for it. He must have seen something he liked."

Walker shrugged. He was quite aware that Jay Mac had been judging him. He had no idea what the verdict had been. More than that, he wasn't all that concerned about it. "I didn't come here because I wanted your father's approval. Or yours."

Skye realized it was what Jay Mac would have liked best about him. Walker carried himself in a quiet, confident way. His indifference about what people thought of him wasn't feigned or a sign of arrogance. Comfortable in his own skin, he didn't care about the opinions of others.

Skye stopped in her tracks and touched Walker's elbow when he would have continued on. She searched his face. "You didn't take any money from my father, did you?"

"No." He watched her struggle with that information. She had been so certain the opposite was true. "And to set the record entirely straight, your father didn't offer any."

Skye looked away. She tucked a tendril of hair behind her ear. The wind promptly nudged it out again. "I don't know what to say."

"Let's go back to your house. When the words do occur to you, I want to be sure the wind doesn't carry them out of earshot." Slipping his arm through hers, Walker led Skye back the way they'd come.

Mrs. Cavanaugh met them at the door. She took their coats. "What you were thinking, stepping outside without a hat or a scarf, I'll never know. Both of you. It's scandalous, is what it is. Don't be surprised if the neighbors talk, Mary Schyler."

"Could we have tea in the front parlor, Mrs. Cavanaugh?" asked Skye. She took the housekeeper's gentle tsking for an affirmative response and showed Walker to the parlor.

"Will the neighbors talk?" Walker asked, when they were alone. He had not had much opportunity to look around before and he did so now, studying the photographs on the mantel with particular interest.

"Probably," Skye said. "When it comes to the Dennehys, they look for things to talk about."

"I suspect you and your sisters gave them reason from time to time." He picked up one gilt-edged frame containing a picture of all five Marys. Photographic portraits tended to present solemn, placid faces regarding the camera. This portrait captured a livelier group. There was wicked mischief in every pair of eyes.

Skye came to stand beside Walker. He was pointing to her oldest sister. "That's Mary Francis. She was seventeen then. You can't see it in the picture because she's standing behind Michael, but she's pulling Rennie's hair."

Walker looked closer and could imagine the smile on Rennie's face was a bit more restrained than the smiles of her sisters.

"That was taken a year before she joined the convent," Skye told him.

"Rennie?"

"No. Mary Francis."

"The hair puller."

"Yes. She always helped keep everyone in line," Skye said. "Rennie was being . . . well, she was being Rennie. That's a good enough reason to have her hair pulled."

"She's a twin."

Skye nodded. "She and Michael. They're fifteen there. You can see that Michael's trying to be serious, but Mary Francis made her laugh at the last moment."

"Michael's married now?"

"Hmm-mm. To a federal marshal. Ethan and Michael live in Denver now. She's a reporter for the *Rocky Mountain News.*"

It came to him then, the connection to Logan Marshall and the *Chronicle.* Mary Michael had been that paper's sole female reporter. Logan could have at least told him that. He wondered what else the publisher hadn't thought was important enough for him to know. "Rennie lives here?" he asked.

"No. She and Jarret live all over. They go where Northeast Rail goes. Rennie designs bridges and decides where track is going to be laid. She's worked for the railroad since she left college."

"And this sister? The pixie?"

"That's Maggie. She was twelve. She does rather look like a pixie, doesn't she?" The chair that Maggie was sitting in was too big for her. Her feet were dangling a full inch off the floor. Michael had one hand on her knee and had probably placed it there to keep Maggie from swinging her legs. "Maggie's studying to be a doctor now. She's in Philadelphia with her husband and little girl."

Walker hardly heard. He was looking at the youngest Mary. She was standing on one foot, leaning beside Rennie's chair with her elbow resting on the arm. "What happened to your other leg?"

"I was scratching. My petticoat was new and so stiff with starch it practically cut me."

"You look like a flamingo."

"My dress was pink. I *felt* like one."

The sepia tones of the photograph couldn't show the contrast between Skye's pink dress and her flame-red hair. He couldn't quite contain his grin. He wished he could have seen her then. "How old were you?"

"Ten."

He would have been sixteen. His interest would have been in Mary Francis or the twins. He would have pulled her fly-away braids if he had noticed her at all. Walker set the photograph back on the mantel. "What about your ambitions, Skye?"

"Oh, I've been careful not to cultivate any," she said flippantly.

Walker's response was interrupted as tea arrived. He waited until they were alone again and Skye had poured something for both of them. "I don't believe you don't have any ambitions," he said.

"I can't help what you believe." She handed him his cup. "I should have asked if you wanted something stronger. Do you? It's no trouble."

"This is fine." He sat down in a large armchair. The parlor was a warm, comfortable room. The fabrics were dark gold and blue. The furniture was arranged in a way that invited conversation rather than forbade it. It crowded around the fireplace in a semicircle and the area was lighted by lamps with frosted glass globes. "Why didn't you tell me who you were?"

"You mean why didn't I tell you I was Jay Mac's daughter?" she asked. "Is it so important? You always suspected I wasn't a housekeeper. I should think you'd be gratified to know your instincts were correct."

Was it important? he wondered. Did it change anything? "It wasn't my instincts," he told her. "It was your hands."

Skye was lifting her cup. She paused and examined her hand, turning it one way, then the other. "What's wrong with them?"

"Nothing. That's the point. Look at Mrs. Cavanaugh's sometime."

She understood immediately and wondered why she hadn't seen it before. Only it wasn't her own hands she was thinking of. "Did you mention it to Mr. Parnell?"

He nodded. "He didn't think it was important. He was willing to overlook quite a bit where you were concerned."

"That doesn't make sense to me."

The gold flecks in Walker's eyes sharpened. "What happened in that workroom didn't convince you? He wanted you. He still does. In the face of that, nothing else matters to him."

Skye's cup rattled a little in her saucer as she set it down. "Don't you think that's laying it on a bit thick? He sent me away."

"I know." Walker's hooded glance shaded his eyes and concealed his thoughts. What should he tell her, and when?

"Did he send you here?" she asked.

"Yes."

Skye had suspected it. Having it confirmed was more disappointing than she'd thought it would be. "I see."

But Walker knew that she didn't begin to suspect Parnell's motives or his own. "Did you know I was on the train?" he asked.

"I saw you get on at Baileyboro."

"Then you deliberately hid from me."

"It wasn't very hard."

Walker's smile was wry. "I didn't fully appreciate the advantage you had until I learned who your father was. I take it you knew that conductor."

"Mr. Pennybacker."

That answered Walker's question. "Northeast Rail," he said softly, still not quite believing it. "I couldn't have known that."

"I don't see how," she agreed. It was more interesting to Skye that Walker seemed to think he *should* have known. "And I don't see that it matters. Not when you found me anyway."

It mattered because he wasn't supposed to make mistakes like the one he'd made. Even with Skye's advantage, he shouldn't have lost her at the station. He wondered now if it was such a good idea to come here. He could have kept his distance, bided his time, and planned what he was going to say to Parnell when he returned alone. But when he saw the house and watched Jay Mac Worth alight from the carriage and take the walk to the front door, when he saw the door open and the great man himself disappear inside, Walker was drawn to the same path. He wanted to meet the man who had sent his daughter to Baileyboro, the man who had placed a higher value on an investment than on his daughter's safety.

Walker put his tea aside. The brew was cold and bitter now. He got to his feet suddenly. "I should be going."

That surprised Skye. "I thought Jay Mac invited you to dinner."

"He did, but I never accepted. Your father assumes a lot."

"He does. He's used to people falling in with his suggestions, doing things his way."

"That's not who I am."

"I know." She drew in a breath and let it out slowly. "I'm sorry."

Walker looked at her sharply. "Sorry? Because I don't kowtow to your father?"

Skye stood. At her sides her fingers nervously pleated and unpleated the fabric of her gown. "No," she said quickly, anxiously. "That's not what I meant. I'm sorry that I misunderstood what I saw earlier. I thought you were reporting to him, telling him I was none the worse for my experiences at the Granville mansion. When you have a father as interfering and protective as Jay Mac . . ." Shrugging, she let her voice trail away. When he didn't respond even after she let a few moments pass, Skye added, "That was an apology."

"I know what it was. I'm trying to take it in."

His dry humor touched her. Skye's mouth pursed to one side as she snorted derisively. The look certainly didn't flatter her. The last thing she'd expected in that moment was for Walker to pull her against him and kiss her hard. Her hands rose, touched his shoulders, retracted, then touched him again, this time holding on dearly. She arched into him and felt his arm across the small of her back. The kiss lingered, deepened. Her breasts swelled against the tight bodice of her gown as she was pulled closer. He supported her body with the hard, unyielding length of his.

Jay Mac and Moira paused on the threshold of the room. They exchanged glances. Moira would have discreetly stepped back into the hallway. Jay Mac elected to loudly and pointedly clear his throat. Moira scolded him, saying his name softly.

Walker heard the throat clearing. Skye heard her mother's admonishment. It was Skye who pulled back, at once relieved and uncomfortable when Walker wouldn't release her completely.

"Just how well are you acquainted with my daughter?" Jay Mac asked.

"Papa, please," Skye said. She spoke to her father, but her eyes beseeched her mother.

"Jay Mac," Moira said gently. "Perhaps we should—"

"I will *not* be shooed or shushed," he said flatly. "I want an answer, Mr. Caine. What are your intentions concerning my daughter?"

"Papa!"

"Jay Mac!"

Over both objections, Walker said simply, "I intend to marry her."

Skye stepped out of the circle of his arms. She was finding it difficult to breathe. There was a tightness in her chest and a knot in her stomach. "You don't have to say that just because he saw us kissing. Jay Mac's not that old-fashioned."

"I am so," Jay Mac insisted. "Tell them, Moira."

Walker raked his hair with his fingers. "I'm not saying it because of what your father saw, but because of what he asked. Those *are* my intentions."

"Were you going to tell me?" she demanded. An uncomfortable pressure was building at the back of her throat. It was easy for Skye to imagine disgracing herself by being sick in front of everyone.

"I am telling you."

"Then let me tell you my intentions, Mr. Caine. I have no plans to marry anyone. Not ever." Having said that, Skye hurried out of the room. Her parents parted long enough to let her through then closed ranks again.

"I can't send you after her this time," Jay Mac told Walker. "She's gone to her room."

"That wouldn't stop me if I wanted to follow her."

Jay Mac considered that. This young man wasn't afraid of him at all. Jay Mac wasn't certain that Walker Caine even respected him. It was an unusual situation for Jay Mac. It didn't make him angry, however. It made him curious. "Mrs. Worth and I came to tell you that dinner is being served. Are you going to join us?"

It was a question now, not an assumption. It changed Walker's mind. "I believe I will, thank you."

Moira threw up her hands. She had been certain until just a moment ago that Walker was going to leave. "I'm sure I don't understand either one of you."

Skye was brushing her hair with hard, punishing strokes when her mother entered her room. "Has he gone?"

"Soon, I think. Your father and Walker are having a drink in the library. I didn't want to be part of that."

She noticed her mother had referred to Walker by his Christian name. That suggested a certain familiarity, at the very least a warming to him that Skye didn't find particularly comforting. "I won't have them planning my life for me," she said. "I watched Jay Mac do it with my sisters. I won't have him do it to me."

"You give your father too much credit," Moira said. "All of you do. He couldn't stop Mary Francis from joining an order. He couldn't keep Michael from working at the *Chronicle*. Rennie worked at Northeast in spite of Jay Mac's wishes, and Maggie's going to be a doctor. Those were not your father's plans for them. They did those things in spite of Jay Mac."

"They did those things *to* spite him." Skye couldn't believe her own temerity. She put down her brush. Her hand was shaking and her throat ached again. She had never felt so much like crying and she was certain her mother had never felt so much like slapping her. "I'm sorry, Mama, but I didn't want it to be such a fight with him. I thought he would make an exception for me. I haven't ever wanted to be anything important."

"Oh, Skye," Moira said sadly. She stood behind her daughter at the vanity and studied Skye's reflection. Her fingers sifted through Skye's hair, absently stroking and braiding. "Is that really what you think?"

Skye's shrug was uncertain. "I can't be like my sisters."

"I know."

"I have my own ideas about what I want to do with my life."

Moira nodded. Her smile was as gentle as her fingers in Skye's hair.

"No one asked what I thought about getting married," she said.

"I think your father and Walker know the answer to that now."

Her mother's dry tone gave Skye pause. "Did I make a scene? I hadn't meant to do that. Sometimes I simply can't think clearly around him."

"Are you talking about your father or Mr. Caine?"

"I was talking about Walker, but sometimes it's the same with Jay Mac. I'm so busy anticipating what he'll say or do that I hardly know what I'm saying myself."

Moira's fingers hesitated. "Have you ever considered that perhaps what you're really not doing is listening to him?"

"What are you saying, Mama?"

"I'm saying that sometimes when you girls are doing things to spite your father, you're only spiting yourselves." Moira's hands dropped away from Skye's hair. She patted her daughter's shoulder. "It's just something to think about."

Skye stared at her own reflection, her expression doubtful.

Moira was on the point of leaving when she paused on the threshold. "I liked Mr. Caine very much, Skye."

"Mother."

"Sure, and it's not me he's asking to marry, but I liked him just the same."

Skye turned on her stool. "Yes, but what do you *know* about him?"

"Not as much as you, I'm sure," Moira said. "He told us about his parents being missionaries. I'm afraid I found that so fascinating that the conversation didn't move much beyond it. Your father couldn't wait to get him alone."

"To finish the inquisition," said Skye.

Moira smiled. "More likely to begin it."

It was late by the time Walker Caine arrived at the St. Mark Hotel. Moira had suggested he might find the accommodations there comfortable. He didn't mention that he had stayed at the St. Mark before. Except for an awkward beginning, Skye's mother had been a gracious hostess and she wanted to be helpful. He didn't take that pleasure from her.

Walker registered at the front desk. The lobby was all but deserted. A couple came in from the street wearing evening clothes. They were smiling, exchanging warm glances. Their figures were reflected in the dark polished wood that paneled the entrance. They stopped at the desk to collect their key then disappeared up the wide carpeted staircase. Walker waited a full minute to give them enough time to get to their room. He had no desire to catch them out in the stairwell or in a hallway. They wouldn't have noticed him if he had, but he couldn't have helped but notice them. He was feeling a little raw, a little

restless, and the after-dinner drinks he'd shared with Jay
Mac had intensified the feelings, not dulled them.

His room was on the third floor. It was small, about a
third of the size of the suite he generally shared with
Parnell when they came to the city. He tossed his valise
on a chair and lighted the bedside lamp. A noise outside
drew him to the room's sole window. He had a view of
Broadway below. Although the lobby of the St. Mark was
quiet, the thoroughfare wasn't. Carriages were moving at
a brisk pace, outdistancing the milk wagons and farmers'
carts. A group of men stepped out of a restaurant. They
were wearing identical black coats and derbies, white
scarves and gloves. Two of them carried ebony canes. The
very look of them defined respectability and importance,
yet Walker wasn't surprised when they walked off in the
direction of a seedier section of town.

Turning away, he unpacked his clothes and prepared
for bed. He did it because it was late and not because
he was tired. When he crawled into bed, he found it
was every bit as lonely as he'd thought it would be. He
reached for the lamp and turned back the wick.

Gaslight from the street filtered into his room. Shadows overlaid the patterned wallpaper, lending it a grayish hue. Walker listened to the activity on Broadway,
the sounds of people moving with purpose and direction. Wagon wheels clicked steadily. Occasionally there
was a shout or the bellow of hearty laughter Mostly the
mix of voices was a tranquil, even hum by the time it
reached his ears. Without his being aware of it, the
nighttime cadence of the busy city lulled him to sleep.

Walker had learned how to sleep deeply and wake instantly. When a singular sound separated itself from the
background noise, Walker sat up immediately and listened, each of his senses heightened by the interruption.
It came again, a scratching sound of metal against metal.
It was irregular, starting and pausing and starting again.

He cocked his head to isolate the origin of the sound and realized it was coming from the door. Walker stood and shrugged into his robe. The light in his room was sufficient for him to find his way to the door without bumping into anything. His passage was silent.

At the door he stopped and listened again. He could identify the sound now. Someone was trying to jiggle his key out of the lock. He hunkered down so that his eyes were level with the keyhole. He could see the key wobbling in the lock as it was pushed from the hallway side of the door. Walker actually considered helping the intruder. He could tap the key and let it fall on the floor, where it could easily be pulled into the corridor. He decided against it, preferring instead to learn something about the burglar's patience.

It took the intruder a full minute to push the key onto the floor. He could have been surprised at any time by someone stepping into the hallway from one of the other rooms or the stairwell, but if he was distracted by that possibility, he didn't show it. He was persistent, if amateurish.

Walker almost jumped when the key finally fell. It landed loudly on the hardwood floor. The sound must have surprised the intruder as well, because the entire door rattled in its frame as the man fell against it. After those noises it became quiet again. Walker could imagine what was going on on the other side of the door, the urge the other man would have felt to quell his own panic, the furtive looking around, wondering if he was going to be discovered.

Walker waited. Had the burglar given up?

No. Walker saw a small metal rod being pushed under the door. It took him a moment to realize the object was a button hook. Rather ingenious, that. It took the intruder several tries to catch the tip of the black skeleton key, but once he had it, he pulled it under the door easily. Walker moved back from the door then and waited.

The key turned again, this time from the hallway, and the lock was released. The door was opened slowly and cautiously.

"Sweet Jesus," he said, raking back his tawny, sleep-pressed hair. The silhouette framed in his doorway was very familiar. "I should have known it was you." He pulled Skye into the room quickly and shut the door. The scream that had been rising in her throat was stifled by his hand across her mouth. "I'm the one who should be raising hell here." He eased his grip when he felt her relax. It wasn't an accident that his hand rested near her neck. He felt like strangling her.

"You scared me!" she said accusingly.

Incredulous, he asked, *"I* scared *you?* What happened to knocking on a person's door?"

Skye drew herself up stiffly. "It's the middle of the night. I thought you'd be sleeping."

Walker let her go. "Your logic not only eludes, it frightens me. But then, to your way of thinking, that probably serves me right."

"Exactly."

He nearly groaned. He shook his head instead. The movement only partially cleared it. Walker pulled on the belt of his robe and lighted the bedside lamp. Skye had already taken off her coat. She hung it beside his just inside the door and was removing her fur-fringed hat. Her bright hair was pulled back loosely, secured by a black grosgrain ribbon. The arrangement was soft and flattering. Her eyes looked impossibly large, the centers of them so dark and wide that they were more black than green. She was wearing a plain hunter-green gown with the tight sleeves cut high on her shoulders and the neckline closing at the base of her throat. Tiny jet buttons fastened the tailored bodice. She was nervously fingering one of them now, trying to gauge his reaction.

Walker pointed to the room's sole chair. "Sit." His tone did not invite argument. He disappeared into the dressing room and returned wearing a pair of black trousers and a wrinkled white shirt that he didn't bother to tuck in. Skye's flush told him that she realized he had been quite naked under his dressing gown. "Does anyone know where you are?"

"Who would I tell?" she asked.

The entire neighborhood, he thought. This was just the sort of thing the gossips would relish. "How did you get out?"

"I walked out. The house only looks like a fortress. There aren't any guards at the doors."

"There should be," he said. "Your father should hire a dozen, just for you." He sighed. It probably had been tried already. "Why are you here?"

"I wanted to talk to you."

"I think I understood that. How did you find me?"

"I asked my mother where you were staying. She told me she had suggested that you come here. It wasn't so difficult after that. I distracted the clerk at the front desk while I looked over the registry. Your name was right there beside room 309. When the clerk was busy with someone else, I came up."

Walker wasn't accepting such a facile explanation. He focused on the one word that was important to him. "Distracted? How?"

"In the traditional way," she said simply. "I flirted with him."

Closing his eyes, Walker rubbed his face with his palm. He let out a slow breath and considered the possibility that it was all a dream. He looked in her direction out of the corner of one eye. She was still there. "What time is it?"

"It was just after two when I arrived in the lobby. I imagine it's close to two-thirty now."

She seemed completely unconcerned by it. "Do you do this sort of thing often?" he asked.

"This would be my first time." She looked around with interest. The room was plainer than the one she remembered Michael having. But that had been years ago. Perhaps they were all so utilitarian now. "Do you have anything to drink here?"

"Water."

"That would be fine." She divined the expression in his eyes. "I'm only thirsty," she said. "I don't need to bolster my courage."

Walker pointed to the dressing room. "I don't think you're lacking in courage, merely in common sense."

Skye found a glass and poured herself a drink of water. When she reentered Walker's bedchamber he was standing by the window, his hands thrust in his pockets. His body was angled forward and he raised himself on the balls of his bare feet. Skye sipped her water, watching him.

He didn't appear to be angry, yet there was a restlessness about him that he was trying to contain. The tawny color of his hair, the length, the thickness, the lithe strength of his profile suddenly prompted an image in Skye's mind of a prowling lion, proud, stately, alone but in command. She was reluctant to go to him.

He sensed her presence and turned suddenly. "I should take you back," he said. "Finish your water and I'll get dressed."

"No. I'm not going with you, and if you try to force me, I'll make it very difficult for you." Skye returned to her chair and sipped her water. "You know I can."

It was the one thing he did know. "All right," he said. "You can stay."

"Thank you," she said softly. She regarded him intently before she spoke again. "You told Jay Mac and my mother that your parents were missionaries."

Of all the things he considered she might have to say to him, Walker hadn't once thought it would be this. She had an uncanny ability to set him completely off balance. He actually felt as if he'd staggered backward, but he knew he hadn't moved at all. Wondering where she was leading, not at all certain he wanted to follow, Walker confirmed her statement. "I told them," he said.

"Why?"

"Why? Because my parents *are* missionaries. Or rather, they were. They've been dead over fifteen years now."

Skye stopped rolling the glass between her palms and gripped it more tightly. "I'm sorry."

Walker knew she meant it. "You shouldn't be. They chose their death when they elected to serve in a leper colony in the South Pacific."

It was not his words that captured Skye's attention, but the lack of inflection in his tone. He wasn't indifferent to their deaths, he was merely pretending to be. He might even have convinced himself. Fifteen years was a long time to practice feeling nothing and capture the essence of it. "Where were you?" she asked.

"They left me on the mainland."

"The mainland?"

"China. Their mission was in Shanghai."

"You never told me any of this before," she said. "Didn't you think it was important?"

Walker took his hands out of his pockets. He folded his arms across his chest and leaned back against the window. He could feel the cool panes of glass through his shirt. "I'm not sure that it's important now."

"But you told my parents."

"Is this what it's about?" he asked. "Is this why you traipsed across town in the middle of the night? You're taking me to task for telling your parents something I didn't tell you?"

"That's part of it."

"Then perhaps you'd better tell me the whole of it, because I don't understand what goes on in that mind of yours."

He hadn't raised his voice, but the cold, sharp edge of it was enough to make Skye flinch. For all that his posture appeared relaxed, she sensed his agitation. His narrow gaze speared her. The gold flecks were splintered and bright. Skye put her glass down and got to her feet. She approached Walker, stopping only when she was within a foot of him. Her hands went to the tiny jet buttons on her gown and she began to unfasten them. She didn't watch her fingers; she watched him.

Walker's eyes dropped to Skye's hands when she touched the first button. The material parted and he had a glimpse of the hollow of her throat. A second button was undone and more of her skin came into view. She undid another. Then another. He looked at her again, a question in his eyes this time. She merely stared back and moved her fingers to the next button.

"Skye." His voice had a deep, raspy quality to it. It also held a warning.

"Mmmm?" She sounded innocent even as she played the temptress.

Walker was looking at the bare curves of her breasts as her bodice gaped wider. "What do you think you're doing?"

"Flirting?" she asked hopefully.

Walker fairly groaned. "I hope this isn't what you did with the desk clerk."

Her smile was a sensual siren's call and she let him wonder. She flicked another button and eased the gown off her shoulders. Skye was naked to the waist. She didn't have to touch another button.

Walker pushed away from the window. His palms grazed her arms, her shoulders. His thumbs passed along her collarbone, then traveled lower, brushing the sides of her breasts. He stroked them, cupping the underside, passing lightly across the nipples. She leaned into him and raised her face. Her lips parted as she stood on tiptoe and reached for him. Her fingers threaded at the back of his neck and she pulled gently, bringing him closer. Her mouth closed over his, hungry and searching.

She was lifted, carried. She felt the edge of the bed at the back of her knees. He pushed the gown over her hips. It spread like a dark green pool at her feet. Her shoes and socks, and finally her petticoat, followed. When she was tumbled backward on the bed, she pulled him with her. The weight of his body held her still for a moment, stealing her breath. He covered her, surrounded her. Her breasts swelled against his chest and her legs rubbed his. She kissed his jaw, his cheek. She pressed tiny, tasting kisses along the length of his neck.

He rolled on his back and she straddled him. Leaning forward, she removed the ribbon from her hair. She shook her head just once, slowly, from side to side, and her unbound hair slipped softly over her shoulders. Her hips moved lower as she slid comfortably over him. Through the barrier of his trousers she felt him straining against the cleft of her thighs. She rocked on him, teasing him again with kisses on the underside of his jaw and just below his ear. She felt his breathing quicken, then catch.

She kissed him again, softly, slowly. She raised her head before she was caught deeply by it. He was searching her face, his eyes dark. She dipped again, grazing his mouth, nudging his nose. Above him, she smiled.

"One of us has too many clothes on," she said.

It was gratifying, Walker reflected, that they thought so much alike.

Twelve

Walker stripped off his shirt and flung it over the side of the bed. He raised his hips as Skye tugged on his trousers. She made it sweet torture, kissing him as she inched the material past his hips and thighs. When she was finished, he was so ready for her that he ached with it.

He twisted them both so that she was under him again, this time on her stomach. She lay still, uncertain now by this turn of events. It was her breathing that became increasingly ragged as he laid his palm on her thigh, then drew it upward over her bottom, past the small of her back, and over her shoulder blades. It was her skin that warmed, even burned, under his touch, and a soft, aching moan parted her lips.

Moving her hair to one side, he kissed her neck and whispered in her ear as she turned her head. His mouth made a trail down her spine and then he moved behind her, lifting her hips.

Skye's fingers curled in the sheets as he entered her. His thrust was hard, the pleasure so intense that she bit her lip to silence a cry. She pushed back against him as he came into her again. She was lifted slightly and his hands came around, sliding under her belly and up to her breasts. They filled his hands. He cupped them. The nipples were hard, harder still when his thumbs passed over them. He urged a hum of pleasure from deep in her throat. Her body fairly vibrated with it.

He clutched her, pressing against her, filling her. His mouth was hot on her skin. He whispered her name. She cradled him, rocking with each thrust, finding his rhythm so they moved together. Her body shuddered first, and when he felt it, he couldn't prolong his own pleasure or hold out to make hers return. His hips moved quick and shallow and his entire body contracted tightly in the moment before he spent himself.

For a long time they both simply lay still, curled like spoons, his arm around her waist. His breath ruffled wisps of her flame-red hair. Lamplight burnished the strands with threads of gold and copper. When she moved slightly, only adjusting her position for comfort, her bottom nudged his groin. His response was a groan that he muffled in her hair. "Don't move," he said lowly.

"But—"

"Not just yet."

Except for the hand she laid across his forearm, Skye stayed as she was. In time Walker slept.

Skye rose from the bed and padded quietly into the dressing room. She washed at the basin. The water was cool on her warm skin and she let it trickle over her shoulders and between her breasts. She dried with a towel that still held Walker's masculine scent. When she was on the point of leaving she saw his dressing gown and slipped it on. The shoulder seams hung low and the sleeves brushed her fingertips. She raised the lapel to her face and rubbed her cheek against the material.

Skye crawled back into bed wearing the dressing gown.

Walker opened one eye. His hand slid over her shoulder and he recognized the texture of his robe. "Why do you have this on?"

"I wanted to wear you."

Once again Walker marveled at her ability to move him off center. He raised himself on one elbow as Skye turned on her back. "When are you going to marry me, Skye?"

"I'm not."

This time her response didn't really surprise him. "Are you going to tell me why?"

Instead of answering him directly, she asked a question of her own. "What is it you imagine I want out of life?"

Walker knew he was in trouble because he had never given it any thought. He did so now, thinking about it carefully because he realized how much depended on his answer. He considered what he knew about Mary Schyler Dennehy, what he had observed, what he had heard. He considered the things she had already told him and the things she had been unable to put into words. He thought about the things that were deeply felt and showed only in her eyes.

The first time he had seen her— the very first time— she had been marching along a Central Park path, a solitary figure who'd left her friends behind. She had been at some risk that night when he was attacked, but instead of running, she had watched the dangerous drama unfold. Knowing her as he did now, he thought that she might even have come to his rescue had events proceeded along a different line.

The next time he saw her was in the entrance hall of the Granville mansion. She was in a room full of other women but she was alone on that occasion as well. He had noticed her immediately, first when she pretended to sleep, and then when she waggled her behind in the air as she leaned over the bench. She was sharp and smart in the interview, tempering her wit so she did not cross the line to insolence. She had managed not only to secure a position for herself but one for another woman who would have surely gone without. He didn't believe she had gone into the meeting with Parnell with that intention. It was a notion that had occurred to her at some point in the interview and she'd seized it. Skye was not one to let an opportunity pass.

She could think quickly, spinning tales that held up under some scrutiny whenever she was caught out. And she didn't shy from danger. Rather, she seemed to embrace it. She was a little reckless, still impulsive, but before he judged her too harshly, he thought back through his own life and realized there was a time he'd have been judged much the same way.

He thought about her upbringing. It was not so difficult to imagine what it must have been like to be the bastard child of a man as powerful and well known as John MacKenzie Worth. In his mind he saw the photograph of the five Marys and understood the faint smiles were deliberate and the eyes were defiant. People must have watched them all the time, waiting for them to make the slightest misstep. Skye in particular seemed to have taken delight in giving the gossips grist for their mill. She had had four lively, lovely sisters to encourage her efforts.

Walker's thoughts eventually wandered to this evening, how she had come to him without reservation, honest in her need and unashamed by it. It was excitement that rushed color to her face, not embarrassment.

Now Walker touched her cheek, tracing the arc with his forefinger and tucking a strand of hair behind her ear. "I think that what you want out of life," he said quietly, solemnly, "is not to waste a day of it. I think you want to embrace excitement when you find it and savor the quiet moments as you come upon them. The worst thing you can imagine is to have each day be like the one before it or know that tomorrow will have no adventure."

Skye didn't speak for a moment. She couldn't. There was a hard knot at the back of her throat that prevented her from saying anything. It was as if Walker had reached into her mind and plucked out her thoughts. In doing so he had touched her soul. "How do you know all that?"

Her voice was both anxious and breathless. There was a sheen of tears in her beautiful eyes. Walker's hand lay near the curve of her neck and now he drew his knuckle along the edge of her jaw. "We're not so different, you and I," he said. "I'm thinking we have a lot in common."

She gave him a hesitant, watery smile and drew his hand to her heart. "I suspected it here," she said. "Long before I could understand it. I kept dwelling on the things I didn't know about you instead of concentrating on the things I did. All my life I've wanted to be judged for who I was, not who my parents were, not the circumstances of my birth, not my address, not my fortune. Yet given the opportunity to see you in that light, I found myself not considering your character but wondering about your past. I think I must be the worst kind of hypocrite."

Bending his head, Walker kissed her lightly on the lips. "You're too hard on yourself," he told her. "In spite of what you don't know, I don't believe you'd have come to my bed on any occasion without concluding something about my character."

It was true. "Yes," she whispered. "But what if I've concluded all the wrong things?"

"Tell me," he said. His grave tone was at odds with the glint in his eyes. "I suppose I'll have to try to live up to them."

She was smiling as she threaded her fingers through his. "I don't think you take yourself too seriously," she said. "You're more casually confident than arrogant. I think you take a position on the important things and shrug off the rest. I think you're secretly amused by most of what you see in others, but you're careful not to patronize. It's interesting that you genuinely don't seem to care what others think of you."

With one exception, he thought. He cared very much, perhaps too much, about Skye's opinion. He almost wished he hadn't encouraged her to talk, and yet he couldn't bring himself to stop her.

"I don't think you enjoy confrontation, but you certainly don't run from it," she said. "You know your own mind. You can listen to others and accept their opinion without trying to change it." Skye was searching his face, studying the line of his slightly crooked nose, the shape of his serious mouth. His brown-and-gold-flecked eyes returned her regard without expression, but this was one time when she thought she understood what was on his mind. Her hand squeezed his gently. "Did you suspect I was going to confine myself to cataloging admirable qualities like bravery, intelligence, and fortitude?"

His low laughter was tinged with self-mockery and his tone was dry. "It's a good thing I don't take myself too seriously." He raised her hand to his lips and kissed her knuckles. His brows were raised and his smile was wry. "Though I really hadn't given any thought to fortitude."

Skye would not be waylaid by his humor on this occasion. "I think you're all those things," she said soberly. "I think you can be protective and patient, kind and cunning. You see more than you reveal and share less than you know. That's both annoying and frustrating." With uncomplicated frankness, Skye added, "It's also intriguing." She watched the shutter close over his expression once more. He was rubbing her knuckles across his mouth again, the gesture more absent than sensual. "But perhaps it doesn't really matter what I feel about it. It's who you are. I can't change it. I can accept it or not. For now I can accept it."

"Tomorrow?" The single word was almost uttered against his will.

"I don't know."

Walker let Skye's hand fall away. He reached for the lamp and turned it back, then lay down fully beside her. He felt her turn toward him, stretch out her body so that she was flush to the planes and angles of his long frame. Her head rested on his shoulder and her arm went around his waist. "You'll stay here tonight?" he asked.

"Until daybreak."

He wondered if it would be enough time. "I'm glad you came," he said, after a moment.

"I thought it could turn out very badly for me," she said.

"You mean if you were caught?"

"I mean if you hadn't wanted me. Or worse, had wanted me then called me a whore for it."

His fingers had been stroking her hair. He paused now. If Skye was confident about some aspects of his character, she also harbored doubts. "That comment is hardly flattering to either one of us," he told her. "Have I made you feel like a whore?"

"No," she said softly. "You made me feel desired. Real and deeply."

"You *are* desired."

"I think I'm beginning to believe it."

Walker didn't understand why she'd ever believed otherwise. "I know I'm your first lover," he said. *Only lover,* he had wanted to say. *Last lover,* he was thinking. "But surely there were—"

"Boys," she said. Then, because she did not want him to feel too smug, she added quickly, "And men." She could imagine he was smiling anyway, seeing right through her, even in the darkness. "I never wanted for an escort, but they weren't lining the sidewalk in front of my house. Some of them were handsome, some were plain. Most of them had an eye on my money. The ones who didn't had an eye on something more intimate."

"What about Daniel? Where did he fit in?"

Had she mentioned Daniel? She supposed she had, because Walker wouldn't have known the name otherwise. He didn't seem to forget anything. "Daniel is my friend. He invited me into his circle, or perhaps he was the one who accepted me when I first barged in." She sighed. "It's been so long I'm not certain I know anymore. Maggie and I were close, but she didn't enjoy joining where she wasn't wanted. I, on the other hand, made it a mission of sorts. Daniel was both my passport and my confidant."

"He loves you?"

Skye shook her head. "No, not at all. Oh, from time to time he got it into his head that he did. He even kissed me once, but we decided we just didn't suit." Her voice lowered confidentially. The husky timbre settled sweetly over Walker. "Daniel wanted to try again, but I think it was just to prove to himself that he could do it better than before. He really likes someone else."

"And you?" he asked after a moment. "What are your feelings?"

"I like him. I hope he'll always be my friend."

Walker winced a little. He never wanted to hear those same words in reference to himself. "There was no one else?" he asked. "No one special?"

She shook her head, wondering why he didn't understand yet. "I'm not very conventional, Walker," she said plainly, without bitterness. "I'm a bastard. I'm Catholic. I'm the daughter of a robber baron and an Irish housemaid. My hair looks as if it's been set on fire, and I'm

not particularly accomplished in any of the usual feminine pursuits."

"And those would be . . ." he prompted.

"Needlework, painting, singing, dancing, playing an
instrument, or playing the hostess."

"I see." He could think of one or two feminine pursuits she had mastered, the least of which was flirting.
"And you don't do any of these things?"

Skye knew she had amused him again, but she had
long ago accepted her shortcomings. Her shrug was
philosophical. "I can do them all, but I'm not passion-
ate about any one of them. Sometimes I wish it were
different or at least that I could accept mediocrity as
my standard."

Walker's fingers paused in her hair again. "That
would be death for you." And he meant it.

"Yes," she said softly. "That would be death." She
turned her face slightly so that she could kiss his naked
shoulder. It was comfortable to be in his arms, to feel
the warmth of his body, the rhythm of his life in the
heartbeat beneath her palm. "My sisters feel the same
way, but then, they all have some talent that was tapped
out by the time I was born." Walker's low and throaty
chuckle vibrated his chest. Skye could feel it against her
cheek. "It's true," she said. "A nun. A writer. An engineer. A doctor."

Walker didn't fill the silence that followed immediately.
He considered his words carefully, not trying to convince,
but simply stating a point of fact. "Your talent is not what
you can do," he said quietly, "but what you are."

"Then I'm— "

"Splendidly, devastatingly unconventional."

Skye shifted her position slightly so her leg stretched
along his. She raised herself to get a better look at Walker.
He let her touch his face with her fingertips. There was
no laughter at the edge of his mouth, no dark irony in

his eyes. His features were as straightforward and honest as his words. "You don't mind it?" she asked.

"It would be like minding the sun for putting color on the horizon when it rises and sets," he said. "Or minding that the tide lays shells along the beach in the course of its flow. How can I mind what *is*? It's your gift, Skye. I appreciate it." Something wet dashed his cheek and he realized it was her tear. It was followed by another. His fingers sifted in her hair as she burrowed against him. He held her in the circle of one arm and stroked the fiery strands of her hair.

Walker was hardly aware of when the cadence of her breathing changed or when her heart began to thrum more loudly between her breasts. He was only aware that those things were happening and that his body was absorbing the same life rhythms. She was moving sinuously against him, kissing his mouth, his chest, the flat plane of his abdomen. His skin retracted. He could feel the hot course of his blood and the tension in his muscles. Her hands were on his thighs, her fingers on the smooth line of his buttocks. She captured him intimately with her mouth.

Sparks of pleasure licked at his skin and pulsed in his groin. Her mouth was hot, insistent, but not hurried. She kept urgency at bay, drawing out the sensation with slow deliberation until he showed her otherwise. His fingertips pressed hard on her pale skin and tangled in her hair. He came in a volley of shudders sinking deep inside her.

Skye sat up slowly. With the slightest tilt of her head, her hair fell backward behind her shoulders. Her right hand lingered on Walker's thigh as she put her legs over the side of the bed. Without a word she padded to the adjoining room and returned with a basin and damp cloth. She washed them both, a ritual as tender as it was intimate.

Skye crawled into bed again. Walker's body instantly curved to accommodate hers. This time when the cadence of their breathing changed it bore the stamp of sleep.

"Open this door," Jay Mac said. His voice was meant to brook no argument, but one was coming anyway.

The hapless desk clerk was protesting even as he was reaching for the key. "Sir, this is the St. Mark. If you'd just let me speak to the manager, I'm certain— "

Sometimes it was a considerable advantage to be John MacKenzie Worth. He had only to say his name to quell the objections. The key was placed in the keyhole and the doorknob was turned. "That will be all," he said, blocking the clerk's entry to the room. He pressed some money into the clerk's hand and waited until the man had turned at the stairs before he let himself into room 309.

Walker was sitting upright in bed by the time Jay Mac entered. Skye was only turning on her side, still buried under a mound of covers, her smile vague as the interruption dislodged her from pleasant dreams.

Beneath his thick, sandy brows and large side whiskers, Jay Mac had a ruddy complexion. He stared hard at Walker, his eyes darting only once to the mound of moving blankets. "Is that my daughter under there?"

"Yes, sir."

The blankets went completely still. "She's not awake?" Jay Mac asked.

"I think she is now," Walker said. He lifted one corner of the blanket. Skye's eyes were no longer bleary. Her expression was stricken. He lowered the blanket. "Yes, sir. She's awake."

Jay Mac closed his eyes and rubbed the bridge of his nose. Although his color was fading, just above the neck of his starched collar his skin was still markedly red. His cheeks puffed as he blew out a hard sigh. His hand dropped away from his face and he took out his spectacles, unfolding them with great care. "She missed breakfast this morning." His mouth was grim. "It appears she slept in."

Walker said nothing. The mound of blankets did not stifle Skye's groan and he let it pass for a response.

"You'll marry her, of course," Jay Mac said.

"I told you those were my intentions yesterday," Walker said. "They haven't changed."

Skye kicked at the blankets, but she didn't come up. *"Nooo!"* she fairly wailed.

"It isn't your choice any longer, Mary Schyler," Jay Mac said flatly. He regarded Walker. "Come by my office at ten. We'll discuss details privately."

Walker nodded and watched Jay Mac turn sharply on his heel. His shoulders were braced stiffly, his spine was rigid. He could have slammed the door on his way out, instead he closed it quietly. Walker winced anyway.

"He's gone," Walker said.

Skye sat up and pushed hair out of her eyes. Her expression was feral. "How could you?"

"How could I what?" he asked calmly.

"Just sit there!"

Walker raised the blankets enough to slip out of bed. He was naked. "I didn't think my current state of dress would do anything to change your father's mind." He picked up the discarded clothes from last night and went into the dressing room. A pillow slammed between his shoulder blades as he crossed the threshold. "Good aim," he said, without pausing.

Skye threw off the covers and got out of bed herself. She put on Walker's dressing gown again and belted the sash tightly. "I'm not marrying you," she told him sharply, pacing the floor at the foot of the bed. Her feathered brows were furrowed and she worried her lower lip between her teeth. "Didn't you hear anything I said last night? Didn't you believe the things you said about me?"

Walker came to the doorway of the dressing room to finish fastening his trousers. "What are you talking about? Of course I listened. I believed everything I said."

Her eyes pleaded with him. "Then you didn't understand!"

Walker reached behind him and picked up a shirt. He shrugged into it. "I suppose I don't."

She stopped pacing. "I'm not going to marry you," she said. "I'll be your mistress, your lover, but I won't marry you."

He supposed it was about love, but with Skye, one never knew for sure. So he asked, "Why not?"

"Because I want to be an adventuress!" she almost shouted at him. "I can shoot and ride and fence and sail. Those are the skills I've been mastering. I've studied history and geography and art and architecture. I want to go places, Walker. That's my purpose. I can't marry you!"

The silence that followed her words could not have been more profound. Unmoving, Walker merely stared at her. His thumbs rested in the waistband of his trousers. His head was tilted slightly to one side. He only blinked once. "An adventuress," he said quietly, "is someone who schemes to marry a rich man, not someone looking for adventure. At dinner last night, while you were sulking in your room, your father said he hoped you would go back to school. Perhaps you should, Skye, and learn the difference between what you want to be and what you are."

Skye felt his words like a blow to her stomach. Air rushed out of her lungs. She sat down slowly on the edge of the bed and willed herself not to look away from Walker. To do so would have been an admission somehow that she was as young and willful and irresponsible as he thought she was in that moment.

"Get dressed," he said. "I'll take you home."

"I can take—"

"I'll take you home," he said again. He disappeared into the dressing room.

In spite of the fact that Walker had arrived at the Worth Building ten minutes early, he was shown into Jay Mac's office without any waiting. He took the chair Jay Mac pointed out to him while Jay Mac himself chose to stand at the window.

"She's my youngest," Jay Mac said, looking out over the city. He had rocked forward on the balls of his feet, his hands clasped behind his back. He looked very much like a captain of industry, only his conversation wasn't about tracks and ties and lines. It was deeply personal and deeply felt. "I don't suppose that means anything to you," he added. "I only meant to nudge her in the direction of going back to school. I wasn't thinking about marriage for my Mary Schyler, not yet. I would have planned better for her than you."

Walker said nothing. He waited.

"I should kill you for what you did to my daughter."

"I thought you were going to," he said, his tone carefully neutral. "You had a gun tucked in your trousers this morning. A Colt?"

"Smith and Wesson." He unclasped his hands and patted his right side. He turned slowly, parting his jacket to reveal the butt end of the weapon. "I still have it, and I still may use it."

Walker didn't believe it was Jay Mac's usual method of handling a conflict. He also didn't doubt that the threat was serious.

Watching Walker carefully, Jay Mac asked idly, "You don't flinch much, do you?"

"Not much."

"Play poker?"

"A little."

"Do you win?"

"Most of the time."

Jay Mac smiled slowly, thoughtfully, the answer just what he expected. "I thought you might." He sat down behind his desk and leaned back in his chair. The Smith and Wesson was still within easy reach. "I'm not going to be fobbed off with those answers you gave me last night. I don't give a damn who your parents were or what they did. It doesn't matter if they brought you up in China by way of Timbuktu or Hackensack. My wife enjoys that sort of thing. I don't care if you were raised by wolves." He paused and let that sink in. Walker appeared to remain unmoved. "There's something you haven't told us, Mr. Caine. Something you've kept from me, from Moira, perhaps even from my daughter. I want to know what it is."

So Walker told him.

Jay Mac's hands were folded in his lap. He tapped his thumbs together as he listened. By the end of Walker's account, they were still. "Does Skye know any of this?"

"No. She suspects something's not right, but she doesn't know what I've told you."

Jay Mac consulted his timepiece. It was almost eleven-thirty now, and still much too early for a drink. For once, he didn't let that deter him. Leaving his chair, he poured himself a small Scotch at the sideboard. "Anything for you?" he asked.

Walker shook his head.

"I don't usually . . ." Jay Mac's voice trailed off. He looked down at his hand that held the tumbler. It was trembling.

"You don't have to explain." Walker could understand why he was shaken. "You didn't know."

"Did you think I did?"

"I wondered."

He swore vehemently. "I would have never sent Skye there! I had a simple agreement with the man about financing his engine. When I saw his notice in the paper, it occurred to me that Skye might discover the progress of the invention, or if it existed at all. My investment wasn't large— not above twenty thousand dollars— and no amount of money would be a satisfactory exchange for my daughter's life. I met Parnell once. He seemed agreeable enough, not the sort who would— " He couldn't finish the sentence. He knocked back a swallow of his drink instead. "I'd hoped that sending Skye to Granville would ground her feet again. I'm certain she suspected other motives, but as usual, she let her imagination take the place of clear, solid thinking."

Walker found it difficult not to smile just then. Jay Mac did not seem to credit that Skye's imagination was rooted in anything so solid as her father's previous dealings with his other daughters.

Jay Mac returned to his desk. He didn't sit down this time, but rested one hip on the edge of it. He looked at Walker consideringly. "You've proved you can keep her safe," he said gruffly, as if the admission were forced rather than willingly offered.

"Yes, sir. I think I've proved that."

"You haven't shown you can care for her though. I'm speaking of finances now."

"Yes. I understood that. I draw a regular wage."

Jay Mac snorted. "That's the only conventional thing about your employment. I can't say that I like it." His eyes narrowed. "Unconventional suits Skye, though."

"Yes, sir," Walker said gravely. "I've come to appreciate that."

Jay Mac's penetrating glance became even sharper. "Why do I think you're laughing about something?"

Walker realized belatedly that a grin was edging his mouth. He reined it in. "I couldn't say, sir."

"More likely you *won't* say," he said. "Never mind. If it concerns something with Skye, I don't think I want to know." He finished his drink. "And you may as well call me Jay Mac. All my sons-in-law do. My daughters, too. Hell, the whole country does. No reason that you should be an exception."

"Yes, sir." The response was automatic, not an insolent ignoring of the older man's wishes.

John MacKenzie Worth had to smile. "Well, it's easy to see you weren't raised by wolves." He studied Walker Caine again, taking in the crown of thick, tawny hair that was perhaps a trifle overlong, the lines in a young face that made it seem older, and the frank, implacable eyes that could challenge or intimidate or reflect on his own sense of confidence. "Does my daughter love you?"

"No. She's curious about me, perhaps a little fascinated, but I don't mistake it for love."

Jay Mac was thoughtful. "That will make it difficult," he said. "Do you love her?"

"Yes."

Jay Mac nodded wisely. "That will make it easier."

Walker did not see Skye again until the wedding. The arrangements were made swiftly and quietly, and no one was invited save the family. At Walker's insistence there would be no announcement in the paper or any acknowledgment in the community that the marriage had occurred. Jay Mac understood the reasoning, and he approved. The bride's mother did not. The bride herself simply didn't care.

The wedding took place in the Worth home, in Jay Mac's study. Seventy-two hours had been enough time to assure that the vows weren't exchanged in Judge Halsey's chambers. Moira had insisted on flowers. Cut glass vases filled with orange blossoms and baby's breath were set out on every available surface. The fragrance was sweet but not cloying.

Walker wore a suit that Jay Mac's tailor quickly put together for him. The black swallow-tailed coat and trousers were cut cleanly along the lines of his lean frame. The evening waistcoat was white on white brocade. The shirt was crisply white, with a stiff wing collar and starched cuffs. His hair had been trimmed, but the edge of it still brushed his collar. A silk handkerchief was carefully arranged in the upper pocket of his coat.

"Mama says you've cleaned up quite nicely."

Realizing he was the target of this statement, though he didn't recognize the voice, Walker turned away from the sideboard, where he had been contemplating getting drunk. He was confronted by a pair of large, forest-green eyes beautifully framed in a wimple and cornet. "Sister Mary Francis."

"And intelligent, too."

Walker's brows lifted a fraction at her dry, caustic tone. "Have I offended you in some way?" he asked quietly.

Mary Francis had the grace to blush. People usually didn't take her on. They were either in awe of her habit or too dumbfounded by her straightforwardness. Mary Francis considered her answer carefully, fully aware of her parents talking to the judge on the other side of the study. When she saw Walker's attention stray in that direction, she knew there was a lull in the conversation. She could almost feel their eyes boring into her back, advising caution and an even temperament. "It's this situation I find offensive," she said, keeping her voice low. She glanced over her shoulder and smiled serenely at her parents and the judge. Their anxiety did not appear to lessen. "This is intolerable," she said, facing Walker again. He was regarding her with polite interest and some amusement. "Can we talk somewhere privately?"

His eyes darted to the door. "Since your sister seems to be late for her own wedding, I don't see why not."

"Good." Without any explanation to the others, Mary Francis led Walker to the front parlor. She closed the double doors securely behind them. "There," she said, satisfied. She looked at Walker, considered him at length, but didn't expound on her thoughts.

He returned her regard for a full minute before he broke the silence. "Are you going to tell me that she's run off?"

"Run off?" Mary Francis was genuinely puzzled. "Skye? Heavens no. That's not her way. She'll be down directly. The maid is fussing with her hair right now and there was some problem with her gown earlier."

"I see," he said, but of course he didn't. "You were with her, then?"

She nodded, smoothing the front of her habit. Her hand fell naturally to her rosary and she sifted through the beads. "Skye thinks I can talk you out of this marriage."

Now Walker felt the fog lifting. "Then you're here on a diplomatic mission."

"Yes. That's something you understand, isn't it?"

Walker said nothing. His interest remained polite, but his thoughts were reserved.

"You *do* play your cards close to the vest."

He shrugged.

"I suppose you're determined to go through with this wedding."

He looked down at himself, then at her. "I dressed for it."

Her full mouth widened in an appreciative smile. "It would be a shame to waste the suit. My father's tailor?"

He nodded. "You're not going to try to talk me out of marrying your sister?"

"I am trying," she said. "It's a feeble attempt, I grant you. My parents and the judge think I'm engaging you in a ferocious argument. Skye hopes I'll break your knees."

If there was a choice, Walker was going to pick physical injury to trading barbs with Mary Francis. "You're not going to do either?"

She shook her head. "But there are always appearances to observe. Which is why I asked you to come in here. Skye wouldn't accept that I didn't want to be placed in the middle. This way she'll think I tried and failed." Mary Francis sighed. "Not that I think this wedding is a good idea. You must know she doesn't want to marry you."

"She's said as much."

"Did Papa really catch you both out at the St. Mark?"

To Walker's way of thinking, Mary Francis's keen interest was not congruent with her habit. He felt uncomfortably warm and wished he had had time to pour himself that drink. He considered simply offering up his kneecaps and finishing the interrogation swiftly. He couldn't answer her questions if he was screaming in pain.

Never one to surrender, he charged. "In bed. In the buff." He watched as her pale, ivory complexion flamed. Under her wimple, Walker suspected she was a redhead just like her sister. "You can blush," he said. "I wasn't certain."

She grimaced. "I suppose I deserved that."

"No supposing about it," he said drily.

"All right. I *did* deserve it." The next time she asked a shocking question she would be better prepared for a shocking answer. There would be no next time with Walker. He was more than able to hold his own. "I think you should return to the study," she said. "I'll go upstairs and inform Skye that you're intractable."

"She knows I'm intractable," he said. *Tell her I love her.*

"What?" Mary Francis asked, halting at the door. "Did you say something else?"

Had he spoken aloud? he wondered. The words had been right there, on the edge of his mind, on the tip of his tongue. "Nothing," Walker said after a moment. "It's nothing. Tell her I'm waiting. Tell her that we're all waiting."

"It won't hurry her, but I'll mention it."

Walker understood. To Skye's way of thinking it was a little like informing the condemned that the crowd had gathered at the gallows. When Skye joined them some thirty minutes later in the study Walker revised his opinion slightly. She had a trancelike dignity about her that made him think of French aristocrats and the cart ride from the Bastille to the guillotine.

As he looked around the room, the vision in his mind took full shape. Judge Halsey had the dour countenance of an executioner. Jay Mac, leading Skye forward on his arm, was the wagon driver who carried the doomed to meet their fate. Moira was an anxious bystander, fascinated and fearful, but rallying in the end. Mary Francis was calm in the storm, her serenity a sharp contrast to the madness she saw all around her but was powerless to stop.

Walker's own role was that of the revolutionary soldier, assisting the *beautiful* victim up the final steps to the steel blade.

He took Skye's hand and drew her close to his side. She came without resistance, but her skin was like ice. "I don't want your head in a basket," he whispered. Incredibly, she looked at him and there was panicked acknowledgment in her eyes. That was when he knew she shared his vision. The last niggling doubt he had about carrying out the ceremony evaporated. He squeezed her hand.

Judge Halsey's words were brief, the directions simple. Honor. Love. Obedience. Richer. Poorer. Health. 'Til Death. Skye's voice shook as she offered up the words. Her hand still held no warmth. She couldn't quite meet his eyes. For his part Walker repeated the vows while he searched Skye's face, willing her to hear him out. He said the words quietly, deliberately, but suspected he hadn't been heard at all. A certain distant expression had returned to her eyes and when she looked at him, she looked right through him.

After the exchange of vows there were congratulations. Jay Mac's and the judge's were the most heartfelt. Moira's best wishes were subdued. Mary Francis managed to raise her sister's smile.

"Thank God," she said, when she saw it. "You looked grim as death."

Skye felt that grim. She looked sideways at Walker. He didn't seem at all affected by the changed circumstances of their lives. "Your compliments will turn my head," she told her sister. "Mama and Mrs. Cavanaugh spent a lot of time on this gown." As much as three days and a shotgun approach to marriage would permit, she thought. She considered saying as much, but some cautionary light in her sister's eye made her think twice. Was Mary Francis actually warning her not to push Walker? She wondered about the conversation the two of them had while she was pacing the floor in her own room. Mary Francis would only say that nothing had changed or was going to change and that Skye should determine how to make the best of it. Oh, and there had been a parting shot—something about being two sides of the same page. What had she meant by that?

"You're lovely."

Skye blinked. It wasn't Mary Francis who offered the observation, but Walker. He had called her beautiful once, but she had been wearing considerably less on that occasion.

Wondering what he saw that prompted a comment now, Skye caught her reflection in the gilt mirror above the mantel. Her gown was weighted silk. It had softness and substance and contrasting colors. The bodice was verdigris, the skirt marine blue. The cut was narrow and revealing in the bust, waist, and hips. The back of the gown was drawn up in an elaborately draped bustle. Gold threads trimmed the heart-shaped neckline and tight cuffs. Another band of gold edged the hemline. A cameo rested at her throat, supported by a delicate gold chain. She wore small gold studs in her ears. Her bright hair was almost tamed in a smooth chignon. The most militant tendrils curled near her ears and temples. A wayward strand had fallen softly against her neck.

"Say thank you," Mary Francis directed firmly. Her eyes darted between the stricken bride and the stoic, impassive groom. "Your husband's made you a very pretty compliment."

Skye hastily looked away from her reflection. Her response was rote. "Thank you."

Mary Francis shook her head and briefly raised her eyes heavenward. She sought both patience and guidance. While Skye appeared to find no humor in her gesture, when she looked at Walker, his faint smile communicated his understanding.

"I hear Irish wakes are festive," he said with severe irony.

That caught Skye's attention. "One could be arranged."

Mary Francis grinned at Walker. "I think she means you could be the dearly departed."

Walker nodded. He hadn't failed to grasp Skye's implication. His attention was caught by Moira, who was talking to Mrs. Cavanaugh at the door. "I believe we're about to be summoned to dinner," he said. Skye stiffened but didn't resist when he took her arm. Walker pretended not to notice. She wasn't prepared to give him any quarter and now wasn't the time to take her to task for it.

"You drank quite a bit at dinner," he said. Each course of the interminable meal was accented with a specially chosen wine. Everyone sipped except Skye. Everyone else also ate between wine tastings.

Skye was sitting at her vanity. She paused in removing the pins from her hair and raised her eyes. Walker was reflected in her mirror. His image seemed soft to her, wavering and blurred at the edges. With some difficulty she searched his features for signs of censure.

"Merely an observation," he told her.

Her eyes narrowed on the slim smile that touched his face. Was it mocking, or amused? Perhaps both. In her off balance state, she couldn't be sure. Skye's fingers returned to the pins in her hair. When they fumbled, failing to pluck out the pin as she wished, she swore softly.

"Let me," he said. He came up behind her and touched her shoulders. He unclasped her cameo and laid it on the vanity. His fingers returned to touch the curve of her throat.

Skye's gaze wandered to his hands on her bare skin. His fingers were long, the nails trim. Next to them the line of her collarbone was delicate. Even the lightest pressure from him was like a brand on her flesh. The length of her neck seemed too slender to support her head. She leaned back, resting the crown of it against his hard, flat belly. His fingertips grazed her throat, sending a shiver through her. Skye closed her eyes and then his hands were in her hair. The pins were removed easily and her hair fell about her shoulders. His fingers combed through it, sifting, releasing the fragrances of lavender and lilac.

"Better?" he asked quietly.

"Mmmm."

He knew how to interpret that. He kept threading his fingers through her hair. Fire crackled in the hearth. It gave sound to the fire crackling in her hair. The strands of gold and orange and red that were like slivers of flame wrapped around his fingers. "You're going to have a sore head in the morning."

Skye didn't open her eyes. She nodded agreeably, unconcerned. The crown of her head rubbed against his hard midriff. "I suppose you'll think I deserve it."

"I'll think you earned it."

"Like I earned this marriage?" she asked.

He didn't reply immediately. "I don't want to argue about it, Skye. What's done is done."

Opening her eyes, Skye sat up and pulled her hair forward, away from Walker's exploring fingers. In the silence that had preceded his words, she imagined she had heard his answer. In every way she had made her bed and would be forced to lie in it. Honor. Love. Obedience. 'Til death.

Skye picked up her brush and ran it through her hair with rough strokes. Her activity was clumsier than she would have wished, and after only a half-dozen ragged passes, she pitched the brush hard at her reflection.

The angle of the toss, more than the anger behind it, shattered the mirror. Glass cracked and splintered. It sparkled as it fell away from the silver paper backing and landed on the top of the cherrywood vanity.

Stricken, Skye stared at the damage she had caused. She raised her eyes slowly and sought out Walker. His reflection had disappeared. Panic caught her breath. In her lap her hands twisted once until her fingers found the plain gold band he had given her to seal his vows. She bent her head, breathing easier. After a moment tears gathered in her eyes, then dripped soundlessly onto her lap. They spiked her lashes. One splattered the back of her hand.

"Take this," he said.

The silk handkerchief that had accented his black tail-coat was placed in the line of her blurred vision. Skye took it, though she hadn't any clear idea what to do with it. She clutched it instead of raising it to her face.

Walker knelt beside her. There were a few shards of glass on the floor, but he ignored them. One crunched beneath his knee. "Like this," he said patiently. He took the handkerchief from her and dabbed at her eyes and cheeks. The prompting helped Skye take over the task but did nothing to stem the flow of tears. Her shoulders heaved once. She was wretchedly unhappy.

Watching her, Walker's own heart was gripped in a vise. He stood up slowly, brushed glass dust from his knees, and went to the adjoining dressing room. "You have a daybed in there," he said when he came out again. "I can sleep on it."

Skye's knuckles whitened as she clenched the handkerchief more tightly. A small hiccup interrupted her sob. She stared at him out of wide, glassy green eyes. "Why?"

"I think it would be better."

Her brows furrowed. "Better?"

A muscle worked in his jaw but he spoke calmly. "I thought you would prefer it."

"You mean you would."

"If I meant that, I'd have said it. I was trying to be considerate."

"I don't want you to be considerate." The last tear spilled over the rim of her eye. She wiped it away impatiently and came to her feet. "You haven't taken my feelings into account before now. Why should you start?"

"I've always taken your feelings into account. It's your thinking I don't credit much." He watched as his retort simply took the wind out of her sails. Skye was visibly deflated. Her shoulders sagged a little, her eyes dropped away from his. She looked alone again, all at once at sea. Alcohol had had a mercurial effect on the emotional tide. The ebb and flow of anger was as difficult to predict as it was to follow.

"I'm going to get ready for bed," she said wearily. She rubbed her right temple with her fingertips. What had happened? she wondered. Minutes ago she had been resting comfortably against Walker, his fingers in her hair. For as long as it lasted, his touch had been soothing. "Sleep wherever it suits you."

Taking Skye at her word, Walker returned to the dressing room.

Thirteen

Skye's clothes were strewn around the bedroom. On his path from the dressing room to her bed, Walker had to step over her gown, the bustle, the train, a corset, a chemise, stockings, two petticoats, and a shoe. The other shoe had been neatly placed under the bed. One could only marvel at how she had managed it.

Skye herself was sprawled on the bed, more covered than not by an eyelet lace comforter, two quilts, and a crisp cotton sheet. One of her bare legs had pushed aside all the blankets and was lying smoothly on top. Her hair spilled across a scattering of pillows. Her head was turned in his direction. Her eyes were closed and her mouth was slightly parted.

Her exhausted, labored breathing sounded a lot like snoring.

Walker stood at the edge of the bed, looking down at her. He was smiling crookedly. A single dimple creased one side of his mouth. It wasn't the wedding night he had imagined. His not-so-virginal wife was sleeping off the effects of hard drinking in her very virginal bed. Her parents were sleeping in another wing of the house, probably lightly, alert to the first sign of trouble from the newlyweds. Thank God Mary Francis had returned to the convent.

Giving Skye a less-than-gentle shove, Walker rearranged her limbs to make room for himself. She murmured something sleepily, something that didn't sound very complimentary, but she allowed herself to be manipulated. Walker slipped in beside her. His grin deepened when he realized she was quite naked. Reasoning he might as well be hanged for a sheep as for a lamb, Walker shed his drawers and turned on his side. Skye's rounded bottom fit snugly against his groin. Her back was flush to his chest. They shared the same pillow and the fragrance of her hair teased his nostrils. He kissed her shoulder lightly, then lay back and closed his eyes.

The band of heat just below Skye's breasts was becoming uncomfortably warm. She moved restlessly, pushing against the weight at her back with her legs and bottom. She came awake abruptly, her eyes opening wide as she realized what she was pushing against and what the inevitable reaction was. Instead of one source of heat, now there were two.

"I'm not going to attack you," he said, his voice thick with sleep.

She whispered the obvious. "You're awake."

"Just."

"I'm sorry."

So was he. It had been a splendid dream. In light of his waking condition, Walker believed it could have been more than that very soon. "Do you want up?" he asked huskily.

"Yes, please. I don't feel well."

He let her go immediately. Skye scrambled out of the bed and rushed to the dressing room. Walker winced at the sounds of her being sick. "Do you want help?" Her moan could have meant anything; he took it as a refusal.

Walker rubbed his eyes, then stretched for the lamp beside the bed. He lit it, replaced the globe, then fell tiredly back on the mattress. A bleary glance at Skye's mantel clock revealed it was four-thirty. That surprised him. He felt as if he'd just gone to sleep. "Are you all right?" he called.

There was no moan this time. There was no response of any kind. Walker pushed himself upright. He was at the edge of the bed when he heard Skye pouring water, then the sounds of her cleaning her teeth. She was fine, then. Walker hooked his heels on the bed frame and rested his elbows on his knees. He was supporting his head in his hands when she came out of the dressing room. She was wearing his shirt. The tails fell below her thighs.

"What are you doing in my bed?" she asked from the doorway.

"I'm waiting for you," he said. "Do you feel better?"

"I thought you were going to sleep in here."

He shrugged. "You said I should wherever it suited me. It suited me here." Walker raised the covers and slipped back into bed. "You must feel better," he grumbled.

"What?" she asked.

"Come to bed," he said. When she didn't move, he added, "Or not. Whichever you prefer." He turned on his side, away from her.

Skye glanced at the daybed in the room behind her. It didn't look particularly inviting. Anyway, it wasn't the bed she had made for herself. Ignoring the litter of her own clothes, Skye joined Walker. She turned back the lamp and lay beside him. He was breathing quietly and evenly. She was careful not to disturb him. Her eyes adjusted to the darkness slowly. A sliver of moonshine that she hadn't noticed before outlined the furniture with a blue-gray cast. "Are you still awake?" she whispered.

"It depends," came the husky reply. "If you want to fight, then I'm sleeping."

Skye considered that was good sense. "I've made a mess of things, haven't I?"

Walker didn't think she was talking about the shattered mirror or the scattered clothes. Still, he didn't
turn toward her. He remained quiet, letting her sort
out her own thoughts.

"When Michael married Ethan, we were all together,"
she said quietly. "Even though it was arranged on the
spur of the moment, we managed to be there. When Rennie was married, Michael was already living in Colorado
and couldn't come east. At Maggie's wedding, it was only
Mary Francis and me. Then it was only Mary Francis."

She sounded wistful, Walker thought, a little homesick
in her own home for the way things used to be. There
had been telegrams from the Marys who couldn't attend,
best wishes mingled with warnings about the action Skye
was about to take. Of course, it wasn't the same.

"I know it's silly," she said, "but I looked around the
dining table this evening and realized how empty it
was." It wasn't just missing the Marys, she thought, it
was that no one was there for Walker, either. "Was there
someone we should have invited for you?" she asked.

"Moira asked me." He turned over and raised himself
on one elbow. The blue-gray cast of moonlight limned
Skye's profile. "There isn't anyone."

Skye felt her heart being squeezed. "Then you're
alone."

His eyes wandered over the spill of Skye's hair. He
raised his hand and gently touched her cheek with the
back of his knuckles. Her skin was smooth, flawless.
She turned into him by just the slightest fraction. "Not
anymore," he said.

Skye didn't respond. She held his hand against her
face a moment longer. She kissed his knuckle.

Without a word passing between them, they stretched
simultaneously. Their bodies turned, adjusted, and finally rested together so her cheek rested on his shoulder
and one of her legs bent and lay across both of his. The

proprietary nature of the arrangement suited Walker. He liked the way her arm slid across his chest, the way her slim figure could insinuate itself against him with perfect feline grace. He watched her raise her left hand slightly and turn it first one way, then the other, allowing the moonlight to catch the edge of her wedding band.

"It's not what you imagined," he said, his voice husky, just above a whisper.

Was he talking about the ring, or about what it represented? Skye let her hand rest on his chest again. "It's odd," she said softly. "All my life I've been chided for my imagination and it failed me here. I never thought about marriage except to think how I could avoid it. I watched my sisters take the march and as good as threatened my father not to turn his attention in my direction. I was so busy watching him I backed right into you." Skye let her palm slide back and forth along Walker's chest. "I'm still not quite sure what happened."

Walker wondered if keeping her off balance was the way to keep her close. "You regret it?"

"Regret implies I had a choice," she said. "I didn't."

He noticed that she didn't move away from him, though. "I'm not sorry," he said.

"I know you're not. But I don't know why. I would have been your mistress."

"So you said."

Skye waited for more explanation. Walker didn't offer one. After a while her eyes closed, the stroking of her hand slowed, the rhythm of her breathing changed.

She was asleep when Walker finally said, "It wouldn't have been enough."

They were served breakfast in their room. Skye watched Mrs. Cavanaugh with some astonishment as she fussed over Walker, asking him if everything was prepared to his liking or if there was anything else he needed. "I wouldn't get too used to that," Skye said, after the housekeeper left. "She's not usually so ingratiating."

The food was set out on a small table near the fireplace. Wearing his trousers and a shirt that was only half buttoned, Walker sat down and began filling his plate. He gave Skye a sideways glance. "Is she the one who trained you?" he asked.

Skye looked at him sharply. She tightened the sash of his dressing gown and sat opposite him. "What's that supposed to mean?"

"Exactly what I asked." He ran a hand through his tousled hair and regarded her with something close to exasperation. "If I intended to say that as a housekeeper you were less than ingratiating, I'd say it. That wasn't my intention. I merely wondered if Mrs. Cavanaugh helped you prepare for your position at Parnell's."

Skye placed two orange slices on her plate. "I suppose I'm being prickly this morning."

An understatement, Walker thought. She woke up out of sorts, her hackles already raised. He would have liked to have believed it was confronting the broken mirror that had set her on edge, but he was more honest with himself than that. Skye had simply opened her eyes, seen him, and been angry.

Skye realized he wasn't going to give her cause for an argument by agreeing with her. Her mood was not improved by the knowledge that even disagreement would have prompted an argument. She seemed to be determined to be a shrew this morning.

Skye tapped the shell of her soft-boiled egg with the side of her spoon. "Yes, Mrs. Cavanaugh helped me prepare," she said. "It was my mother's idea. Jay Mac hadn't seemed to consider that I might not be qualified for the position." She began peeling away the cracked shell and placed it carefully on the side of her plate. "It made me more suspicious of my father's real reasons for sending me to Baileyboro. He seemed so certain that I only had to arrive there in order to secure the position."

"You thought it was all arranged between Parnell and your father."

She nodded. "It wasn't outside the realm of the possible. The same could be said of you and Jay Mac."

Walker paused in raising his coffee cup to his mouth. "You know that's not true."

"I know it wasn't true then," she said. "It didn't take the two of you long to work something out later." She ignored the narrowed watchfulness of Walker's eyes. "I saw Jay Mac take you aside after dinner. Is that when he paid you for me?"

"That's when he warned me that you and alcohol didn't suit."

Skye flushed but she didn't look away.

"In China," Walker said, "marriages are arranged all the time. No one thinks anything of it. Just the opposite, in fact. The bride is quite happy that her parents are able to find a suitable partner for her poor, miserable, worthless self." He saw that he had her complete attention now. Her mouth was slightly parted, her eyes had widened. She wasn't certain if she could believe him, and if she could, she wasn't certain what exactly he was saying about *her.* "Brides don't come with a dowry," he went on. "The bridegroom's family gives her gifts instead."

Skye was about to remark that it was a good custom when Walker continued.

"The gifts aren't hers to keep," he said. "They stay with her family. It's a bride-price. Her family has lost a valuable worker while the groom's family has gained both a worker and a childbearer. The bride-price is supposed to offset the loss."

Skye's mouth pursed to one side. She snorted softly,

derisively. "I don't like the idea of being bought by you, either."

"I didn't expect that you would." He set his coffee cup down. "Your father and I didn't exchange any money. Does that satisfy you?"

She supposed it would have to. She shrugged diffidently and applied herself to her meal. Walker, she observed, was quite comfortable with her silence. He unfolded the paper that Mrs. Cavanaugh had brought with their tray and read it while he ate. Perversely annoyed by his lack of attention, Skye tapped her fingers on the edge of the table.

Walker was oblivious to Skye. An article in the *Chronicle* announcing a science and technology exposition held his complete attention. Frowning slightly, a small crease between his brows, he reread the account, making note of the location and schedule of events. Jonathan Parnell was a scheduled speaker. Walker wondered if he knew it. The arrangements for the engagement had probably been made months earlier, even before Walker had been hired by Parnell. In all that time Walker couldn't remember Parnell mentioning this upcoming exposition or the fact that he was supposed to deliver a lecture on the physics of internal combustion.

Skye's curiosity was roused by Walker's expression. She could see he was disturbed by something he was reading. She couldn't discern if he was angry. "What is it?" she asked. "Our marriage announcement?" She knew that he hadn't wanted it reported in the paper. And she didn't take issue with it, either. She was satisfied that as few people as possible should know about the marriage. There would be less stigma surrounding the divorce if it came to that. "Walker?"

Still frowning, he looked up. "What?" he asked absently, closing the paper. "Did you say something?"

"I asked about what you were reading."

"Oh."

When he didn't expound, she put down her fork and rested her hands on her hips. "Well? Are you going to tell me, or do I have to read it for myself? I can, you know. I went to school long enough to learn how to do that."

His frown faded completely. He regarded her with some astonishment, realizing for the first time how deeply she had been stung by his comment about not knowing the difference between an adventurer and an adventuress. On that occasion he had told her to go back to school. She certainly hadn't forgotten. "You're welcome to read it," he said, pushing the paper toward her. "I have to get dressed and leave for a while." He saw her surprise. "I didn't think you'd object. You've never indicated that you expected a real honeymoon, and you seem to prefer your own company this morning."

That was plain enough. "Then I won't ask where you're going." She picked up the paper and opened it, studiously ignoring Walker while he prepared to leave.

On the point of going, he inquired, "Shall I ask Mrs. Cavanaugh to take care of the broken mirror?"

Seven years' bad luck, she was thinking. "She's probably already asked one of the maids to see to it."

"Very well. You should consider packing some things. I don't intend that we should spend another night here."

She looked up from the newspaper. "Not spend another night here?" she asked. "But where—"

"We'll discuss it when I get back."

They certainly would. Her sharp glance told him as much.

Walker was unaffected. "I shouldn't be gone more than a few hours."

Skye stared at the paper again. The words blurred in front of her, but she gave every indication that she was immersed in her reading. It wasn't until the door closed that the first tear slipped past her lower lashes.

* * *

Walker's first order of business took him to the telegraph office at Broadway and 34th Street. He sent off a quick message to the station at Baileyboro for Parnell, mentioning the article that had appeared in the *Chronicle*. It would be enough to whet Parnell's interest and confirm in his mind that Walker was still in his employ. The brief message was the only communication Walker had had with Parnell since leaving Baileyboro. He could well imagine that his employer wasn't pleased about that. Parnell must have wondered what was taking so long.

Walker's second stop was the offices of the *Chronicle*. He had to wait almost an hour to see Logan Marshall, but he was in no particular hurry. He spent the time in the busy editing and copy room, observing the frenetic activity of the reporters and press men with interest and amusement. It didn't give him the time to dwell on the difficult morning he'd spent with Skye.

The meeting with Logan was brief, and Walker was able to gather more information about the exposition. The material for the story had been supplied by the sponsors of the event and Walker was given the name of one man in particular to contact.

Everything about Franklin Dover was large except for his voice. His proportions were perfectly suited to his six-foot-six frame, which made it all the more surprising that he was so soft spoken. One anticipated a voice that would echo in his barrel chest and bellow from his lungs. Instead, Walker found himself leaning forward in his chair, straining to hear what Mr. Dover had to say.

"You're quite right, of course," Dover said. "The initial plans for the exposition were made well over a year ago. The idea was to present something for scientists and inventors, a forum for discussion and consideration of new ideas."

"And the response?" Walker asked.

"Overwhelmingly favorable. We're expecting attendees from all over this country and possibly fifty or more from Europe." Franklin Dover sat back in his chair. He might have dwarfed it, but it had been specially made to support him. His dark side whiskers widened an already broad face. He stroked one side with his thumb, his expression thoughtful. "What's your interest in the exhibition?" he asked. "Do you have something you wish to enter?"

Walker shook his head. "No, nothing like that. I expect it would be too late anyway, wouldn't it?"

"The planning committee is still considering some items for inclusion. Only something very noteworthy could be added at this time. There is no altering the lecture series. After all, the exhibition is only a month away."

"Then the list of men scheduled to speak has been confirmed?"

He nodded. His large hands came together in front of him and formed a steeple. His index fingers tapped together. "That's right."

"Including Jonathan Parnell?"

"Everyone." His brows knit slightly. "Are you interested in his topic?"

Walker had introduced himself to Franklin Dover as representing John MacKenzie Worth's interests and those of Northeast Rail. Worth's name had appeared among those who were bankrolling the exhibition. The group of powerful and wealthy men were politely referred to as "contributors," but Walker recognized their concern was self-interest. They were moved to add their money to the kitty by an entrepreneurial gambling spirit, definitely not the same spirit with which they contributed to libraries and the arts. "Jay Mac is interested in Parnell's topic," he said, correcting the impression that the questions were entirely his own.

"As far as I know, Parnell plans to attend. At least, I haven't heard anything to the contrary."

"You've met Mr. Parnell?" asked Walker.

"No. He's something of a recluse. That's why we were pleased to have his confirmation. He must be very excited about his work and quite far along if he's prepared to share his advances." Dover's own excitement could not quite be contained. His pale blue eyes burned with a particular brightness. "I take it representatives from Northeast will be there."

Walker smiled faintly at the question Franklin Dover would not ask directly. "I think you can count on Jay Mac attending."

"That's very good indeed."

Levering out of his chair, Walker extended his hand to Dover. His fingers were engulfed immediately in the other man's large, powerful hand. "Jay Mac wondered if you might have a list of those planning to attend," he lied shamelessly.

"I'm sure I do." He hesitated. "But I'm not— "

"To conduct business," Walker explained. "Jay Mac is hoping to meet with certain individuals there."

Franklin Dover gave in easily. There couldn't be any harm in releasing the list. If it made Jay Mac happy, then there was something to be gained through cooperation. "I'll get it for you."

When Walker left he had a neatly copied list in his pocket. He presented it to Jay Mac at his office at the Worth Building. Jay Mac looked it over carefully, adjusting his spectacles several times during his slow perusal.

"What is it you want to know again?" he asked, lowering the paper a mere fraction so he could see Walker over the edge. "It's hard to see that anyone in industry's been left out."

Walker sighed. That was his first thought when he had seen the list. "I need to know which ones are most likely to have been interested in Parnell's work. Who'd have the most to gain?"

Jay Mac placed the list on top of his desk, then rooted through his middle drawer for a pen. He jabbed it in the inkwell and began checking off names. "Rockefeller. Vanderbilt. William Barnaby. Stanford. Fisk. Gould. Rushton Holiday." He glanced at Walker. "Perhaps you'd rather I checked who's *not* likely to be interested."

"No, sir; you're telling me what I need to know."

Jay Mac continued to work. He said casually, "My daughter suffered no ill effects from her bout of drinking?"

"Not after she was sick."

Jay Mac chuckled. "Serves her right. She was behaving badly, sullen and spoiled."

"She was lonely," Walker said. "Missing her sisters."

Pausing, Jay Mac looked up. "They would have been there if they could have."

"She knows that. As comfort, it went only so far."

"I see." He went back to work. "When are you going to tell her about you?"

"Tonight. I know I haven't been fair to her, but I'll tell her tonight. I have to return to Parnell's. I can't say what he's going to do about the exhibition. I should be there. I *have* to be there."

"Skye won't like that."

"I know." Even before the announcement in the paper, Walker had been thinking about returning to Baileyboro. He knew he was going to have to explain it to Skye. He wondered if she'd want to return with him or if she'd be glad to see him go. "We're going to take a room tonight at the St. Mark," he told Jay Mac.

Jay Mac nodded. "That's probably wise. You have to work things out for yourselves. Does Moira know?"

"I didn't see her this morning." It was an easier explanation than admitting he'd only just decided where he and Skye would go.

"I'll have a suite reserved for you," Jay Mac said. "A wedding gift."

"That's kind of you. We both appreciate it."

He held up a hand as he slid the list across the desk to Walker. "Don't thank me yet. You could be sorry that Skye won't have anywhere to run."

"Skye's not a runner," Walker said. "I've learned that about her." He was surprised that Jay Mac didn't know his daughter better. "Damn the torpedoes. That's Skye."

Jay Mac considered Walker thoughtfully. "You're right," he said after a moment. "I was thinking of her sister. Maggie's gentle, more of a peacemaker . . . more like her mother. Skye's more . . ."

"Like you?"

Removing his spectacles, Jay Mac shook his head. "No," he said. "Not like me. Skye's like . . . Skye. All my daughters are unique, but I can see myself or Moira in each of them, except for Mary Schyler."

"She thinks the talent was tapped by the time it was her turn to be born."

Jay Mac's eyebrows rose. "She told you that?"

Walker nodded. "Almost her exact words." He picked up the list but didn't glance at the checked names. He folded it once and slipped it in his pocket. It was clear he had given Jay Mac something to think about. Now Walker decided to give him the time. "I may not see you this evening," he said. He tapped his pocket. "Thank you. You've been helpful." Jay Mac nodded absently. Walker showed himself to the door.

Skye had not packed anything. Walker knew he couldn't blame indecision for her lack of cooperation. What to pack wasn't the problem; taking orders was.

Walker found Skye in the library. She was alone, curled in a chair with a blanket over her legs. A heavy book rested partially in her lap and partially on the arm of the chair. Her feathered brows were furrowed in concentration. She was pulling a strand of hair through her lips as she read. The damp tip was dark. Walker stood just inside the door, watching her for several minutes before she sensed his presence.

"You're back," she said. Her tone was without inflection.

Walker thought she might actually go back to reading, but she slipped a leather marker in the book and put it on the table beside her. He recognized the book as the same one she'd been reading at Parnell's. "You took that from the Granville library." It wasn't an accusation, merely a comment.

Skye's guilty conscience made her answer a little defensively. "I plan to return it."

He almost offered to take it back with him, but the timing was wrong. "I've been to your room. I noticed you haven't packed anything."

She tucked the heavy plaid blanket about her legs. "There's nothing wrong with your powers of observation."

"Where's your mother?"

"She's gone to see Mary Francis. Why? Are you going to beat me?" She flinched as he raised his hand, although he only ran it through his hair. He looked as if he was seriously considering how to respond to her question. "I'm sorry," she said after a moment. "I shouldn't have said that."

Walker pushed away from the door and sat down opposite her. His eyes fell to the blanket. "Are you feeling well?"

"I'm fine. No lingering effects from last night. I was chilly, that's all."

He rose, briefly stoked the fire and added wood, then returned to his seat. "Better?"

Skye shrugged. "It was fine before," she said. "There was no need to—"

"Damn it, Skye! I'm not your enemy. Our marriage doesn't have to be a war. Even the simplest exchange is a battle with you, every glance is a skirmish."

She glanced at the clock. "And it's been just a little over twenty-four hours," she said drily "Can you imagine years of this?"

"No," he said firmly.

Her smile held no warmth. "Neither can I." She got up and tossed Walker the blanket. "I'm going to pack now. I'll go wherever you'd like, Walker, and show you I can be compliant in my own fashion. You should know, however, that I don't intend to share a bed with you."

"You're a trifle late coming to that decision," he said. "It would have been more timely four days ago, when you showed up at the St. Mark wearing a gown and little else." He watched blood suffuse her pale complexion. "Still, I'm not averse to the idea myself." If anything, her color darkened with this announcement. Clearly she hadn't expected him to agree with her. She thought she had established battle lines that he couldn't ignore only to find he was willing to do just that. "We'll leave as soon as your mother returns. Jay Mac is reserving a suite for us at the St. Mark and knows not to expect us this evening."

Skye turned to go. "I might have known," she said, under her breath.

They didn't go immediately to the St. Mark. The hansom cab that Walker hired took them on a slow, meandering tour through Central Park. The pond was still frozen over and there were a few skaters taking advantage of the ice. Skye watched a couple making several graceful turns. The colors of the setting sun were captured in the ice beneath their feet. Bands of rose and orange and mauve and gold glinted on the surface and blended in a kind of winter rainbow.

Inside her muff, Skye's hands folded and tightened. She made no comment about anything she saw. Walker appeared not to expect one. The cab circled the pond slowly and more skaters gathered. Lanterns were lighted on the edge. Laughter rose from one of the benches where a mother had collected her young children and was preparing to launch them onto the ice.

The cab turned down a path she recognized instantly as the one she had taken on a certain fateful night. She hadn't heard Walker give the driver any special instructions, yet Skye couldn't believe the route was entirely accidental.

"This is where we first met," Walker said softly. He wasn't looking at the path. He was looking at Skye.

She had the oddest sensation that Walker was courting her. She could feel the intensity of his gaze and had to will herself to continue to look out the window. "I remember," she said. "There were two men chasing you that night." She refused to ask the question that hovered at the forefront of her thoughts. By Walker's own admission, he was better at keeping secrets than at sharing them. It was something he was going to have to change.

"Before I came to New York I was a—" Walker paused, searching for the right word. "I suppose you would call it a diplomatic aide." Skye had become very still and Walker knew he had her attention. "I was attached to our embassy in London. One of our officials at the embassy had gotten himself neck-deep in trouble and I was asked to extricate him."

Skye's head had tilted slightly to one side. She had removed her hands from her muff and now they lay still. She was no longer twisting her wedding band.

"He had involved himself with a married woman. The wife of a powerful member of the House of Lords, as it turned out. He gave her a ring, a family heirloom that was easily identifiable as his. When her husband found out about the affair, he didn't confront it openly either with his wife or with our embassy man. He began blackmailing them both."

In spite of Skye's best intentions, she heard herself ask, "His own wife?"

"His own wife," he repeated. "She had money in her own right, a fortune he was trying to tap. Our embassy man was similarly well connected but didn't want to pay. Neither of them knew it was her husband orchestrating the blackmail— he worked through intermediaries— but they knew the ring had been found and taken and was what the blackmailer was holding against them. I was directed to get it back."

He made it sound so ordinary, Skye thought, as if it were not beyond his usual duties. She wondered if that was true.

"It took some time," Walker continued, "but once I confirmed who was holding the lovers as financial hostages, finding the ring wasn't too difficult."

"What did you do?" She was looking at him now, her eyes searching his face.

"I stole it back," he said simply. "People don't expect you to do that sort of thing, so they don't plan for it. The husband wasn't aware he had been found out and he hadn't taken any particular care to hide the ring. It was in a box in his safe with some other valuables. Getting it back was the easiest part of the assignment." He sighed, shrugging faintly. "Everything was handled very quietly, discreetly. No one wanted the episode brought to light. I suspect my part in it was discovered because of our embassy man's gratitude. I think he recommended my work to someone he shouldn't have. It got back to his lordship and he proved he could hold a grudge. His hired thugs have trailed me for months. I don't think he intends to kill me, but he certainly wants some kind of satisfaction for the difficulties I caused him."

"Difficulties *you* caused him?" she asked, surprised. "But you weren't the one having the affair!"

Walker's smile was faint. "True enough. But his lordship didn't care so much about the affair. He could tolerate his wife's indiscretion and probably had. He had a mistress himself in Mayfair. What he couldn't stand for was the interference in his scheme. In effect, I killed the goose that laid the golden eggs."

"You said they've been after you for months. Then that evening in the park wasn't the first you met up with them?"

"No, not at all. It's never the same men. That makes it difficult for me to know that I've really lost them. There were three encounters before I left England. What you witnessed was my second confrontation here in New York. No one's been able to track me to Bailey-boro, it's only— "

"In the city that you're in danger," she finished for him. Her eyes were troubled. "Every day you're here it's a risk."

Her concern warmed him, gave him hope, but he couldn't let her make too much of his situation. "It's not as dangerous as all that. They may have even given up."

"You can't know that."

She was right, of course. He couldn't know. "I'm not worried about it," he said. "And I didn't tell you so that you could worry for me."

"Then why *did* you tell me?"

Walker didn't answer immediately. He wanted to lean over the space that separated them and take her hand. He wanted to kiss away the small crease between her brows and the downturned corners of her mouth. He did none of these things. "It's part of your life now," he said. "Because it's part of mine. You have a right to know these things."

"Sharing a secret with me," Skye said gravely, quietly, "is the same as keeping it to yourself. You could learn that in time, or you could just believe me now. Nothing you tell me is going to go anywhere else. Not ever."

Tension began to slowly seep out of the cords in Walker's neck. He put one hand to his nape and rubbed, feeling the pressure ease. The carriage swayed gently as it left the park and took the main thoroughfare toward the heart of the city. Walker leaned back against the soft leather cushions. It was dark enough now that the driver had lighted the outside lamps on the carriage. A mixture of twilight and lamplight bathed Skye's face. Her features were more relaxed than they had been at any time since waking this morning. Most notably the edge of anger that had sharpened her eyes had disappeared. No glance in his direction any longer held an accusation.

"I always assumed," she said thoughtfully, "that our first meeting was somehow related to Parnell. It's odd to discover he had nothing to do with it."

"Only indirectly," he told her. "I was in the city with him on business. He required some supplies for his work and I had gone to a number of places to order them. I suppose I was seen then."

"You don't seem convinced."

He wasn't and he should have realized she would see it. "I returned once to the hotel room where Parnell was supposed to be waiting for me. He wasn't there. I had an idea where he might have gone, so I made some inquiries. No one admitted that they had seen him, but I'm fairly sure that's how I was seen."

"I'm not certain I understand. Where did you go?"

"Brothels."

"Oh."

He saw she was trying to be very worldly about this information. Only the faint flush in her cheeks betrayed her. "He told me later that he had been to the Seven Sisters, but the madam denied it when I was there. I don't think it really matters. The men who came after me could have seen me there or at Josie's or at any of the other places I visited. When I realized I was being followed, I couldn't return to the St. Mark." The memory of the chase that had ensued prompted a small smile. "I led them back and forth across lower Manhattan for over an hour before heading north to the park. They weren't easily frustrated. I finally had to turn and make a stand."

Skye pressed her hands against her middle. It was easy to call up the vision of that night and it still had the power to make her insides clench. "And now you're here again," she said. "They could find you."

"I haven't been frequenting any brothels on this trip," he reminded her. "I've spent most of my time at your place or at the St. Mark."

"Until today," she said. "Today you went out."

He was saved replying as the cab slowed then stopped. "We're here," he said.

Skye had been too absorbed in Walker to take note of their surroundings. She looked out now. "That isn't the St. Mark," she said.

"Delmonico's," said Walker. "Dinner first."

They were shown to a secluded table, a place where they could see others but not necessarily be seen. It wasn't for social status that Walker had arranged for dinner at one of New York's premiere restaurants. Walker gave the steward the wine order soon after they were seated.

Skye smoothed the edge of the crisp white tablecloth with her fingertips. She was finding it difficult to meet Walker's eyes. "Are you certain you wanted to order that wine?" she asked, risking a small glance in his direction. "I could make a fool of myself again."

"You've never made a fool of yourself," he said. "Even when you were pie-faced."

"Gallant," she said. "But a lie, I'm afraid. I'll do better this evening."

"I'm not worried." And he wasn't.

The wine arrived and Walker tasted it and approved it. The steward filled glasses for both of them. Skye waited until the steward had disappeared before she tasted hers. It was a cautious sip. She set the glass aside while she examined the menu and didn't pick it up again until Walker had ordered for both of them.

"Was this Jay Mac's idea?" she asked, raising her hand in a sweeping gesture to indicate the restaurant.

Walker's eyes followed the graceful turn of her wrist and fingers. She could make the most mundane movement take on extraordinary beauty. She seemed totally unaware of it. Heads had turned when they'd entered the restaurant and Walker would never believe it was because they all recognized Jay Mac Worth's bastard daughter. It wasn't her tarnished pedigree that people noticed; it was the powerful, unaffected spirit of her life they responded to. The wide smile. The bright eyes. The energy of her gestures. Skye, at her most demure, wasn't entirely successful in smothering these attributes. She fairly radiated life.

Delmonico's, it seemed, had been a good idea. And it had been his own. "I thought you might enjoy it," he said. "Was I right?"

Skye realized that he wasn't entirely sure of himself. Yes, she thought, he was definitely courting her. She wasn't immune to that sort of flattery, but she was also wary. She hadn't drunk enough wine to forget their earlier conversation. Was he trying to save their marriage, or simply to get her back into his bed? And, Skye wondered, would she know the difference? "I'm enjoying myself," she told him. "I like Delmonico's. Their ballroom is spectacular. Have you seen it?"

"I've never been here before."

Skye noticed he was perfectly at his ease. On the occasions when she had dined with Daniel he had been so worried that he would make some gastronomic *faux pas,* like ordering the wrong wine or asking for a sorbet flavored with rum when Maraschino was considered the correct choice, that their pleasure in the experience was dimmed. Skye didn't care that much for convention, but in his own way, Daniel could be mired in it. She forgave him that because he was also willing to flout it enough to bring her to Delmonico's in the first place. "You must have been to places like it in London," she said.

"Not in London," he said. "In Paris."

"You've been to Paris?" She could not keep envy out of her tone. "I begged Jay Mac to let me make a European tour, but he was adamant that I should finish school." Cream of artichoke soup was set before her. Skye raised her spoon and skimmed the surface. She encouraged Walker to do the same. It was delicious. "A good choice," she told him. "Tell me about Paris."

He began to describe the city, the people, but Skye held up her hand and shook her head.

"I can read about that," she said. "In fact, I have. I want to know why *you* were in Paris."

"Before I was sent to London, I was attached to our embassy in Paris."

"Diplomatic aide?"

"For lack of a better description."

"Another affair to set right?" she asked drily.

He shook his head, his smile wry. "The French don't care about that. I was asked to help them recover a painting stolen from the Louvre."

She was skeptical. "They entrusted that to an American?"

"It was agreed I had the best chance of getting it back, since the theft had been perpetrated by Yanks. There was a fair amount of national honor at stake."

"I never heard about the incident."

"I'm not surprised. No one wanted it brought to the attention of the public. The French were embarrassed by their failed security measures, and you can understand the embassy's embarrassment. The theft was the mastermind of an assistant to the ambassador himself. No one knew that in the beginning. When it came out, it was decided that it was in everyone's best interest to keep the entire incident quiet."

"How did you recover the painting?"

"I stole it."

She couldn't temper her smile. "You're not a diplomatic aide," she said. "You're a thief."

Walker wasn't offended. His tone was more philosophical, revealing he had long ago come to terms with his particular talents. "It's probably more true than not." He watched her carefully, but Skye gave no indication that she found the information troubling.

Their soup was whisked away, their wine was refilled, and a light bass filet was placed in front of them. It flaked easily under Skye's fork. "I'm not aware that we have an embassy in Baileyboro," she said.

For a moment he didn't understand. "Parnell," he said heavily, with some reluctance. "Parnell is personal. I took a leave to come here and work with Parnell."

Skye didn't understand what that meant, but their location wasn't conducive to discussion. Although they enjoyed a modicum of privacy, the waiters moved in and out of hearing range. Their conversation was easily detectable by anyone who wanted to listen. "It can wait," she said, then added significantly, "until we're alone."

Over the next eight courses, Skye absorbed everything Walker shared with her. It was like putting together a quilt with diverse and colorful patches of fabric. The pattern took shape slowly, but it existed when one looked for it. It was held together by a common thread and the undeniable order of the arrangement. As unlikely as it seemed in the beginning, in the end, the colors and small scraps of fabric shared a singular harmony.

"I was five when my parents decided to become missionaries. Until that time we shared a house with my mother's mother on Beacon Hill." The address indicated old money, prestige, and acceptance in the upper stratum of Boston society. Walker knew that Skye would understand. "My mother's younger brother was there also. Most of what I recall about my childhood includes him one way or another. Grandmother was everyone's idea of a matriarch. She was the absolute ruler— fierce, stern, cold. I rarely saw her. She was uncompromising about the role of children in a home. The main rule was to have as little to do with them as possible. I can't say that I minded. On the rare occasions our paths crossed, I remember being quite afraid of her. I swear, the only reason she knew my name was because I was her sole grandchild."

Skye didn't believe he was exaggerating. She ate slowly, taking in his every word.

"My father and mother spent much of their time involved with the church. That didn't find any favor with Grandmother. She believed in Sunday duty and generous contributions. Her Protestant ethic was about work and not about faith. She removed my parents from her will just hours after they announced their decision to take up a China mission. I celebrated my sixth birthday in Shanghai."

"What about your uncle?"

"He had his own interests and didn't want to come with us. I know my mother asked him. He felt obligated, I think, to stay with Grandmother, though they didn't get along in any fashion. The family money was in shipping and my uncle was the first to admit he had no business sense. Grandmother was forced to sell off pieces of it after my father withdrew, when my uncle wouldn't take it up. The money supported my uncle's projects over the years. He always had something he was working on. None of it suited Grandmother. She thought he was a wastrel, perhaps even a little mad. She was astonished, I think, that she had sired him."

Skye could hear it in Walker's voice, the assurance that his uncle was the least mad person he knew. "You must have written over the years," she said. "To know so much about him."

"We did. Mail delivery was inconsistent at best. We would go for months at a time without hearing anything from Boston, then we would be flooded. I cared more about the news from home than about my parents. They were very satisfied with our life in Shanghai. The mission consumed them. They counted themselves responsible for over two thousand converts."

"Two thousand," she said softly. "They must have been enormously pleased."

Walker's tawny brows were raised. He shook his head. "Not with millions of souls to be saved," he said. "And that was only in the province of Nanking. My parents felt that their life's work could never be accomplished. It didn't stop them from trying, however. Even then I was part of the diplomatic corps." Walker's smile was wry. "My father liked to think of himself as an ambassador of God's."

Skye smiled because she expected it and because she wasn't expecting her pity. She imagined that Walker had been more alone in Shanghai working beside his parents than he had been in Beacon Hill with his uncle. "You never had any brothers or sisters?"

"None who lived." His voice lowered. "My mother miscarried at least two times that I know of while we were in

Shanghai. She thought it was because she hadn't done enough. It led directly to her decision to join the leper colony. It was her way of atoning for some imagined sin."

"So they left you behind on the mainland?"

"I was supposed to return to Boston, but money for my passage never arrived. My uncle could be a little vague at times. I imagine he forgot he was supposed to send it."

"A little vague!" she exclaimed softly. Skye was amazed by what had happened, as well as by Walker's calm acceptance of it. "But you were just a boy. How could he forget his responsibility to you that way?"

"He forgot most things when he was working. He had a passion for his projects that rivaled my mother's. The focus was simply different."

"What sort of work?" she asked. "You never said."

"Didn't I?" A sampling of cheeses and fresh fruit had been set in front of him. Walker chose an apple slice and chewed it slowly while Skye waited for an answer. The time had come. "He was a tinkerer," he said.

"A tinkerer?" she asked blankly. "An inventor, you mean? Like Jonathan Parnell?"

"Not *like* him," Walker said. *"Exactly* like him."

Skye frowned. "What?"

"My uncle *is* Jonathan Parnell."

Fourteen

The carriage ride to the St. Mark was made in silence. Skye found it easier not to talk than to talk and not raise her questions. For his part, Walker was not in a particular hurry to complete the account. He took his time at the desk, registering them as Mr. and Mrs. Walker Caine with a little fanfare and flourish. The clerk was the same one who had been on duty several nights before, the same one with whom Skye had carried on a flirtation. Now Walker noticed that his wife did everything she could to avoid the poor clerk's eye. As for the clerk, he seemed to be the victim of a tickle in his throat. It was the only thing that could account for all his incessant clearing of it.

Their suite was on the fifth floor and they rode the steam lift with three other hotel guests and the lift operator. The crowd kept Skye from saying what she thought of Walker's lingering at the front desk. She didn't have difficulty communicating it with a sideways glance.

On the threshold to their rooms, with the bellboy looking on and the lift operator still poking his head into the corridor, Walker picked up Skye and carried her inside. The action actually rendered her speechless. Her eyes, on the other hand, were flashing.

Their bags were deposited inside their bedroom and Skye looked around while Walker tipped the young man. Jay Mac had seen to fresh flowers in all the rooms. There was a bucket of champagne chilling on the bedside table and a box of chocolates in the sitting room. The bathing room had a large enamel tub and an entire shelf filled with bath salts and perfumes. Fresh towels were stacked beside the washbasin. A single red rose lay on top, imparting its fragrance into the fabric.

The bedroom was large. Even so, most of the space was captured by the enormous bed. Skye didn't spend any time dwelling on that feature. Her eyes skimmed past it to the balcony, then the armoire, the dresser, and the oval mahogany table and Queen Anne chairs. Every piece of furniture gleamed with polish and reflected the deep burgundy and cream accents of the wallpaper, bedspread, and mantel shawl.

The sitting room had several conversational areas that were defined by the arrangement of wing chairs and sofas and a love seat. After Skye had removed her hat, gloves, and coat, she selected a chair beside the fireplace. Walker was still in conversation with the bellboy in the other room. She couldn't imagine what he had found to discuss, but when the young man came through the room on his way out, he was having a difficult time controlling his smile.

"What was that about?" she asked Walker, as he began to lay the fire.

He didn't answer her. When he finished with the fire, he brushed off his hands and removed his jacket. The silver threads in his vest glinted in the firelight. "Would you like champagne?"

"I'd like to be able to think clearly," she said.

"Champagne is good for that." He brought in the bucket from the bedroom and two crystal glasses. "This was your father's idea," he said. "In case you were wondering." He uncorked the bottle.

Although she was prepared for the popping, Skye still

flinched. She ran for a towel when the bubbles spilled over the lip of the bottle and mopped up the excess on Walker's hand and sleeve. "You've got some right here," she said, then dabbed at his jaw with the edge of the towel. She drew it away slowly, aware his eyes had darkened and his body was still.

"And you have some here," he said lowly. He bent his head and touched the corner of her mouth with his lips.

Skye didn't move. Even her breath was held. She didn't respond to the kiss in any way that he could see. Only she was aware that her heart had skipped a tortured beat. "Walker," she said softly. "I don't think—"

"All right," he said. He took a step back, poured the champagne, and handed Skye her glass. He didn't touch his rim to hers, having no idea what a proper toast might be for this occasion. He doubted Skye would toast her own seduction, and it was premature to hold out for a happy marriage, not when his wife had set down rules about sharing the bed. Walker put down the champagne. Skye had returned to her chair, but Walker chose the sofa. He loosened a button on his vest and rolled up his sleeves. His long legs were stretched out in front of him. "You have more patience than I would have credited," he told her, after he had tasted his champagne.

"You'll tell me in your own time," she said. "I've learned that much. I don't know that I like it, but I can respect it." She raised her champagne glass and wrinkled her nose as the bubbles floated upward and tickled her. Skye rubbed the end of her nose and curled her legs beneath her. Yards of hunter green fabric spilled around her. She smoothed the fabric over her lap and waited even longer for him to speak.

When he began, she realized that not only would it be in Walker's own time, but in his own way. His first comment wasn't about Jonathan Parnell at all.

"I was free to go most everywhere I wanted," he said.

"With my parents involved in the mission, I enjoyed fewer restrictions in China than I had endured on Beacon Hill. Most foreigners stayed close together and didn't venture into the countryside. Except for the missionaries, there wasn't much of an effort to learn about the people who were their hosts. Some countries, like England, actually negotiated spheres of influence."

Skye's brows rose briefly in question.

"Those are geographic areas where foreigners can operate under their own set of laws and mores. It's all separate from Chinese culture and Chinese expectations. Essentially, it means foreigners govern themselves and the Chinese have no control. The United States didn't bargain for that privilege. Not because we particularly respected the Chinese, but because we wanted an open door to pillage the whole country."

She didn't comment on his cynicism, believing he had good reason for it. "So the world was your oyster," she said softly.

Walker smiled at that, remembering. "Something like that. I know I satisfied my curiosity about most things Chinese. I learned enough of the language to engage in conversation and translate for my parents, who never quite grasped it. I spent a lot of time observing people going through the routines of their lives, the births, marriages, deaths. Ritual and religion fascinated me. I absorbed everything I could." He sighed. "Over time I began to understand how little my parents appreciated the people they were trying to convert. The concept of a single God, for instance, is not easy for the Chinese to accept. Their religious history embraces Tao and Confucius and Buddha. They can embrace many things, but not just one. To my parents, the Chinese were pagan. To me, they were deeply spiritual."

Walker raked back his hair. "There was an older man in the village who allowed me to work beside him. He had no sons, only daughters, and they were both married and living elsewhere. In exchange for my labor, he taught me things. Each of us thought he had the better part of the bargain."

There was no mistaking the affection Walker had for his mentor. "Your parents couldn't have liked it," Skye said. "They were there to save souls, not lose yours."

"They forbade it."

"And you did it anyway." Skye could see that she and Walker shared a rebellious nature. The strictures placed on him as the child of missionaries couldn't have been so different from those that had been placed on her. She began to understand how it was he knew her so well.

He nodded. "I got away whenever I could and joined Han-sheng. He would never have permitted it if he had known my parents were against it. In truth, it never occurred to him that I would defy my family. It was something he simply couldn't have understood."

"Han-sheng," she said quietly, testing the unfamiliar name. "And you learned Tai-Chi from him?"

"I learned about patience and discipline and the nature of order from him. Tai-Chi is a way of expressing those things."

"I thought it was a way of fighting."

Walker grinned. She sounded disappointed. "Tai-Chi can prepare one for the fight. The exercises mirror the movements of Chinese self-defense. Han-sheng called it Kung-Fu."

"And that's what I saw you do in the park?"

"That's what you saw," he told her. "When my parents left me behind, it was with the expectation that I would return to Boston. As I told you, the money didn't arrive. While I waited for some news I continued to live at the mission but spent most of my time with Han-sheng. My parents' replacements were less accepting of the arrangement than even my mother and father had been, but they also had less control. They put up with me because they believed it was their duty. When we learned my parents had died, they felt released from any promises and sent me to an American shipping merchant. The plan was for me to earn my passage back to Boston by working for him. The man was trading in opium and K'u-li labor for the Central Pacific Railroad. I ran away instead."

Skye was leaning forward in her chair, the champagne glass in her hand untouched. She didn't have to imagine what life must have been like on Shanghai streets. Walker told her. A picture began to form in her mind of a boy who'd become accomplished at living by his wits, who'd abandoned the teachings of his parents and his beloved Han-sheng, to steal and cheat and beg from the local merchants. He greased his beautiful tawny hair with bootblacking and lived in alleyways and slept with dogs. He had to defend his territory and his spoils from other thieves, and the fighting made him strong, sharp, and agile.

It had never been much of a charade. Even with the bootblack and a pigtail, the stolen clothes and bowed head, Walker was simply too foreign looking to be mistaken for anything else. He was quick enough and bright enough to elude the authorities for almost six months, but when he was caught, he came within minutes of paying dearly for his crimes.

"I convinced them I was British," he said, affecting a credible accent.

"British?" she asked. "But— " Skye stopped as she realized she had the answer to her question. "The sphere of influence."

He nodded. "They were afraid to touch me then. I was taken to the British Embassy. It was obvious to the Brits that I was a Yank, but they didn't hold it against me. I was given food, clothes, shelter, and severe lectures. Eventually I was turned over to William Elkins, the American consul in Shanghai. Mr. Elkins was engaged in some very delicate negotiations with T'zi Hsi." He saw Skye's questioning look and explained. "The emperor was only a child at the time. His mother ruled. She still has powerful influence, but then it was absolute and Mr. Elkins had no idea how to engage her cooperation."

"And you did," Skye said. Walker had absorbed the culture, the religion, the way of thinking that was a mystery to the West. Of course, he understood what the men in power did not.

"And I did," he agreed. "I helped him arrange a profitable treaty which gained him a great deal of favor with President Grant. When he realized that I was more asset than liability, he stopped thinking about sending me away. I stayed with him for three years, helping him with the local government officials, assisting him in making the best trade agreements. I listened to everything. None of the Chinese officials suspected I understood the language. Foreigners hadn't bothered to learn before. I was young, of no consequence to them, and they were indiscreet. I knew who could be bribed and who would consider it an insult. Sometimes the negotiations would require communication among several powerful families. I was often a messenger between them, trusted simply because they thought I was ignorant and inferior."

Walker shook his head, his mouth drawn to one side in a derisive, mocking smile. "The Chinese believed in their superiority as much as Mr. Elkins and others like him believed in theirs."

"You could read the language," Skye said.

"Not well," he admitted. "But well enough."

"You were the consul's spy."

Humor touched Walker's smile now and the gleam of it sharpened the gold flecks in his eyes. "I think I was referred to as a second assistant to the consul's aide."

"You were a spy," she said firmly.

He shrugged. "Mr. Elkins rewarded my service by getting me sponsored to West Point."

Skye's eyes widened. She swallowed some champagne. "West Point," she repeated.

"Hm-mmm," he murmured, enjoying Skye trying to take it all in. "I was being groomed for a position that would take into account my special talents."

"Those would include stealing, lying, and fighting," she said drily.

Walker didn't blink. "I'd like to believe they noticed I had an ear for languages, I was interested in other cultures, I was resourceful, and I'd demonstrated I could take care of myself, but I think stealing, lying, and fighting sums it up nicely."

Skye nearly choked on the champagne she was swallowing. She put the glass aside, though she was uncertain if a clear head was an especially good thing right now. Walker's revelations were something more than she'd expected.

"After West Point, I thought I'd return to China. Mr. Elkins had hoped for it, but I was assigned to Washington first, the White House specifically."

Skye didn't try to hide her astonishment. "You spied for the president?"

"I reported to President Grant," he corrected her. "The work wasn't so different from what I had done for Mr. Elkins."

She pulled a face at him for splitting hairs. "You may as well call a spade a spied," she said, her tongue tangling over the words. "I mean a spied a spade. Oh, you know what I mean. You just as well should say it."

A single brow arched and his smile was wry. "One of us should." What he wanted to do was kiss her. Champagne had made her mouth damp. The taste of her and the drink would be a heady mixture. With some difficulty, Walker reined in his thoughts. "I might have stayed in Washington longer, but I was loaned out for a special assignment in New York."

Something niggled at Skye's memory, prompting her to say, "Logan Marshall."

"That's right. Parnell told you at your interview that I had once worked for the publisher."

Her tone was a touch accusing. "You didn't offer much clarification."

"You weren't entitled then," he said, without remorse. He paused, sipping his own drink, as if thinking about it now.

"Beast," she said, when he didn't say anything more. She tossed her head. "Perhaps I don't want to know."

Walker reached across the space that separated them and took her wrist. Without much urging on his part, he was able to pull Skye from her chair and onto the sofa beside him. She was wedged between Walker and the arm of the sofa and turned slightly in his direction. He leaned toward her and rested his forehead against hers for just a moment, looking her straight in the eye. "You're eaten up with curiosity," he said.

Skye knew that if she said anything at all she would find herself kissing him. She was saved from losing her resolve when he drew back and began to explain.

"I worked for Logan Marshall briefly when his wife returned to the stage. She received threatening letters, from an understudy, as it turned out, that were quite graphic in their description of the harm that was intended her. I'm not certain how it came to pass that Grant himself heard of it. I know he admired Katy's acting when she was in Washington, and Marshall himself is certainly powerful enough to command the president's notice. I do know that it was Grant who recommended me to Marshall."

Something else became clear to Skye. "That's how you found me after I left you at the station."

He nodded. "If it's any consolation, Marshall didn't give you up easily. It was only because he knew me that I was able to discover anything about you."

Was it consolation? she wondered. Was she sorry that Walker had found her so easily? He hadn't let go of her wrist. His fingers circled her skin in the small embrace of capture. Not once had she tried to pull away. "And after Marshall?" she asked.

"I returned to Washington, then Paris, then London."

"And back to New York."

"That's right," he told her. "Because of my uncle." He released her now and was surprised to find that Skye caught his hand and threaded her fingers through his. "The money for my passage back to Boston arrived six months after I began living with Mr. Elkins. It was put aside for me. My uncle didn't mind that I decided to stay, but my grandmother hoped I would change my mind. I think she believed that I could be compelled to take over the shipping business. It was a bone of contention until she died."

"When was that?"

"I was in my last year at West Point," he said. "Soon after, my uncle bought the Granville mansion in Baileyboro. He had a little money from the sale of Grandmother's business, and he had had some success with a number of patents. It was several more years before he finally moved there. I wrote to him regularly and received a reply every third or fourth time. I met him in New York on two occasions when I was working for Logan Marshall, but he liked to remain in Baileyboro. I gathered from him that he knew he was considered a recluse by the villagers but that he didn't mind. It suited him in some ways. He had a groundskeeper and cook who looked after the house and him. No one bothered to interrupt or ask questions. His work was everything."

Walker smiled. "He was as happy as I've ever known him."

"I've never thought of Jonathan Parnell as a particularly happy man," Skye said.

"That's because you didn't know him."

Skye looked at him oddly, searching his face. "You mean I didn't know him as well as you," she said.

"No," said Walker. "I mean you didn't know him at all."

She frowned. "But you said—"

"I said Jonathan Parnell is my uncle. The man *you* know isn't Jonathan Parnell."

Skye simply stared at him. Questions flooded her, but the words would not be formed. It was too astonishing.

"You believe me?" he asked.

"I believe you." It never occurred to her that she couldn't.

"I received a few letters from him when I was in Paris. You have to understand that my uncle always addressed the letters to Hsia To. It's Chinese for 'Little Too Many.' Sometimes a daughter is given that name as a joke."

"Because daughters aren't valued."

"Exactly. In my case, I once overheard my uncle comment that I'd been born only because my mother had had a little too many." He saw Skye glance at her own glass of champagne and look relieved that she hadn't drunk more. "Years later, when I understood his comment, I wrote to him about the name. The next letter that arrived, and every letter after that, was addressed just that way. He even took to using it in place of my name when he spoke about me."

"Your uncle has a peculiar sense of humor."

Walker could tell she was thinking he had inherited the trait. In spite of that he felt her squeeze his hand, encouraging him to go on. "The letters I received from him while I was in Paris bothered me. There were some things he mentioned rather offhandedly that I thought bore a closer look. I suppose by then I was feeling rather protective toward him, but I was also caught up in what I was doing. I didn't write back. When I was in London, the letters stopped altogether."

He leaned back and rested his head against the back of the sofa. Skye's thumb was lightly passing back and forth across his knuckles. In the other hand he held the champagne glass. He gave it to Skye and let her put it aside. "I can't explain what made me sure something was wrong. Before that I had gone for months without hearing from my uncle, but this time I was alarmed."

"So you came back."

Walker was silent for a long time. "Too late," he said at last.

Skye's hand tightened on his. She had been expecting it, but somehow it still had the power to wrench her. Walker's own features were taut, the line of his jaw cleanly defined. A muscle worked in his cheek. "You're certain?" she asked.

He nodded slowly, almost imperceptibly, closing his eyes. "Certain of everything but where they put the body." Walker turned his head to the side and looked at Skye. Her face was pale but she was holding up.

"The groundskeeper and the cook," she said.

"That's right. His name is Morgan Curran. She's Corina Curran."

"Wife?"

"Sister. Stepsister, actually. Reading is her married name. She's a widow." Skye's expressive eyes were easy to read. "No, he wasn't murdered. At least, not that it was obvious or suspected. He drank a good deal."

"Liver disease?"

Walker didn't mince his words. "He drowned in his own vomit."

Skye blanched. "How do you know all this?"

"It's what I *do,* Skye. I ask questions. I observe. I listen. I discover. It's not so difficult. Most of the time it's not even dangerous. It requires patience and discipline and an occasional bit of luck."

She thought it probably required a great deal more than that. She reached up and touched the side of his face, brushing back the hair near his temple. The hard lines of his face softened a bit.

"It was the middle of summer when I arrived in Baileyboro," he told her. "I asked for directions to the Granville place at the train station. I was pointed to a man pacing at the far end of the platform. He was waiting for an approaching carriage, his shoulders hunched, hands in his pockets. 'That's Mr. Parnell there,' I was told. 'Good piece of luck,' they said, 'to run into him that way.' "

"It was Morgan Curran," said Skye.

Walker let out a long, heavy breath. "It was. There was no resemblance at all, yet it became clear that no one in Baileyboro thought he was anyone but Jonathan Parnell. I went out to the Granville mansion later but never announced myself. I looked around the property, watched people come and go, and heard Curran being addressed as Parnell. I knew I had to come up with some way to get into that house, some way that would keep me there for a while. I wasn't confident that a simple search or a confrontation would turn up anything. The small chance that my uncle was still alive also meant I had to act quickly. No one was being hired at the house so I couldn't present myself as looking for work. I needed another plan."

Skye's hand fell away from Walker's face as understanding came to her. "You threatened Parnell!" she said. "Those attempts on his life were your doing! You made him think someone was after the engine and that he was in danger."

"Guilty." The single word was said without regret. "He hired me to protect him."

"But how did he find you? He could have hired anyone."

"I made myself known in Baileyboro. Cautiously, of course. A bit mysteriously. It's a small village, and it was precisely the kind of thing that got everyone's attention. After two threats, Parnell sought me out. I pretended to come reluctantly, which made him want me more. I had references from people I could trust. They were sufficient to impress Parnell."

"How can you call him Parnell?"

"That's how I think of him, how I have to think of him. To do otherwise would show my hand. I could make a mistake so easily. Anyway, it's not as if I called my uncle by his last name. He was Uncle Jon. Curran is Parnell."

"And Parnell is not an inventor," she said.

"No. Not an inventor. He's only played at it. Quite thoroughly, too."

"That's why you didn't care that I had drawn a picture of the engine."

"You knew I saw it?"

She nodded. "You folded the paper differently than I did. I knew you had to have looked at it and decided I could keep it. I wondered why. Now I know. It was a worthless piece of paper, anyway."

Walker was reminded again it was the incidental things that could trip him up. He was fortunate that it was Skye who had caught him out. "Your father found it interesting."

"Those were his exact words when he saw it, but he didn't explain. After what I had been through, I suppose he didn't think he'd better."

"You're not entirely right about it," Walker said. "The engine *is* the beginning of a working model. It's just that what you showed your father is exactly what Parnell showed him when Jay Mac agreed to finance it. Your drawing proved to Jay Mac that Parnell's first rendering of the invention wasn't a fake, but it also proved there'd been no progress."

"Because your uncle's dead," she said quietly.

"He wouldn't have stopped working otherwise. He *couldn't* have."

Skye turned and laid her head against Walker's shoulder. She felt his arm come across her back. He rubbed her arm. "Did you know right away?" she asked.

"Within twenty-four hours of getting inside. There was noplace they could have hidden him. I was everywhere in the house."

"But you never found the body."

"No, I've never found it. I've been over the grounds a score of times, but I can't find anything like a grave. Now that winter's almost over I can look again. The ground may settle over it. That may be the only clue I'll have."

Skye was struck by the memory of Walker's trip to the swan pond with Annie's little boy. "You've considered the pond?" she asked.

He nodded. "And the river. Nothing has ever surfaced."

What a grim task it was for him, she thought. Her skin prickled with cold that came up from her bones. She felt his arm tighten on her shoulder as if he knew what had caused her shiver. "Why have you done it all alone?" she asked. "Can't you make a case to the authorities? Curran is impersonating your uncle. Apparently he has for some time, certainly as long as they've all been in Baileyboro. Surely he should be held accountable for some explanation."

"I considered it," Walker said. "But without the body, I can't prove murder. Depending on the manner of murder, I may not even be able to prove it then. There's also the possibility that Uncle Jon died of natural causes. Morgan Curran saw an opportunity to use my uncle's identity and took it."

"I'm not certain I understand what Parnell and his sister have to gain by assuming the identity. The engine isn't working and Parnell can't make it work. Did you ever notice that when he comes up from the workroom his hands are clean? Oh, he has a spot of grease on him here and there, and his sleeves are rolled up. He even looks a bit distracted and harried, but under his nails there's not any grime."

He had noticed, but he didn't know she had. "You're amazing," he said softly.

She glanced up at him. Her smile was self-depreciating. "Not so amazing. I saw it but the significance didn't register until you told me about my own hands." Skye rested her head against him again. "So, if you don't think you can find your uncle's body, then what is it you hope to prove against the Currans?"

"Fraud."

"Fraud? But who—"

"Your father, for one. Parnell entered into a contract with your father to help finance his work on the engine. He also entered into a contract with Rockefeller, Holiday, and Westinghouse. Those are the only ones I know about for certain. I suspect that the list is much longer than that. He received thousands of dollars from each man in return for the promise of the exclusive patent rights."

"My God," she breathed softly. "Does Jay Mac know?"

"He does now."

Skye shook her head from side to side, feeling for her father. "Poor Jay Mac."

"He wasn't pleased. He thought he owned Parnell."

Skye became very still. "What?" she asked in a small voice. "What did you say?"

"Your father wasn't pleased."

She sat up and away from Walker. "No, the other."

"I said he thought he owned Parnell."

"Did Jay Mac say that?"

Walker tried to remember. It was obviously important to Skye. "It was the same morning Jay Mac came to the St. Mark to find you," he said slowly. "I went to see him later and he asked me about my work. I told him everything. That's when the matter of the contract came up. He even showed his copy to me." He paused, thinking back carefully on the conversation. "I think those were his exact words."

Skye didn't have any trouble believing her father would have thought it or said it. It was so like him to think that the contract for patent rights as ownership of Parnell himself. "My father probably wrote as much to Parnell when he wasn't getting satisfactory answers about the engine. It must have frightened Parnell." Skye made a small grimace. "Even my father's correspondence can be threatening."

"I'm not certain I understand the significance," Walker said.

Skye was filled with restless, anxious energy. She stood and moved away from the sofa. Her hands smoothed the midriff of her hunter green gown before her arms crossed protectively in front of her. "I told you about the intruder I surprised in my father's study."

Walker nodded. "I remember."

"He was looking for something in Jay Mac's desk and when he didn't find it he asked about a safe. Before he left, he said, 'Tell Jay Mac he doesn't own me.' But when I gave my father the message, it didn't mean anything to him."

"You're sure?"

"Jay Mac wouldn't have lied about that. Not when I'd been placed in danger. If he'd associated the words with Parnell, he wouldn't have sent me to Baileyboro. That's what makes me think he probably wrote them to Parnell. Jay Mac had no face-to-face contacts with him after the contract was signed." Skye stepped closer to the fire. She couldn't get warm enough. "It was Parnell who was in my home that night. He's the one who . . ." Her voice became hardly more than a whisper. ". . . the one who touched me."

Walker got to his feet, but he kept his distance from Skye. He thought that if he touched her now she would come out of her skin.

"He was in the city that night," she said. "You told me that yourself. He wasn't in the hotel room when you got there."

"Parnell went to a brothel."

She shook her head. "You didn't find him at one, did you? He was probably at our home already, on the property, just waiting for everyone to turn in for the night. He was looking for the contract. He wanted to end it with my father. Jay Mac must have been giving him too much trouble, asking for too much information about the engine. He probably thought it was too risky to stay in business with my father."

Walker thought back to the night in question. He recalled sitting in the hotel room, very much like the one they were in now, waiting for Parnell after the search of New York's seamier sections had turned up nothing. Walker looked toward the door, imagining Parnell coming in as he had done that night.

Skye watched the gradual change in Walker's features. The crease between his brows disappeared. The vague, distant expression of memory retrieval faded. And as knowledge came to him, so did the taut lines of tension and splintered sharpness of his gold-flecked eyes. "What is it?" she asked. "What have you remembered?"

Walker continued to stare at the door as if his vision of Parnell could become real. "The side of his face was reddened. I suppose I thought that it had something to do with an encounter with a whore. Parnell said he'd been with two." Now he turned to Skye. "You left that mark on him."

"I suppose I could have. I slapped him hard."

He swore softly under his breath, berating himself for not realizing it before now. The clues had been there and he hadn't been able to piece them together. "I should have known when you first told me about the intruder. I should have made the connection. Even when I knew it was Parnell going into your room, I didn't—"

"You knew?" she asked, stricken. "You knew Parnell was coming into my room and you—"

Now Walker approached her. When he saw her take a step back, he stopped. He could have reached for her, touched her, but his hands remained at his side. "Skye, I didn't know until the night that I stayed with you in your room. I was hit on the head, remember? No ghost did that. And I didn't suspect you. Who else could it have been?"

"But you didn't say anything."

"I made sure you spent the remaining time with me, in my room. I told you I was protecting you. What could I have said, what else could I have done? If you recall, you weren't honest with me. I didn't know why you were at the mansion or how far I could trust you."

Skye's chin came up. Her eyes accused him. "It didn't stop you from sleeping with me," she said.

Walker stared at her hard. "It didn't stop me from loving you, either."

She became perfectly still. "What?"

The rough gravel-edge of his voice changed. It was husky with feeling now. "It didn't stop me from loving you."

"You've never said . . ."

"Neither have you."

Skye's hands dropped to her sides. She was careful not to let her fingers twist the folds of her gown. She wanted to command presence, to preserve calm. "I didn't think you would welcome that sort of declaration," she said quietly. "I was afraid you would think I was trying to hold you with it, bind you to me."

"I married you, Skye. Love is supposed to bind us." His eyes narrowed. He tried to see past her shuttered expression. "Are you certain you didn't want it to bind *you*? You're the one who doesn't want this marriage. You're the one who wants the freedom to take your leave as you please. You would have been my mistress, my lover. You didn't want to be my wife."

She couldn't deny it, not the way he had put it to her. But he didn't understand everything. "It doesn't mean I didn't love you," she said. "Or do you think I'd be anyone's whore?"

Walker sucked in his breath. The edge was back in his voice. "I've never treated you like a whore."

Skye had the grace to look away. "I'm sorry. I shouldn't have said that." She raised her eyes to him again. "But you never mentioned marriage until you knew I was Jay Mac's daughter."

"It doesn't mean I didn't think about it," he said. "Or do you think I'd be anyone's whore?"

Skye's head retracted as if she'd been slapped. When he reached for her, she stepped back. "I suppose you think I deserved that," she said. "But I didn't. It wasn't an accusation, merely a point. I know you didn't accept money from my father, yet I don't see how my being Jay Mac's daughter couldn't have influenced your proposal."

Walker sighed. The hand he had held out to her was raised now and he rubbed the back of his neck, shaking his head slowly. "It influenced the timing, nothing else. You could have been the Cavanaughs' daughter and it would have been the same." She wanted to believe him, he could tell, but a lifetime of suspecting the motives of others had made her doubt herself. "I don't need any money you bring to our marriage," he said. "Not only don't I need it, I don't want it. I earn an adequate wage. Not to your father's standards, but sufficient for our needs. Jay Mac asked me if I could care for you. I satisfied him on that account. How do I satisfy you?"

"Oh, Walker," Skye said softly. She stepped toward him, tentatively at first, then again, and then a final time that put her within the slender space of a moment from him. She raised eyes that glistened with unshed tears. "You satisfy me so well it frightens me."

"I didn't mean—"

She raised a finger to his mouth. "Shhh. I know what you meant." Her hand dropped away and rested on his shoulder. She laid her forehead against his chest. "Be patient with me, Walker. I've never loved anyone before, not this way. I wasn't expecting it. I certainly wasn't expecting it to be returned." She felt his hands go around the small of her back. "I don't seem to know what to do with myself." Skye's breath caught on a sob that she couldn't quite contain. Her tears were making a wet track on his shirt. "Except make both of us miserable. I'm getting good at that."

Walker rested his chin against the crown of her hair. He held her close. "I thought you were only curious about me," he said quietly. "I was afraid to mistake your interest for love. I thought once you had your questions answered, you'd be bored and be done."

Skye found a handkerchief in his pocket and used it to dry her eyes. "You must think I'm shallow."

"I thought you were infatuated."

"If you're trying to extricate your foot from your mouth, you're not doing a very good job of it." She pushed the handkerchief back in his pocket. "I've been infatuated before, but never once with you."

Walker didn't know whether to be alarmed or pleased.

"I love you," she said, raising her face. The depth of

her feeling was in the gravity of her voice, in the darkening centers of her somber eyes. "How do I satisfy you?"

"I'll show you." His head lowered. His mouth came across hers. The kiss was soft, searching. He felt the fullness of her response as she raised herself on tiptoe and leaned against him. Her arms circled his neck. Her breasts were pressed flush to his chest. Their lips parted, their tongues exchanged a touch, a taste. The fragrance of her hair was released when he took the combs from it. It spilled down her back. His fingers sifted through the silken, fiery threads. It was like a flame licking at his flesh.

Still holding her, Walker drew back slightly. Skye's mouth was damp and swollen from the kiss. Her face was flushed. The black centers of her eyes were dreamy and unfocused. "Tell me you don't regret this marriage," he said.

She was off balance enough that had he wanted to hear the sky was green, she would have complied. It was comforting to know that she wasn't compelled to lie. "I don't regret this marriage," she said huskily. She touched his lips briefly with hers. "No regret." She kissed him again. "None." Her arms fell away from his neck. She took him by the hand and led him into the bedroom.

The bed was already turned down. The lamp on the table beside it was lit. A few flowers from the vase had been removed and were lying on the plump pillows. Skye looked at Walker sideways. "Wishful thinking?" she asked.

He shook his head and answered solemnly. "Prayer."

She loved that he could make her laugh.

Skye was still smiling when he laid her back on the bed and covered her with his body. He nudged her nose with his, growled lowly, and swept away her amusement with a hard, hot kiss. Their naked bodies twisted under the sheets. His mouth traveled from her lips to her jaw. He made a damp line along her neck to the base of her throat. He went lower, taking the tip of her breast into his mouth. She arched as fire radiated from her nipple to her belly. Her legs parted around him. He came into her.

He didn't move immediately. She liked the stillness of him, the heaviness filling her, the denial that made his face taut and the anticipation sweeter. In the end it was Skye who lifted her hips, Skye who set the rhythm of their joining. It was her hands that gripped his shoulders and held him close.

She whispered in his ear, "I love you."

His climax was hard. The shudder that released the tension and pleasure was absorbed by Skye and her body vibrated in turn. Her heart thrummed. Sensation washed through her limbs in undulating waves. There was a rush of sound in her ears and the delicious taste of his mouth on hers. Champagne kisses were intoxicating.

Walker rolled away and lay back on his own pillow. He lifted his head, pulled a crushed flower from under it, and handed it to Skye. She smoothed the damaged petals and tucked it behind her ear. He wished he had thought of it. The effect was exotic, beautiful.

"You're staring at me," she whispered.

He thought he could do it for the rest of his life and never get his fill. "I know," he said. He lifted himself on one elbow when she lay back. "I like looking at you." Walker dropped a kiss on her mouth. The flower's fragrance mingled with the scent of lavender in her hair. "You're going to have to get used to it."

"It will take a long time."

That suited him. "I'll give you a long time," he said. "Years. Scores of them."

She turned into him and Walker accommodated her body, slipping his arm under her head. "How soon do you have to go back to Baileyboro?" she asked. She felt him tense. "Did you think I didn't know you'd have to return? That's what you were trying to tell me this evening. It's what you were leading up to." His fingers were trailing across the outer curve of her breast. "Well," she said slowly, slyly, acknowledging that his seduction had been successful. "Part of what you were leading up to."

He grimaced. "I'm that transparent?"

"Like glass." One of her hands slipped under the sheet and she patted his chest consolingly, just above his heart. "But I think it's because I love you."

He had to trust that she meant it. Taking her hand, he squeezed gently. "I should go back tomorrow."

She nodded. "In the morning?"

"I don't know the train schedule. If there's something in the afternoon, I can wait until then. Parnell's expecting you to return with me," he said. "I didn't tell you that. I was supposed to follow you, find out who you were working for, then bring you back to Baileyboro. Parnell suspects the threats on his life are because of the multiple contracts."

Skye sat up suddenly, drawing the sheet to her breasts. The flower dropped on her lap and she picked it up and twirled it between her fingers, using it as an extension of her hand to make a point. "Parnell knows I work for Jay Mac. He was in the house, remember? He thought I was a servant when he gave me the message for my father. I never saw him but he saw me. When I arrived at the Granville mansion, when I walked into the interview, he had to have been suspicious."

"When you walked into that room, he wanted you. That's why he hired you. It's why he wants you back." Walker sat up and leaned against the headboard. "I'm sure he remembered you from that night because he wouldn't accept that I didn't believe you were a housekeeper. I didn't understand that he had evidence that pointed to the contrary." Walker watched Skye's twirling slow. The flower petals ceased to be a blur of color. "He suspects now that you were sent there by Jay Mac, that it has to do with the engine, but a lot of that's my doing. From the beginning I tried to convince him that you were a threat."

"But why?"

"To get you away from there. I saw how he looked at you. He never bothered any of the other servants. Jenny Adams is too old. The twins were always together. No one except Corina lived at the house. I'd heard rumors about the housekeeper before you, though. She left without notice and I never could find out where she went."

"You tried?"

"I thought she might know something that could help me. I didn't try very hard. There wasn't much opportunity."

"I don't remember her name."

"Mrs. Givens. She was a widow."

"Like Annie," Skye said softly. "Do you think Annie's in any danger?"

He shook his head. *You're* the one who'd be in danger. If I took you back, that is."

She frowned. "If? You're considering not doing it?"

"I'm not considering it at all. I've decided. You'll remain here with your parents. There's some work you can do for me." He got out of bed and walked naked to the armoire. He opened it and took out his dressing gown. He shrugged into it while he hunkered down and pulled his valise from the bottom of the wardrobe. He opened it and took out the list he had reviewed with Jay Mac earlier in the day. Sitting on the edge of the bed, he handed it to Skye and watched her unfold it. "It's an attendance list for the science and technological exposition. Those are the men who've indicated they plan to be there for some part of the three-day event. It's a partial list at best. I'm sure there'll be others who arrive unannounced." Her finger was trailing along the column of names, pausing briefly when she came to one that had been circled.

"I want you to go to every circled name and find out who has a contract with Parnell. If you can find out what they've financed, that would be better. You can ignore the names I've checked. I've overheard Parnell discussing contracts with those men with Corina."

"The contracts are in his desk in the library," Skye told him.

"I've looked there. There's nothing."

"I'm sure they're there. What else would agitate Parnell when he found me sitting at his desk? I wasn't poking around. I didn't know then to look for anything, but he didn't realize that. His behavior didn't make sense to me, but I know I didn't imagine it." She tapped the flower against her chin as she thought. "You looked in the hidden drawers, didn't you?"

"Hidden drawers?"

Her mouth pulled to one side as she looked at him out of the corner of her eye. "I suppose that means you didn't." She sighed. "Parnell's desk is a copy of one I'm familiar with. It's riddled with secret drawers. They're not even hard to find if you know what you're looking for."

"How did you come by this information?"

She permitted herself a smug smile. "I told you I've studied lots of things. Antiques are a particular interest. So is the Granville history." She placed the flower on the bedside table and gave Walker back his list. "You need me," she said. "And Parnell wants me. I'm going back with you."

"No."

"Jay Mac can speak to all the men on your list. He'd do it better than I. They'll meet with him. Even if they gave me an audience they wouldn't believe me."

"No."

"This isn't only about an engine, Walker. It's about a treasure."

He didn't say no this time. He didn't say anything at all.

Skye was encouraged. Coming up on her knees, she let the sheet drop and slid her arms around his neck. The list slipped through Walker's fingers. She tumbled him onto the bed and whispered in his ear. "I'll tell you all about it on the train."

Fifteen

"It's all right here," Skye said. The Granville family history lay open on her lap. The movement of the train jounced the heavy volume. Skye steadied it with two fingers. They were past West Point now. She had refused to open it earlier, afraid Walker would find some excuse to put her off the train. It would be more difficult now and he had to know she would follow him.

"Show me," he said. His voice was clipped. She didn't seem to care that he was angry with her. She hadn't cared about the danger, either. Skye put a lot of stock in his ability to protect her. He wasn't certain all her faith was justified. "What did you mean, this was about a treasure?"

"I think Parnell and his sister have read this historical account of the Granvilles. There's information early on about a treasure ship that was abandoned on the Hudson by Edward Granville. My first impression was that the ship was raided, then sunk. The more I read, the less convinced I became. The family historian certainly was intrigued by the idea that the ship may have been sunk with its treasure on board."

"Is there evidence, or is this just some kind of family myth?"

Skye was satisfied that she had captured Walker's attention. She trusted that he would listen with an open mind. "A little of both, I'm afraid. Until the time of Hamilton Granville, it seems, it was part of the family lore. The idea that so much wealth could possibly be buried under water . . . well, you can imagine they found it intriguing. It's hard to tell who might have been stirred enough to act on the idea, but it was Hamilton Granville—"

"The Granville ghost."

"The very same," she said. "He gave his young mistress an unusual piece of jewelry. Some of the family believed it came from the sunken treasure ship. It was a necklace fashioned from the beaten gold of Spanish doubloons. It's more correct to say that it was in her possession after Hamilton killed himself. It's assumed that he's the one who gave it to her. She certainly never wore it openly while he was alive. His wife wouldn't have approved."

"What happened to the necklace?"

"His mistress, who was also a servant, ran off after she was discovered to have it. The account doesn't say, but I'd think she was probably accused of stealing it. The family would have been desperate to have it back. It was worth a fortune even then, and the Granvilles were having financial difficulties. In only two more generations they lost possession of the house and the land."

"To my uncle."

"I don't think so. When I was a little girl, my family summered in the valley. There were no Granvilles living at the house then." She cast him a sideways glance. "Except for the ghost, of course."

"Indeed," he said drily. "If only it were that simple. It's not a ghost causing our problems." Walker pointed to the open book on Skye's lap. "Was there more treasure found?"

She shook her head. "Never. Not for lack of trying, though. No one attempted to recover the necklace by looking for Hamilton's mistress. Over the next forty years, people looked for the treasure source. The efforts were concentrated along the Hudson. Quite naturally, the history isn't clear on exactly where or how, but I have the impression that old tunnels from the house to the river were excavated."

"Tunnels?"

"Hmm-mmm. There were at least two of them, both laid during revolutionary times to give the Granvilles a way out. They were Tories, you know, and not particularly well liked by the neighbors for their politics. They lodged British soldiers." She tapped the book. "This account claims that Benedict Arnold passed a night at the house."

Walker was skeptical but not dismissive. "You think these tunnels exist?"

"It's likely. I've always thought the house was built with secret passages, so tunnels wouldn't surprise me. It would explain what Parnell does all day in his workroom."

"When he's pretending to work on an engine he knows nothing about."

"Exactly."

Walker thought about it. "It doesn't explain his clean hands."

"Gloves and a change of clothes," she said simply. "I'd wager if we searched the workroom we'd find both, or at least, a passage leading to them."

He turned on her sharply and said under his breath, "Don't entertain that thought again. We will not be searching. I will."

"Walker," she said softly, beginning to object. "I thought we—"

"No," he said. He didn't add anything to the single word. As far as he was concerned, it wasn't necessary.

Aware of nearby passengers, Skye said, "I'm not going to argue about it here."

"I'm not going to argue about it at all." He picked up the book. "May I?"

"By all means," she said, with little grace.

Walker ignored the icy tones. "Tell me about these passages," he said. "How do you know they exist?"

"I don't know," she admitted reluctantly. "I suspect. I might have been able to confirm it had I stayed longer."

Walker frowned, drawing on a memory. "That's why you were sketching floor plans of the rooms," he said with sudden insight.

"Well, yes," she said slowly. "You saw those?"

He leaned back hard. What his single swearing utterance lacked in volume it made up for with intensity.

"What is it?" Skye asked, her eyes anxious. "Walker?"

"I found your sketches in your apron pocket . . . in that little notepad you carried around. I showed them to Parnell. I didn't understand their significance. I really thought it was your manner of doing a thorough inventory. I let Parnell believe you were using the floor plan to memorize his room so that he wouldn't be safe, even at night. I thought it would make him more eager for you to leave." He closed his eyes a moment and rubbed his lids, thinking. "If you're right about the passages, then he may have suspected what you were doing. Jesus. He and Corina are going to watch you all the time."

She could almost hear what he was thinking. "I'm not going back to the city," she said. "This doesn't change anything. If they're watching me, then they can't watch you. This isn't a problem, it's an opportunity."

He grimaced and shot her a wry glance. "You'll understand if I don't quite see it that way." He sat up again. "Do you think Parnell used a passage to get from his room into yours?"

"There isn't a passage between the rooms. My sketches and measurements showed that to me. The rooms fit together like two pieces of a puzzle. They interlock. There's a connecting door that hasn't been opened in years. He had to have come in from the hallway." She hesitated. "Or we have to accept another explanation."

"Hamilton Granville?" Walker shook his head. "It wasn't a ghost."

Skye's eyes dropped to her lap. The faint flush to her complexion was evidence of her pained thoughts. "It would be easier to accept," she said quietly. "The way he . . . the way he touched me . . ."

Walker slipped his hand under one of Skye's. His fingers threaded with hers and he squeezed gently.

"To pretend it wasn't quite real," she went on. "That would be better than accepting Parnell's hands on me." Her voice trailed away. Skye moved closer to Walker, drawing comfort from his solid frame. She did not see the splintered coldness of his gold-flecked eyes or the remoteness of his expression. She did not know the manner of death he was planning for Jonathan Parnell.

Parnell came up from his workroom to meet Walker in the parlor. His first question was about Skye. "Where is she?"

Walker noticed that Skye's observations were accurate. Parnell's hands weren't stained from his work, but his sleeves had smudges of oil and grease, and, as Walker looked more closely, even a fine layer of dust around the collar. "I sent her upstairs to her room until we could talk."

"Her room?" asked Parnell. "Or your room? Is she still playing the whore for you?"

"She's in the room next to yours," he said, without inflection.

Parnell poured himself a drink. He did not offer one to Walker. "This is interesting," he said, motioning Walker to sit. His pale blue eyes were narrowed as he raised the tumbler of liquor to his lips. "You wouldn't let her out of your sight before. What's changed your mind?"

"She works for Jay Mac Worth." Walker saw Parnell's fleeting expression of satisfaction because he was looking for it. That flash of acknowledgment confirmed for Walker that Skye was right about the identity of the intruder in her home. At the same time, Walker realized that Parnell placed more confidence in Walker's own competence and judgment. "I followed her from the station to Worth's home at 50th and Broadway. You don't appear surprised."

"No," Parnell admitted tightly. "I'm not. Worth has been a supporter of my work. The fool thinks he owns me. Do you know why he sent her here?"

Walker shook his head. "I'm not sure that he did. If he's involved, it wasn't with the intention of harming you, though. It could be that he wanted to have information on the progress you're making on the engine. If he's invested in your work, then that would make sense." Walker would not reveal that he knew other men had invested as well, or that he had known it for some time. He wanted proof before he confronted Parnell. "Wouldn't you say?"

Parnell shrugged. He knocked back another swallow of his drink. "What makes you think Worth isn't behind the threats on my life?"

"I can't find any support for it. Or even that Miss Dennehy works for him in another capacity. He doesn't appear to conduct business in that manner. Miss Dennehy was a servant in his home, a maid, not the housekeeper. That's the position she returned to when she left here. Mrs. Worth was the one who hired her and she's the one who took her back."

Parnell didn't want to hear about Jay Mac's wife. "She's nothing else to Worth?" asked Parnell.

"His spy, you mean?"

"I mean his whore."

Walker's eyes remained shuttered, his expression remote. "I couldn't find anyone who would say so. In the course of her duties Miss Dennehy rarely saw her employer. I talked to the housekeeper, the groundsman. I spoke to the neighbors' servants. I was discreet."

Parnell's head bent in a slight bow, acknowledging his dry appreciation of Walker's work. His smile was as faint as his sarcasm. "Of course." He refilled his glass. "But she returned with you. Willingly, it seems. How did that come to pass?"

"I told her you regretted your decision to dismiss her and I said you were offering more money if she'd return to the position. I gave her your apologies for the incident in your workroom." Walker watched ruddy color spread across Parnell's face. It was clear Parnell thought an apology was unnecessary and shouldn't have been offered. "She's also running away. It suits her purpose to be out of the city right now."

"Running away? From what?"

Walker paused a beat, letting Parnell's imagination reinforce the lie he was about to tell. "She was involved with a married man."

Parnell nodded thoughtfully, his eyes focused on a point beyond Walker's shoulder. "Marshall? Turner?"

"She worked for them. I confirmed that much. The rest I couldn't find out."

"Did you ask her?"

Walker shook his head. "You wanted her back here. I didn't see the point in antagonizing her with questions like that."

Parnell speared Walker with a glance. "What do you really think, Mr. Caine? Don't talk to me about the evidence. I don't want to hear what the neighbors' servants report. Tell me what that instinct of yours says about Miss Dennehy."

"Don't trust her."

Parnell nodded, satisfied. "I was thinking the same thing."

"He believed you?" Skye asked softly, when Walker passed her on the stairs.

Walker nodded. "Be careful."

Skye touched him briefly on the sleeve and continued on her way to the parlor. It would not be an easy audience with Parnell. Her heart was slamming hard in her chest and her palm was slippery on the door handle when she twisted it.

"Come in," Parnell said, when Skye hovered in the doorway. "I didn't know if you'd agree to return with Mr. Caine. He tells me you had already engaged other employment."

"Mrs. Worth was kind enough to take me back."

"I don't remember seeing the Worths as a reference when I hired you."

"I didn't put them down. I had worked there only a short time. I had no chance to prove myself. Now that I've returned here, I doubt I'll ever be able to go back. They won't tolerate a second defection."

Parnell's lightly colored brows were raised. He stared at her consideringly. "Then you'll have to make a success of it here."

"That's my intention."

"Of course you'll apologize for that regrettable situation in my workroom."

Skye's mouth went dry. He expected an apology from *her*? Even had she been able to think of something to say, she wouldn't have been able to force the words out. "I . . . I don't think I understand," she finally managed.

"You encouraged me," he said. When she still didn't respond, he said, "Do you make a practice of it, Skye?

That's what Mr. Caine believes. He says you were involved with a married man."

Skye wondered how she would respond to the accusation, whether she was up to the task of playing out her role. She felt heat rising above her collar and up her throat, finally searing her cheeks. The doubts she harbored about her abilities vanished. "Mr. Caine's lying."

Parnell's regard was almost pitying. "I don't think I believe you. You haven't the knack of telling a falsehood. Your face is too expressive." He watched her flush become deeper. "Was it Dr. Turner?" he asked. "Or Logan Marshall?"

"I never had an affair," she repeated.

He waved one hand dismissively. "It doesn't matter. I'd hoped for something else from you, but I can accept the disappointment. You'll begin your duties immediately. Walker says that you're in the room next to mine, is that right?"

Skye felt her heart knocking again. She rubbed her palms in the folds of her plain gray skirt, twisting the fabric just a bit between her fingers. "That's correct, but—"

Parnell was leaning against the sideboard. He straightened now, the simple action cutting Skye off. He took a step forward. "Let's be frank, Skye. We both know the reason you've come back here. It wasn't the additional money, though I'm certain you're greedy enough to have appreciated it. And it wasn't the work, though I think you've shown a certain aptitude for it. I don't believe it's Walker Caine, either. You came back because you've decided that I may be worth pursuing."

Skye couldn't help her little start. "Mr. Parnell," she began. "I think you have the wrong—"

"We'll talk about it this evening," he said.

Realizing she was dismissed, Skye all but fled the room.

* * *

Skye's reinstatement to her position went awkwardly. Annie Staplehurst couldn't hide her resentment. Though she welcomed Skye back and said all the right things, she was visibly hurt and unhappy. Rose and Daisy Farrow snickered a great deal between them. They had their own ideas about Skye Dennehy's return and the glances they traded spoke eloquently for their silence. Jenny Adams was more blatantly disapproving, tsking a great deal as she bent over her sewing. Hank Ryder was polite but reserved.

Corina Reading's expression was the most difficult for Skye to discern. She was the most guarded in her reaction to meeting Skye again. Suspicion and anger would flash suddenly, giving Skye a glimpse of the emotion that simmered beneath Corina's cool surface.

Young Matthew Staplehurst was the only one genuinely glad to see her again. He hung on her skirts throughout the day as she directed the running of the household. He also provided her with an opportunity to leave the house and meet privately with Walker.

Walker came upon them by the swan pond. Skye gave Matt a handful of crusts and let the boy continue pitching them in the direction of the elegant, preening white birds. "I told Annie that I would get Matt," he said.

"Was she angry?"

"No."

Skye wanted to touch Walker's face, to feel the shape of his jaw in the heart of her palm. Afraid someone would see, she didn't dare. "Annie's hurt that I've come back. She thought her position was secure. I hadn't expected she would resent me."

"We don't have time to talk about Annie," he said. He glanced at Matt, made certain the boy was safe on the edge of the icy pond, then turned his attention back to Skye. "How did your interview with Parnell go?"

"He thinks I came back because I want to be his mistress."

Walker's mouth flattened. Wind ruffled his uncovered hair and he raked it back impatiently. "He's testing you, Skye. I hope you didn't appear too flattered by his proposition."

"Flattered?" Her voice rose a notch. "How can you think I'd be flattered?"

"I don't think you'd be flattered. I simply didn't know what you would reveal to him. If you seem too eager, he may think it's odd. You rebuffed him before."

"I threatened to kill him before. I may do it again. He expects me to give him some sort of answer this evening and I think he intends to come to my room to get it."

Walker rubbed the back of his neck. The cords of tension there were so tight that his head ached. "This is no good, Skye. You should have stayed in the city. I was out of my mind to let you come back here."

"I just can't leave now," she said. "There has to be another way."

"You can come to my room."

She shook her head. "We agreed that wasn't the answer. If I do that, we'll always be watched. You won't have a chance to explore on your own, and neither will I." A swan hissed behind her. She held out her hand toward Matt. "Come along, Matthew. We're going back to the house now." The boy tossed his last bread crust and came running. He slipped his hand into Skye's outstretched one. "I'll tell him no," Skye said to Walker. "He'll have to accept it. If he's really testing me, then he'll accept it."

"And if he's not?"

"I have a gun." She turned, tugged on Matt's hand, and began walking.

"What the hell are you talking about?" Walker demanded. He felt Matt look up at him anxiously and realized he was scowling. "You never said anything about a gun."

She shrugged. "It's Parnell's. The one with the cutaway trigger that he aimed at you. You hid it in your wardrobe and I found it when I was packing. I put it in my trunk and I've had it ever since." Her beautiful features were serene as she turned her head in his direction. "Don't worry, Walker. I know how to use it. I'm really quite an excellent shot. I thought it was proper training for adventuring." She smiled. "Seems I was right."

He wasn't amused. "Three days," he said tightly "If we have nothing at the end of three days, I'm sending you back to the city. In that damn trunk, if I have to."

Walker didn't like to admit that Skye's presence made a difference in his search. In the months prior to her coming to Granville he had found himself all too often under Corina's watchful eye. Mrs. Reading wasn't easily distracted, disarmed, or charmed. She kept a close eye on her brother and a closer one on him. He couldn't recall her having an easy smile for anyone or a glance that wasn't suspicious. She would have allowed him to take her to bed. There had been overtures in the past, and he had been tempted. In the end, he never pressed for her favors, afraid it would be too difficult to extricate himself.

Now Corina was too busy watching Skye to pay attention to his movements around the house. He was no longer so concerned that she would come upon him unexpectedly. If she was prowling now, at least she had other prey in mind. Walker slipped into the library unnoticed. He considered locking the door behind him but decided to do so would give rise to too many questions. There was always the possibility that someone would try to get in.

He had also thought about waiting until night and mak-

ing his visit to the library while everyone was sleeping.
That posed its own risks. The lamp he would have had
to have carried could have roused someone. Sometimes
it seemed that the more openly a thing was done, the
easier it was to conceal. Who would suspect him of being
foolish enough to rifle Parnell's desk in broad daylight?

Skye had described the desk to him in perfect detail
and explained how to access the panels that uncovered
small pocket drawers. No special equipment was required
to unlock the desk's secrets. The craftsmanship was ex-
quisite, relying on springs and weights and counter-
weights. As the first panel opened up under his light
touch in the righthand corner, Walker acknowledged to
himself that he couldn't have found it without Skye's
guidance. He wasn't so certain he was going to admit it
to her.

Walker held his breath as he eased the panel open.
The pocket drawer was only a few inches high but more
than eight inches deep. It held two rolled documents.
His fingers had closed over one when he heard footsteps in the hall. They paused just outside the door.

Shutting the panel quickly, Walker opened the book
he had brought in the event of an interruption. By the
time the door was cracked he was comfortable in Parnell's
large chair, his legs stretched in front of him, looking for
all the world as if he were a man of leisure.

It was Corina Reading's small, flawlessly featured face
that appeared in the opening. "I didn't think I was going
to find you," she said. Her eyes dropped to the book in
his lap, but she said nothing. Her disapproval was in her
cool tone. "Hank requires your help in the stable."

"Oh?" Walker shut the book and laid it aside. "Did
he say why?"

"He didn't say and I didn't ask. I only offered to look
for you because I didn't want him tracking stable muck
through my kitchen."

Walker got to his feet. "I suppose a few minutes to myself was too much to ask."

Corina's smile was brittle. "You work here, just like the rest of us. It's only right that you should have to earn your wage."

"That's what I was doing," he said calmly. "That's the Granville history I was reading."

"I know what it was. I don't know why you're suddenly interested in it."

"I'm interested in whatever poses a threat to Mr. Parnell." He gave her an easy smile as he passed her on the way out. "And that includes the ghost of Hamilton Granville."

Jonathan Parnell looked over the schedule for the science and technological exposition while he sipped an after-dinner drink. He held his comments until he had read everything. Watching him closely, Walker tried to detect an edge of panic in Parnell's expression. Except for lifting his glass more frequently, there was nothing notable in his reaction.

"It was good of you to bring this," Parnell said. "I read the *Chronicle* article you sent me, of course, but this covers the event more completely. It's quite an impressive gathering. You'll arrange for additional security, won't you?"

"What did you have in mind?" asked Walker.

"I'll be very exposed. There may well be another attempt on my life. I know there hasn't been one here for months, but I don't think we've frightened anyone off. It's more likely that it's being planned." Parnell set the schedule aside. "I think a search of every man who attends my lecture is in order."

"A search?" he asked. "Of every man? *These* men?" Walker had always known Parnell would think of some way to keep from attending the exposition. The surprise was only that he was being so clever about it. He wondered how much of the idea was influenced by Corina. "You can't be serious."

"Are you saying you can't arrange it?"

"I can arrange it," Walker told him. "I doubt that I'll gain anyone's cooperation in carrying it out. Can you imagine someone like Morgan or Rockefeller submitting to a search?"

Parnell shrugged. "They'll have to, won't they? If they want to hear me speak, they'll have to do it."

"If you insist, naturally I'll see what I can do, but I think there's no sense in it. You'll be speaking to an empty room. The men who plan to attend your lecture won't stand for the indignity."

"You're probably right." Parnell rolled his tumbler between his palms. "I'll have to cancel the engagement. There's nothing else I can do."

And that was that, Walker thought. Parnell had used him to neatly avoid appearing at the exposition. Had Walker agreed easily to making the arrangements, had he supported Parnell's ridiculous idea, Parnell would rightly have been suspicious. "Perhaps if you had mentioned the exposition earlier," he said. "There may have been some way to provide the security without an individual search of all the participants."

"I forgot about it," Parnell said carelessly. "I can't be expected to remember these things when I'm involved in my work. There should have been a reminder."

"Of course," Walker agreed. "It's just too bad about the timing. I could have planned something if I'd known." Relief flashed briefly in Parnell's eyes. "Go ahead and send your regrets, but I'll be working on the problem. If there's a way for you to be there safely, I'll pursue it. I know you're disappointed." Walker had to temper his smile as he saw an edge of panic return to Parnell's expression.

A scratching at the door interrupted Parnell. "What is it?" he demanded impatiently.

Walker stood as Annie Staplehurst appeared on the threshold. She was clearly uncomfortable, her pale gray eyes darting uneasily between Parnell and him. "What is it, Annie?" he asked.

She couldn't quite meet his eyes. "I'm wanting to speak to Mr. Parnell," she said.

Parnell sighed. "Well? What is it?"

When she didn't answer immediately, Walker began to suspect he was the reason for her discomfort. "I think Annie means she wants to speak to you alone. It's no problem. I have to get back to helping Hank. There's a broken axle on the carriage." Before Parnell could object, Walker took his leave.

"Well?" Parnell demanded again. "What is it, Miss Staplehurst?"

Annie's fingers fidgeted in the folds of her gown. She cleared her throat. "I don't wish to appear forward, sir, but I've come about something that concerns you."

Parnell held out his empty tumbler and indicated with a careless gesture that she should refill it. "You can speak freely," he said as she rushed to take the glass. "Don't top it off," he told her. "Half will do."

Annie poured the drink. It was difficult to do because her hands were shaking. Some of the liquor dribbled over her fingers. She hastily wiped them on her apron before giving the tumbler back to Parnell. "I've come about something I heard today," she said. "I thought it was important enough for you to know." She felt his keen eyes on her and began to wish she hadn't come at all. "I believe Miss Dennehy has a gun," she blurted, looking everywhere but at him. "I thought you'd want to know."

One of Parnell's lightly-colored brows kicked up. "A gun?" he asked. "Have you seen it?"

"No, sir."

"No? Then how did you come by this information? Did Miss Dennehy tell you this herself?"

"Oh, no. She doesn't suspect I know. Matthew told me." Parnell's expression was skeptical, and Annie went on quickly to explain. "I know he's just a boy, but he's smart as a whip, and he hears and sees things that surprise me all the time. I suppose it's the way of children. No one pays the least attention and then suddenly you hear yourself quoted by them." She stopped abruptly, realizing she was rambling. "Miss Dennehy took Matt with her to the swan pond this afternoon. It wasn't long after that he started talking nonsense about a gun. I didn't pay him any mind at first, but when he kept it up, I began to take notice."

Parnell sat up straighter. "He actually said Miss Dennehy had a weapon?"

"That's what I got out of it."

"Perhaps I should talk to the boy."

Annie shook her head quickly. "I don't think he'd tell you," she said. "And if he did, I don't think you'd understand him."

"But you had no such difficulty," he said skeptically.

Annie's reply was forceful and inarguable. "I'm his mother."

Parnell pushed aside the uncleared plates from his dinner and rested his forearm on the table. His fingertips followed the embroidered pattern in the linen tablecloth as he thought. "Did your son see the gun?"

"I don't know. Do you think Miss Dennehy is carrying it on her person?"

Parnell refrained from answering that question. "Was she alone with your son?"

Annie nodded. "They weren't gone above twenty minutes. I was on the point of going to get Matt, but Mr. Caine offered to do it for me."

"Mr. Caine," Parnell said softly. "So he and Miss Dennehy were there together."

Annie felt as if Parnell was missing the point. It was not her intention to involve Walker Caine. "Only a few minutes. He brought them both right back."

Parnell had heard enough. "Thank you, Miss Staplehurst. You can go." He waited until she had made a small curtsy before he added, "And keep on going. I expect that you'll be gone as soon as Hank and Walker repair the carriage. Hank will take you into town. I'll have Mrs. Reading arrange it."

Annie's stoic features were shattered by this announcement. Tears welled in her eyes and her complexion went from ruddy to ash. "But, sir, I didn't— "

He held up one hand, stopping her. "You've betrayed your friend," he said. "Miss Dennehy was responsible for you gaining a position in this house and she treated you fairly. Now that she's returned you've proved to me that you can't make room for her. Since I have no intention of dismissing her, you'll have to leave."

"But I did it for you, sir!"

Parnell shook his head, his lip curling derisively. "I'm not a fool, Miss Staplehurst. You did it for yourself." He came to his feet. "I'll prepare a letter of reference for you to take and there will be severance pay. I'll expect you in the library at the end of an hour. Both will be waiting for you. See that you're not late." He went to the door and held it open for Annie. He heard her sob as she passed.

Skye tensed when she heard footsteps outside her own door. The sun had gone down hours earlier and every lamp in the bedroom flickered. The heavy drapes were drawn against the inky sky and a fire was laid as much for the light it provided as for the heat.

She paused in unpacking her clothes. The armoire stood open, half-filled now with the items from her trunk. "Yes?" she asked. "Who is it?" There was no response. Skye set her gown aside and moved closer to the door. "Is someone there?" There was no single word Skye could identify, but she recognized the sound of someone's pain.

She had used a chair to reinforce the locked door and now she pushed it aside. As soon as the door was opened, Annie stumbled into the room. Skye caught her by the elbow and supported her. Annie's solid, yet somehow frail form rested against Skye. She was sobbing uncontrollably, her grief so profound that Skye felt it as a wound on her own heart.

"What is it, Annie?" Skye patted the back of Annie's heaving shoulders. "Annie, you have to tell me what's wrong. Is it Matthew? Has something happened to Matt?" The door was pushed wider and the little boy in question came into the room. He pressed himself into his mother's skirts, holding onto them with pudgy fists.

Annie straightened and stepped away. Tears spilled from the corners of her eyes, but a single shudder helped her gain control. She was grateful for the handkerchief Skye pressed into her hand. She blew her nose.

Skye knelt and pried Matt's fingers away from Annie's gown. The boy was frightened by his mother's distress and Annie was unable to comfort him. He went into Skye's arms with only a little prompting. She looked up at Annie. "Can you tell me what's wrong?" she asked. "You know I'll help you if I can." For reasons that Skye couldn't divine, her offer prompted another bout of tears. She felt Matthew grow restless in her embrace. He was losing interest now, more confident perhaps in her ability to help his mother. She gave him a small pat on the bottom and let him wander away. He went directly to her writing desk and began plucking papers from the top.

Annie watched him out of the corner of her eye. "He'll make a mess," she said.

"Never mind about Matt. He's fine." Skye rose and led Annie over to the bed to sit. "Tell me why you're crying and what's to be done."

Annie pressed the balled handkerchief against her mouth to stifle a sob. "He's dismissed me."

The words were almost unintelligible and Skye strained to hear them. She frowned, not certain she'd heard correctly. "Annie, I don't think I understood. It sounded as if you said you've been dismissed."

Annie's nod was violently affirmative. Her tightly closed eyes squeezed out another round of tears. She knuckled them away. "He says I'm to go. Right away. Tonight. I've done a terrible thing, Skye," she said miserably. "A terrible thing."

Skye couldn't fathom the behavior that would have prompted Annie's dismissal. "You'd better tell me the whole of it."

"It's a betrayal," she said. Her eyes pleaded with Skye for understanding. "Just like he said. I didn't do it for him. I did it for me. Oh, that I could be so selfish. Even if you can forgive me, I won't be able to forgive myself."

Alarmed, Skye placed her hands on Annie's shoulders and gave her a little shake. "Tell me, Annie. What have you done?"

"I told him about your gun. I know you have one. Matt told me. It's true, isn't it? Matt wouldn't have lied."

"It doesn't matter now," Skye said. She let her hands fall away from Annie and crossed her arms in front of her. She felt cold suddenly. "You didn't give me an opportunity to explain. You went directly to Mr. Parnell. Why didn't you ask me about it?" Skye watched Annie's eyes dart away and the flush of pained embarrassment color her complexion again. "Oh, Annie," she said sadly. "You thought he'd dismiss me."

Annie nodded. "I thought he'd be grateful that I was lookin' out for him," she whispered. "Instead he saw right through me. Matt and I have got to leave and you'll be staying." She dabbed at her eyes again and risked a glance at Skye. "I'm sorry. I truly am. I should have learned my lesson the first time."

Skye was still thinking hard, wondering how to handle Parnell when he confronted her. It was inevitable that he would. She would have to lie, and it would have to sound plausible. "What do you mean?" she asked absently. "What lesson?"

"That you always land on your feet."

It wasn't what Skye expected Annie might say. She frowned. "What are you talking about?"

"The time you went to the cellar," Annie said. "One of the first nights you were here. I was on my way to the kitchen myself, and I glimpsed you going in that direction. I thought you probably didn't want company, so I let you go on. When I went down a little later, your pan of milk was warm by the stove and you weren't around." Annie sniffed. She brushed the tip of her nose with the handkerchief. "I heard you in the cellar. You knew you weren't supposed to go down there. We've all been warned off right from the start. It came to me suddenly, just a thought that I should have pushed to the back of my mind. But I couldn't."

Now Skye knew what she was going to hear. She remained quiet, letting Annie say it.

"I shut the door and locked it. I knew it was wrong— you'd been so very good to me— but I thought if I could secure your position, things would be better for Matt and me."

"Is that all you did?" asked Skye. "Did you tell anyone?"

Annie shook her head. "I didn't think I'd have to. I thought you'd be discovered there and the matter would take care of itself. I was glad when I realized the next day that you'd got out. You have to believe me. I felt terrible about what I'd done."

"Not so terrible that you let me out."

"But I didn't give you away when I had the chance." At Skye's questioning look, she explained, "Mrs. Reading came through. I could have told her where you'd gone, but I didn't."

"She asked about me?"

"She asked about the milk on the stove."

Skye remembered putting the milk on to warm. She was going to have graveyard stew to help her sleep. The sugar and cinnamon were sitting out on the table. So were a few crusts of bread. She had prepared the same thing for herself the evening before, the first night at Granville, and Mrs. Reading had watched her. "Did you tell her the milk was yours?"

"I did," Annie said. "But I told her I didn't want it any longer. I was going to put it away, but she told me to leave it."

"And then you left."

"That's right. I could have told her where you were. Surely it counts for something."

"It's all right, Annie. What's done is done. There's no sense making yourself sick over it." It was clear to Skye that Mrs. Reading hadn't believed Annie about the milk. Corina might not have realized that she was in the cellar then, but the cook knew she had been around recently. "You'd better begin packing your things. There's nothing I can do for you here. Mr. Parnell isn't going to change his mind."

"I don't want him to change his mind," she said. "I didn't come here for that. I wanted you to know what I've done. I wanted to tell you how sorry I am. I wish

I could take it back." She saw Skye's skeptical expression. "And not because I lost my position. This is a frightening place, Skye. There's part of me that's glad to go. I can't sleep most nights for hearing the Granville ghost pace the floor."

Skye didn't want to hear Annie's stories about the ghost. "Annie," she said firmly. "If Mr. Parnell is telling you to leave tonight, then— "

"Do you forgive me?"

"Yes, I forgive you." She took Annie's large, hardworking hands in her own. She captured Annie's gaze, held it, then spoke deliberately and slowly. "Listen to me. I'm not angry with you. Of course, I forgive you. I want you to pack your things and go to Baileyboro. Get a ticket for New York and present yourself to a house at 50th and Broadway. Ask for Mrs. Cavanaugh."

Annie was uncertain. "What sort of house?" she asked. "You know I ain't the kind that— "

Skye squeezed her hands. "Annie, it's not a brothel. It's a family home, and I'm known there. Mrs. Cavanaugh. Can you remember that, or shall I write it for you?" Annie repeated the name. "Good. You'll do fine. Tell them I'd like you to have work there. They'll take you in and let you stay as long as you behave yourself."

"Oh, I will. I *will.*" She leaned forward and hugged Skye. "The others think you like Mr. Parnell's attentions," she said. "I know it's different with you. That's why I could believe Matt about the gun." She drew back and glanced around. "Where'd he go?"

Skye swiveled around on the bed and looked for Matt. "He must be hiding. He hasn't left the room. The door's still closed." She dropped on her knees beside the bed and looked under it. Matt hadn't crawled there. "Where are you, Matt?"

Annie was up and looking behind the chair. She tried Skye's trunk next, lifting a few of the topmost belongings. Her son's little tow head didn't appear. "Matthew Staplehurst! Show yourself right now!" Both women listened. There wasn't so much as a giggle to reveal the whereabouts of the boy.

Hands on her hips, Skye surveyed the room. "This is silly," she said. "He can't have disappeared." Her eyes fell on the armoire. The door to it was still ajar from when she had been interrupted. She placed one finger over her lips and pointed it out to Annie.

Annie nodded, understanding. She tiptoed quietly toward the armoire and opened the door fully. Without any warning, her hand snaked in. Her plan was to come out with a handful of boy. She pulled out crumpled linens instead. "I'll be darned," she said, staring at them. "I was sure—"

Skye was sure, too. "I had those folded," she said. "The little scamp must have made a nest for himself." She dropped down in front of the deep armoire and leaned in, rooting around for an ankle or wrist that wasn't hidden as well as the rest. "Matt, come out—" Her voice broke off abruptly when her hand seemed to go through the back of the wardrobe. "Annie, go next door to Parnell's room. See if Matt's there."

"Why in the world—"

"Just go, Annie." As soon as she heard Annie leave the room, Skye pressed forward, crawling into the armoire in just the manner she was sure Matthew had. The panel at the back was already open, swinging outward into Parnell's room, or more specifically, into Parnell's own armoire. The opening was small but easily negotiated by someone on their hands and knees. Skye had no difficulty moving through it. She understood now that Parnell had had no difficulty either.

Skye yanked on her gown as it caught beneath her, then she pushed the rest of the way through, opening the outer doors to Parnell's armoire. She grinned when she saw Annie sitting on Parnell's bed with Matthew in her lap. "Look at that. You've got him. As soon as I found the opening, I knew he'd be in here." It took Skye a moment to realize that Annie wasn't sharing her satisfaction. Even Matthew looked unusually subdued.

"What is it?" she asked. She started to climb out of the wardrobe. It was an awkward journey and her gown impeded her progress. She was startled when she felt herself being hauled upward, a firm hand grasping the coil of hair at her nape. Her hands went automatically to the back of her head to keep her hair from being torn out by its roots.

Skye was yanked hard to her feet and brought flush against Parnell himself. His fine, distinguished features were sharply etched. His blue eyes were like chips of ice, burning her with their coldness. He turned her around so that her back was pressed flatly against him. One of his arms locked under her breasts, making struggle almost impossible. His touch made Skye want to retch. For a moment she couldn't see clearly. Darkness pressed in on the edges of her vision and she realized she was in danger of fainting. An odd thought crossed her mind then: the thought that her sisters would laugh if she fainted in the midst of her first real adventure. The ignominy of it was like smelling salts, pushing back the darkness.

"Hold still," he whispered in her ear. His arm tightened as did the fingers in her hair.

Skye forced herself to quiet though she couldn't relax. She looked at Annie. Had it all been planned just this way?

Annie understood the question in Skye's eyes and knew she deserved to be doubted. She shook her head. "I didn't have anything to do with— "

"Quiet," Parnell said. "Give your boy to Skye."

Annie's eyes widened. She held Matthew more tightly and didn't move.

"So help me God, I'll kill you right in front of him." He saw Annie recoil. "Now, give him to Skye."

Annie slid off the bed and approached Skye and Parnell slowly. "You go to Skye," she whispered to Matthew, ruffling his hair. "Skye wants to hold you." Parnell released Skye enough to allow her to take the boy. Annie still gave him up reluctantly. Her eyes were anguished. "I don't understand," she pleaded. "I don't—"

"Go to your room and pack your things." His smile held no sympathy. "Yes, I can see you wish you'd done that right away. It's too late now, and regrets won't solve the problem. Go on with you. Pack everything. The boy's things, too." As an afterthought, he added, "And don't talk to anyone." Annie fled the room. Parnell released Skye and gave her a push at the small of the back toward the bed. "Sit there." He closed the door and locked it.

"Why are you doing this?" Skye asked. "Annie was getting ready to leave."

"Not fast enough to suit me. This will move her along *and* keep her quiet." He reached into the armoire and pulled all the panels shut. Anyone entering Skye's room would no longer know that she had exited through the wardrobe. "I thought she might come running to you."

"You listened."

He nodded. "You can hear quite well through the back of the wardrobe. The panel doesn't always have to be opened."

Skye struggled for calm. "Matt must have surprised you."

Parnell didn't reply. He leaned against the closed wardrobe and watched her silently. The picture of her with the child in her lap intrigued him. Her hair was like a copper aura about her head. Madonna and child, he thought. It was a false picture, of course. At one time he might have mistaken her for pure. No longer.

Matthew squirmed in Skye's lap. He could sense her uneasiness as the silence went on. She stroked the back of his head and felt Parnell's eyes narrow on the movement of her fingers.

It seemed hours passed before Annie returned. Skye knew by the mantel clock that it had been less than twenty minutes. Parnell brought Annie into the room. He took Matt from Skye and gave the boy over to his mother. "I want to show you something, Annie."

With no more warning than that he brought back his fist and clipped Skye on the chin. She fell back on the bed without a sound. "Now come with me," he said. He led Annie and Matt out of the room and locked the door behind him.

Sixteen

The touch was light but strangely insistent. Skye shrugged, trying to avoid the sensation that caressed her from throat to shoulder. The strength of her panic forced awareness.

Skye's eyes flew open and she was confronted by Parnell. He was standing over her holding a long silk scarf in his hand. One corner of the gray silk was being drawn across her bare arm. He was smiling. It was a cold greeting and it did not touch his eyes.

"Your ghost, I'm afraid." It wasn't an apology. He let the scarf trail along her arm, dipping lightly in the curve of her elbow. "But you liked it. I know you did."

Skye rolled away and sat up quickly. She was still on Parnell's bed, but when she tried to scramble to the far side, he grabbed her leg and pulled her back. Her dress was unbuttoned to the waist and now the hem was rucked up to her knees. Skye found herself clutching the bodice while she kicked ineffectually at Parnell.

He straddled her easily, drew her hands away, and pinned her wrists to the headboard. "You're more responsive when you're sleeping," he said.

"Drugged, you mean."

He ignored that. "I like you compliant." He looked at her closely. "But this is good. Your fear is very satisfying."

"I'm not afraid of you."

His faint smile was pitying. "I should have taken you the first time I saw you," he said. "It was in the Worth home, but you didn't know that, did you?"

Skye merely stared at him, refusing to play to his hand.

"There wasn't any time then. I had come for other purposes and you were a distraction." He sighed. "And then, when you unexpectedly came here, there was always Walker Caine between us. He enjoyed watching you as much as I did."

Skye twisted but couldn't dislodge Parnell. His hands were so tight on her wrists that her fingers were numb. He was staring at her with darkening eyes. The look was sexual and predatory.

"Walker's no longer a problem," Parnell said. "He won't be watching either one of us now. I have you to myself . . . for as long as I want . . . in any way I want."

"What have you done to Walker?"

Parnell was of no mind to answer Skye's questions. His head bent. When his mouth was close to hers, he whispered, "I can make you want me. I can, you know. I have."

Skye spit at him.

Parnell reeled back. His reaction was instinctive. The flat of his large hand sent pain screaming through Skye's head and delivered the oblivion she had prayed for.

This time Skye's waking was accompanied by her own pained groan. Her jaw ached miserably. Tentatively pressing her tongue against her teeth, Skye knew a moment's relief that she hadn't lost any. Encouraged, she tried to raise a hand to her face and discovered it was impossible. Her wrists were bound tightly at the small of her back. She gave in to her first instinct to yank at the bonds. The silken knots tightened. She rotated her ankles and found them similarly bound. This time she did not attempt to force a release. Instead Skye willed herself to quell the panic, relax, and think. She had brought herself to this pass, she thought, by enraging Parnell. She had to believe it was worth it. If he came for her again, she would be prepared. She would kill him if he touched her.

The room was dimly lit by a single oil lamp. A glance at her surroundings told Skye she had never been in this particular room before. She was lying on a cot not much wider than she. It shook slightly as she rolled awkwardly off her back and onto her side so she could face the light. The new position relieved the pressure in her wrists but forced her head to rest at an odd angle. Her jaw began to thump.

Skye sat up slowly, dropping her bound legs over the side of the cot. The oil lamp rested on the dirt floor and cast its small circle of light over her legs. A tide of panic swept through her again as she realized she was no longer wearing her gown. She had been stripped to the plain white shift she wore under her day dress. Even her shoes had been removed. The bonds that cut her across the ankles were her own stockings.

The floor was cold and damp on her bare feet. She lifted them a few degrees so they didn't rest directly on the floor. The cot creaked under her shifting and she could feel the canvas give with her movement. It struck her that the cot hadn't been placed here specifically for her but had been a furnishing of the room for a long time. The canvas was rotten from the damp and she would be fortunate if it didn't tear under her weight.

Three walls of her prison were whitewashed stone. The green-veined marble look was the product of patches of mold and moss along the surface and in the crevices. The fourth wall was dirt with an opening squared off with timber like the adit of a mine. Lamp-light did not extend to the tunnel beyond. The darkness was like a wall itself, hard and impenetrable.

Panic did not assert itself again; hopelessness did. Except for the cot there was no furniture, and except for the adit there was no way out. When the oil lamp burned itself out she wouldn't be able to see at all. The movement of her wrists was desperate this time. The stockings Parnell had used merely tightened further.

She wondered about Annie and Matt. Had Parnell really let them leave, or were they similarly trapped in another part of the mansion? The possibility of their plight left Skye with no pity for herself.

She had no idea how long she had been unconscious. More than a few minutes, she was sure. Perhaps as long as a half hour. It hardly seemed possible that she had only returned to Granville this very morning. Parnell had moved quickly. She wondered if Annie's disclosure about the gun had forced his hand, or if he was acting on a plan that was well thought out. Was it true she couldn't expect help from Walker, or had Parnell been bluffing? Skye found she didn't want to think about the answer to that.

She stood carefully, testing her balance on her bound feet. The slightest misstep would have her toppling face forward on the floor. She inched away from the cot toward the adit. By pushing with her toes she was able to nudge the lamp in front of her.

"Careful. You'll catch your shift on fire."

She nearly fell then. The sound of Walker's voice somewhere behind her made Skye lose her precarious balance. She managed to catch herself against the wall and use it for support. Her heart slammed hard against her chest and for a moment it was difficult to breathe. Her eyes darted anxiously around the room.

He wasn't there. Fear was already pushing her to the

edge of madness, she thought. She had imagined his voice. The cruelty of it made it impossible to hold back a single sob.

"Skye?" Walker realized she hadn't seen him. Her sob cut him to the quick and made him curse his own carelessness. "Down here," he said softly. "Under the cot."

Skye's eyes dropped immediately. Walker was indeed stretched out beneath the cot. His wrists and ankles were similarly bound. He flashed her a smile that was more grimace than grin as he inched his way out from under it and sat up.

Skye sagged a little against the wall as she realized the scope of their predicament. This was not the manner in which she had expected to see Walker. Her rescuer was in need of rescuing. Her expression was easy to read.

One corner of Walker's mouth was raised in a self-depreciating smile. "Not quite the knight on a white charger, am I?" His eyes went swiftly over Skye. Except for a slight swelling along her jaw, she looked to be unharmed. In fact, she looked quite beautiful. A touch of color had returned to her cheeks, and her unbound hair spilled over one shoulder. Her own eyes were bright now with a mixture of relief and hope, and the unrelieved whiteness of her shift made her seem wraith-like, almost ethereal. "Although when I dream of a damsel in distress . . ." He didn't finish the sentence. Skye was not at all flattered by the comparison.

"Hmmmph," was what she said.

"Do you know where we are?" he asked. Walker's tone was merely conversational, without any thread of panic.

Skye shook her head. "Not really. I imagine somewhere close to Parnell's workroom. Probably just on the other side." Still using the wall for support, she hunkered down. "How did you get here?"

"I had just finished helping Hank with the carriage. Parnell came down to speak to Hank about something.

I wasn't needed or wanted, so I excused myself and went to the house. When I walked into the kitchen, Corina offered me cake and coffee and I accepted. That's the last thing I remember." As he talked, Walker began to shift his position slightly, moving his bound hands so they rested under his buttocks, then under his thighs. He drew himself up, folding his legs close to his chest so that his chin touched his knees, and brought his wrists under his knees, his calves, and finally past his feet until his hands were in front of him, resting comfortably on his lap. Concentrating on the knots now, he didn't notice Skye's look of complete astonishment. "I only came around when you started moving the lamp toward that opening." His long, agile fingers worked the damp rope that secured his wrists. When he felt himself forcing the movements, he relaxed and went at it again patiently. "I don't like to admit it, but at first I thought you were a ghost. When I realized it was you, all I could think of was that you were going to go up like a candle wick if you tipped that oil lamp. I didn't mean to frighten you."

Sky was stating at Walker's hands. The knots seemed to be unraveling of their own accord, melting at his gentle coaxing. When he had moved his bound hands from back to forward, the length of his body was possessed of a singular fluidity. Tension dissolved in the face of his graceful contortions. Now his fingers plucked the knots loose and Walker was able to release his hands through an opening smaller than her own wrists. When he was free he stretched his fingers, clenching and unclenching his fists. It didn't take him any time at all to release his ankles.

Tossing aside the ropes, Walker went to Skye's side. He gently touched the side of her face with the back of his hand. "What happened?"

"Parnell. I didn't see it coming the first time." She

let herself be turned so that Walker could work on the stocking binding her wrists.

"The first time?" he asked.

"The second time I made him do it. I wanted him to leave me alone." She didn't have to explain. Walker's tension, his silence, told her he understood. "It worked," she said softly. "He put me here with you."

Walker found his voice slowly. "Tell me from the beginning," he said.

Skye drew a calming breath, more for Walker than for herself. "He found out I have a gun. Matt overheard us at the swan pond this afternoon, and he innocently told Annie."

"Who not so innocently told Parnell." Anger edged Walker's voice. "She was looking out for herself."

"Don't blame her," Skye said. "She has Matt to think of, too. And I'm afraid it all may have ended badly for her. We have to find both of them." Quickly, while Walker worked to free her, she told him about Annie locking her in the cellar and the armoire that opened between Parnell's room and her own. "That's how he was able to move back and forth," she said. "There is no passage between the rooms, at least, not a corridor, but the wardrobes are flush on either side of the same wall. Mine's in my dressing room, but his is so big that it remains in his main bedchamber."

Walker massaged her wrists once they were free. He felt her wince as circulation returned. "Matt found it?"

She nodded. "By accident. Parnell was furious. He was listening to Annie tell me what she'd done, and when I realized where Matt had gone, he caught us all. He had Annie pack her things and it seemed as if he was going to let her and Matt go, but I don't know if that's what he did."

"We'll find her," Walker said. "And Matt." He turned her again and began working on her ankles.

"First things first. We have to find a way out ourselves."
He glanced at the lamp. "And we don't have much time.
Thirty minutes' worth of oil at the most."

"What do you think Parnell and Corina are doing?
Will they come here to check on us?"

"I wouldn't if I were them," he said matter-of-factly.
"I don't think we're prisoners. This is supposed to be
our crypt. Once Parnell realized that Matt knew about
the gun because of our conversation, he understood I
was still involved with you in some way. It's hard to
imagine what he knows, or what he thinks he knows,
but he clearly decided he wasn't taking any chances. He
decided it was time to get rid of us both. Corina might
have encouraged him."

"Will they leave the house?"

"That's harder to say." He rubbed Skye's ankles. "It
depends how greedy they are. Parnell and Corina have
all the money they can collect from their invention
scam. I found the contracts. They were in the desk,
where you said they'd be. I didn't have time to examine
them, but I'm confident that's what they were. We need
to get them before they're destroyed." He helped Skye
to her feet. His eyes ran over her quickly. The state of
her undress and the reason for it raised his anger again.
It was a tangible thing, with heat and substance.

Skye touched his forearm and felt the hard cords of
tension drawing his muscles taut. "He didn't . . . nothing happened. I told you I made him angry. And he
didn't drug me this time."

"Did you know he was drugging you?"

"I suspected. Corina had opportunity and motive.
She did it for him." Skye raised her hand to the side
of her face. "Except for this, he didn't touch me."

Walker placed his arms around her waist and drew
her close for just a moment. His lips touched her forehead, then the slight bruising on her jaw. "All right,"

he said softly. "Help me find a way out of here. Do you think you know where the tunnel goes?"

Skye drew back. "Nowhere. If there were a way out in that direction we wouldn't have been put here. Look at us. Neither one of us is very dirty, we weren't carried in that way. I think Parnell's workroom is on the other side of one of those stone walls. There's a way in that isn't obvious, but it's there if we can find it. This is the tunnel Parnell's been working on."

"The one leading to the treasure?"

"The one he *thinks* is leading to the treasure."

Walker wasn't going to take issue with Skye's theory about the treasure or split hairs with her about what Parnell was thinking. The existence of the tunnel made him believe there was more fact than fantasy in Skye's ideas. "Is it worth investigating?"

"Only if we split."

He nodded. There was just one light and two directions. He glanced at the cot. "This will only take a moment." The cot broke up easily under his hands. He tore the rotting canvas into strips and wrapped them around one of the wooden cot legs. He divided their precious supply of oil by dripping half of it onto the canvas, then lighting it. "You use the lamp. I'll take this torch. Yell for me if you find something." He kissed her hard on the mouth, then disappeared into the tunnel.

Skye began hunting immediately, running her hands over the rough whitewashed stones, looking for one that could be moved. She worked systematically, top to bottom, left to right. She pushed and probed with her fingers, the heels of her hands, and sometimes her shoulder. Except for loosening bits of mortar and peeling away some of the whitewash, the exercise was fruitless. When she had completed one turn of the three walls, she began again, even more slowly this time, pulling on the stones as well as pushing them.

Walker's torch flickered as he moved along the narrow passage. The tunnel was shored at regular intervals with timber, but there was enough loose dirt along the perimeter of the walls to let Walker know it was inadequate support at best. He proceeded cautiously, looking for any source of light that wasn't coming from his own torch.

Less than twenty yards from the entrance Walker found Parnell's boots and gloves and duster. A pick and shovel rested beside the garments. A wide-brimmed black felt hat was hanging on the end of the pick handle. It was all evidence that Parnell had taken the Granville family myths seriously. Shaking his head, Walker tossed the hat and took the pick with him.

The tunnel had a gradual downward slope. Walker could almost feel the weight of the earth above him pressing down. There was no hope of digging up, and when the tunnel ended abruptly another twenty yards from where he'd found the pick, Walker realized here was no hope of digging out. If the tunnel had ever extended beyond this point, it had collapsed in on itself. There was no telling how much of Parnell's work was undone by the shifting earth. Disappointed in spite of the fact that there had been almost no chance of success, Walker turned and began to retrace his steps.

He would never be able to say what drew his eyes downward. Perhaps it was the sudden softness of the earth beneath his feet. Perhaps it was the play of light as he lowered the torch. It could have been that the pick caught a stone as he dragged it alongside him. Walker recognized happenstance as the source of his discovery. He poked the butt end of the torch into the soft dirt wall and raised his pick overhead. Then he began digging.

Intent on his task, he almost didn't hear Skye's approach. "Stay back," he warned her.

She took an immediate step forward. "Walker? What is it? What are you—"

His face was stony, his eyes fierce. "Stay back," he repeated. He swung the pick. Clumps of dirt were sprayed as he yanked it out and plunged it in again. "You don't need to see this."

But she already had seen. Thanks to Walker's pick marks, the outline of the grave was clear. He hadn't found a way out; he had found his uncle.

Skye turned away and went back to the anteroom and waited. He came upon her ten minutes later. His torch had only a few threads of flame lighting it now. He leaned the pick against the stone. There were deeply carved lines around the corners of Walker's mouth.

"Is it— " She didn't need to finish the question. Walker was nodding. "I'm sorry," she said softly. "I know you hoped it wouldn't be true."

He *had* hoped. Aloud he had said he knew his uncle was dead, but quietly, in his thoughts, he had hoped for a different outcome. "It happened some time ago," he said. His voice was quiet, gritty. Emotion edged the words. "I don't think I was here then. I don't think I could have saved him." His gold-flecked eyes were anguished. "I'll never know— "

Skye's arms went around him just as the torch burned itself out. "Don't," she said. "Don't do this to yourself. You've done every— "

Walker put Skye from him. "Have you found anything?" he asked, without inflection.

"Walker."

The set of his face was grim, the planes and angles sharply chiseled. He raked back his hair and repeated his question. There was no time to bask in Skye's comfort even if he could accept it.

"Nothing," she said. "I can't find a way out."

Walker wouldn't accept it. "That's not possible. There was a way in."

It was that knowledge that had kept Skye going as

long as she had. "I've tried every stone. There's no
secret spring, nothing that will be turned or manipulated. I've been over the floor. Perhaps there was a way
out through the tunnel and Parnell closed it with a
landslide."

"The slide is older than that. Dust has already settled.
We were brought in another way and we just haven't
figured it out."

Skye shook her head. "God knows," she said, raising
her face upward. "I don't."

They thought of it simultaneously. "We're not behind
Parnell's workroom," Walker said.

Skye finished his thought. "We're below it."

The lamp was sputtering now, but neither of them
paid it attention. Walker lifted Skye on his shoulders
and traced a thorough spiral path starting at the center
of the room. Skye pushed at the timbered ceiling until
she felt one section give way. It shifted but would not
be moved. "It's no good, Walker. He's put something
over the top. I can't lift it."

"Yes, you can."

"But I—"

She *had* to lift it. The height was too great for Walker
to reach it unassisted and Skye couldn't support his
weight. She was the one who had to do it. The lamp
supplied only a flicker of light. In the dark they might
not be able to find the trapdoor again. "Stand on my
shoulders, Skye."

She responded to the command in his voice. As he
hunkered down she grabbed his raised arms and was
hoisted standing onto his shoulders. Walker raised himself slowly, forcing Skye to bend at the knees to keep
from hitting her head on the ceiling. When she was
directly under the trapdoor she began to rise, pushing
with all her strength against the door while Walker absorbed the pressure of her weight.

The door gave a quarter of an inch. She could feel the object on top shift as she inclined the door. She pushed harder, using her entire body like a lever to force the opening.

"More, Skye," Walker said. The force of her pushing almost buckled his knees. He held steady, grasping her ankles tightly. "You can do this."

It was more than his body that supported her. Skye felt his absolute confidence. He believed in her as perhaps no one else ever had. She applied more force and lift and gave it all sound with an unladylike grunt that would have appalled her mother and that had Jay Mac shaking his head in disbelief.

There was a grating noise as one leg of the worktable overhead was pushed off the trapdoor. It burst open so suddenly that Skye unfolded like a jack-in-the-box through the opening. Bracing herself on the floor of the workroom, Skye hauled herself through easily. "Pass me the lamp," she said. "There's bound to be another one in here."

Walker raised it to her. With its last thread of light she was able to fire the lantern hanging just inside the door. She set the lantern near the opening. Walker looked up at her sweet face looking down at him. He was grinning. "I love you," he said.

Her smile was serene. "Just for that, I'm going to pass you a ladder."

"There's a ladder?"

Skye nodded. "Parnell must have hoisted it up after he was done with it." She disappeared long enough to get the ladder that was leaning against the wall. She lowered it a few feet until Walker was able to grab and support it. She kissed him as he came out of the pit. "Did you really think I could lift that door?" she asked, lending him a hand.

"Of course," he said simply. "You can do anything."

Grinning now, Skye picked up the lantern. "What now?"

"Where's that gun?"

"It was in my trunk."

"We need to get it. If Parnell and Corina are still in the house, we might be able to move up the backstairs unnoticed."

"All right." Skye followed Walker out of the workroom. They didn't speak at all as they worked their way quietly up the stairs to the kitchen. At the top of the steps Walker paused and listened for sounds of conversation or movement. With a single glance at Skye he communicated that it was safe to continue.

The backstairs were deserted as well. Walker made Skye wait on the landing until he was certain the hallway was safe. When he reached the door to her room, he motioned to her to follow.

"Where are they?" Skye mouthed the words.

He shrugged and rooted in her trunk, coming up with the gun after a few seconds. He checked the barrel. It was empty. He raised both brows and gave her a telling look.

"I never said it was loaded," she whispered. "And you never asked."

"I have shells in my room." He indicated she should go first this time and he would back her. Skye took a step out of the dressing room and stopped suddenly. She placed a finger to her lips. With the other hand she pointed to the armoire.

Voices could be heard from the other side. Walker huddled in front of the armoire while Skye knelt beside him. Parnell and Corina were arguing, their raised voices and sharp tones perfectly audible through the thin partition of the wardrobes.

"And I'm telling you we can't stay here any longer," Parnell said. "Can't you be satisfied with what we have?

We've already been wildly successful, more than I dreamed. Why must you always want more?"

"Your dreams are paltry, that's why," Corina snapped. "I'm the one who got us this far."

"And I'm the one who took the risks. You're the cook. I've been impersonating another man. It's my signature on those contracts."

Walker touched Skye's wrist. With a series of gestures he told her he was going to load the gun and get the contracts. She was to stay just where she was. Skye agreed and watched Walker go out of the corner of her eye as she continued to eavesdrop on Parnell's conversation with his sister.

"If you don't want to pack your things, Cory, then don't," Parnell said. "We have enough money for you to buy everything new. You can travel anywhere you want. Do anything. Seventy thousand dollars can make you very happy if you'll let it."

Corina's small oval face was mottled with angry color. "It's nothing compared to the treasure!" she said furiously. "Nothing."

"A treasure that doesn't exist is worth exactly that—nothing." He reached under his bed, withdrew two valises, and tossed both on his bed. "I've been searching for it for months now. *I've* been searching. There's nothing there, Corina. The tunnel can't be excavated. Parnell told you and you wouldn't listen. You sent that man to his death, making him dig. It could have been me who was buried alive." He saw it in her eyes then, that fleeting wish that it *had* been him. "Watch yourself," he warned her. "I can put you in that cellar as easily as I put the others there."

Corina snorted. "You couldn't have done it at all without my help. Or do you think Walker would have just followed you down there like a sheep to the slaughter?" She crossed her arms in front of her, her pose more impatient than defensive. "You needed me. You've always needed me. *I'm* the one who took the position with Parnell. *I'm* the one who saw the opportunities with the contracts. *I'm* the one who read the Granville history and understood the potential. What have you done except to complicate every plan we have because of your own vile needs?"

His head jerked back under her verbal blows. Angry color flushed his face unnaturally. "Shut up, Cory."

But she would not be silenced. "You caved in to those death threats and hired Walker Caine against my advice. Instead of simply having a few servants to worry about, we had to contend with someone whose very job demanded he watch you! In all the time he's been here you've hardly made any progress on the tunnel. You're barely to the point Parnell was when the landslide occurred. And then there was Mrs. Givens."

"Shut up, Cory."

"And when you frightened her off, you had to have another whore. You couldn't wait to have that Dennehy bitch, could you? I was drugging her from the first just so you could get inside her!"

"I never—"

"That's it, isn't it? You never get inside! You only touch. What kind of man are you?"

Parnell's hand came up.

Corina's eyes blazed. "Don't you hit me," she bit out. "Don't you dare!"

Rather than let his hand hover in the air, Parnell raked back his hair in an angry gesture.

"You have to pay for them or drug them and you still can't do what a real man does. You'd have tried with her again tonight if I hadn't stopped you—and you'd have failed."

"Go get your things, Cory. We're leaving this place. It's over. If there *was* a treasure, it's not going to be yours."

"It's because you still want me, isn't it?" she asked baldly, needling him. Her voice was husky and quiet, a throaty whisper. "Just like when we were children. I've spoiled you for other women. You didn't only touch me. I let you do other things. I let you do anything. Is it because I'm your sister? Is that what made it different for you?"

"Stepsister," he said quietly. "You're my stepsister."

"I know. But Mother still said it was wrong. Do you remember when she—"

This time when Parnell raised his hands, he put them over his ears. "I'm not listening to you," he said tightly.

"What a child you are," she whispered. "It's small wonder that you need me to show you what needs doing."

Parnell turned away and went to his armoire. "I'm leaving here, Cory. You can go or stay as it pleases you. I'm taking half the money." He yanked open the door to the wardrobe. "And you can have—"

Just like Alice-through-the-Looking-Glass, Skye Dennehy fell forward into the opening. She tried to scramble out of the way, but Parnell was too quick. His fingers caught the shoulder of her shift and he pulled hard. To prevent him from ripping the material, she was forced forward on her knees.

Corina threw up her hands. She was very close to tears. "Can't you do anything?" she demanded. "I thought you said she couldn't get out! You should have killed her!" She glanced quickly over her shoulder to the open doorway. "You know what this means, don't you? *He's* out, too."

Parnell's hand moved from Skye's shoulder to her hair. He twisted his fingers in it and jerked her to her feet. "Is that right?" he fairly growled. "Walker's out?"

Skye remained mute.

"Of course he's out," Corina snapped. "I hope you did a better job with Annie and her brat." Her full mouth flattened, then became a sneer. "Or can we expect more company?"

Parnell slipped his forearm around Skye's throat. He kicked the wardrobe door shut. "I think it's safe to assume he won't be coming at us that way," he told Corina.

Her voice rose an octave. "He shouldn't be coming after us at all!"

"Do you have your pistol?"

She shook her head.

"Get it."

"What if he's out there?" she asked. "What if he's waiting for me?"

Parnell's laughter was short and without humor. "It's not so easy being the one to take the risks, is it? Well, dear *sister*, I have my protection. What are you going to use? Walker Caine was never much interested in your cold charms."

"Bastard."

The pressure on Skye's throat made every word a struggle. "If you let her go, she won't come back," she told him. "And not because Walker will find her. She'll betray you again."

Parnell's arm didn't loosen. It tightened on Skye's throat as if he could force answers from her. His cold blue eyes had narrowed on Corina. "Explain yourself," he said. "What betrayal?"

Corina shook her head. "It's a play for time," she snapped. "I'm going to get my pistol."

"Don't let her go," Skye told him quickly, imparting urgency into her warning. "She'll leave you."

"Stay where you are, Cory. I want to hear what she has to say."

Corina ignored him. "Walker must be somewhere

else," she said. "She's just trying to give him time to get here." She hesitated on the threshold, looking up and down the hall before she hurried away to her own room.

"You've lost her," Skye whispered hoarsely. She brought her hands up to Parnell's forearm and tried to get him to ease his grip on her throat. She managed to turn her head slightly to one side and draw a deep, cleansing breath. "She's been playing you for a fool. You must have suspected."

Parnell gave Skye a small shake before he urged her toward the door. "Talk to me," he said. He emphasized his words by forcing her up on tiptoe. Had he pressed further, her feet would have left the floor.

Skye sought purchase on the forearm that held her securely against him. Her fingers bit into Parnell's shirt and the hard muscle beneath. "All the time she's been making you dig in the cellar, she's been looking for the treasure abovestairs."

"Where? Here, on this floor?"

She could only choke out a single word. "Higher." Parnell moved Skye into the hall and toward the main staircase. When they stood on the precipice of the landing, he paused. Skye held her breath, afraid he meant to push her. "On the servants' floor. She went up there at night . . . when you were . . ."

"With you."

"With me," she agreed. "She wanted you to be with me. She had an opportunity to get rid of me and she didn't take it." Skye knew she had Parnell's complete attention. His arm loosened slightly to let her breathe. "Corina covered for me."

"What are you talking about?"

"I went into the cellar. Annie locked me in and Corina figured it out. Instead of exposing me, she drugged my milk that night and later went back to the cellar and locked

the door I used to get out. She never told you. I was valuable to her as long as I proved a diversion."

Parnell placed a hand at her back and forced her to
take the first step down. "Cory says I shouldn't have
let you read the Granville history," he said quietly. His
mouth was very close to her ear. "But you know why I
wanted you to have it."

Skye did know. Parnell had wanted to convince her
it was Hamilton Granville's ghost making nightly visits
to her room. He wanted her to be seduced by the idea
of the ghost, a little afraid, a little intrigued, and thoroughly in its thrall. "Did you do the same thing to the
housekeeper before me?"

He didn't answer her question and his hold tightened
so she couldn't ask any more of her own. She was effectively silenced, unable to cry out to Walker, unable
to warn him of their approach. Parnell urged her forward over the lip of the next step.

Skye didn't immediately understand Parnell's intent.
At first she thought he meant to move her out of the
house entirely, using her as a hostage to make his escape. It wasn't until he turned her in the direction of
the library that she realized her mistake. She had forgotten about the money, had never considered where
he might have kept the fortune from his investors.
Parnell wouldn't have entrusted it to a bank, not with
bankers among the businessmen he had deceived.
Parnell would have kept it close by so that he could
look on it occasionally, have it close so he could take it
on a moment's notice.

The doors to the library were closed. He made Skye
open them. The arm at her throat was cutting off her
circulation. Her fingers felt numb and clumsy because
of it. Even her thinking didn't seem sharp any longer.
She should have found a way to warn Walker.

The room was empty. Parnell made certain of it by

turning himself and Skye in a slow circle to investigate the area. He pushed her to the desk and forced her into the chair behind it. He shoved the chair forward, caging Skye between the desk top and the chair arms, and stood over her, behind her, and made her open the panels under his direction.

One by one the pocket drawers were sprung open and each in turn revealed nothing. The contracts and money had all disappeared.

"Damn her!" he swore. His fingertips pressed whitely into Skye's shoulders. "She's taken it all! Taken everything!"

Skye gasped at the pain. Her hands slipped from the top of the desk to her lap. From his hiding place under the desk, Walker placed a loaded gun in her palm. Her fingers closed over it.

Parnell yanked the chair away from the desk and hauled Skye to her feet again. This time, when he turned her toward him, he found himself facing the barrel of his cutaway trigger Colt. He took a step backward without any urging from Skye. Her two-handed hold on the weapon was steady. Walker crawled out from beneath the desk.

"Keep it on him," Walker told her. "If he moves, shoot." Then he hunkered down at her bare feet and tore a strip off the hem of her shift. Skye didn't flinch. Walker straightened after he produced a second strip and held one in each hand. His next order was for Parnell. "Turn around and put your hands behind your back." There was hesitation. Walker added calmly, "Shoot him, Skye."

The movement of her finger was almost imperceptible, but Parnell saw it. He spun on his heel and presented his hands behind his back. Walker tied him quickly, then forced Parnell to kneel and added a length that bound his wrists to his ankles. When he was done, he pushed Parnell's shoulder so he toppled on his side. Watching

Walker work, Skye realized Parnell had to be considering his own mistakes in binding both of them. Walker's method of securing Parnell made it impossible for Parnell to move his hands forward as Walker had done.

"I'm going to get Corina," said Walker. "I want you to stay here."

Skye relaxed her grip on the Colt. "You'll need this. Corina went for her gun."

He shook his head. "Keep it. And don't think twice about using it."

"I won't."

It wasn't Skye who responded. Both Skye and Walker turned toward the open doorway. Corina Reading stood there. Her small hands held her gun as steadily as Skye and she was aiming it squarely at Walker. Sixteen feet separated Corina and her target. Her delicate features were sharply set, her sloe eyes coldly focused.

Skye's own weapon remained leveled at Parnell's chest. She eyed Corina's gun critically. "That's a single-action pocket revolver," she told Walker. "A Smith and Wesson .32. The range is fair; the accuracy is poor. She has only one shot. She has to be very good or very, very lucky."

Corina's flinch was centered in her eyes. "I only want the money."

Skye's position hadn't changed. Even with her gun pointed in another direction, she remained perfectly poised and said, "I can get the drop on her."

A faint smile curved Walker's mouth as he held Corina's eyes with his own. His words were issued with the slight edge of a challenge. "You heard her, Corina. She says she can get the drop on you."

Corina's hands tightened.

Skye elbowed Walker aside and pivoted in the same motion, squeezing off a shot as the lead ball from Corina's revolver split the air. She felt the Colt's recoil charge her muscles and shudder her bones and the infinitesimal sensation of something hot and hard whispering past the curve of her shoulder. In the same moment Skye saw Corina Reading's feet leave the floor and her shoulders heave backward. She was thrown against the far wall of the hallway, her features registering both surprise and pain as she remained suspended there for a second. Her collapse followed, her body folding forward like a rag doll until she lay face down on the hardwood floor.

The single-action Smith and Wesson slipped out of her hand and skittered across the floor.

Silence held them all still. Parnell's limbs were rigid against his bonds. Skye's extended arms were locked in the action of firing. Walker's frame remained in the half crouch that Skye had forced on him.

Walker was the first to recover. He straightened slowly and removed the gun from Skye's hands. He laid it on the desk. "Are you all right?"

She nodded. Her face was pale and her heart was slamming, but she was all of a piece. "I'll see to her," she said quietly. "Watch Parnell." Skye crossed the room to Corina's side and knelt. Blood was pooling on the floor near Corina's shoulder and Skye was gentle in turning her over. She opened Corina's bodice and eased it off her wounded shoulder. Ripping more of her shredded shift, Skye bound the injury. "We need to take her to a doctor," she said.

"It's a clean wound?"

"All the way through."

"What about Annie and Matt?"

Skye glanced at Corina. Her color was ashen but her pulse was steady. The flow of blood had slowed and was no longer dangerous. "There's time. It's not life threatening." Corina moaned softly as if to object, but Skye paid the theatrics no attention. She pointed to Parnell. "He can help you find them."

Parnell struggled to sit up. "Hank drove them to Baileyboro."

"He's lying," Skye said. "I heard Corina say that she hoped they couldn't get out. They argued about it. Annie and Matt are trapped somewhere in this house."

"You need me to find them," Parnell interjected quickly.

Walker ignored the interruption and looked at Skye. "Do you know where they might be?"

She shook her head. "One of the locked closets . . . a passage I've never had time to investigate . . . another cellar. I couldn't find them quickly. Young Matt . . ." Skye's bright green eyes glistened as tears rose unchecked. "Annie will be so frightened."

"Then we need this bastard," Walker said.

Skye didn't look at Parnell. "Be careful."

Parnell jerked at his bonds. "You'll have to untie me. I won't tell you anything unless you untie me."

Walker hunched down beside him. His eyes were sharply splintered, cold in their remote indifference. "I can make you tell me anything I want," he said softly. He watched a bead of sweat form on Parnell's upper lip. Walker had made his point. "In the interest of time, I'll let you up."

"Is it the money?" asked Parnell. "Is that what you want?"

Walker took a letter opener from the desk and used it to undo the knots securing Parnell's ankles. "My uncle was Jonathan Parnell," he said. "That's what this is about, Mr. Curran. A good and decent man is dead, buried in a shallow grave below this house, and you'll have to answer for it." He paused a beat, releasing the last knot and tossing the opened letter back on the desk. He hauled Morgan Curran to his feet. "Does that sufficiently explain my purpose here?"

The man who had been known for months as Parnell was reeling. "You know who I am?"

"I've always known."

"The threats on my life?"

"I'm the only threat on your life."

His throat was dry. Morgan Curran didn't have enough saliva to spit. He thrust his chin in Skye's direction. "Is she your partner?"

"She is now."

"Your uncle's death was an accident. The tunnel collapsed."

Walker was unmoved. "He shouldn't have been in there."

"That was Corina's idea. She thought the Granville fortune was buried at the end of it, just like some damned pot of gold at the end of the rainbow."

"And you always follow your sister's lead."

Curran blinked. "My stepsister," he corrected. "But yes, I follow her lead. She's a very forceful woman. Not easily subjugated." His eyes shifted pointedly to Skye again. The stare she returned was filled with loathing. Curran's reply was delivered with a mocking sneer. "Some women are more easily mastered."

Skye could not remain quiet. "You drugged me!" she accused him. "I wouldn't have let you— " Too late she realized the danger. Walker's attention had shifted in her direction and Morgan Curran's conversation had had a purpose. The bonds on his wrists were loose now. "Walker!"

Walker sidestepped Curran's lunge only to realize that he hadn't been the intended target. Curran meant to have the gun.

Walker and Curran laid their hands on the Colt simultaneously. They wrestled for control of the weapon, sliding across the desk, toppling the chair and an unlighted oil lamp. Broken glass ground into Walker's back when they rolled off the desk and onto the floor. Curran came away with the weapon and scrambled to a crouching position. Walker's foot shot out, but Curran retracted his hand in time. He fired in Walker's direction, missing by inches when Walker pushed the fallen chair at him and upset his balance. It was enough time for Walker to come to his feet.

Curran reacted immediately, swinging his aim toward Skye to hold off his adversary.

It was a mistake. Walker's rage was a controlled explosion. From perfect stillness he became a blur of motion. He leapt feet first. Curran fired as his wrist was struck while Skye flattened herself against the floor. The shudder she felt didn't come from her own body. The cry she heard didn't come from her own throat. She looked up in time to see Walker's sharp hand blow send Curran to his knees. A second thrust, delivered with the heel of his hand, pushed Curran's head backward. His shoulders slammed against the floor. Walker's foot made contact with Curran's chest, pulling back at the last possible second, breaking two ribs instead of bruising his heart. Curran groaned painfully as he tried to draw his next breath.

Walker stood over him, winded more by the strength of his anger than by the struggle. He glanced at Skye. She was rising to her knees, her hands attending to Corina, not to herself. "Is she—" He didn't have to finish his sentence.

Lowering her eyes, Skye shook her head slowly, the message clear.

Walker heard Curran's anguished moan as he understood what was left unsaid. It was then that Walker's splintered glance shifted downward. Unmoved, his voice was quiet, intense. "Annie and Matt," he said.

Skye listened, her heart easing, as Walker, true to his word, made Morgan Curran tell him everything.

Epilogue

For the second time in their short marriage Walker Caine carried Skye across a threshold. Although she made a small protest that the deed had been done before, she did so while looping her arms comfortably about his neck and snuggling against him.

"It's not the same," he said. "That was the St. Mark. This is our home."

Skye liked the sound of that. Her lips brushed Walker's cheek as he set her down in the entrance hall of the Granville house. He turned his head so the kiss could settle more fully on his mouth. The contact was brief. Skye drew back, smiled, and gave him a knowing glance. "This way," she said. She was eager, slightly breathless. Taking his hand, Skye pulled Walker toward the wide staircase. He barely had time to kick the front door closed behind him.

The Granville mansion was deserted. Skye's light footsteps up the stairs took on a faintly hollow sound. Her laughter, when Walker tried to grab her from behind, echoed along the corridor. Not that either of them noticed. Having the house to themselves was liberating, not eerie. During the two-month investigation into the death of Corina Reading and the trial of Morgan Curran, Walker and Skye found themselves with little in the way of privacy. Jay Mac's palatial granite home at 50th and Broadway could have quartered an army brigade with more ease. The endless parade of attorneys and bankers and investors and reporters and police touched everyone's nerves. As a scandal it held the city enthralled. It was not often that men the likes of Worth and Rockefeller and Gould and Carnegie were duped. The public took no small measure of glee at poking fun of the men who ruled industrial empires and were relieved of their pocket change by a brother-and-sister team of thieves.

During the course of the trial, as the details were brought to public attention and public ridicule, Jay Mac alone received more than eight hundred requests to invest in inventions ranging from machines that were supposed to reproduce the human voice to newfangled clothing fasteners. "What's wrong with buttons?" Jay Mac asked on more than one occasion.

It was left to Skye to sort through the pleas for money and separate fact and fancy. It was a difficult task, but one perfectly suited to Skye's wonderfully fluid imagination. Inventing, by its very nature, combined elements of what existed with what might exist, and Skye found herself intrigued by the possibilities. She dedicated herself to finding the requests that deserved funding and making recommendations to her father.

"Why should I give anyone a nickel?" Jay Mac was moved to ask. He held up the morning edition of the *Herald* at breakfast and showed everyone the headline: ROBBER BARONS ROBBED. "It says right here that greed was our downfall."

"Oh, then it must be true," Moira said drily. "If it's there in the paper for all the city to see."

Jay Mac snorted, but he was moved to see reason in the end. While other men who were similarly gulled into investing with Morgan Curran received the same mountain of requests as Jay Mac, he was the only one to respond with financial support even to a select few.

"It's always been about risks," Skye had told him.

Her green eyes were bright, her voice earnest. "That's what I learned from you. The real Jonathan Parnell had an idea that would have caused a revolution in our lives. You invested in a possibility, tried drawing to an inside straight. Had circumstances been even a bit different, you might have been holding a patent for an engine that would have brought thousands of people something better than they have now. It didn't work this time and we're all a little poorer for it. But do you really want to leave the game altogether?"

When it was put that way, Jay Mac wasn't about to refuse. He had looked at Walker then. "She wins a lot of arguments," he said.

"Yes, sir."

"You have years of this ahead of you."

Walker glanced across the table to Skye. His eyes held a smile and a challenge. "I know."

"You might think you've caught her," Jay Mac said, "but she's going to lead you a merry chase the rest of your life."

"I look forward to it," Walker had said.

Those words came back to him as Skye eluded his grasp when she turned the corner on the landing. She passed the master bedchamber, which had been Curran's, and then moved quickly past her own. She shot him a siren's smile over her shoulder, beckoning him with a sultry green glance that held a fair amount of mischief.

"This way," she said huskily. "Hurry."

That suited Walker fine. It seemed just this side of forever since he'd held his wife in an intimate embrace. He had spent long hours in court, helping the prosecution prepare the case against Morgan Curran, then later testifying. Although Walker wasn't responsible for making reparations to the financial victims of Morgan and Corina's scheme, he felt honor bound to do so for his uncle's sake. A substantial amount of money was recov-

ered from Curran's desk and Walker personally saw to it
that each investor received seventy-five cents on the dollar.

There was also the matter of funeral arrangements
for his uncle. Walker was gone from the city for a week
while he saw to Jonathan Parnell's burial in the family
plot in Boston. In his absence, Skye arranged for a memorial service to be part of the gathering at the science
and technological exposition. Men who would have
come together to hear Jonathan Parnell speak observed
a moment of silence instead and paid tribute to the
tinkerer whose grasp of the possible had set him apart.
Walker arrived in time to be part of the service, touched
beyond words by Skye's thoughtfulness and the condo-
lences of those who understood the scope of the loss
of a man like Jonathan Parnell.

"Where are you going?" Walker asked. Skye had just
flitted past the door to the room he had occupied and
they had briefly shared.

She grinned again and crooked a finger at him, the
come-hither look clear in her darkening eyes. Just outside the door to Corina Reading's room Skye let herself
be caught. She was brought flush to Walker's body, his
mouth full on hers, the kiss hungry and urgent. It was
hard to remember her purpose. "Time enough for
that," she whispered against his mouth.

"Time enough— " Walker's husky, surprised response
was cut short as Skye opened the door to Corina's room
and pulled him inside. He reached for her again but
she turned easily out of his embrace and held up one
hand to keep him back. For the first time Walker understood it was adventure his wife had on her mind,
not romance. With some difficulty he reined in his
thoughts. "What are you after, Skye?" As if he didn't
know. "Still thinking about the treasure?"

She nodded, her smile only a little guilty. "It's not about
the money," she said. There was never any question that

Walker couldn't provide for her. With his uncle's death everything that remained of the family fortune fell into Walker's hands. It wasn't the shipping money that provided the bulk of the wealth, but the patents that Parnell had on his myriad inventions. While Walker's grandmother had decried the loss of her shipping line and the lack of business sense of her son, Jonathan Parnell had been quietly amassing a fortune he never cared about. Even Jay Mac had been astonished by the size of the estate once it was settled. There had been a great deal of laughter at Skye's expense, the gist of it being that she was an adventuress, after all. "You know I don't care about the money," she told him.

Walker grinned. "It's about the mystery." He reached for her hand, took it, and brought her close long enough to kiss her on the forehead. "I married a kindred spirit. Show me what you're thinking."

"Corina found a way leading from this room to the servants' quarters abovestairs." As Skye explained, she began looking around the room for the inlaid walnut panels that would move under her touch. With no encouragement, Walker began to do the same. "While she kept her brother busy digging under the house, she used the opportunity to look elsewhere. I think she was getting close to finding what she wanted when I arrived here and brought Annie with me."

"How do you know this?"

"Something Annie said to me when she made her confession about the gun. She told me that this was an evil place, that she could hear the ghost walking at night." Skye drew back the curtains and secured them. The afternoon sun brought the gleam of copper to her hair. The spring light warmed her face. The edge of the wood was bordered by daffodils and the bright yellow blossoms swayed gently in the breeze. Looking out now, seeing springtime and sunshine on the lawn, it was hard to imagine that Annie's words could have been fact. Skye turned to Walker. "It wasn't you upstairs. And it wasn't me. We know it wasn't Curran she heard walking around."

Walker made a slight grimace. The only place Morgan Curran had been going to was Skye's room. His confession had been made before the trial, privately, to Walker alone. It hadn't taken long to get. Corina Reading was her brother's accomplice, making certain Skye was available to Curran by lacing Skye's milk with a narcotic. It kept Curran occupied and gave Corina the opportunity to search for the treasure herself. "So if we believe it wasn't actually Hamilton Granville, then— "

"Then it had to be Corina. Annie and Matt's presence upstairs would have frustrated her efforts. She moved around up there to frighten Annie. I think that's what sent Annie downstairs looking for something to eat or drink in the middle of the night. She was scared by what she heard."

Walker hunkered in front of Corina's armoire. Hoping to find a panel like the one in her brother's room, he pushed at the back of it. It was solid. "Damn," he swore softly, sitting back on his haunches. He looked around the room. Nothing had been touched in almost two months. Dust had collected around Corina's perfumes and pots of cream on her vanity. A delicate spiderweb had been woven from the curtain rod to one corner of the room. The bed was made. Some of Corina's clothes were scattered on the floor where she had left them in her rush to find her gun. The bottom two drawers of the highboy were still open. The mantel was crowded with figurines and a few photographs. Logs were stacked neatly in the fireplace, ready to be used. The dull black fireplace tools stood at attention in their rack. The marble apron had lost its gleam with a thin layer of dust.

Walker's attention strayed to the paintings on the wall as Skye lifted them one by one. Although he watched her, his thoughts kept straying back to the fireplace. Something was wrong, out of place. He shot to his feet suddenly as the realization hit him. "It's here, Skye."

She turned around. Half expecting to see an opening yawning in the wall in front of her, she was disappointed to confront Walker standing beside the mantel looking very full of himself. "It's where?"

"Here. Don't you see?"

"Don't be smug, Walker. Anyway, you're supposed to say 'Eureka.' "

He laughed and knelt in front of the cold fireplace. "Two months ago it was still plenty cold enough to have a fire in this room. You can see for yourself that except for a little dust, the tools are clean, the apron's clean, the hearth is clean. Where are the ashes? Even if Corina had cleaned the hearth and the apron, the tools would still be gray with residue. She wouldn't have bothered cleaning them." Skye was kneeling beside him now, caught by Walker's irrefutable logic. "Where should we try first?"

"The logs," she said. Careless of the dust, Skye scooted forward on her knees and helped Walker take out the wood. They lifted the iron grate and andirons together and put them aside. Skye raised the damper.

The rough brick wall at the back of the hearth moved a fraction of an inch. They exchanged glances, then identical grins. Skye's delighted laughter was cut off by Walker's quick kiss. She would have been happy to have it go on a little longer, but he had broken it off to push on the wall. She threw her own slight weight into helping him.

Skye was the first to crawl into the narrow passage behind Corina's hearth. She batted away a few cobwebs, stood, then held out her hand to help Walker up. The corridor was too small for them to stand side by side and the stairs in front of them were steep. There was just enough light coming from the attic windows above for them to find their footing. Walker stayed at Skye's back to make certain she didn't fall and braced himself firmly on either side of the passageway as they climbed.

As Skye had anticipated, the passage led to a small attic room. It was empty except for a few tools and a lantern that Corina had left behind. Skye bent over the crowbar and hammer. "Corina must have thought at first that the treasure would be in this room," Skye said. "Look, most of these floorboards have been pried loose and reset. You can see that the nails are bent and scraped."

Walker saw that Skye was right. Corina's search had led her to loosen most of the wood shirring on the walls. A close inspection of the rafters proved that they had been shifted as well. "Mrs. Reading was nothing if not thorough," Walker said. "No treasure."

"Not here," Skye agreed. "Which is why she wanted to get rid of Annie. I think Corina began to suspect the treasure was next door."

Walker looked at Skye with something very much like disbelief. "Are you telling me that after all this we're going to end up in Annie's room?"

"Well, yes," she said simply. "What did you think?"

"I think we could have taken the backstairs straightaway and avoided crawling through fireplaces."

Skye snorted softly, dismissively. "Where would have been the fun in that?" She consoled him with a light pat on the arm. "Help me find a way through. There's bound to be one." She ignored the fact that Walker rolled his eyes. As soon as she started working, he was beside her again.

This time it wasn't cleverness that brought about discovery; it was clumsiness. Skye dropped the crowbar she was using and its hollow thud against the wall helped them find a trapdoor. Easing themselves through the opening, they entered the room that Annie and Matt had been given for their use at Granville.

There was nothing of Annie's left behind or anything belonging to her son. She had managed to gather everything she owned when Morgan Curran gave her the opportunity. What she hadn't understood was that Curran wasn't going to let her leave Granville. Walker found Annie and Matt trapped in a closet on the second floor. Matt was sleeping soundly in his mother's arms. Annie was plainly terrified. Two months away from the mansion had scarcely settled Annie's fears, though her new position in the Worth home meant she had the benefit of Mrs. Cavanaugh's kind and patient care.

Looking around, Skye pronounced herself quite satisfied with their progress. "It's really quite amazing, don't you think?" she asked, brushing herself off. "This is the room where Hamilton Granville's lover slept. And where he came each night to see her."

"Not by the route we just took," Walker said drily. "A man only has so much strength."

Skye noticed that in spite of his words he was eyeing her with a particularly wicked look. She felt herself go hot and cold and her resolve waver. For good measure she took a step back, out of arm's reach and harm's way. "I'll wager he used it to make his escape, though. Probably more than once. By all accounts his wife was suspicious and not above trying to catch her husband out."

"Mmmm."

His noncommittal murmur didn't fool Skye. "What are you thinking?" she asked.

Walker chuckled. "I'm thinking that if she'd been as good as you, she'd have caught him right off."

"If she'd been as good as me," Skye said saucily, "he wouldn't have strayed in the first place."

He didn't blink. "You're referring to your skill with a firearm, of course."

"Beast," she said, completely unoffended. "I'll show you to what I was referring." Skye crossed the small distance that separated them and placed her arms around his waist. She raised her face.

"I thought your wanted to find buried treasure," he said.

In answer Skye loosened two buttons at the top of his vest and plucked at the tails of Walker's shirt. "I do," she said softly. Her fingertips deftly slipped beneath the waist of his trousers. His skin was warm and smooth. The flat plain of his belly retracted slightly in anticipation of her touch. She raised herself on tiptoe and laid her mouth against his. "I have."

Walker's groan was a whisper against her lips. Their mouths fused. The kiss deepened. Without breaking the intimate play, Walker carried Skye to the small bed where Hamilton Granville had lain with his lover. It creaked loudly under their combined weight. They stilled abruptly, waited, then shared husky laughter at the thought of what could happen.

"Worth the risk?" he asked, rising on his elbows above her. His darkening eyes teased Skye as her body was already shifting to accommodate him. He didn't wait for any other response. Walker's fingers moved over her bodice, releasing the buttons and parting the material. Their clothing was flung aside or pushed out of the way. Her arms slid around his neck and then she felt the heat of his mouth on her breast.

Her body was sleek and faintly musky. Her red hair fanned out brilliantly on the faded quilt beneath her head. She bit back a sound of wanting as Walker's mouth trailed across her skin and took her other breast. He raised the nipple beneath the damp, rough edge of his tongue. Her fingers threaded in his hair and the hot suck of his mouth brought a cry that she did not try to restrain.

He covered her with his body and she rose to meet him, taking him into her with the fierce, unashamed passion that joined their hearts and touched their souls.

In loving's aftermath their breathing quieted slowly.
The muscles of his back and shoulders had a faint sheen.
Skye's fingers trailed along the lean whipcord length of
him and she felt his body shudder with an aftershock of
pleasure. He pressed a kiss into the curve of her throat,
then slipped off her and onto his side. The splendid afternoon light covered their bodies in bands of sunshine.
If they had been satisfied with that, the bed might have
held. It was Skye's searching and shifting to have the quilt
over her that contributed to the bed's collapse.

They thumped hard to the floor as the bed slats broke
like broom straws. Dust motes rose and scattered. The
bed frame split and the headboard groaned. They
watched it warily as it teetered for a moment before it
tilted back against the wall instead of toppling on them.
Then they looked at each other. Skye's bright laughter
exploded from her as Walker pounced. They fought for
possession of a quilt that neither of them really wanted
and ended up making love amid the broken slats and
collapsed frame, half on the mattress, half off, and this
time it was the floor that creaked, not the rickety bed.

"Goodness," Skye sighed, rolling into Walker's arms.
She folded her arms across his chest and raised her face
to look down on his. The lines of tension that had creased
the corners of his eyes and mouth in recent weeks were
absent now. The tawny eyes were no longer splintered and
strained. When he lifted his hand to push back a lock of
hair the movement was not edgy or restless. She leaned
forward and kissed him on the mouth. "You look like a
very happy man," she whispered.

"Hmmm."

The touch of his mouth was soft, his murmur a caress.
"These past weeks have been hard for you," she said. Skye
had watched him chafe at the restrictions the trial had
posed. His extraordinary patience was tested by the court
preparation and the demands of the investors who wanted

to know why Morgan Curran wasn't exposed earlier. There were those who weren't satisfied with the reparations that Walker made and wanted to have their losses completely covered. "You must be glad it's behind us."

Walker raised his hand and lightly touched the side of Skye's face. Her fiery hair was like silk against his fingertips. "No more than you."

"It wasn't so—" She stopped, abandoning the lie. "I was so afraid they wouldn't find him guilty. At night—"

He placed a finger over her lips. "I know," he said. He had held her night after night when she had been afraid to go to sleep, afraid that Morgan Curran would enter her defenseless, wandering thoughts as easily as he had entered her room. He had held her until exhaustion had claimed her body if not her mind. The shadows beneath her eyes had been fading since Morgan Curran received his unpardonable sentence two days earlier. The tip of Walker's finger traced the arch of her cheek. "I wasn't certain if you'd want to come back here. We didn't have to."

"I did."

It was just like Skye to face a thing head on. Her courage moved him. He was absolutely sure he had made the right decision about their future together. "I have my next assignment," he said after a moment.

Skye sat up now. "Assignment?" Skye was uncertain what that meant. She reached for her discarded shift and slipped it over her head. If he was going to tell her terrible news, then she wanted a bit of protection against it. "You didn't tell me," she said. Hurt, she avoided his eyes. There was nothing she could do about the slight quaver in her voice.

"I was saving it for the right moment." Standing, Walker slipped into his trousers. "I've known for a week now."

"A week." All that time, she thought. He must have

been thinking how to tell her he was leaving. "When does it begin?"

"I've booked passage already. The *Eastern Star* leaves in ten days."

Skye swallowed hard and smoothed her shift over her hips. "*Eastern Star?* Then it's the Orient."

"I thought you'd be happy."

She shrugged. "It will give me time to renovate this house, I suppose. And search for the treasure. Perhaps Mama or Mary Francis will come and stay a while."

That's when Walker backed her right up against the wall. Her bottom pressed against the precariously tilted headboard as he braced an arm on either side of her shoulders. He bent his head slightly and gave her the full force of his level stare. "You have exactly ten days to find the treasure, pack your things, and say goodbye to your family. I'm not giving you a choice about this, Skye. You're coming with me."

Skye stared at him open-mouthed. Using this moment to tell him he was being high-handed was a little like cutting off her nose to spite her face. There would be two oceans to cross, time enough to let him know what she thought of not having been consulted. And it wasn't as if she didn't have a secret of her own, she thought a trifle smugly. Mary Francis had been correct about the fertility of the Dennehy women. Right now she launched herself into Walker's arms and spread kisses over his face.

"I take it this means you're happy," he said. Somehow she had managed to attach herself to him like a limpet. His hands cupped her bottom and her thighs cradled him intimately. "I guess I found the right moment."

Skye let him enjoy that thought. She would take issue with it as they were riding out the stormy waters around Cape Horn. Somehow, it seemed fitting. She buried her face in his neck and her smile against his skin. "I love you," she whispered. Skye raised her head and searched his face. Her eyes were solemn. "You won't regret this."

"There was never any possibility of that," he said.

She felt his words as a physical force. Pleasure rippled through Skye and she leaned into him again. The movement was unexpected and challenged his balance. Walker took a step backward, caught his heel on the edge of the mattress, and moved forward, bumping Skye into the headboard this time. With a grating, scraping sound it began to slide down the wall. Walker, with Skye still in his arms, managed to jump out of the way and protect his bare feet from injury. The headboard thudded to the floor.

They didn't notice that it had cracked in the center. They were looking at a hole in the wall that had been hidden for the better part of half a century. They peered inside together. A slim beam of sunlight made the interior visible and revealed a single ironbound chest. The lid was open. Yards of dusty silk draped one corner where the material had been lifted to reveal the richer treasure beneath.

Sunshine winked across the golden surface of a thousand Spanish doubloons.

"Eureka."

Neither of them was surprised that they said it as one.

About the Author

JO GOODMAN lives with her family in Colliers, West Virginia. She is currently working on her newest Zebra historical romance, once again set in the Regency period. Look for it in August 2005! Jo loves hearing from readers, and you may write to her c/o Zebra Books. Please include a self-addressed stamped envelope if you would like a response. Or you can visit her website at www.jogoodman.com

Discover the Romances of
Hannah Howell

BOOK YOUR PLACE ON OUR WEBSITE AND MAKE THE READING CONNECTION!

We've created a customized website just for our very special readers, where you can get the inside scoop on everything that's going on with Zebra, Pinnacle and Kensington books.

When you come online, you'll have the exciting opportunity to:

- View covers of upcoming books
- Read sample chapters
- Learn about our future publishing schedule (listed by publication month *and author*)
- Find out when your favorite authors will be visiting a city near you
- Search for and order backlist books from our online catalog
- Check out author bios and background information
- Send e-mail to your favorite authors
- Meet the Kensington staff online
- Join us in weekly chats with authors, readers and other guests
- Get writing guidelines
- AND MUCH MORE!

**Visit our website at
http://www.kensingtonbooks.com**